About

Maisey Yates is the *New* … bestselling author of over one hundred romance novels. An avid knitter with a dangerous yarn addiction and an aversion to housework, Maisey lives with her husband and three kids in rural Oregon. She believes the trek she makes to her coffee maker each morning is a true example of her pioneer spirit. Find out more about Maisey's books on her website: maiseyyates.com, or find her on Facebook, Instagram or TikTok by searching her name.

Louisa Heaton is a married mother of four (including a set of twins) and she lives on an island in Hampshire with her four adult children, husband, dogs and cats. She can often be found walking her dogs along the beach and local trails, muttering to herself, as she works out plot points. In her spare time, she reads a lot, draws, or chooses from a myriad of crafts. Usually when she ought to be doing something else! You can follow her on X @louisaheaton

Amalie Berlin lives with her family and critters in Southern Ohio, and she writes quirky, independent characters for Mills & Boon Medical. Her favorite stories buck expectations with unusual settings and situations, and the belief that humour can powerfully illuminate truth – especially when juxtaposed against intense emotions. And that love is stronger and more satisfying when your partner can make you laugh through the times you don't have the luxury of tears.

Princess Brides

December 2024
Enemies to Lovers

January 2025
A Second Chance

February 2025
A Marriage of Convenience

March 2025
Friends to Lovers

April 2025
A Cinderella Story

May 2025
A Royal Baby

THE PRINCE'S CINDERELLA DOC

LOUISA HEATON

To Becca, with all my love.

You are the strongest young woman I know. xxx

CHAPTER ONE

FOR YEARS DR KRYSTIANA SZENAC had walked along the beach with her dog Bruno, allowing her gaze to fall upon the faraway façade of Il Palazzo Grande—the Grand Palace. It was like a fine jewel in the warm sunshine. A glittering building set atop a hill, with every window, every white wall, reflecting the light. She'd often wondered about what it would be like to live in such a place, but had never imagined for one moment that she would ever pass through the arched gates into the royal sanctuary where the King and his son the Crown Prince lived.

He didn't know it, but she felt a kinship with the Prince, and every time she thought about their connection—which was often—she would smile to herself, knowing it was ridiculous because he didn't even know she existed!

But he was about to.

Krystiana sucked in a breath as the large armoured car drove her through the gates and into the palace grounds. She gazed out of the window, feeling like a silly little tourist as she took in the guards in their dark blue uniforms and the white sashes that crossed their chests, the flower displays—perfectly tended, not a weed in place—and the architecture: solid white walls rising high, the crenelated roof with the billowing flag of the royal family and the circular towers in each corner.

It had all the hallmarks of the castle it had once been, even down to the other guards she saw at the top of each tower, ever watchful, even though there had been no threat to Isla Tamoura for hundreds of years. It was pomp and circumstance for the tourists who flocked to the island in their droves, keen to explore this jewel off Italy's south-eastern coast.

Did Crown Prince Matteo feel safe behind these walls? She couldn't see why he wouldn't. All the barriers… All the guards… Security was high. She'd already had her bags searched before she was even allowed in the car. A rugged, dark-suited secret service agent had frisked her down too—the most bodily contact she'd had in years.

It had made her feel uncomfortable, but she'd bitten her lip until it was done and then smiled politely at the agent as he'd opened the car door for her. *'Grazie.'*

The agent hadn't said much. He'd had that mysterious, moody, steely exterior down perfectly, getting into the car and saying into his phone in Italian, 'I have the parcel. Delivering in fifteen minutes—that's fifteen minutes.'

She'd raised her eyebrows, having never been referred to as a parcel before. She'd been called a lot of other things in her life, but never a *parcel*.

The car purred its way through another set of arches and then came to rest outside a columned terrace. The agent got out, adjusted the buttons on the front of his dark suit and looked about him before opening her door.

Krystiana stepped out, her nerves getting the better of her at last, and wished she'd had something to eat before leaving home. Just something that would have settled her stomach. But there'd been almost no time to prepare. The call had come in unexpectedly. She was needed immediately. There had just been time to pack a bag for an overnight stay. To call her neighbour and ask her to feed and walk Bruno.

A day of living in the palace! It was almost a dream. That a woman like her—a woman who had been raised initially in Krakow, Poland—should find herself hobnobbing with royalty.

Well, it wasn't exactly hobnobbing. It was work. Standing in for the royal doctor to run the Crown Prince through his yearly physical. She'd been chosen because she shared a clinic with Dr Bonetti, the King's private physician, and had already had her background checked. That was what happened when your colleague was the King's doctor. There could be no chance of any impropriety connected with the royals.

They'd already had enough excitement, after all.

A red carpet led from the car up to the white stone steps and into the palace proper.

On wobbly legs she ascended the stairs, aware that the agent was following along behind her. She assumed someone else would bring her bag. As she neared the top of the steps and saw the opulent interior of the palace she felt her pulse quicken, and her mouth went as dry as the Dune Dorate—the Golden Dunes.

She tried her hardest to appear nonchalant as she walked across the marble floor towards a man dressed like a butler, who had the rigid stature of an old soldier.

'Dr Szenac, welcome to the Grand Palace. It is a pleasure to welcome you to these halls. My name is Sergio and I shall be your attendant whilst you are here. Have you been to the palace before?'

She shook her head, her long golden plait swinging at her back. 'No. It's my first time.'

'Oh! Well, please don't let it be your last. I'm reliably

informed that the public tours are very entertaining and informative, if you wish to know anything of its history.'

She'd never been one to study history. History should stay in the past, where it belonged. Not be dragged back into the present at every opportunity. She could appreciate beautiful architecture, and respect the amount of time a building had stood in place, but she was far more interested in the people who lived in it now.

'Thank you. I might do that one day.'

Sergio led her up a curved stairwell, adorned with portraiture of Kings and Queens of the past. She could see the familiar glossy black hair and beautiful blue eyes of the Romano family in most of them. Occasionally there was a portrait of someone who had married into the family, including the one she stood in front of now: Queen Marianna, sadly passed.

'She was beautiful, wasn't she?' asked Sergio.

'Most definitely.'

'And not just in looks. She had a very kind heart. It broke her when her son was taken. She died never knowing of his safe return.'

Krystiana nodded. It was tragic. Crown Prince Matteo's kidnapping had been a story she had followed with bated breath, praying for his safe release. It had been a couple of years ago now, but still, she knew in her heart that it would never be forgotten by those involved.

'The Prince must have been devastated when he got home to discover his mother had died?'

Sergio nodded sadly. 'They were very close. Ah, here are your quarters.'

He stopped in front of a set of double doors and swung them open wide, and once again she tried to appear unaffected by the riches within, simply nodding and smiling.

'Thank you, Sergio. These look wonderful. I'm sure I'll be very comfortable.'

'Your initial appointment with the Prince is at three this afternoon. Take time to settle in. Pull this red sash—' he indicated a brocade sash that hung by the white marble fireplace '—if you want anything and I'll be with you momentarily.'

'Thank you.'

'A servant will bring up your bag. Are there any refreshments I can get you? A drink, perhaps?'

She *was* thirsty, and now that some of her nerves were settling she felt that maybe she could eat. 'Some coffee would be wonderful. And some water? Maybe a bite to eat? I had to come here in rather a rush and I'm afraid I didn't get a chance to dine.'

'I'll have a selection of food brought up to you immediately. Do you have any allergies or food preferences?'

'No.'

He bowed. 'Then I will be back shortly. Welcome to the Grand Palace, Doctor.' And he departed, closing the doors behind him.

Krystiana spun around, headed straight over to the doors in the far wall and flung them back, allowing in the bright sunshine, the freedom of the outdoors, as she stepped out onto a large terrace and breathed in the scent of bougainvillea, jasmine and columbine.

An array of flowers grew in small ornamental pots, framed by clipped firs in taller blue pots. A table and six chairs were sheltered by a large umbrella. Below her were the private royal gardens and she took a moment to take in the sight. They were simply gorgeous: a low maze with a water feature at its centre—a stone horse crashing through stone waves—an ornamental garden, a lily pond, a mosaic. Little paths ran here and there—one down to a grotto, another through a set of rose arches to a circular bench and a bust.

Someone had poured a lot of heart and soul into this

garden. She wondered who. Some gardener? A series of them? Each of them adding something new during their term, perhaps?

Beyond the palace walls she saw olive groves, small terracotta-coloured churches, roadside shrines and undulating hillsides that shimmered with heat from the overhead sun. It was something she could paint. She often turned to creativity when she was stressed. She'd never had such a view before—she *had* to sketch it before she left.

Not that I could ever forget this.

The view had a timeless quality. She almost felt she could stand there all day admiring it. But reality beckoned, and so she turned to observe her rooms more carefully. It was the most sumptuous suite—all white marble and silver accents. A large bed occupied the centre of the bedroom, with pristine white sheets and a gold counterpane. There was a desk and chair in the living room, a comfortable pair of sofas in palest cornflower-blue and vases of fresh flowers on almost every surface. A door in the corner of the bedroom led to an en-suite bathroom, with a sunken bath in the centre, a walk-in shower, a toilet and bidet and a huge assortment of toiletries in a room that was all mirrors.

Briefly, she wondered about the poor maids who had to clean it each day, buffing it to a shine, because not a single surface had a fingerprint or a smudge on it anywhere.

But what would you expect in a palace?

The opulence was meant to make her feel good. Treasured and important. But Krystiana had always preferred simplicity and rustic touches. Wooden bowls, plain knives and forks for her food. Simple cloth mats beneath her plate. Watercolours. Plain whitewashed walls—the minimalist look, with stone and driftwood she'd collected from the beach where she walked each day, barefoot, her trousers rolled up as she paddled in the water.

All of this was nice. Amazing, in fact. But it wasn't real.

She felt like Alice through the looking glass, looking at a world she didn't quite understand. But she was keen to know more.

Crown Prince Matteo Romano shook the hand of the cultural attaché from Portugal and bade him a safe journey home. He was looking forward to the future visit he would take to Lisbon, to see for himself the amazing artwork said to be displayed in Galleria 111. The attaché had done a fine job of convincing him the place was worth fitting in to his schedule, especially as he was such a fan of the surrealist painter António Dacosta, the work of whom the gallery had confirmed they had a huge stock.

As soon as the attaché had left, Matteo let out a breath and relaxed for a moment. He was almost done with his schedule for today. A few brief moments alone, and then he would meet the new doctor who had been brought in due to Dr Bonetti's family emergency.

He hoped everything was all right with the man's family. He'd known Dr Bonetti for years, and had met his wife and children. They'd all dined together on occasion and he thought very well of them all. He envied the doctor his happy marriage and his smiling children. They all seemed so *together.* So…*content.*

None of them had the stresses that were placed upon *his* shoulders. Who could understand the burden of being a prince, a future king, without having lived in his shoes?

He reached for the coffee that Sergio had brought in earlier, along with the news that the stand-in doctor had arrived and was settling in. The drink was cooler than he'd like—his meeting with the Portuguese attaché had gone on longer than he'd expected—but he continued to drink it until it was finished. Then, needing the freshness of the outdoors and the calm that viewing the gardens gave him, he stepped out of the terrace doors onto the balcony to gaze down into the palace gardens.

As always, he felt serenity begin to settle in his soul and he closed his eyes and breathed in the warm, fragrant air. *Perfezionare.* Perfect. His hands came to rest on the rich stone balustrade and for a moment he just stood there, centring himself. Grounding himself.

Behind him there was the gentle sound of Sergio clearing his throat. 'Dr Krystiana Szenac, sir.'

'*Grazie*, Sergio.'

He turned and there she was. Dressed in a black knee-length skirt and an emerald-green blouse, her blonde hair flowing over her shoulder in a long plait. A hint of make-up and an amazing smile.

She curtsied. 'Your Highness.'

'Dr Szenac. It's a pleasure.' He stepped forward to shake her hand. 'I appreciate you coming at short notice and hope our pulling you from your schedule hasn't disrupted your life too much.'

'No. Not at all. I was able to make new arrangements. When your country calls, you answer.'

He smiled. 'Indeed. I take it your journey was uneventful?'

'It was wonderful, thank you.'

'And Dr Bonetti?'

'His wife has been taken into emergency surgery, but I'm afraid that's all I know.'

Emergency surgery? That didn't sound good.

'Let us hope she pulls through. Alexis Bonetti is a strong woman—I'm sure her constitution will hold her in good stead.'

She nodded. 'I hope so.'

'May I offer you a refreshment before we settle down?'

'I'm fine, thank you. Sergio had some coffee brought to my room.'

'Excellent.'

He stared at her for a moment more and then indicated that maybe they should sit down at one of the tables on the sun terrace. He pulled out a chair for her, and she smiled her thanks at him as she sat down.

He sat opposite. 'Well, I'll try not to keep you here too long. I just need my yearly physical to be carried out. Dr Bonetti usually does the deed, but this year it will be down to you—if that's all right?'

'Absolutely.'

'He usually runs a barrage of tests—I'm sure there's a list somewhere. And then, if I'm all okay, he signs me off for another year.'

'I know what to do—don't worry. He emailed me your file, with a list of assessments I need to put you through and the paperwork that needs filling out.' Dr Szenac smiled. 'According to your file you're in very good health, and your last couple of physicals had you back at full health after your…' she looked uncomfortable '…blip.'

'My *kidnapping*. Yes. Well… Two years in a cave, will do that to any man.'

She nodded. 'Yes. My apologies for bringing it up.'

'Not at all. My therapist says it's good to talk about it. The more often the better.'

She smiled her thanks.

He didn't want her to feel uncomfortable, so he tried to change the subject. 'You're originally from Poland?'

'Yes. Krakow.'

'I've never been there. What's it like?'

'I don't know. I haven't been there for years. I just remember the grey and the cold.'

He saw her shiver and it intrigued him that she could still feel it, all these years later, just *thinking* about it.

'When did you move here?'

'When my mother died. My father was…away, and I had no one else except for my Aunt Carolina, who lives here.'

'On Isla Tamoura?'

'Yes.'

'Well, I'm very glad you're here.' He smiled.

She nodded. 'Yes. Me too.'

CHAPTER TWO

WHEN KRYSTIANA WOKE the next morning, the first thing she did was reach over and turn off her night-light. It was an automatic thing—something she hardly noticed doing—but today when she did so she stared at it for a moment, wondering if Crown Prince Matteo had one too.

For two years he'd been stuck in a cave. Was he now afraid of the dark?

Throwing off the bedcovers, she got up and threw open the double doors to the sun terrace. The fragrant air poured in and she closed her eyes for a moment as the warm rays from the sun caressed her skin. This was what she loved about living here. The warmth. The colour. The heat. The beauty of this treasured isle.

How fortunate that her aunt lived here. It had been exactly what she had needed after her experience at the hands of her father—to leave such an ugly existence behind and come to a place that only had beauty at its core. There had been a new language to learn, but wonderful, loving, passionate people to support her. New friends. A new life. Isla Tamoura had given her a new beginning, a new hope, and she loved it here so much.

Krystiana took a quick shower and braided her long hair into its usual plait, donned a summery dress and sat down to eat the breakfast that had been brought in on a tray. She was used to eating breakfast alone. She quite enjoyed it. But this time, before her day started, she grabbed her pad and pencils and began sketching the view from her balcony. This afternoon she would be going home again, so there was no time to spare.

Her sketch was vague. Outlines and shapes. She would fill in the colour later, allowing her imagination to take flight. She took a couple of quick photos using her phone.

She almost lost track of time, and when she did glance at her watch she saw there were only a few minutes until nine o clock—her scheduled time to give the Prince his yearly physical. She left her pad and pencil on the bed, finished her orange juice and then pulled the sash to call Sergio. She wasn't sure exactly where in the palace the examination would take place.

Sergio arrived, looking as perfectly presented as always. 'Good morning, Dr Szenac. I hope you slept well?'

'Very well, Sergio, thank you. I have my appointment with His Highness Prince Matteo, to start his physical, but I'm not sure where I have to go.'

He nodded. 'I believe you are expected in the private gym. Dr Bonetti always carries out the yearly check-ups there.'

'Thank you.' She'd had no idea the palace had its own gym—but, then again, why wouldn't it? Matteo and his family could hardly pop out to the local leisure centre if they wanted to lift a few weights, could they?

Sergio led her through the palace, down long tapestry-filled hallways, past vast vases so big she could have climbed inside and not been seen even standing upright. They passed a coat of arms, a suit of armour, and fireplaces filled with flowers, until he brought her to a set of double doors.

'The gym, Dr Szenac. All of Dr Bonetti's equipment

has been laid out for you, and the computer has been set up for you to enter the results of each test for the record.'

'Thank you—that's very kind.'

'The computer isn't likely to be difficult, but if you do have any queries we have an IT expert on hand.'

'That's marvellous.'

Sergio smiled and opened the doors.

The gym was filled with all types of equipment—treadmills, stair-masters, weight machines, free-standing weights, workout equipment, yoga mats. Anything and everything seemed to be here, and one wall was made of glass that revealed a room beyond filled with a full-length swimming pool.

Pretty impressive!

But she didn't have time to linger. The Prince would be here at any moment and she wanted to be prepared.

She was running her eye over what she needed to achieve today, reminding herself of the assessments, when she became aware of a presence behind her.

'Dr Szenac.'

She turned and bowed slightly. 'Your Highness.'

'I'm ready, if you are?'

Smiling, she nodded. 'Absolutely. Ready to begin with the basics? I'll need to do blood pressure, pulse and SATs.'

'Perfect.'

'All right. Take a seat.'

She began to set up her equipment—the pulse oximeter that she'd place on his finger to measure not only his pulse but the oxygen levels in his blood, and the arm cuff around his upper arm that would measure his blood pressure.

His basic measurements were perfect. Exactly what she'd expected them to be.

'Okay, now I need to check your height and weight.'

'I don't think I've shrunk.'

She smiled. 'Glad to hear it.'

Again, his weight was perfect for his height.

'Now I'd like to set you up for a treadmill test. I'll need to attach you to a breathing tube, so we can measure oxygen intake, heart-rate and lung capacity whilst you run up a slight incline for three minutes.'

He nodded. 'Can I warm up first?'

'By all means.'

She looked at his previous measurements and typed them into the computer, aware that Matteo was stripping off behind her and beginning to stretch.

When she turned around she noted that he was in excellent physical shape. Clearly he used the gym often to keep fit. His muscle tone was almost beautiful. His figure was sculpted, without being overly worked. It seemed almost wrong to look at him and admire him like that. Not least because he was a prince.

'Right, I need to attach these electrodes, if that's okay?'

Does my voice sound weird?

He stood still whilst she attached the electrodes to his chest and body, trying her hardest not to make eye contact, then attached the wires that hooked him up to the machine for a reading. She fastened a breathing mask around his nose and mouth, and suddenly there was that eye contact thing.

She could feel herself blushing. 'Okay… For the first minute I want you just to walk at a steady pace and then, when I tell you, I'm going to increase the speed and I want you to jog.'

'All right.'

'Ready?'

He gave her a thumbs-up and she started the treadmill and the EKG monitor that would read his heart's electrical activity. The machine began printing out on a paper roll and she watched it steadily, keeping a careful eye out for any issues, but it all looked fine.

She glanced up at him as he ran with a steady pace, his body like a well-oiled machine as he tackled the jog easily. His oxygen intake was perfect; his heart-rate was elevated, but not too much.

When the three minutes were over she switched everything off and then laid a hand on his wrist to check his pulse. She felt it pounding away beneath her fingertips and kept count, then made a note of the result.

'You're doing brilliantly.'

He pulled off the mask. 'Good to know.'

'You work out a lot?'

'Can't you tell?' He raised an eyebrow.

'Well, I…er…yes… You look very…er…'

He laughed. 'I meant can't you tell from my results?'

She flushed even redder and laughed with him. 'Oh, I see.' She nodded. 'Yes!'

'I try to do thirty minutes every other day, alternating with the pool. Lifting weights. Half an hour of cardio…'

'You do more than me.'

'It's easier for me. My life is scheduled to the minute, so I know when I can fit things in to get everything done.'

She was curious. 'Is that a perk or a drawback?' she asked. She wasn't sure she'd want to be so regimentally scheduled each day. What about free time? What about spontaneity?

'It depends on the day.' He laughed again, wiping his face with a towel.

'And today?'

He shrugged. 'Well, I have this, and then I get to spend some time with my daughter.'

'Princess Alexandra? She's beautiful. How old is she now?'

'Five.'

'You must be very proud of her.'

'I am. But I don't get to spoil her as often as I would like.'

Of course not. She didn't live with him. The Princess lived with her mother, at her family's private estate.

'That must be hard for you?'

He stared into her eyes. 'You have no idea.'

Oh, but I do, she thought. *I know how hard it is being away from those you love. I know only too well.*

She blinked rapidly and turned away, forcing her mind back to the assessment. 'Next test.'

'I'm all yours.' He did a mock bow.

Krystiana smiled and then indicated that he should move to the next machine.

They were just about finished with their testing when the doors to the gym opened and in walked Sergio, looking grave. It was the most solemn Matteo had ever seen him.

He finished towelling himself down and raised an eyebrow. 'Sergio? What is it?'

'I have some unfortunate news for Dr Szenac, sir.'

She looked up from her notes and frowned. Was it about Dr Bonetti's wife?

'I'm afraid there's been an accident at your villa. A drunk driver tried to take the corner near your abode too fast and ploughed into your home. I'm afraid your living area and bedroom have been almost destroyed, and the property is not safe for you to reside in just yet.'

Matteo was shocked and looked to Dr Szenac. 'I'm so sorry!'

Her face was almost white. 'Is the driver all right?'

He was impressed at how her concern was immediately for the driver.

'I believe he got away quite lightly, all things considered. He's being treated by the medics now.'

'Okay. Good. That's good.' She turned away, her thoughts in a distant place. 'Oh, my God. What about Bruno?'

'Bruno?'

'My dog. He's a rescue.'

'I believe your neighbour was out on a walk with him at the time,' Sergio replied.

'Oh, thank goodness!'

She sank down into a chair, her legs obviously trembling, and put her head in her hands. Matteo felt for her. Was her home ruined?

'You must stay here with us. Until everything is fixed.'

She looked up, tears in her eyes. 'I couldn't possibly do that.'

'Nonsense! It's done. Sergio, could you arrange for Dr Szenac's clothes and anything she needs to be brought to her quarters here in the palace? Including her dog, who I'm sure will bring her great comfort. We're going to have a guest for a while.'

'I don't know what to say…' she said, beginning to cry.

He smiled. 'Say yes.'

She looked at him for a long moment and he saw gratitude. 'Then, yes. Thank you. Yes.'

He nodded. 'Sergio? Make it happen.'

'I'm so lucky I was here when it happened, she said later. Otherwise I might have been injured!'

'Well, you were here, and that's all that matters.'

'But—'

'No buts. There's no point in wondering about what *might* have happened. You just need to worry about what *is* happening.' He smiled. 'I learned that in therapy. Look at me—spreading the knowledge.'

She smiled as she stroked Bruno's fur. They'd had a joyous reunion when Sergio had returned with her dog, her clothes, her computer and some rather startling photographs of the damage to her villa.

'That's going to take weeks to repair,' she'd said.

'Let me take care of that,' Matteo had offered.

'I couldn't possibly let you do that! It will cost a fortune!'

'Are you insured?'

'Yes.'

'Then don't worry about it. Let me do something good for you. You were kind enough to step in at the last minute and help me out when I needed a doctor—let me step in and help you out when you need a…'

'A builder?' She'd laughed.

He'd smiled back. 'A knight in shining armour. Didn't you see my suit of armour downstairs? It's very polished.'

So of course she'd thanked him profusely, feeling so terribly grateful for all that he was doing to help her out.

'I appreciate that. I really do.'

'Nonsense. It's what friends do.'

And she'd smiled. *Were they friends?* 'Thank you.'

Matteo had invited her to dine with him that evening.

'You can bring Bruno. If he's lucky we might be able to feed him titbits under the table.'

'He'll never want to leave this place if you do that.'

And now they sat on his sun terrace, awaiting their meal, staring out across the gardens below and watching the sun slowly set.

'By the way, I don't know if you've heard but Dr Bonetti's wife has pulled through. She's in a stable condition and expected to go home soon. He phoned from the hospital. Let my secretary know.'

'That's excellent news! Wow. So good to have such great news after earlier. And the driver who hit my home? Do we know about him?'

'Already home. And already charged by the police for drink driving. He's to attend court in a few days' time.'

'If it was an accident I'm sure he's very sorry.'

Matteo sipped his water. 'Unfortunately, from what I've discovered, the man is a known drunk. He's already had his licence taken from him and the car wasn't even his. It was his son's and he'd "borrowed" it.'

'Oh.'

'We'll get him into a programme.'

'We?' She raised an eyebrow.

'My pack of royal enforcers,' he said with a straight face, knowing there was no such pack at all.

'Enforcers?'

He laughed. 'I'm sorry. I don't really have enforcers. I was just… Look, he needs help. Someone will go and visit him and make sure he enrols into a programme that will get him the help he needs. Before he kills someone next time.'

'Maybe I could go and see him myself?'

'Is that wise? You're emotionally involved.'

'Which is why he might listen to me. Meeting the actual victim of his crime might make more of an impact.'

'Was hitting your wall not enough?' He cocked his head to one side. 'How do you know so much about crime and victimology?'

She looked down and away from him then, and he realised there was a story there. Something she wasn't willing to share.

'I'm sorry—you don't have to answer that.'

She laughed. 'Don't therapists suggest that talking is good for the soul?'

He nodded. 'They do. But only when you're ready. *Are* you ready?'

'I don't know.'

He sipped his drink. 'You'll know when it's the right time. And, more importantly, if it's the right person to talk to. You don't really know me, so I quite understand.'

She stared back at him. Consideringly. Her eyes were cool. 'I think you'd understand more than most.'

He considered this. Intrigued. 'Oh?'

She paused. Looked uncertain. And then he saw it in her face. The determination to push forward and just say it.

'I was six years old. And I was taken.'

'Taken?' His blood almost froze, despite the warmth of the sun.

'My father buried me in a hole in the ground.'

CHAPTER THREE

SHE STARED AT HIM, trying to gauge his reaction. 'Surprised?'

The Crown Prince opened his mouth as if to say something, but no words came out. He was truly stupefied. Shocked. His mind raced over the fact that she'd been kidnapped too.

'Of course I am! Your *father* did this?'

'He planned it. It wasn't a spur-of-the-moment thing. My parents had split up and had a bitter custody battle over me. Their divorce was not amicable.'

'That must have been upsetting for you.'

A nod. 'Yes. My mother was awarded full custody, but my father got to see me once a month. Just for one day. This particular weekend he told me we were going to play a game in the woods, where he worked as a gamekeeper. I was going to help him snare rabbits.'

Matteo listened intently, his face showing how appalled he was that something like this had happened to her.

'We went deep into the woods. It was dark and damp and there almost wasn't any light…the trees were so thick.'

'Were you scared?'

'Not to start with. I was comfortable being in nature. I'd played in those woods. I was with my father. I thought I was safe. And then he showed me a bunker he'd made.'

'A bunker…? What was it like?'

'Not very big. Maybe the size of a single bed? Thc walls were lined with wood. Old pallets, I think. He told me we were going to play a game, and that to play I had to get inside the bunker and wait whilst he went and chased rabbits towards it. He told me the roof would open easily. That I'd be able to push it open and the rabbits would jump into the dark for me to play with.'

'Mio Dio...'

'Once he put the roof down I heard a padlock click. He said *"Przepraszam"*—I'm sorry—and then he left me.'

She took a sip of water, reliving that moment once again in her mind, hearing her father's footsteps as he walked away and how it felt for her tiny fists to beat against the solid roof above her head, lined with soil.

'He would come back when he could, to bring me food and water. I tried to escape, but…he was stronger than me. Once he brought a book and a candle, so I had light to read.'

'How long were you underground?'

'Six weeks.'

He looked sick. 'How did you escape?'

'I was found. My father had reported me missing, of course. Said I'd disappeared when he'd left me outside a shop. After a few weeks the police began to suspect him and followed him into the woods. Dogs found me. I'll always remember hearing them come closer, their barks echoing above me. I began to scream. I screamed so much I had no voice for three days.'

'And your father?'

She swallowed hard. 'He's in prison now.'

He nodded. 'Do you visit him?'

Why did he not know about this? She worked with his father's doctor! How come none of this had shown in her background searches?

Because she'd been a child. The records would be sealed.

'No. I've never gone back to Poland.'

'Do you think you should?'

Her head tilted to one side as she assessed him. 'Have you ever visited your captors in jail?'

Matteo thought for a moment, then smiled, caught out. 'Fair point. But my captors were strangers—yours was your father. You must have loved him?'

'I did. But not any more. It's not the same.'

'And…' He cleared his throat and took a sip of water. 'Do you have any flashbacks? Any issues from your captivity?'

'Not really. Apart from needing a night-light.'

'That's understandable.' He looked out at the broad expanse of rich orange-pink sky, cloudless and still.

'So, Your Highness, as you can see we are both injured birds.'

'I guess we are. But we're resilient and we'll both fly again.'

She looked uncertain. 'I hope I already am flying.'

He nodded. 'You are. Believe it.'

She smiled back, thankful for his understanding and support. Who'd have thought it? That she'd be sharing her story with the Crown Prince?

How many times had she gazed at these palace walls, wanting to let him know that she understood what he had gone through? How many times had she considered writing him a letter but decided against it? Assuming that he wouldn't actually see it, and that it would be dealt with by a private secretary.

They were probably the only two people on this island who shared such an experience. It bonded them. And here she was. Sitting across from him, watching the sunset, sharing with him her darkest nightmare.

'You're a good man, Your Highness.'

He smiled back at her, his blue eyes twinkling. 'Call me Matteo.'

She nodded. 'Krystiana.'

She lay on her bed, staring at the ceiling. Had she been a fool to blurt it out like that? She'd never told anyone here about what had happened. Only her Aunt Carolina knew—no one else. Until today, anyway. She hadn't even told Dr Bonetti, and he was her partner in the medical practice they ran in the town of Ventura.

But sitting opposite Matteo like that, being that close to him, she had wanted him to know. It was as simple as that. Being kidnapped was such a unique experience, and she'd needed him to know that she understood it. That she'd been through it, too.

He'd been so kind.

'Thank you, Krystiana. For sharing that with me,' he had said. 'It must have taken great courage to share something so…personal.'

She'd pushed her *tagliatelli* around her plate, biting her bottom lip. Trying to work out why she'd told him everything. Was she being selfish?

'I've kept it inside for so long… It felt good to get it out. I guess I knew you'd understand.'

She'd looked up, expecting to see sympathy or pity on his face, but he hadn't looked at her that way at all.

'Other people don't. Not truly,' he'd said. 'They couldn't.'

'No.' She'd sipped her water.

'I don't want you to feel bad for telling me. I can see it on your face that you're uncomfortable now.'

She'd smiled wryly at his perceptiveness. Was she an open book? Could he read her? Was she so obvious? Or was it that only he could see, because he'd been through the same thing?

She'd given a short laugh. 'I'm normally so private. I keep myself to myself. My best friend doesn't even know. There's no alcohol in this water, right?' she tried to joke.

Matteo had nodded. 'I'm honoured you shared it with me.'

Krystiana continued to stare at the bedroom ceiling. So different from the one in her villa. Back home she had a ceiling fan in the centre of the roof; here she had a chandelier, reflecting the brightness from her night-light around the room.

Her conversation with Matteo hadn't been uncomfortable because she'd shared her story with him—it had become uncomfortable because she hadn't realised what sharing it might make her *feel*. She'd entrusted him with something of herself and she didn't like it. Okay, it was only a small piece of her past, but still… If she'd told him that, what else might she say?

She felt as if she'd given him some of her power and that felt wrong. It was an unexpected emotion.

She got little sleep that night, and when she did finally wake in the morning she vowed to herself that maybe it would be a good idea to stay away from the Crown Prince for a while, He had a busy life, anyway—she probably wouldn't see him any more, and she would have to leave the palace to go to work each day at her practice and see her real patients.

She'd told him about her kidnapping because she'd often thought he would be intrigued to know, but that was as far as it went. That was all. Their lives were separate.

It was as if she was just renting a room and he was her extraordinary new landlord.

A car was waiting to take her to work. A sleek, black armoured vehicle, with its engine idling and one of those dark-suited Secret Service guys behind the wheel.

Krystiana trotted down the steps, ready for work, but also ready to drive past her old home and see the wreckage for herself first. She was anxious, her belly full of a twisting apprehension so that she hadn't been able to manage any breakfast and had only had a single cup of coffee.

'Come on, Bruno! Hurry up!' Her dog, a middle-aged pooch of indeterminate breed, with the character of a grumpy geriatric, ambled after her.

Sergio opened the car door for her. 'Have a good day, Dr Szenac.'

'*Grazie*, Sergio.' As she got into the car, she almost jumped out of her skin. 'Your Highness! What are *you* doing in here? I thought this was the car that was going to take me to work?'

He smiled. 'Matteo—remember? And good morning to you, too. I thought I would come with you to survey the damage to your house.'

'B-but…' she stuttered. 'Aren't you busy? Surely you have more important things to be getting on with? Like helping to run a country?'

'One of my citizens has had her home destroyed by a fool who should never have been on the road in the first place. I am doing my duty by attending the scene of the tragedy to see if there is anything I can do.' He leaned in. 'It's called being supportive—so accept that fact and close the door. Bruno!'

He patted his hands against his lap and her dog jumped in, up onto the car's expensive leather seats and smoothly onto the Prince's lap. He gave her a smile that was cunning and smooth, sliding his sunglasses down onto his face.

'Is that your disguise?' she asked.

'No. I have a baseball cap, too, and when we get to your villa both of us will have hard hats. The site manager will show us around.'

'They're working on it already?'

'From first light this morning.'

She pulled her legs in and Sergio shut the door behind her. 'That's impressive.'

'It's what I do.'

Krystiana smiled at him and then she laughed. He really was very kind. And going completely above and beyond anything she'd expected of him. Not that she *did* expect anything of him. He'd been her patient for one day. Now he wasn't. And, although he'd said they were friends, she wasn't sure how to negotiate that particular relationship.

She didn't have the best track record with men, and she hadn't been kidding when she'd told him she kept to herself. She'd only got one friend and that was Anna Scottolini, her next-door neighbour. She'd neglected to tell him that the best friend she'd mentioned was a senior citizen in her ninety-second year of life.

'You passed, by the way.'

'I'm sorry?'

'Your yearly physical. With flying colours. You're fit as a fiddle.'

'How fit *are* fiddles?'

She shrugged. 'Very, it would seem. Bruno! Don't be embarrassing!'

Bruno had decided the lap of the Prince was a very good place to begin washing his nether regions and had set to with gusto. Feeling her cheeks flame red, she reached over to grab the dog and pull him onto the seat between them.

'Sit there. Good dog.'

Matteo smiled at her and she felt something stir within her. Whatever it was, it made her feel incredibly uncomfortable.

Matching him, she pulled her sunglasses from her handbag and slid them over her face and turned to look out of the window.

If I don't look at him, I won't think about him. Yeah. Like that's going to work!

Krystiana's villa sat atop a small hill on the road into Ventura—or out of it, depending upon which way you were going. When Matteo stepped out of the vehicle in a simple white shirt and dark trousers, and donned his baseball cap and sunglasses, he could see the palace far in the distance, shining like a pearl. White and glittering.

He wondered briefly, now he knew exactly where she lived, if he would be able to spot her home from the palace walls?

Because of course he would always think of her now. No matter what happened in the future, he would feel a kinship with this woman at his side because of what they'd both been through. After she'd told him what had happened he'd initially been shocked, but drawn in by her story. So similar and yet so different from his own.

Six weeks underground. Alone and in the dark.

Kindred spirits. That was what they were. So he was glad he'd made her the offer to stay at the palace whilst her home was worked on, and he did want to see the damage for himself—but had it only been that? Concern for one of his citizens? Concern for someone he'd like to think of as a friend? Or something more?

He felt at ease when he was with her. There was something relaxing about her. But that in turn worried him, simply because it *was* so easy to be with her. He could be himself—and he hadn't been himself for a very long time. It was confusing and alarming, because what did it *mean*? For so long now he'd held himself apart from everyone. Ever since he'd returned home. And yet he'd spent one day with her and had discovered that…

He turned to look at her house. At the metal fencing around the perimeter and the crumpled mess beyond it. Because that was what it was. A crumpled mess of brick and rubble, mortar and plaster, glass and wood. He'd seen something similar when he'd once gone to help during the aftershocks of an earthquake the island had experienced a few years back.

Thank goodness she hadn't been inside when it had happened. If Dr Bonetti's wife hadn't been ill he'd have done his physical as usual and Krystiana would have been at home.

Fate? He didn't believe in that any more.

Pure luck? Maybe…

A man in a high-vis vest and a yellow hard hat came around the corner. He raised a hand and ambled slowly over the loose rubble before coming to the metal fencing and opening a panel. 'Your Highness.'

'Carlo?'

'Si.'

'This is Dr Szenac—she is the owner of this property. Could you walk us through it? Let us know what's happening?'

Carlo nodded and led the way. The ground was uneven, loose bricks and rubble everywhere, so Matteo turned to offer her his hand.

'I'm fine,' she said. 'Watch where you're going and I'll follow.'

He nodded. It was probably a good thing that she hadn't accepted his hand. After all, he was meant to be keeping his distance.

I really must work harder on that.

Her kitchen and bathroom looked untouched by the collision, but the rest of her downstairs rooms and to some degree the rooms above had pretty much collapsed down on top of each other. The vehicle that had smacked into the villa had been a large four-wheel drive, and the driver had been going at some speed. She'd expected to see a car-shaped hole in her wall, or something, but not this. This was…*shocking*. This was the home she had built up since moving out of Aunt Carolina's…

'I'm so sorry, Krystiana,' Matteo said as they surveyed the wreckage.

She didn't want to cry. She had done her make-up for work later. Now she was going to look like a panda.

One of her sofas seemed to be missing. Some framed photographs lay on the floor, their glass cracked and missing fragments. Bending down, she went to pick one up. The only picture she had of her mother. Her eyes welled up again and she began to sob, her hand clamped over her mouth as she tried to cry silently.

'Hey, come here…' Matteo pulled her towards him and she huddled against his chest, the photograph of her dead mother in her hands.

He was warm and comforting. Soothing. And although she wanted to remain there for ever she sniffed hard and pushed away from his chest, stepping out of his arms. She couldn't. No. It wasn't right.

'I'm fine. Really. Show me everything, Carlo.'

Carlo looked at Matteo for permission and she saw him give a terse nod.

She followed him around, listened as he gave complicated observations about lintels and weight-bearing walls and nodded, pretending she understood everything he said. They couldn't go upstairs. It hadn't been made safe yet, he said. But she'd got what she needed. The one thing that mattered. There'd been no way she was leaving her mother in the rubble. In the darkness. Like a piece of discarded litter.

'Thank you. You've been very informative.'

'How long should the work take?' asked Matteo.

'If we can get the supplies we need, four weeks minimum. But it may be longer than that.'

'Do what you can. Money is no object—do you understand me?'

'Yes, Your Highness.'

Matteo turned to her. 'I'll walk you back to the car.'

And he followed her through the building site that was now her home, occasionally putting the tips of his fingers on the small of her back, guiding her through.

When they reached the car, he sighed. 'Are you all right?'

'I'm fine.'

'Maybe you shouldn't return to work today?'

'I have to. I have my own patients *and* Dr Bonetti's. I can't let them down and I won't.'

'All right. I'll have the car drop you off and then pick you up again tonight.'

She shook her head. 'You don't have to. You have work too, remember?'

Matteo nodded. 'Yes. You're right. But it seems wrong leaving you when you're upset.'

'I'll be fine. We're strong, aren't we?'

He smiled. 'We're strong. Yes.' He glanced at the back seat of the car. 'Want me to take Bruno?'

'He sits in the office with me. Patients seem to like it.' She shrugged.

'Interesting medical student…'

'He has a passion for bones.'

It was a lame joke, but she was trying to make light of the situation. It had been a stressful twenty-four hours, but she'd been through worse.

Matteo smiled dutifully. 'I'll see you at home, then.'

Home.

She got into the car, waiting for him to slide in next to

her. Bruno gave a wag of his tail and licked some dust off the back of her hand.

'Don't wait up.'

Krystiana spent the day treating patients, and for almost six hours barely gave a thought to her ruined home or her palatial sleepover. She treated an infected jellyfish sting, a child with chicken pox, two bad sunburns, a bad case of laryngitis, gout, completed a newborn baby's assessment, and checked a wound on the foot of a Type Two diabetic—all before lunch.

It felt good to get back to her normal routine, to see her patients' faces and to slide back into the routine of consulting and issuing prescriptions. There was a rhythm to it, a logic. Medicine was often a puzzle, with the patients the clues, and there was nothing she loved more than to solve the puzzle and heal the patient. Helping people was what she did best, and it made her feel good about herself that she could do so.

A therapist would no doubt say that it was down to her feeling so powerless and impotent when her father had kept her below ground. That the fact that she hadn't been able to help her mother when she died fired her soul now.

Maybe it was true. Who knew? Perhaps that was why she was so anxious to leave the palace? She'd done her thing. She'd helped out when Dr Bonetti hadn't been able to make it and now her part was over. She wasn't needed at the palace any more, but she had to stay there because she needed a place to sleep.

Or did she? Maybe Anna, her next-door neighbour and best friend, could put her up until the work on her house was done?

No. I can't ask her to do that. She's in her nineties! And besides, how would I pay for the repairs? I'm insured, but that would take ages, and Matteo is getting the work done quicker than I ever could.

It felt wrong. He was being so generous and she wasn't used to someone helping her like that. She was used to standing on her own two feet. Being independent.

She was mulling this over when her next patient arrived. Sofia De Laurentis. Sixteen years old and the daughter of a duke. A lot of her patients came from among the upper echelons of society, but class and prestige were not enough to keep away disease.

Sofia was Krystiana's last patient of the day, and she entered her consulting room looking nervous, fidgeting with her backpack.

'Hello, Sofia, what's brought you here today?'

Sofia couldn't meet her eyes. 'You can't tell anyone, but… I think I might be pregnant.'

Krystiana didn't react. 'All right. What makes you think that?'

'My period is late. A few weeks. And I feel weird.'

Krystiana took some details. The date of her last period and how long they usually lasted. 'Have you taken a pregnancy test?'

'I bought one. I had to go in disguise—can you believe that? There were two tests inside and I used them both.'

'Positive?'

Sofia nodded.

'And do you know who the father is?'

Another nod.

And then she asked the most important question as her patient was only sixteen. 'Did you consent?'

'Yes.'

She believed her. 'Okay. Let's get you up onto the bed.'

Krystiana felt her tummy, but it was still too early to feel the fundus—the top of the womb—above her pelvic area. She smiled, and helped pull Sofia back up into a sitting position.

'Take a seat.'

She prepared to take her blood pressure, wrapping the cuff around her arm.

'So, I can take a blood sample to confirm the pregnancy if you wish. Do you want to keep the baby?'

Sofia shook her head, her eyes welling up with tears. 'I don't know. My father will be furious.'

'You live with your father? What about your mother?'

'She died when I was young.'

Oh. Krystiana knew a little of that pain. She had been left with no parents at a young age, whereas this young girl still had her father.

'You have time to make a decision. You have options. You could keep the baby, or have it adopted. And of course you can also have an abortion. But *you* must be the one to make the decision—no one else can make it for you and no one can force you to make it. Do you understand?'

'Yes.'

'But, again, that's *your* decision.'

Sofia nodded. 'So what do I do now?'

'You think. The first trimester can sometimes be difficult, and not all pregnancies make it through. Take some time to think what you would like to do, and in the meantime I'll book you in with a midwife for a visit. If you'd like to tell your father in a safe environment then you can always do so here, with a member of staff or myself attending. Are you feeling sick at all?'

'A bit.'

'Try nibbling on something as often as you can. Hunger can trigger nausea. Have a biscuit or two at the side of your bed for first thing in the morning, before you get up. Nothing chocolatey—something plain. A ginger biscuit, or something like that.'

Sofia stood up. 'Thank you. You've been very understanding.'

'It's my job.'

When Sofia had left the room Krystiana sat for a moment and pondered her young patient. She had a difficult time ahead of her—a future that no one could predict just yet. And she felt in a similar situation, with her home in disarray. Her living area open to the stars.

She realised that she had always struggled in every area of her life. It was a state of affairs that she had become used to. Perhaps that was why the richness and opulence of the palace made her so uncomfortable? It hid the real world. It wasn't reality. It was a mirage.

Krystiana liked her minimalism. Her stone. Wood. Brick. She wasn't used to marble and crystal and silk. She wasn't used to servants and having things done for her. She enjoyed the simplicity of making her own breakfast. Chopping up fruit and adding it to a bowl of oats gave her pleasure. She liked looking after her own home. Polishing it. Sweeping the floors, cleaning her bathroom.

At the palace those sorts of chores were done by servants. And she didn't like the idea that someone else was having to pick up after her. It didn't feel right. It felt as if parts of her everyday life were being taken from her. And since moving to the island Krystiana had started relying on her gut feelings and instincts, because she'd realised rather swiftly that they were the only things she could trust.

She reached for the phone, intending to dial the palace and tell them not to send her a car because she was going to make her own way. But then she realised she didn't know the number, and that all her things—her clothes, her personal computer, everything she valued—were there. She had to go back. Maybe just for one more night? And then she would pack her things.

She wasn't Matteo's doctor any more. He didn't need

her. She'd told him about their shared experience and she didn't need to share any more. Because she knew that if she did stay his friendship, his easy nature, would cause her to share more. But she couldn't do that. Because sharing with him would mean *trusting* him.

And she couldn't trust anyone ever again.

Visiting the building site that was Krystiana's home, Matteo had felt incredibly disturbed. One half of the villa looked fine, the other a total wreck. They had picked their way through the rubble, being careful not to stumble, and then Krystiana had found her mother's photograph.

Watching Krystiana crumble like that had opened his own scars. They had both lost their mothers. They both knew that kind of loss. His heart had gone out to her and before he'd been able to stop himself he had pulled her into his arms and held her tight.

He had wanted to make her feel better—wanted to let her know that she wasn't alone. That was all. But listening to her cry, feeling the wetness of her tears seeping through his shirt, he hadn't wanted to let her go.

Realising that had disturbed him. What was he doing? Getting involved in her life like this? Inviting her to stay? Offering to rebuild her home? Sheltering her not only with his house but with his arms, his embrace? He didn't need to be worrying about someone else like this. He did *not* need another emotional crisis in his life. He'd had more than enough to last a lifetime! Getting involved with others, caring for them, only caused him pain in the long run.

And then she'd stepped away from his arms and he'd felt relief. Relief that she was trying to be strong all by herself. It was a clear sign that she did not want to depend upon him and that was fine by him. He didn't need anyone depending upon him personally like that. He knew he could never give anyone what they'd want from him. He'd vowed never to love again, so if he couldn't care for someone like that what was the point? He'd been humiliated once.

He'd felt some of the pressure he'd been putting on himself dissipate. But of course then he'd felt guilty for acting so selfishly. Princes were not meant to be selfish. They were not meant to look out only for themselves, but to look out for their people. And wasn't Krystiana one of his people?

After the car had dropped her off at work he had returned to the palace to carry out his duties. He'd had a pile of reports that needed to be read and signed off, and he'd also needed to meet with his secretary to discuss his schedule for the next few months.

He had a busy time coming up. His father, the King, was going to abdicate within the year—on his seventieth birthday. These next few months would be a whirlwind of appointments, visits, public walkabouts and royal duties. Everybody wanted to see the man who would soon be King.

But as he'd sat at his desk he hadn't been able to concentrate. All he'd been able to think about was Krystiana. How displaced she was. The disruption in her life and what he could do to make it better.

He'd ended up pacing the floors and constantly checking his watch. She'd finish at six p.m. and then the car would bring her home.

He knew he needed to sort his head. Clear it. He knew he needed to create more distance between them. He couldn't let her in past his defences. The risk simply wasn't worth it.

He'd already lost his mother, his wife, and almost his child. That was too much loss for one person to deal with. Letting someone in, letting them get close, was dangerous. Matters of the heart were terrifying in how vulnerable they could make a man. They were a weakness. One that those guerrillas had used with impunity, making him think that his wife and child had been killed.

He would let Sergio deal with Krystiana from now on. He didn't think she would be upset by that. Hadn't she been the one to push him away in the villa?

He was only doing what they both wanted.

So why did he feel disturbed by it?

Krystiana came back to the palace after work and hoped that she would be able to get to her quarters without being seen. If she did meet Matteo she would be politeness personified, but she would tell him that she was tired, that she needed to take a shower or a long bath and then she would be going to bed. It was best all round if she left him to get on with being the future King and she got on with being a doctor. She'd helped him out for one day—that was all. She had told him about her past and that was it. It didn't need to go any further than that.

He was a very nice man—kind, considerate and clearly compassionate. Plus, he had the warmest blue eyes she had ever seen. The type of eyes, framed in dark lashes, that invited confidences. She knew without a shadow of a doubt that if she spent any more time in his company, as his friend, she would grow attached to a man who couldn't possibly remain in her life. They were on two separate paths.

He was Crown Prince. She was a medic. And those two things did not have any future unity.

Krystiana hurried to her quarters, closing the doors behind her and walking straight over to her bed. Sitting down on the mattress, she pulled her mother's photograph from her bag, dusted it off with her fingers and placed it on the bedside cabinet, staring at it for a brief moment.

If only you could see me now, she thought. *Living in a palace in Italy.*

It was far removed from where they had lived in Kraków. What would her mother say?

He's handsome. Is he single?

She smiled at her mother's imagined voice and, raising her fingers to her lips, kissed them and pressed her fingertips to her mother's photo. *'Tęsknię za toba,'* she said. *I miss you.*

A knock at the door had her wiping her eyes and sniffing before she called out 'Come in!'

Sergio walked into the room. 'Good evening, Dr Szenac. His Majesty King Alberto has invited you to join him and his family for this evening's meal.'

'Oh, that's very nice of him but I'm rather tired. It's been a stressful day and I'd really like to just turn in—maybe have a tray brought to my room, if that's okay?'

Sergio nodded. 'I understand.' He turned and made to go, but then stopped, as if changing his mind. 'It would not be wise to turn down the King's invitation, Dr Szenac. I believe this very morning he approved the finance for the renovation of your villa and he wishes to meet with you. I fear he would not take kindly if you did not come.'

Of course. It wasn't just Matteo paying to fix her home. It was coming out of the royal family's purse. To live in their home, to take their money and then not even show her face at dinner would be incredibly rude.

She glanced down at Bruno, who had settled into his doggie bed and was chewing on his toy.

'Right. I understand. Please tell the King that I will be happy to join him and his family at dinner. What time should I be ready?'

'Dinner is at seven.'

'Perfect. Thank you.'

'The dress code is smart casual.'

She wasn't worried about the dress code. She was worried that they would sit her opposite Matteo and she would end up looking into those deep blue eyes of his all evening.

He didn't always eat dinner with his father. They both led such busy lives, on such different schedules, it was rare for both of them to be home at the same time. But his father had just come back from a short break in Africa and wanted to catch up with his son before a tour around Europe took him away again.

It was a good thing they both enjoyed travelling and meeting new people.

'It was a great shame to be informed about Dr Bonetti's wife. I hear that she has pulled through?' his father asked.

'Yes. My advisor tells me that earlier today she was moved off the critical care unit and on to a ward.'

'That's excellent. I must send them a token of my affection. Remind me to tell my secretary.'

Matteo smiled. 'I will.'

And that was when the doors to the dining room were opened by Sergio.

'Ah! This must be our new guest. Dr Szenac!' The King got to his feet. 'Welcome! I'm so pleased to meet you, though it is such a shame it has to be under such difficult circumstances. How is your home looking?'

Matteo watched his father greet Krystiana, kissing both her cheeks and smiling broadly. Krystiana looked tired, but her eyes were sparkling still.

She curtsied. 'Your Majesty. Thank you. The work has begun, so hopefully I won't have to impose upon you and your family for too long.'

'Nonsense! Our home is your home. We wouldn't have it any other way. Please—take a seat.'

Sergio held out a chair for her and she settled into it—directly opposite Matteo.

He smiled at her. 'How was work today?'

'Interesting. Though it always is. You never know who's going to walk through the door.'

'Keeps you on your toes!' his father said.

She nodded.

Sergio filled her glass with water and laid a napkin over her lap. 'Can I get you a drink, Dr Szenac?'

'I'm fine, thank you, Sergio.'

'We must introduce you to everyone. You know who I am, and my son, but on your right is my sister Beatrice, and opposite her is her husband Edoardo. They're here on a flying visit from Florence.'

Krystiana smiled at them both. 'I'm very pleased to meet you.'

Matteo could see that she was nervous. Surrounded by royalty. Hemmed in by titles. A king, a prince, a duke and a duchess. She was blushing, her face suffused with a rich pink colour in both cheeks, as she struggled to make eye contact with anyone. He hated seeing her looking so uncomfortable.

Knowing how badly her day had started, he decided to rescue her. 'How's Bruno doing with the change in his home-life?'

She looked up at him, grateful. 'He's adapting very well. Almost as if he always suspected he was meant for palace life. I think he likes having servants.'

He laughed, enjoying her smile.

'And how are *you* adapting to being back in palace life, Matteo?' asked his Aunt Beatrice. 'It must be such a relief for you to get back to normal?'

He nodded. 'It is, but I expected it to be different… getting home.'

'How do you mean?'

Beatrice looked extremely interested, but then again she would be. He hadn't seen her since before his kidnapping, and he hadn't had much chance to talk to his father's side of the family about what had happened.

'When you're in that situation, held captive, what keeps you going is the thought of returning home. Of getting back. Of everything being all right again.'

'But…?'

'But it's not that way at all. You feel like you've been held captive in time, and that although everyone else has moved on you're still in the same place. You want to process what has happened, but it's difficult.'

'Your father tells me you had some *therapy* afterwards?' She said it as if therapy was a bad word.

'Yes.' He looked at Krystiana and smiled. She would know what that meant. 'I still am.'

'Really?'

'I've found it to be helpful.'

Beatrice raised a perfectly drawn-on eyebrow, but didn't ask any more.

He shared a look with Krystiana. 'There are some… after-effects you don't expect.'

'Like what?' asked Edoardo, sitting back as the first course arrived and the servants laid steaming bowls of soup in front of them all.

'Bad dreams. And being enclosed in any small space is a little unnerving now. Being afraid of the dark.'

Krystiana looked up at him. He knew. Knew that she was the same. That she had the same fear as him. And suddenly he didn't want to be at this dinner any more, surrounded by the others. He wanted to be somewhere talking to *her*. Asking her about how she dealt with the same things. Whether she'd beat the fears or still struggled with them.

'And, of course, there was all that business with Mara,' said Beatrice, with a snide tone to her voice. 'I always said she wasn't the one for you.'

Yes, well... 'She was my best friend, Aunt Bee.'

'So she should have waited for you.'

'She was alone and afraid.'

He tried to stand up for his ex-wife, despite his feelings. He knew what she'd gone through. They'd talked about it many times, and as far as he could see she'd done what any person would. The humiliation he'd felt, expecting to come home to a wife when in fact she was actually his ex-wife, had been his to work through.

His aunt sniffed and dabbed at her lips with her napkin. 'Well, so were *you*, I'd imagine.'

'She had no idea if I was alive or dead. She was trying to raise a baby, all alone, and she was grief-stricken and needed comfort.'

'So she turned to Philippe? An old boyfriend?'

'He was there for her when I couldn't be. Come on, Aunt Bee. You know Mara and I weren't a true love-match. We had an arranged marriage. I would never have stood in the way of her finding her true love.'

'She'd just had your *child*!' Beatrice was clearly appalled by Mara's behaviour.

'That's enough, Bee,' said his father, bringing order to the table. 'I do apologise, Dr Szenac. We are a passionate family and often our get-togethers can be a little...heated.'

She smiled at him. 'That's all right. Please don't apologise. I'm sure it's the same in any family.'

'I'm grateful for your understanding. Is your family like this?'

Matteo saw her take a sip of soup, her hand trembling, and knew it would be difficult for her to answer. Her mother was dead. Her father was in prison.

'I have only my Aunt Carolina, and though we love each other very much we do have our moments.'

His father guffawed. 'So we are normal, then?'

Krystiana laughed, too. 'Yes, you are.'

Edoardo leaned over. 'You're a doctor, I believe?'

'Yes. I have a practice in Ventura, which I share with the royal physician, Dr Bonetti.'

'Ah, yes. I think someone told me that earlier...before you came. Are you married, Doctor?'

She blushed. 'No.'

'Planning on it?'

She shook her head. 'No.'

'Why ever not?' interrupted Beatrice.

Krystiana looked uncomfortable. Again. Matteo understood that his family could be a bit much. They were inherently nosy and thought they were the authority on most subjects.

He interjected for her. 'Marriage isn't the be-all and end-all of life, Aunt Bee. Plenty of people remain happily single.'

'But what's the point of *being* here, then?'

Krystiana looked at him in a panic. 'How did you and Mara meet?' she asked, clearly wanting to divert the topic of conversation away from herself.

'We were distant cousins and we had known each other since we were children.'

'You grew up together?'

He nodded. 'Her father is an earl. We were best friends. Went to school together. I loved hanging out with Mara—it seemed the most obvious thing that we should marry, and of course it strengthened the relationship between our families.'

'You had a happy marriage?'

Matteo shrugged. 'It seemed to be. We had our ups and downs, but all couples do. Our friendship was something that neither of us wanted to lose. And we haven't—despite what happened.' He flicked a look at his aunt, who clearly still disapproved.

'You weren't worried that marriage to one another would change your friendship?' Krystiana persisted.

'No. We knew we loved one another and had done for years. We didn't expect marriage to change that.'

She nodded. 'That's good. I'm glad you were happy together.'

He smiled, feeling they were in some kind of a conspiracy together. 'Me too.'

'And then you had a child together,' added Beatrice, raising her eyebrows as if she doubted the wisdom of that decision.

'Alexandra. She's beautiful, by the way, and I can't wait for you to meet her.' He directed his answer to Krystiana.

'I look forward to it.'

His face was stretching into a broad grin as he looked at her, and he was almost forgetting there were other people around the table. When he did remember, he looked at them to see they were looking at him rather strangely. He looked away and sipped at his wine.

He could remember the look on Mara's face when she'd told him that she was pregnant. She'd looked so happy! And he'd been thrilled too that he was about to be a father. But he'd known Mara wasn't the soul mate he'd always hoped for. Mara had always talked about having children, and about how she hoped to be a good mother to her baby. How she hoped to care for it herself as much as she could, and not let royal nannies get in the way and take over. They'd both had such dreams for their child, and it was disappointing that it hadn't worked out.

But he was pleased for Mara and the happiness that she had found with Philippe. He was pleased that, despite the kidnapping trauma, she had managed to move on with her life and find true joy with a man she loved. A proper love. Romantic love. Something he'd once yearned for but had now vowed to stay away from.

He'd been hurt by what had happened between him and Mara. But he couldn't imagine being in love with someone and losing them, the way his father had lost his mother, the love of his life.

If anything, he was a little envious of Mara. But he knew he wouldn't find anything like that for himself.

Couldn't find that for himself.

Because what if he lost it all again? It had hurt to let Mara go. To let another man help raise his child. And he'd seen the devastation romantic loss could cause.

He didn't ever want to go through that pain.

He'd had enough pain already.

Krystiana asked to be excused at the end of the meal, as she had a long day at the practice tomorrow, and Matteo offered to walk her back to her quarters. She was a little anxious about that, but figured it was only a short distance and she could hardly refuse him in front of his family.

And as they walked Matteo began to tell her more about his kidnapping.

'…and then they just came out of nowhere.'

'The people who took you?'

He nodded, those blue eyes of his now stormy and dark.

'Yes. They emerged from the side of the road, holding machine guns and wearing masks. I had to stop the car. Mara was in the back, pregnant, breathing heavily from her contractions.'

'I remember she was in labour. It was on the news.'

'They approached, threatened my men with guns to their heads and pulled me from the vehicle, binding my hands with rope and pulling a dark bag over my face.'

'You must have been terrified!'

'I was. I thought they might do something to Mara, too. That we might lose the baby. I remember struggling, trying to free myself, trying to do what I could to distract them from my wife and unborn child.'

'But they left Mara behind?'

'Yes. They were just after me. I was hit over the head with something. A rifle butt—maybe something else. I think I passed out and they dragged me to another vehicle.'

She shook her head in amazement. 'I don't know how I would have coped with that.'

'We drove for a long time. I tried to remember which way the vehicle turned—right or left—whether I could hear anything outside that might help—like trains or traffic, the sea…anything!'

'And did you?'

'No. We headed deep into the country and I was dragged into somewhere dark and cold.'

'The cave?'

'Yes. I was chained like an animal to a metal post and kept there, underground, for two years.'

Krystiana swallowed hard as they arrived at the door to her quarters. She was imagining it all too clearly. How it must have felt. The panic inside him. The loss of control. The helplessness. Being at someone else's mercy. She knew how that felt *exactly*.

'Two years… I thought six weeks was a long time.'

'You were just a child.'

'I know, but…'

He looked down at the floor. 'It makes you realise the resilience of the human spirit, doesn't it?'

She nodded, biting her lip. His story reminded her so much of her own, and she'd never had anyone who had been through something similar to talk to about this. The need to share with him was intense.

And that was exactly why she had to go into her room. She'd thought she'd said goodbye to all these memories. Had put all the pain in a box and stored it right at the back of her brain, where it couldn't hurt her any more. But being with him, listening to him talk about his own experiences, made her want to bring it back out again and pick over it. Analyse it. Try to make sense of it.

'Well, I have a long day of work tomorrow. I need to be up, bright and early.'

'Of course.' He nodded, then looked at her. 'How do you sleep?'

She looked into his eyes then, and knew she couldn't lie to him. 'With a night-light. You?'

He smiled, but it was filled with sadness and empathy. 'The same.'

Krystiana nodded. She should have known. She'd always been embarrassed about having one, and she'd never dreamt she would ever tell anyone about it—because why would she need to? No one would ever get that close. But telling him had been easy. *Easy.*

'Well, goodnight, Matteo. I hope you have pleasant dreams.'

'You too, Krystiana. You too.'

She woke early, disturbed by a dream in which she'd found herself back in that bunker, back in that hole in the ground, screaming for someone to find her, to save her, when suddenly the roof had opened. She'd shielded her eyes from the light as she saw someone kneel down and offer her a hand. When she took it, and when she was pulled from the earth, it was into Matteo's arms, and suddenly she'd found herself against his chest.

She'd woken with a start, her heart pounding.

Needing some fresh air before work, Krystiana stepped out into the morning sun and stopped in the gardens for a moment, just to breathe in the warm summer air, her eyes closed.

She'd expected to be alone. No one else awake but the

servants, busily working away behind the scenes, but she suddenly felt a presence by her side.

She opened her eyes and saw Matteo. 'Morning.'

'Good morning. Couldn't sleep?'

She couldn't tell him about her dream. 'I just needed some fresh air. I've never enjoyed being cooped up inside.'

He looked out over the gardens. 'No. Nor me. Come on—let me show you everything.'

He walked her down a path that lay before her like something in an exquisite painting. Green hues of olive and emerald, fern and lime, pine and sage, were layered and interspersed with shots of fuchsia, gold, white and rose. Someone talented had landscaped these gardens, and as they walked past lily ponds and bubbling water features, fountains and grottos, she marvelled at all that she could see.

'This is a beautiful place. Are these gardens open to the public?'

'No. They're my own private project.'

She looked at him, amazed. '*You* designed them?'

He smiled. 'Designed them, helped build them, planted almost every seed.'

'But this is *years* of work!'

'I started young. I always had—what do they call it?—green fingers!'

She laughed. 'Yes! Wow. I had no idea. You must have missed it incredibly when you weren't here.'

'I knew they were in good hands. And the thought of them kept me going when I was captive.'

'The memory?'

'I kept imagining myself walking along the paths, lifting a flower to smell its scent. I tried to remember how I'd built it. Created it. In my head I lost myself here many times. But by losing myself here, I *kept* myself. If that makes any sense?'

She nodded. 'It does. It anchored you.'

'Si.'

He led her down a curving stepped path, bordered with bushes she couldn't name that were higher than her head, flowering with tiny blue and white flowers, until they emerged in a sun garden that had a sundial at its centre. The floor had been laid with coloured stones—a mosaic depicting a knight fending off a giant green dragon.

'You did this, too?'

'It came from a book I read as a child. The tale of St George and the Dragon. A story that fascinated me. This mosaic was a birthday gift from my mother when I was ten years old.'

'A whole mosaic? My mother used to buy me socks for *my* birthday.'

He smiled. 'Socks are useful. Was it cold in Poland?'

'Only in winter.'

'Was your birthday in the winter months?'

She laughed. 'No. July.'

She went over to look more closely at the sundial. It was made of a dark stone, slate in colour. But marbled with white. She had no idea what it actually was, but the dial itself was exquisite, with a hand casting a shadow to one side.

She checked her watch. 'It tells the correct time.'

'Of course.'

She looked around them, saw that the palace was hidden by trees and bushes. 'You could almost imagine the palace isn't there,' she said.

Matteo smiled.

'If I lived here permanently I'd want a reminder of this at all times of the year, so that even in winter I'd know that spring was coming,' she said.

'Don't you know that anyway?'

'Yes, but…sometimes it takes a long time to get what you want. I'd want to capture this. This beauty.'

'You could take a photograph.'

She looked at him then. 'You know what? I can think of something better!'

He frowned. 'What is it?'

She smiled. 'Just you wait!'

'You want me to *paint*?' Matteo looked at Krystiana, doubtful.

He could plant a flowerbed, landscape a garden, and would eventually rule a kingdom, but to paint a picture? With his fingers? He wasn't a child…

But something about Krystiana's smile made him willing to give it a go. There was something about her. Something compelling. But for the life of him he couldn't work out what it was.

She was lit up from the inside at the thought of painting, and she'd had a servant at the palace fetch her painting equipment from her room. There were easels and palettes, and paints in acrylic and watercolour in all the colours of the rainbow.

'Remind me again why we're not using brushes?'

'Because this is much more fun. Touch the canvas as you create. Be at one with your picture. I want you to paint the garden. Not just what you see, but what it makes you *feel* as you look at it. I want you to try and use colour to feed your emotions into the work.'

'How do I do *that*?'

'Don't think about it too much. Go by instinct—it's what I do.'

He looked at the blank white canvas. 'I feel ridiculous.'

'Forget I'm here.'

'Are you going to be watching me?'

'No, I've got to go to work. But I would love to see your painting when I get back.'

He looked at her doubtfully, but then he closed his eyes for a moment, enjoying the soft breeze over his face, the warmth of the sun upon his skin, and tried to think about how this garden made him feel.

Before he knew it the soft, warm, fragrant breeze of the garden had awakened his senses. And he began.

Krystiana watched him for a moment, mesmerised by the tentative smile appearing on Matteo's handsome face, and when she realised that she was watching *him* more than she was watching the painting, she quietly slipped away.

CHAPTER FOUR

PRINCESS ALEXANDRA ROMANO was a dainty little thing and cute as a button. With her father's features, she had the cutest large blue eyes, framed by thick, long, dark eyelashes and the sweetest smile.

Her father carried her on his hip. 'Alex—meet Krystiana.'

Krystiana gave her a little wave. 'Hello, Alex. You didn't have to meet me from work, Matteo. I'm sure you have plenty of other things to be doing.'

'We were out for a walk. I saw the car pull up and thought I'd introduce you two.'

Behind her, Bruno jumped out of the car and Alex squealed with delight. 'Doggy!'

Matteo put her down so that she could give Bruno a cuddle. He happily rolled over onto his back, tongue lolling.

'I can't compete with a dog!'

'Can any of us?' She smiled at him, then reached into the back seat to grab her bag.

'How was work today?'

'Good. You?'

'Good. I finished my painting, by the way. I'm not sure you'll think it's Picasso, but…it's done.'

'Maybe you could show me later?'

He nodded. 'Sure. Alex? Come on, now, sweetheart. We must go.'

'But I want to play with the puppy!'

Krystiana smiled at her. 'I'm sure Bruno would love it if Alex took him into the garden. I've got some bags if he misbehaves.' She pulled from her handbag a small pouch filled with blue plastic bags.

Matteo took it. 'Thanks. Maybe you could join us later? Collect Bruno before my darling daughter wears him out completely.'

'Sure. I've got some work to do on my computer first.'

'Okay. I'll see you later.'

She nodded, anxious to be away. She'd spent the day worrying about their time in the garden that morning. About how pulled towards him she often felt. Was she a moth? Or was she the flame? Either way, allowing herself to get close to Matteo was dangerous. He was a very attractive man and he was far too easy to talk to, far too easy to care about.

She knew she would fall deeply if she allowed herself. It was a fatal flaw. She was too trusting. And she simply couldn't allow that. She wanted to love and be loved, but she was scared of it. All the people that she had loved had been lost. And the one person who should have loved her the most had hurt her irreparably.

Love did something to people. It twisted them in ways they did not expect and there was no guaranteeing who it might happen to. She didn't want to take any risks with her heart.

'I'll see you later.' He picked up Bruno's lead, and with his daughter began walking the dog away from her.

And that's how easy it is, she thought. *For you to be discarded. For people to move on and leave you behind.*

Her father had loved her so much he had tried to hide her underground, but now that he was in prison did he ever try to contact her?

No.

Some love! And that from the man who should have loved her the most.

Krystiana did not need to be loved so little or so much that someone wanted to ensnare her. Or lie to her, convincing themselves that what she didn't know wouldn't hurt her. Because they'd be wrong.

A relationship with an aunt and a dog was as far as she would go. Matteo could be a friend, an acquaintance, and nothing more.

Matteo stood watching his daughter play in her sandbox outside. She had such joy in her face as she scooped sand, trying to make herself a sandcastle and then arranging her carved wooden dinosaurs into position, as if they were protecting it.

Alex made all her own sound effects, too. 'Grr...' she said, and made roaring noises as she stomped them around the base of the castle.

He couldn't help but feel his heart swell with his love for her. She was just so perfect. He and Mara might not have been perfect, but their little girl was. As long as she was in his life, then nothing else mattered. She was all he needed and his whole heart was hers. There would never be anyone else and that was okay. She was the most honest person he knew. An open book. He didn't have to worry about Alex breaking his heart. At least, he hoped not.

He knelt down, suddenly feeling the need to be close to her. He smiled—because how could he not when he was with his beautiful daughter?

'Are you building a castle? Or a palace?

'A palace.'

'Ah, I see. Like this one?'

Matteo settled down onto his knees and continued to watch his daughter play. He was so proud of her. Of the way she'd grown so big and strong without his help or influence in her early years. He was so sad that he'd missed them, but he knew that Mara had not let their daughter forget him. His ex and her new love had raised Alex wonderfully. And even though Mara had left him, she'd never taken away his daughter.

Alberto, his father, wouldn't have stood and watched idly as Mara took away the future heir to the throne. And it saddened him that his own mother hadn't lived long enough to see her grandchild grow up. An undiagnosed brain aneurysm had ruptured one evening after she had gone to bed.

'She looks like you when she concentrates.'

He jumped at the voice and stood up, noticing Krystiana holding on to Bruno's lead.

'Krystiana. I thought you were still working?'

'I needed some fresh air. Being inside for a few hours always makes me feel this way. It's so beautiful out here, I'm amazed you ever go back indoors.'

He nodded. 'If I could spend my life out here then I would be a very happy man.'

Kneeling again, he began to build his own sandcastle and situated the dinosaurs around it. He created a small moat and made one of the dinosaurs fall into it. He made an 'ahh…' noise as it fell.

Alex chuckled.

He and Krystiana shared a smile and he felt something inside him—a warmth he hadn't felt before, something weird that made his heart pound—and he had to look away from her, focus on what was happening with Alex.

But he was totally aware of the very second that Krystiana left with Bruno. He momentarily stopped what he was doing and watched her go…

He knew it was late, but she was needed. *Now.*

Matteo banged on her door. 'Krystiana! Are you awake?'

There were some muffled sounds and then he heard her call out.

'I'm coming—hang on!'

He waited, aware of the clock ticking onwards and trying his best not to be impatient. When she finally opened the door he tried not to notice her delightful bed-head and sleepy blue eyes. Nor the fact that she wore a short white robe, tied at her waist, revealing very bare, shapely legs.

'A boat has sunk just off the coast, carrying Syrian refugees. There were families on board. Children. A team has been assembled on the beach, and a rescue operation is underway, but as one of the few medics on the island—'

He didn't need to say any more. The tiredness was instantly gone from her face and instead it was filled with a determination.

'Give me two minutes!'

She ran barefoot across her quarters to the bedroom and yanked open the wardrobe, grabbing a pair of jeans, a soft tee shirt and a jacket, and pulled everything on over her pyjamas. At the bottom of her wardrobe, was a bag that she grabbed, and in much less than the two minutes she'd asked for she was ready to go.

'What do you know so far?'

The royal car raced the team of helpers down towards the beach, where an impromptu camp had been set up to appraise and assess the refugees as they were rescued and brought to shore.

Overhead lights had already been erected, lighting up the coastline, revealing the massive operation already at work. To one side was a tent with a white flag with a red cross on it, and it was to this that she raced.

Matteo had leapt out of the vehicle when they'd arrived and headed straight across the sand towards a small motorised boat that was waiting to take him out to assist with the rescue. It was such a small island, but she was aware that the royal family had helped out in a crisis before. It made them more beloved of their people, showing that they didn't just sit behind the protective walls of their palace but that they got their hands dirty and helped out whenever there was a problem.

Years ago there'd been a small earthquake in Italy, but the tremors and aftershocks had affected Isla Tamoura, bringing down buildings and trapping people in the rubble. Alberto and his son had gone to help there—she could remember seeing it on the news.

She had to assume he knew what he was doing now and that he was in safe hands. Right now she had patients who were wet and cold and in danger of hypothermia.

Krystiana entered the tent and was thrilled to see Dr Bonetti already there, assessing a bedraggled patient. Giving him a quick nod of greeting, she got to work to check on patients of her own.

A woman sat in front of her, huddled in a blanket, shivering. Her eyes were wide and terrified.

She gave the woman a reassuring smile and showed her the stethoscope. 'I'm a doctor. Krystiana. What's your name?'

'R-Roshan.'

'Roshan? I need to listen to your heartbeat, okay?' She patted at her own chest and her patient nodded.

Her chest sounded fine. Her heart-rate was a little fast, but she put that down to the situation. Slowly she tried to communicate with Roshan, explain the examinations she needed to carry out. Blood pressure. Temperature. Pulse. Oxygen saturations. She moved more slowly than she would have liked, but it was important not to frighten this woman any more than she already was.

Her body had been under huge amounts of stress, but

all she found was that Roshan was soaked through, a little dehydrated and also very hungry.

As the examination went on Roshan began to cry, saying things in Arabic that Krystiana didn't understand. She seemed to be asking her about something. Pleading. Her words were a cacophony of sounds. What could it be?

Krystiana could only imagine how scared she was. So far away from her home. A place she'd had to flee from for whatever reason. Was her life in danger? What had she offered the captain of the boat in exchange for her passage? Had she given him everything she had? All her money?

It made her sick to think about it.

She gave Roshan an extra blanket, and was just about to check on another patient when Matteo came barging through the tent entrance, a soaked child in his arms.

Roshan cried out and threw off her blanket. *'Qamar!'* she screamed.

Krystiana pointed at an empty cot. 'Over here.'

She watched as Matteo carried the child over and carefully laid him on the bed.

'He's not gained consciousness since we picked him out of the water but he's breathing. I noticed a lump on the back of his head.'

'Ask Dr Bonetti for warm IV fluids. He'll show you where they are. And fetch some more blankets.'

Matteo raced off to do her bidding whilst she examined Qamar and tried to gain venous access.

He was indeed unconscious, but breathing at a steady rate. The lump on the back of his skull indicated that something had hit him hard, knocking him out, though thankfully she couldn't feel any fracture, or a break to the skin that would need stitching.

She peeled him out of his wet clothes—Roshan helping when she realised what Krystiana was doing—and then covered him with the blankets that Matteo brought over.

'I have the IV.'

'I've inserted a cannula—let's get him hooked up.'

'What can I do to help?' he asked.

'Look after Roshan for me. I think she might be his mother.'

She got in the cannula and started the warm IV running. Then she checked to make sure he had no other visible wounds or any broken bones. She checked his heart-rate and it was steady and sure, but he was thin and bony and she didn't know how strong he was. She'd be happier getting him to a major hospital, where they could give his head a scan to make sure there were no brain bleeds or contusions.

She looked over at Matteo, who was doing his best to communicate with Roshan. His clothes were soaked from carrying Qamar, but he wasn't complaining. She was so grateful to him. For getting involved like this. She could see that he was doing a wonderful job with Roshan, who now sat beside the bed of her son, clutching her prayer beads and dabbing at her eyes with a tissue.

'Shukraan! Shukraan...' she said to them both.

Krystiana looked at Matteo. 'What does that mean?'

'I don't know. Perhaps she's saying thank you?'

'Maybe. Are there any more?'

'The boats are going to stay out in the bay for a few more hours, but it looks like we got everybody.'

'How many people in total were on that boat?'

'So far, twelve.'

Twelve people in the water.

Dr Bonetti came over to greet Matteo and thank him for his assistance.

'What's the status of the other patients?'

Dr Bonetti looked grave. 'Mild hypothermia in some cases. A couple are a little malnourished, but that can be easily sorted out over the next few weeks. One had a dislocated shoulder that I've re-sited. We did lose one, though.'

'Who?' Krystiana asked.

'An old man. The coldness of the water was too much for his heart.'

She felt awful at the news. What these people must have gone through—trying to find freedom, doing everything they could, even something that was dangerous, to try and achieve it. What must it have been like for them, travelling on that boat, all huddled together without enough rations to go around?

Had Roshan given up her share of fresh water so that her son would survive the journey? Parents did that, didn't they? Loved their children so much they would gladly give up their own lives if it meant their child survived. That was what they were meant to do, anyway, if the situation arose. She'd like to think she would do the same thing.

'What's going to happen to them?'

'We'll keep them here overnight. Make sure everyone is stable. And then they'll have to be transferred to hospital—'

Matteo frowned. 'They'll have to go on another boat?'

'We have a shuttle boat that can take them. We've used it before—they'll make it there safely.'

Matteo frowned. 'A shuttle boat? I have a ship they could use. It would be larger and more comfortable. Faster, too. I imagine they won't want to spend much time on the water again.'

Krystiana looked up at him. 'That's very kind of you.'

'It's the least I can do. I'm just ashamed it's not more.'

She smiled at him, her gaze dropping to his wet shirt. 'You must be freezing. Here—take a blanket.' She offered him one of the warm blankets from the pile and draped it around his shoulders.

He looked down at her as she did so. 'Thank you.'

Krystiana looked up into his blue eyes and fireworks went off in her belly. Those hypnotic eyes of his…those thick dark eyelashes… His soft, full lips…

Blinking rapidly, she cleared her throat and looked away. 'Well, I must get on. Neuro obs and…stuff.'

Matteo also looked awkward. He nodded. 'Of course. I'll go and make arrangements for the ship to escort these people tomorrow.'

She nodded and turned away, feeling the skin on her face flaming with a heat that she'd never experienced before, her heart pounding, her mouth dry.

What on earth was happening?

And why did she feel like this?

CHAPTER FIVE

SHE DIDN'T SLEEP much that night when she got back to the palace. Her mind was a whirlpool of thoughts.

I'm attracted to Matteo.

It had to be that. She knew what the first flames of attraction felt like and what she'd felt hadn't been flames but a raging fire, out of control.

There'd been another man once. When she'd been at university. Adamo… She'd studied with him and he'd been nice. They'd gone out on a few dates—dinner, dancing—and he'd had the ability to make her laugh.

She'd begun to think she'd found the one. Something that had started as a slow burn had quickly become a flame. She'd fallen in love with him and, determined to be the one who took control of everything, had asked him to marry her.

And that was when her world had come crashing down around her ears again. Because he'd said no. He couldn't marry her. He was already married! Krystiana, to him, had been nothing but a fling.

It had made her feel used and stupid and ashamed. She had let her attraction to him roar out of control as she'd sought the happiness she felt she deserved, but she'd been a fool!

It had taken weeks for her to sleep again, to think straight again. It had been as if she'd been thrown back in time to when nothing made sense and she'd hated that—because she'd always kept herself safe by controlling everything in her life.

After what had happened with her father—and then Adamo, who had humiliated her—she had vowed to herself never to give her power away again. Never to give her heart to anyone. Because those who had your heart had the power to hurt you and she'd been through enough.

But this thing with Matteo…she didn't feel she had a choice. It felt like something that was happening without her having a hand on the steering wheel. She was in a car and it was careening out of control, down a sheer mountainside, and the brakes weren't working.

How could she stop it?

I could leave. I could rent a place. Nothing is stopping me. And that would be my choice, then, wouldn't it?

That seemed a good idea, and it was still a good idea after breakfast, when there came a knocking at her door. Hoping and praying that it wasn't Matteo, she opened it to see a woman she didn't know holding the hand of Princess Alex, his daughter.

She beamed a smile at the little girl and crouched down to her level. 'Hello, Alex! What are you doing here?'

'I'm going horse-riding!'

'Horse-riding? That sounds fun. I've never done that—aren't you lucky?'

'One day, darling, Krystiana, you will ride a pony of your own.'

She tried to ignore the voice of her father in her head.

'Could you come? Bruno, too?'

She thought about it. She could. After the hullaballoo of last night's rescue she needed something nice and settling. It was the weekend, she didn't have work today or tomorrow, and she really liked Alex. Perhaps it could be the last thing she did before she packed her things and left?

'All right. But I'm going to leave Bruno here. I'm not sure how he is around horses and I don't want there to be an accident. Is that all right?'

Alex nodded. 'Come on, then! We're going *now*!'

'I'll meet you there. I just need to change.'

Alex and the woman who was clearly her nanny nodded and headed off, whilst Krystiana checked her wardrobe for the right gear. What did people wear to ride horses? She hoped she'd get a gentle one. She'd hate to be stuck on the back of a galloping horse she couldn't stop…

She'd had enough of that kind of terror already.

Krystiana reached up her hand to stroke the mane of a beautiful grey horse. 'She's gorgeous!'

'Her name is Matilde.'

She jumped, not having expected to hear Matteo's voice. She'd thought it would just be Alex and her nanny. Maybe a groomsman, but no one else.

'Matteo…'

He smiled at her and patted the horse on its neck. 'She's a gentle beast and she will look after you.'

'Good. I'll need that. I haven't ridden before.'

He looked surprised. 'No? Then I'm glad you agreed to come along. Everyone should ride a horse at least once. Horses spark a passion that often consumes.'

Horses weren't the only thing that sparked a passion… She'd lain await all night thinking of him.

'Well, I could hardly turn down a princess, could I? And give up the opportunity of a lifetime?' She'd always wanted to ride a horse.

He laughed. 'No one can turn her down! Once she turns that smile upon you, you're lost.'

She knew the feeling.

'And the dark horse? Is he yours?'

He smiled. 'Galileo? *Si*. A very proud beast.' He could see the uncertainty in her face. Her anticipation. 'Nervous?'

'Yes. A lot.'

'Do you trust me?'

How could she answer that? To say anything but *yes* would be rude. 'Sure.'

'Don't worry. I'll lead Matilde with a guide rope and Sofia will guide Alex's pony. We're only going for a gentle walk through the orchard. No galloping.'

He smiled to reassure her.

'Alex, *mio cara*, let's get you up in that saddle.' He lifted his daughter up onto the horse's back, making sure she was secure and steady before letting go. 'Your helmet is on tight?'

'*Si*, Papà.'

Krystiana looked uncertain. 'I may need help getting up on this beast. How do you do it without falling off the other side?'

Matteo smiled at her. He held Matilde's reins firmly and showed Krystiana how to put her foot into the stirrup and hoist herself into the saddle.

She did it quickly, not wanting him to have to hold her around the waist or touch her bottom, because if he touched her anywhere below the belt line she feared for her heart-rate.

He mounted his own steed.

'Are we all ready?'

The two women nodded.

'Alexandra?'

His daughter nodded, her eyes on her horse's neck.

He made a small noise of encouragement to his horse and used his stirrups to urge the animal into a walk. The other three followed behind as he led them into the orchard.

The sun shone down on them from above, warming her bare arms and feeling good. As she adjusted to the horse's gait Krystiana found herself relaxing somewhat, beginning to enjoy the adventure.

It was everything she'd hoped it would be. The horse's motion was almost a rocking movement, hypnotic in its rhythm, and with the warmth of the sun and the beautiful orchard all around them she felt herself wanting to just relax and drift off—especially as she'd lost a lot of sleep last night.

It was such a strange world, she thought. That one moment she could be attending refugees on a beach, and the next moment be horse-riding. What were Roshan and Qamar doing now? And the others? Were they already in hospital? Were they feeling better?

Matteo led the parade of horses down a steep slope and along a small grassy path that would take them into the main thicket of trees.

As they moved along she listened to the birds singing, and then she heard the steady trickle of water and smiled when he led them towards a small babbling brook. Picture-perfect.

They stopped for a moment, and the horses sniffed at the water but chose to nibble on the tall grass alongside it.

'Is everyone all right?' asked Matteo.

Krystiana nodded—as did Sofia, the nanny.

'*Si*, Papà,' said Alex.

He smiled and urged the horses onward.

He'd not known Krystiana would be horse-riding with him and Alex. He'd thought it was just going to be himself, the nanny and his daughter. It had been a surprise to see her standing there at the stables, in figure-hugging jeans and a checked shirt. All she needed was a Stetson and she would look like a proper cowgirl.

Her long hair was in its usual plait. He'd spent the entire night, tossing and turning in bed, wondering what her hair would look like spread out over a pillow.

That moment they'd shared in the refugee tent had been…*electric.* He'd felt it. He'd noticed that she felt it too, but luckily she'd done something to avoid it.

He didn't need the complication of another relationship. He'd married his best friend and hadn't made that work—what hope would there be for anyone else? Plus, he couldn't contemplate the *idea* of another relationship. If you loved someone, you lost them, and the pain of that was too much.

His father was a different man since losing Matteo's mother, and when he himself had come home to find his mother dead and that his wife had moved on and begun a new relationship, he'd decided there and then that the only person he would ever love again would be his daughter.

He wasn't looking for love. Or a fling. His position dictated that a fling would be very bad news indeed. The Crown Prince of Isla Tamoura did *not* use women in such a way. He had standards. And morals.

Any deeper relationship was a no-go, so…

But seeing her here this morning had fired his blood once again, and he was glad that she was a novice with horses—it meant that he could lead without having to look at her or make eye contact, and everyone seemed quite content to just ride along and view the scenery in peace and quiet.

Not that his mind was peaceful. Or quiet. It was coming up with a million and one thoughts about Krystiana that he kept trying to push away.

I am not risking my heart again. No way.

The kidnapping, and then coming home to find his marriage over, his mother dead, were three huge stresses he'd already had to cope with, and there was his coronation coming up at the end of the year…

He just wanted to relax whilst he had the chance. He did not need the added complication of a forbidden crush. Because that was what it would be. They'd shared an experience. They'd both been glad to find someone else who knew how that felt—that was all.

A mind trick. The body playing games.

He knew he was stronger than that. He'd spent two years wondering if this was the day he was going to die and carrying on anyway. If he could get through *that*, then he could get through *this*.

A few more weeks and she'd be gone from his life. Any future physicals would be conducted by Dr Bonetti, and if he retired he would ask another doctor to take over that particular duty.

He could resist his feelings for a few more weeks.

CHAPTER SIX

'SHE'S BEAUTIFUL...' WHISPERED MARA.

Matteo looked over at his ex-wife, who lay on their daughter's bed as she went off to sleep. 'She is.'

Mara smiled. 'I wasn't talking about Alex. Though she is *very* beautiful, of course. I meant the woman I saw you with.'

He decided to play ignorant. He didn't need his wife playing games. 'You've already met Sofia. You hired her.'

'The *doctor*, Matteo.'

He raised an eyebrow. 'Krystiana? She's just staying here until her place gets fixed.'

'Is that all?'

He picked up the book they'd been reading to Alex and quietly slid it back onto his daughter's bookshelf. 'Of course that's all.'

'Are you sure, Matteo?'

He raised an eyebrow. 'Yes.'

'*Krystiana?* Not Dr Szenac?'

'We're friends. You call friends by their first name. Remember, Mara? We're friends—it's what *we* do.'

She nodded. 'Of course! Of course that's what friends do. I'm just not sure I've ever seen *friends* look at each other the way you two do.'

'I barely know her.'

'You barely know her or you're friends?'

His ex-wife slowly got off the bed, hoping their daughter wouldn't wake. They both crept from the room and Mara pulled the door almost closed as they headed into the next room.

Matteo handed his ex-wife the glass of wine she'd started earlier. 'Please don't, Mara.'

She stared him down. 'Don't what?'

'Don't try to matchmake.'

'I'm not! But I *am* asking you to be careful.'

'You're hinting. Just because you're all loved up, and you feel guilty about giving up on me, it does not mean I'm your responsibility.'

'I'm not trying to fix you up, Matteo. I'm asking you to think carefully about what you're doing.'

He shook his head at her, amused. 'Nothing's happened.'

She smiled. 'Keep it that way—or you're going to hurt a lot of people.'

The next day Krystiana found herself standing outside her villa with Aunt Carolina, who had agreed to meet her there. Some progress had been made. A lot of the loose rubble had been cleared and the first-floor ceiling had been propped up by scaffolding and made secure, whilst a lot of the loose brickwork had been hacked back, so that the hole in her wall had become almost twice the size. Inside, her furniture looked forlorn and strange, open to the elements, but she thanked her lucky stars that there'd been no rain and therefore no water damage.

'Carlo!' She waved to the foreman and he waved back, jumping down from a digger that was removing debris to another part of the site. 'How is everything going?'

'It's going as well as can be expected. My team are working hard and at all hours round the clock.'

'Are we still looking at a few weeks' work?'

'Three...four weeks, maybe. As long as there are no more surprises.'

'You've had surprises?'

He smiled. 'Not yet.' He turned to look at her aunt and she realised she hadn't introduced them. She did so.

'Buongiorno.'

She noticed the interested smile on Carlo's face as he looked at her aunt, and saw that Aunt Carolina was smiling back.

'You're working hard all day, every day? Seven days a week?' Carolina asked.

'Si.'

'Perhaps I should bring you and your crew some food? Some drinks?'

'That would be very kind of you—thank you. We lose a lot of time on lunch breaks, going to find food to eat, so that would help us work faster.'

Carolina beamed. 'Well, I'd like to think I was helping...'

Krystiana looked from one to the other and found herself smiling. Who'd have thought it? Carolina and Carlo? Her aunt had lived alone ever since her divorce, years ago, and had always said that men were more trouble than they were worth.

Clearly she was having a change of heart!

'Come on. We need to get going or we'll be late for lunch ourselves.' Krystiana interrupted.

'Of course. I'll see you later, Carlo.'

Carolina waved as she walked away with her niece back to their car.

Once inside, Krystiana turned to her. 'Well, *you've* changed your tune!'

'He was a very nice man!'

'They all are. To begin with. You tell me that all the time.'

'Maybe so—but being alone isn't all it's cracked up

to be. You have to give someone a chance to prove you wrong.'

Did she? Her father had proved her *right*. Those who had your heart could hurt you the most. As Adamo had. Did she have to give Matteo a chance? He seemed nice and kind. He seemed a good, strong, caring man. But what if that was just his public persona? What if he was someone else entirely?

The smile on her aunt's face put doubt into her mind for the next couple of hours, and she found herself wondering, as she was being driven back to the palace, whether she'd been too harsh in her decision-making and ought to give Matteo the opportunity to show her that he was not going to break her heart.

Perhaps if they went out once or twice, and the excitement of something new died down and the fear dissipated somewhat, she'd discover that they didn't have much in common anyway—so what was she worried about?

It could hardly become anything, anyway. He was a prince! He wouldn't enter a relationship lightly, either.

When she got back to her quarters she stared at the suitcase in the bottom of her wardrobe and decided she would leave it there just a little bit longer.

CHAPTER SEVEN

MATTEO HAD INVITED her to dinner in his quarters. He wasn't sure whether he should have or not, but he'd figured, *What the hell?* He was a grown man, they were both adults and they were friends. It wasn't as if he didn't have any self-control. He liked her. He could spend time with her. But that was all it would be.

It wouldn't be a late night. She was bound to be busy, would no doubt have some work to do in her quarters, and he'd only just said goodbye to Mara and Alex, who had gone back to their own private estate in Ventura. There was a load of work for him to catch up on.

He knew he might be playing with fire, but he also knew he couldn't spend the next few weeks jumping out of his skin every time he had to spend time with Krystiana. Best to have a couple of hours in her company and cool the heck down. Okay, so she had beautiful eyes and a nice smile. She was kind and generous and easy to be with…

I'm not exactly talking myself out of this, am I?

He put on some dark trousers and a white shirt. Simple elegance. Something he could feel relaxed in. He didn't want to look as if he was trying to impress her. Because he wasn't. But any gentleman showed respect for the woman he was with by dressing nicely for her.

Krystiana arrived on the dot of seven, her gentle knock

at the door signalling her arrival. His heart hammered in his throat and he paused before answering the door, but then he took a deep, steadying breath and swung it open.

And there she stood, looking gorgeous and summery in a blue wraparound dress, that long plait of hers over one shoulder.

'Hi. Come on in!' He stepped back.

'Thanks.' As she stepped in he automatically leaned forward to drop a kiss upon her cheek. He held his breath as he pressed his face close to hers, and his heart almost leapt from his throat as his lips pressed against her skin. She smelt of flowers and soap and something he couldn't quite put his finger on. Whatever it was, it was delicious.

And then he was pulling away and he could breathe again.

She'd flushed a beautiful pink in her cheeks and, clearly trying to distract him from it, she pointed. 'What's that? The painting you promised to show me?'

He nodded at the canvas on the easel, draped with a cover, smiling, but looking apprehensive. 'I'm no Da Vinci, but, yes. Here you go. What do you think?'

He pulled the cover off with a flourish so that she could see it.

An explosion of colour leapt out and he watched her face carefully as she picked up the canvas to consider it properly. Clearly he was new to painting, but he had tried hard and his use of colour was good for an amateur. Even if he said so himself. He'd enjoyed doing it and considered doing so again.

No, he wasn't Da Vinci, or Picasso, or any other famous painter. But it was definitely a Romano. Rich in texture and colour, a riot of green interspersed with cobalt blue, scarlet red and sunshine-yellow. A vast blue sky clear of clouds sat overhead, and he'd even attempted the mosaic floor, using his fingertips for each tile.

'Matteo, it's marvellous!'

'Thank you.' He was pleased that she liked it—he took pleasure from *her* pleasure.

'Are you sure you did this? It's beautiful! You've done a wonderful job for your first time.'

'Imagine what I'd be like with practice.' He smiled.

She looked at him, her smile uncertain.

'Yes! Yes, I imagine you would be brilliant!' She laid the canvas back upon the easel and admired it better by stepping back. 'You've captured the very essence of the garden. Full of life and joy. This will keep you going in the winter months when there's less in bloom.'

And suddenly he knew something. 'I'd like you to have it.'

'Me?'

He nodded. 'I can look at the real thing every day. You'll be going home soon and I'd like to think you will remember your visit.'

It saddened him to think of her leaving. She was a kindred spirit. Someone who had experienced the same thing as he and that was important. Who else would understand what he had gone through?

But it was more than that shared experience. There was a naturalness about Krystiana. Something about her that spoke to him. And it was confusing and worrying and exciting in different ways. But that was the whole point of tonight. To show that he could deal with that and not act on it. Krystiana could never be more than his friend, and that was the thing that he needed to remember more than anything else.

Besides, princes could not be with commoners. It was against the law of his country. So…that was that. As Mara had tried to forewarn him. And it was a *good* thing, because it kept him safe. She was out of bounds and men like him did not have flings. The media would have a field-day if he did. But thankfully his heart was boxed away. To all intents and purposes it was still in that mountain cave and he had to leave it there.

'I'm honoured. Thank you.'

He smiled, and being caught in her gaze once again was exhilarating. Everything else faded away and all he saw was her. He blinked and stepped back, indicating they should go further out onto the terrace, where the views were impeccable in the late evening light.

'Would you like to take a seat? Sergio will be here momentarily with the first course.'

'What are we having?'

A dash of attraction with a hint of lust and a heavy dose of desire.

'I told him to surprise us. I'm sure he won't let us down. He has quite the palate.'

'Really?'

'His family own a winery. Up in the Auriga Hills.'

Good. That's better. Talk about Sergio. The most unromantic topic you can think of. Wine and grapes and feet squishing grapes in age-old barrels. Sergio's feet. Yes, now, there's an image.

'I didn't know that.'

'I'm sure he'd love to show you around one day.'

'Have you ever been?'

'Yes. A few years ago now, though. Before I was kidnapped.'

She nodded. 'How do you feel about it now?'

He didn't mind talking to her about that, either. 'Sometimes it's like a dream. Like it never really happened to me. Other times it's like a nightmare and I remember everything. How about you?'

'Well, it's been a lot longer for me since it happened. But I understand what you mean. I tried to make sense of it once, by going to the place where it had happened. I thought if I confronted it then it wouldn't have any power over me.'

'What was that like?'

'Strange. The landowner agreed to walk me out to the spot where my father had created the bunker. He was very sweet to me. Very kind. Asking after my well-being, wanting to know that I was all right. He even apologised to me for not knowing. For not realising that I was out there. And then he pointed at a dip in the ground. It just looked so normal and inconsequential. No different from the rest of it. And yet in my mind it had held such power. The hole had been filled in, and scrub and mulch covered it over, but I stared at it, trying to imagine myself in such a small hole, shivering in the cold, clutching a book for comfort.'

He could imagine it all too easily. 'Did you have nightmares before?'

'Every night.'

'And going to the place...did that help get rid of them?'

'It did. I saw it was just a place that meant nothing any more. It wasn't the bunker that had harmed me—it was my father. That takes longer to get over. Someone close hurting you. But, yes, it was a good thing for me to do. It exorcised the ghosts that lingered. Gave me closure.'

'How so?'

She glanced at him. But thankfully not for too long. Her eyes were like welcoming pools he wanted to stay in.

'I think it's because it was the place I wanted to escape from so much. A place I told myself I would never again go near. I'd built it up into this huge thing. So that place... it haunted me. By returning I showed that I was stronger. I proved to myself that *I* was in control.'

Matteo nodded. He understood. And he was in awe of her bravery and courage.

'You could go back too, you know. I believe in you. If

you could get through two years in that place, then you can get through anything.'

'I don't have to go back. I've thought about it, but the bad dreams are only occasional and my therapist has been helping me a lot…sorting through my feelings.'

'Good. Talking therapy works really well. I'm glad you're getting a lot from it.'

He nodded. 'I am.'

At that moment Sergio arrived, carrying a tray, and laid down a small bowl in front of each of them. 'Butternut squash risotto,' he intoned. 'Do enjoy your meal.'

'Do you think being held hostage made you a different person?' she asked after a while.

'I'm still me.'

'Of course—but are you a stronger you now?'

'I'd like to think so. I've been given a different perspective on life. On trauma and struggle and just wanting to survive. I'd like to think I have taken that and learned from it, so that I can be a strong king when I take the throne.'

'You'll make an *excellent* king,' she said emphatically.

He was pleased at her confidence in him. It was something he shared. 'Thank you. I shall certainly try my very best.'

She nodded. 'I've no doubt. What other royal opens up his palace to a homeless woman? Helps search for survivors under earthquake rubble? Goes out to rescue asylum seekers? You're not afraid to get your hands dirty. You care. You're compassionate. You'll make an excellent monarch.'

She clearly meant every word. He was truly touched by her confidence in him. 'Thank you. That means a lot to me.'

She stared back and he found himself caught in her gaze. What *was* it about her that did this to him?

'Eat your risotto before it gets cold.'

She nodded, smiled and picked up her fork.

She imagined, as he spoke, what it might be like to be with him. Who wouldn't? He was a prince. Handsome and charming. A presence with an overwhelming masculinity that made itself known whenever she was with him. He was a good listener, a caring and thoughtful person, and she could see that he liked people.

He was always courteous and considerate to the servants in his employ, chatting to everyone the same way, no matter whether they were another member of the royal family or a gardener. She could appreciate his kindness, his heart, and his concern for his people and the future he might bring them. Clearly being King was something he took seriously.

But her body responded to him in ways she did not want. Her heart fluttered with excitement every time she saw him and she yearned for something more than what they had. But that was just her being foolish. A remnant from a previous time in which she'd trusted people.

'How do you see your life changing when you become King?' she asked, genuinely interested.

He shrugged. 'I imagine it will be pretty much the same. Just my title will be different. I'll be expected to attend more events. To do more touring, perhaps.'

'Isn't it hard for you to be away from your family?'

'It can be. The kidnapping made me see how important family is. Material things—possessions—those don't matter at all. It's people who count. Being with the ones you love. Leaving them hurts me, but it gets easier each time I do so.'

He ate a mouthful of their next course—a rich lasagne, oozing with béchamel sauce.

'What about you? You left your childhood home and moved to another country. Don't you ever miss Poland?'

'Sometimes. But I'm not so sure it's the country I miss as much as the people I knew there. Friends I made at school. The therapist I saw who became a good friend. My school teachers.'

'You enjoyed school?'

She smiled. 'I did. Very much so. I even thought I'd become a teacher when I was little—I loved it that much.'

'What made you become a doctor?'

'My mother dying the way she did. Hit by a bus. When I got to the hospital and saw how they were trying to save her, I…' Her mouth dried up and she had to take a sip of water. 'I felt in the way. I wanted to help too, but there was nothing I could do but cower in a corner. It wasn't until much later—after I'd moved to Isla Tamoura—that I decided I would never feel that helpless again and so I trained as a doctor.'

'You had focus?'

'Yes. It helped me a lot. Knowing I was working towards something.'

'I feel the same.'

'How so?'

'I grew up knowing I would become King one day. They train you for it, you know. Special lessons in law and etiquette and the history of tradition. They school you in politics and languages and even body language.'

She laughed. 'Really?'

'Really.' He smiled. 'I've always wanted to be a good king. As good as my father and loved by my people. But I've always known I don't want to be just a title behind the palace walls. I want to be involved—I want to get right down at the grass roots and know people. Be an active king who achieves things and is not just a figurehead. I want to be seen doing worthwhile work, not just waving at crowds from behind bullet-proof glass. Being a man of the people means a lot to me, and I intend to get it right. The kidnapping showed me just how much people matter, and if I can help them then I will.'

'Like housing homeless doctors?'

Matteo smiled. 'Exactly.'

She ate another mouthful of food, contemplating her next question.

'What?' he said.

She looked up at him.

'I can tell you want to ask me something.'

Krystiana dabbed at her mouth with a napkin. Then sipped her water. 'Do you ever get lonely?'

He looked straight back at her, considering her question. 'Do *you*?'

'I asked first.'

Matteo sat back. 'There's an element of being a royal that makes you lonely. People put you on a pedestal—they think you're above them so they don't try to reach you. They just admire you from afar. I'd like to think that I'm accessible to everyone, but… I have my father and my daughter. And my extended family, like Beatrice and Edoardo.'

'That's not what I meant.'

'What *did* you mean?'

'Do you miss being married?'

'My marriage to Mara was never a true love-match. Not romantic love, anyway. We were best friends and we still are, despite what happened. I haven't lost her. What about you? Do you ever see yourself settling down?'

She shook her head. 'No. No way.'

'Why not?'

How to answer? Krystiana looked out across the terrace, past the gardens and deep into the countryside, where the setting sun was making everything look hazy and dark. Should she tell him about Adamo? *No.* That was a whole embarrassing situation she never wanted to be in again.

'I don't think I'm capable of giving myself wholeheartedly to anyone. Not any more.'

'Why not?'

'Because I'd have to trust them, and that would make me vulnerable, and I promised myself I would never be made to feel vulnerable ever again.'

She stared back at him as if daring him to challenge her. To argue with her. Perhaps to laugh at her silly fears.

But he didn't do any of that.

He simply nodded in understanding. 'Okay. Good enough.'

'Well, thank you for inviting me to dine with you. I've had a wonderful time.'

Matteo nodded. 'It was my pleasure.'

They stood together by the doors, awkwardly trying to work out how to say goodnight to each other.

He felt that the right thing to do would be to kiss her on the cheek as he said goodbye, but when he'd done that earlier he'd inhaled her scent of soap and flowery meadows and felt a surge of hormones flood his system with arousal and attraction. If he did it again he simply wouldn't get to sleep tonight, and he'd already spent enough sleepless nights lately.

'It will be my turn to entertain you next.'

'I'll look forward to it.'

'All right. Well…goodnight, Matteo.'

'Goodnight, Krystiana.'

He hesitated, and reason told him it would be impolite just to walk away, strange to shake her hand and downright rude to do nothing at all. *Friends* kissed each other goodnight—and they were friends, weren't they?

Leaning in, he kissed one cheek, then the other, trying his hardest not to breathe in her delicious scent.

That would be wrong.

For him *and* for her.

It was just attraction. Nothing more. He couldn't be with her. Nor did he want to be. Being with Krystiana would mean falling hard for her and he wouldn't let that happen. He lived his life in the public eye. She'd be scrutinised down to her every blood cell by the press. And hadn't she just told him that she would never be vulnerable again? Nor trust anyone? Plus she'd already said that she didn't want to get into a relationship anyway, so…

Being in the public eye made you vulnerable. Being in a relationship made you vulnerable. It laid you out bare and then fate would tear you to pieces. Life was cruel and impossible to win. He wouldn't even try to put either of them through that.

But he knew he was attracted to her. She was so easy to talk to. He felt relaxed when he was with her. His true self. He could tell her things that he would never tell anyone else…

He shook his head vehemently as he closed his door. Nothing could come of it. No matter how much his body cried out for the intimacy of hers.

He could fight instinct. He could fight attraction.

And what would be the point in getting involved with someone he knew was not suitable? Falling for Krystiana would *destroy* him. He knew it. She was the type of woman he would fall hard for and he didn't want to be laid open to hurt again. Or humiliation when it all went wrong. And why wouldn't it? Everything else had.

Her life was going in one direction and his in another. They were in a fake bubble right now, and it wasn't sustainable.

Matteo turned and walked straight into his bathroom. He needed a cold shower.

Krystiana smiled at Mara, who sat opposite her in a splendid pure white tailored dress. The dress showed off Mara's sylph-like figure, all long limbs and elegance and grace. They'd met in the corridor of the palace as Mara had dropped off Alex and they'd come for a coffee in the royal gardens.

'What was it like for *you* when Matteo was taken?'

Krystiana was intrigued. She wanted to know what it had been like for those left behind. She was thinking specifically of her own mother, as they'd never had much time to talk about it before she died.

Mara let out a slow sigh. 'It was very difficult. No one knew what had happened to him and I feared the worst. Especially as I'd seen their treatment of him when he was taken. They hit him over the head with a rifle. The sound it made will haunt my dreams for ever.'

'Didn't you have guards? A convoy of any kind?'

'Yes, of course. But they took out the lead car and then surrounded us with armed men. And there'd been a new guard riding with us, who was actually one of them, and he had his gun at Matteo's head. They had no choice but to back down.'

'And then what happened?'

'Then he was gone. I screamed. I cried. I had to get into the front of the car to use the emergency radio. I was still contracting. Still in labour. It seemed an age before help arrived.'

'You gave birth *alone*?' Krystiana could hardly imagine that. At least her mother hadn't seen her being treated roughly. Had never seen inside the hole in the ground. Had not had to go through something like childbirth afterwards.

'My mother came, and my sister. They were able to get to the hospital in time.'

'And it was an easy birth?'

'My blood pressure was high, but the doctors felt that was because of what had happened. The trauma of Matteo's kidnapping. The violence. I delivered in Theatre—just in case it became an emergency and they needed Alex out quick.'

'You must have been frightened?'

'Very.'

'Alex was all right?'

'Yes.' Mara smiled. 'She was beautiful.'

'She still is.' Krystiana smiled too. 'Is Alexandra the name you both chose?'

'It was one of Matteo's choices. I'd not been sure about it, but with him gone like that… I had to choose it. And now I love it. It suits her perfectly.'

'You had no doubt that he'd return?'

'At the beginning? None at all. But when time kept passing. Days into weeks. Weeks into months. A year… I began losing hope. I wanted my child to have her father.'

'That must have been hard for you.'

What had her mother felt as each day passed? Each week? A month? Had she feared her daughter dead?

Mara nodded. 'It was. To lose my best friend, the father of my child… I felt incredibly alone. But I was expected to carry on. Be a representative of the royal family. Appear brave in the face of the *paparazzi*. It became too much, and I began to lean on an old family friend.'

'Philippe?'

She nodded. 'I know a lot of people hate me for it. For moving on. But when you're so alone…your heart cries out for comfort.'

Krystiana considered that. The need to be held *was* a powerful one. To be listened to. *Heard*. When was the last time someone had given her a long hug? When had she last snuggled against someone? Bruno didn't count. He was a dog. But perhaps she felt she could do it with Bruno because dogs loved unconditionally? Dogs didn't trick you, or let you down, or bury you in a miserable hole.

And as she gazed at Mara she wondered. Wondered how she could seem so content, so happy, knowing that life could be unfair and take your loved ones away from you so quickly?

'You and Philippe are happy?'

She smiled. Beamed, in fact. 'Very.'

'I'm glad for you. That you found Philippe.'

Mara nodded her thanks.

CHAPTER EIGHT

'Ouch!' Krystiana whipped her hand from the rose bush, shaking it madly to take away the pain. One of the thorns must have pricked her as she'd knelt down to smell the scent of the misty blue bloom.

The rose was called Blue Moon. Her favourite. Her mother had grown Blue Moons in her small patch of garden, and as Krystiana had wandered through the gardens that gave Matteo peace she had hoped to find some for herself. Spotting the familiar bloom had drawn her to it, and she had reached for it without thinking.

'Are you all right?'

She spun to see Matteo coming towards her. He looked very handsome today. Dark linen trousers and a white shirt, the sleeves turned up to the elbow.

She glanced at her finger and saw a small drop of blood forming. 'I'm fine. I just caught myself on the thorns.'

'Let me see.'

She shook her head, backing away. 'No, it's all right. I—'

But he had her hand in his, examining it carefully, his touch gentle, yet commanding.

She had to stand there, breathing shallowly, trying not to stare at him as he looked at her hand. She did not want this. Did not *need* this. His proximity. His tenderness in looking out for her.

'Really, it's all right.' She insisted.

'You're bleeding.' He reached into his pocket and withdrew a white handkerchief.

'It'll stain…' She tried to protest, but he wrapped it around her finger anyway. She sagged, feeling him apply pressure. She also winced.

'Does it hurt?'

She shrugged. 'I don't know. Maybe a little.'

'Perhaps you have a thorn in it?' He removed the handkerchief for a closer look, but it was hard to see as blood kept coming.

She really wanted her hand back. Having him being this attentive to her was really playing with her mind.

'I've got tweezers in my bathroom. I'll check later.'

She yanked her hand free from his and gave him a brief smile, trying to appear grateful when in reality, she felt anything but. No. She *was* grateful. But that was just one of the many things she was feeling.

'What are you doing out here? I thought you had a meeting?'

In fact that was the reason she had come out here in the first place. She knew it was his sanctuary, but she'd known he was meant to be busy and she'd needed space to breathe and think.

'It got cancelled.'

'Oh.' She bit her lip, trying to think of something to say. 'You didn't want to go and see Alex instead?'

'She's napping. I'm planning to spend some time with her when she wakes up. I came out to find you because I thought you might like to hear about what happened with Roshan, Qamar and the others.'

She was very interested. 'Oh, yes?'

'They made it safely to the hospital. Qamar regained

consciousness quite quickly and his dehydration issues and malnutrition are being thoroughly taken care of by a specialist team of dieticians.'

That was wonderful news. 'I'm glad. What will happen next for them?'

'They'll be found homes, once the doctors give them the okay to leave, and I've put out a few feelers with the authorities to see what we can do—maybe get them some work, places in schools, that kind of thing.'

She smiled. He was so good. So generous. Selfless. She liked that about him. 'That's fantastic. I hope they find the peace that they deserve.'

'Me too.'

'And you? What are you going to do today, now you're free?'

'We're going to go swimming in the pool.'

'Oh, that's nice.'

He smiled. 'Well, I don't get to go to public pools, and I love swimming. Mostly in the sea, but the pool will do. You should come too.'

Krystiana in a pool? In a swimsuit? With Matteo, who'd be wearing nothing but shorts? That was a little too intimate for her liking.

'I…er…think I'll pass.'

'Come with us. It will be fun.'

'Not for me, it won't.' It was out before she could censor it.

He frowned. 'Why not?'

A million excuses ran through her head and she considered them all. But her hatred of lying convinced her to tell him the truth. If he knew, then he would leave it alone and not force the issue.

'I can't swim.'

'What?' He looked at her incredulously.

'I can't swim. I never learned.'

'You had no one to teach you?'

'No.'

She felt her cheeks flush. After her kidnapping she had been too busy with her head stuck in books, and swimming had seemed a luxury that she didn't want to pursue. What would have been the point? She never intended going near water, except to maybe admire it. She never wanted to go in it.

Yes, she now lived on an island, surrounded by water, and after seeing what had happened to those refugees they'd rescued perhaps she ought to, but…

Matteo beamed and his smile melted her heart.

'Then I will teach you.'

'No.'

'Come on. You'll thank me for it.'

'No, I… I don't even have a costume!'

'We'll buy you some.'

'No, honestly, Matteo, it's fine—'

'I won't take no for an answer.'

She could see in his eyes how much he wanted to help her learn to swim. How much he wanted to give something back to her. How excited he was by the idea.

She thought of her pale, pasty body next to his tanned, glowing sun god look and cringed inside. It would be embarrassing, wouldn't it? And spending some downtime with him would only add to the feelings she was already having. She couldn't let that happen.

How on earth am I going to get out of this?

He had to admit to himself that he hadn't quite thought this through—offering to teach Krystiana to swim. He'd just blurted out the invite. It had seemed the right idea at the time and he hadn't been able to get past the knowledge that she didn't know how to. Swimming was something he had always done, and he found a freedom in the water that couldn't be found elsewhere. It was soothing. Good for the mind. And he wanted to share that with her, knowing that she had been through the same kind of trauma as he.

As she entered the pool house, looking nervous, wearing a thin robe, he saw her long, elegant legs and got a flash of intensity through his body. There was something about her. So innocent. So vulnerable. So alone. He could connect with those feelings. He'd felt the need to surround her and protect her this afternoon in the garden, when she'd hurt herself. When he'd seen her bleeding. He'd felt his heart pound and blood rush through his veins.

Okay, it had only been a small puncture wound, but it had been enough to awaken his protective side. He'd wanted to keep the world out so that he could help her, and then, up close to her, holding her hand, inhaling the scent of her, looking into her warm blue eyes it had made his senses go wild—into overdrive—and he had not wanted to let go.

When she'd pulled away he'd seen it in her eyes that she felt something too, and that knowledge had made him stop. She didn't want to get involved with anyone. Nor did he.

He had to back off. To stay away from her. But something kept him there. The need to teach her something. To enjoy the time they had left before their lives reclaimed them. There'd been that look on her face…one that he couldn't resist…and then she had told him she couldn't swim. She lived on an island! And he didn't want her to go without helping her in some small way.

Getting to the pool before anyone else, he'd pounded out a couple of lengths already, hoping that by doing so he would exhaust his body enough not to react to hers. Because he was aware of just how much he did react to her physically, and being in the pool would be a lot more intimate than dinner on the balcony.

He pulled himself from the water and went over to meet her. 'Hi. Thank you for joining me.'

She looked uncertainly at him, then at the surrounding pool. 'Where's Alex?'

'She'll be here soon. I thought you might appreciate some time one-to-one before she gets here. No one likes to see a five-year-old swim better than them.'

'Oh, that's thoughtful. Thank you.'

'Soon you'll be splashing around like the rest of us.'

'I don't imagine you splash much.'

He smiled and ran his hands over his hair to keep it from his face. 'Maybe not.' He laughed.

'So…' She gazed at the pool, at the way the water rippled, reflecting against the walls and the ceiling. 'How do we make a start?'

He looked at her, feeling his blood surge at the thought and trying to control it. 'You take off the robe.'

She looked at him uncertainly. Hesitant. Torn between wanting to spend this time with him and being afraid of what time with him like this might do.

He was a majestic, gorgeous hunk of man, who seemed oblivious to the effect he was having on her. Which was a good thing—because imagine how embarrassing that might be?

She felt shy about taking off her robe. He might assess her body. Krystiana knew she wasn't considered *unattractive*, but that didn't mean she oozed confidence. She still had her doubts and her insecurities, and being in just a swimsuit would make her feel terribly exposed. Vulnerable. And that feeling was something she tried to avoid.

'Would you mind turning around?'

'Of course not.' He turned his back on her so that she could slip off the robe, and for a brief moment she just stood there and gazed at the broad expanse of his bronzed back. At the width of his shoulders and down to his narrow waist, to the swimming trunks that showed a wonderfully toned backside, and then the long, muscly thighs, darkened by fine hair.

Would he chance a look at her?

No. He's not like that.

Krystiana quickly tugged off the robe and slipped into the pool.

He turned when he heard her moving in the water and slipped in next to her. 'All right?'

She nodded. The water had felt cold at first, but now she was in she realised it was perfect.

'How do you feel about putting your face in the water?'

She looked at its rippling surface. 'I won't be able to see anything.'

He nodded, understanding her fear. 'I have goggles.' He reached over to the steps behind him, where a pair hung. 'Best to wet your hair first, before you put them on.'

She nodded, dipping her head back until the full length of her braid was dripping.

'Here.'

He stepped towards her and she had to suck in a breath as he stood close, helping her with the goggles. They were a bit loose, so he tightened them for her. She was just inches away from his marvellous masculine form and she didn't know where to look. Or to put her hands. He was wearing almost nothing.

'I must look silly.' She blushed.

'You look perfect. So, do you want to try putting your face underwater now? Take a breath and then just lower yourself down for a moment and see what it's like.'

'Okay.' She sucked in a couple of deep breaths before pinching her nose and lowering herself beneath the water's surface.

The world sounded strange from underneath. Muffled and weird. She could see Matteo's ripped abs and long legs, his feet standing sure on the bottom of the pool. She took a quick glance at his shorts, at the line of hair from his belly button that disappeared beneath the fabric.

She stood up again with a rush.

'How was that?'

'Fine.' She lifted the goggles onto her forehead and laughed, blushing. 'It was good!'

He smiled back, clearly enjoying her success. '*Fantastic.* I'll get you a float.'

She watched as he easily heaved his form from the pool, the water rushing down his body, and fetched her a blue square of solid foam from the side before he hopped back in.

'Right—now you're going to try to glide.'

'Glide?'

'You're going to hold this float in front of you. Arms nice and straight, face in the water. And with your feet you're going to push off from the wall and see how far you can glide across the pool.'

That sounded simple enough. 'Okay…'

'Deep breath, face down, then push.'

'Sounds like you want me to give birth.'

He smiled, clearly following her line of thought. To give birth you had to be pregnant, and to be pregnant you had to have had *sex*.

She felt tingles inside. Her belly was fluttering and she was beginning to realise that she was *enjoying* this. Something she'd been dreading since he'd suggested it.

Sucking in a breath, she held the float in front of her, put her face down and pushed off the wall behind her. She surged forward, gliding swiftly and surely through the water until her breath ran out, and then she stood up suddenly, gasping for air. 'I did it!'

'You did! You're a natural! Do it again. But this time kick with your feet as you're gliding.'

'Okay.'

She made her way back to the side of the pool and carried out his instructions, and this time she made it almost halfway across.

'I'm doing it! Did you see?'

'I did! Try it again.'

She did it over and over again, kicking her way all the way across the pool, occasionally lifting her head for a gasp of air, until she reached the other side.

'Teach me something else!'

'Okay. Let's try it without the float.'

'Without?' She wasn't too sure about that. How would she stay on top of the water?

'Yes. Watch me.'

She watched him dip under the water and push off from the wall, and smiled in relief as his body naturally drifted up and glided across the surface, before he stood once again to look at her.

He brushed his wet hair back from his face. 'Easy—see?'

'Easy for *you*, maybe.'

'Have faith, Krystiana. See if you can swim out this far to me.'

He was just over the halfway mark. Technically, it wasn't that far, and she knew that with the goggles she'd be able to see under water just how far away he was. He could be with her in a second if it went wrong.

'I'm trusting you to catch me if I start to drown.'

'You won't drown. You can do this.'

'Okay.'

She adjusted her goggles once again, then sucked in

a deep breath and tried to do what she'd seen Matteo do. Head under, push off the wall, kick with her feet, hands out in front of her… Under the water, she could see him. His reassuring torso, his hands out in front of him, ready to reach for her when she got close.

And she made it!

Grabbing his hands and feeling him pull her towards him, she got to her feet, laughing and beaming with joy. 'I did it! Did you see me?'

'You were great!'

He was holding her close. Her hands lay wet and warm upon his chest. And suddenly she realised she was staring into his eyes, and he into hers. Their bodies were touching and she gazed up at his lips, studded with water droplets, and realised, intensely, that she wanted to kiss them so very much.

The realisation hit her with the force of a wave and she glanced up at his eyes to gauge what he was thinking. She thought she saw the same desire in his gaze, too.

The desire, *the need*, to kiss him was just so strong, and as they closed the gap between them, inching ever closer, infinitesimally, she felt her heart pound and the blood roar around her body as if in triumph.

He'll hurt you. Everybody hurts you.

She silenced the voice. Not wanting to hear it. Not in this moment. Not right now. All she wanted right now was…

His lips touched hers and she sank against him, feeling her body come alive. Every nerve-ending was sending sparks. Her heart was pounding with exhilaration at the feel of him beneath her hands as she pulled her even closer.

Nothing else mattered there and then. To be swept away like this was indescribable. The real world dissolved. Fears were silenced. And the hot, sultry desire that she'd tamped down for so long was given free rein.

* * *

'Krystiana?'

Matteo's voice called to her as she hurried to her quarters, her hair still dripping.

She turned. 'Yes?'

Stop blushing. Why am I blushing? Oh, yes, I just kissed a prince!

'I forgot to say, what with…' His cheeks reddened and he looked uncomfortable. 'My father has invited you to the ball tonight.'

Her heart sank. 'Ball?'

'It happens every year.'

'Oh.'

She didn't have any outfit suitable for a ball. But how to get out of it without upsetting anyone? Events were moving far too swiftly for her right now. That kiss in the pool had been madness!

'I…er…don't have anything suitable to wear for a ball.'

'I'll get some dresses sent to your rooms for you to try.'

'Erm…'

'Or Mara might have something you could borrow?'

She nodded. 'Okay.'

'Excellent. I'll see you later, then?'

She watched him walk away, wondering just what the hell she was doing…

CHAPTER NINE

MATTEO SAT SWIRLING the wine around in his glass, mesmerised by its movement and colour, though not yet having touched a drop. He just needed to do something with his hands—anything, really—to keep his mind off that moment in the pool with Krystiana.

I kissed her.

She'd emerged from the water, smiling, laughing, so pleased with her progress, and she'd lifted her goggles onto her forehead and beamed at him—a smile that had gone straight to his heart and made it beat like a jackhammer against his ribs. And something—something he hadn't been able to fight—had taken over his common sense and all reason and logic and he'd somehow convinced himself that just one kiss would be okay!

Hah!

He'd fought against it. They'd only known each other for such a short time, and he'd been determined since returning from his kidnapping not to get involved with anyone. Was he so weak? That all it took was a nice smile and a long braid and a shared experience to make his resolve crumble?

He thought over their time together, looking for clues. When had he first begun to succumb to her charms? But he couldn't see the exact moment. He couldn't discern it at all and that frustrated him.

Krystiana had looked at him in shock afterwards. Had quickly waded away from him, clambered up the pool steps, apologising all the way.

No matter what had happened, he'd not wanted things to be awkward between them. He'd wanted to put it right. So he'd chased after her and *asked her to the ball*—as if his mouth had been operating on a different system to his brain.

It hadn't been his place to invite her, and he hadn't meant to ask, but he hadn't been able to bear her running from him like that. He'd wanted to apologise, to put things right, but when she'd turned to face him the invitation had popped out instead.

Matteo pulled the cord that would summon Sergio, and when his servant arrived he asked him to fetch him a canvas and paints. Sergio bowed and disappeared, returning about thirty minutes later with the equipment he needed. Painting the garden had felt good before. Freeing. It had eased his mind and he needed that right now.

He set up the easel out on the sun terrace and thought about how he felt inside. And then, using his fingers, as he had before, he began to daub the surface of the canvas with paint.

He was so carried away with what he was doing he almost didn't hear the footsteps behind him, and he started somewhat when Sergio spoke.

'Dr Szenac, Your Majesty.'

Matteo turned, shocked to see her standing there, but he smiled, glad to see her. Glad that she didn't seem to have been made uncomfortable by what had happened.

'You caught me. I thought I'd try this thing again.'

She smiled back, but it was brief. Fleeting.

'That's good. That you're getting something from it.

Those colours look great, but you were great with them last time, so…'

He could sense she had something to say. 'Are you all right?'

'I'm going to leave.'

His heart thudded painfully and the smile dropped from his face. 'What? Why? Because of what happened in the pool? I'm sorry if I've made you uncomfortable, I—'

'I'm going to a hotel. I need to take back control of my life, Matteo. It's slipping away from me here.'

He didn't know what to say. Had he caused this? By kissing her? She had to know that it had been an accident. That it wouldn't happen again.

But those words weren't said. He couldn't. It wasn't as if he was going to beg her to stay. Princes didn't beg. He had to respect her decision, and it was probably best in the long run anyway. Neither of them needed to get involved.

He felt the need to preserve his dignity and he lifted his chin. 'When will you go?'

'Tomorrow morning. I just thought it polite to let you know. As you were so kind as to let me into your home.'

'It was the right thing…' There was more he wanted to say but he was struck dumb, the words caught in his throat. He couldn't say any of them out loud. The one person who soothed his soul, who made him feel he could genuinely smile again, was going because he'd screwed up?

'It's for the best. For both of us, I think,' she said.

He agreed. It was for the best. But he didn't feel ready. He'd thought he'd still got weeks left with her. Weeks in which they would talk and develop their friendship. In which to get her out of his system. But for her to leave now, so abruptly… Because he'd overstepped a line he'd never intended to cross…

This was why he didn't get involved with people any more. Relationships got complicated.

'I'll always consider you my friend, Krystiana. I hope our…moment hasn't jeopardised that.'

She shook her head. 'It hasn't. I've always felt connected to you and I think I always will. It's been an honour to know you.'

He nodded.

She seemed to want to say something more, but no more words were forthcoming. Was she struggling to speak as much as he? Did she want him to fight for her to stay? Or just to let her go? *What do I want?*

She nodded a goodbye and walked away.

Matteo swore to himself, his anger and frustration rising. He turned back to his painting, looked at the happy colours, the swirls of green and yellow. His palette lay off to one side and he dipped his hand in black and swept his hand across the canvas. The black cut a swathe through the light—sorrow darkening the joy.

And he stared at it until his anger abated.

'Which one do you want to try first?' Mara spread her hand out at the array of dresses she'd hung up on the rail she had prepped for Krystiana. 'I think the blue would really bring out your eyes.'

Krystiana was in no mood for any colour bringing out anything. Least of all her eyes. She didn't want anyone to notice her. Didn't want anyone to see the sadness that was in her soul.

'What about the black one?'

Mara looked at her as if she was crazy. 'The black one? No, no, *no*, Krystiana! The black is too safe. It's wrong for you. How about the red?'

No. Red would be too much. Everybody would look at her.

'What about that one?'

Mara hefted it from the rail. 'This one? I think this one will look lovely on you. Try it on!'

Krystiana took it, draping the pale grey silk over her arm and going into the bedroom to try it.

The grey was perfect. Almost silver, but not quite. Sleeveless and with a sweetheart neckline. It was understated. The kind of dress that wouldn't make her stand out. And despite it having been designed for Mara, who was sylph-like in build, it fitted Krystiana perfectly, moulding her curves.

She twisted and turned in front of the mirror, admiring it but telling herself to not get too excited. Tonight, she would hug the wall, a glass of wine in her hand, which she probably wouldn't drink, and after an hour or so she would slip away, unnoticed.

She was sad that she had made the decision to leave, but it was for the best. Matteo was getting too close. Getting under her skin. And she didn't know what to do with that!

She'd kissed him in the pool.

She could feel her attraction for him growing and it hurt. Pained her that she could do nothing about it because it wouldn't be right. Getting involved with a man like him… Losing control… Giving him power over her…

If she went into a relationship with a powerful man like him she'd lose. Her heart and her soul. She'd be open and out of control. That short kiss had shown her how out of control she had become in such a small amount of time. One kiss and already she'd knocked down the walls keeping him out.

He belonged to his people, not her, and if she tried to be with him in any way the media would want to know who she was. They would begin to dig into her background and her life—her history would be revealed to all.

No one on Isla Tamoura except for Aunt Carolina and Matteo knew about her past, and that was how she wanted it to stay. She had built a new life here. People didn't look at her with the knowledge of her past in their eyes. She wasn't pitied. She wasn't asked about it and that was the way she wanted it.

'How does it look?' Mara called from the other room. 'I hope you're going to show me.'

Krystiana pulled open the door and stepped out, smiling at Mara's obvious glee. 'What do you think? Does it look all right?'

Mara gazed at her in awe. *'È bellissimo!'*

'It's not too much?'

'No! You look breathtaking.'

Krystiana gazed down at the gown and bit her lip, reconsidering. She didn't want to look 'breathtaking'. At all.

'No, no! Don't look like that. You're wearing it. I've even got a clutch to match it. And shoes. What size are you?'

Krystiana told her.

'Perfect! You'll be the belle of the ball!'

'I don't want to be the belle. I'm not a guest of honour—just a friend, that's all.'

'Oh, come, now. That's *not* all!'

She frowned. 'What do you mean?'

'You like him, yes?'

Krystiana blushed madly. She couldn't tell Mara! Mara had once been his *wife*!

'Not like that.'

Mara raised an eyebrow. 'I wish I could believe you.'

'There's nothing between us. In fact, I'm leaving tomorrow.'

'You're leaving?' Mara looked shocked.

'Tomorrow morning. I have to.'

Mara nodded. 'Maybe that's wise…'

Krystiana turned away and began to unzip the dress.

Even Mara could see that she and Matteo would be a bad thing.

Mara laid a hand upon her arm, stilling her. 'I know it will hurt you to leave.'

'It's the best thing for both of us.'

Mara nodded her head solemnly. 'It's a pity, but I admire you for being so sensible.'

'I'm not being sensible. I don't know *what* I'm being.'

'What do you feel for him?'

Krystiana blinked. Unsure how to answer. 'I like him. Maybe too much,' she said.

Mara nodded. 'He's easy to like. Easy to love.'

Krystiana stared at her. 'I don't *love* him, Mara.'

That was just ridiculous!

She'd read somewhere that when you felt attracted to someone you could blame your medial prefrontal cortex, because that was the part of the brain that was responsible for any *love at first sight* activity. The inferior temporal cortex reacted to visual stimuli, the orbitofrontal cortex reacted emotionally, the anterior cingulate cortex caused physiological responses and the right insula dictated arousal.

Basically, it meant that most of your brain was going overboard, so no wonder you couldn't think straight!

But as she got ready in her room, trying to sort out her hair and make-up for this, her last evening at the palace, she tried to tell herself that she was doing the right thing—even though she strongly suspected her thoughts and decisions were based on her emotional responses.

She liked Matteo. More than she should. So getting away from him was the obvious solution. Besides, he probably wouldn't want to speak to her much tonight, anyway. She'd clearly shocked him when she'd told him she was leaving, so perhaps tonight would be okay? They could avoid each other all evening.

She put in her diamond drop earrings and stood in front of the mirror, checking her reflection. The grey dress was actually very beautiful. Understated and classic. It was a pity it was on loan, because she loved it very much.

Krystiana checked her watch. Nearly time to go.

Why do I feel so nervous?

There was a tentative knock at her door and, suspecting it was Sergio, she went and opened it. Only it wasn't Sergio at all.

It was Matteo.

Her heart leapt into her throat when she saw him standing there in dinner jacket and black bow tie. He looked gorgeous! She almost took a step back. Not sure why he was here.

'I've come to escort you to the ball. On your last night here with you as our guest it seemed right. No hard feelings?'

'Oh. Right. Okay.'

'We're okay?'

She nodded. 'Absolutely. I can't thank you enough for all that you've done for me.'

Matteo gave her a short smile. 'You look *bellissimo*. Truly.'

She flushed at the compliment. 'Thank you. So do you.'

He held out his arm for her to slip her hand through, and they walked arm in arm down the palace corridors.

For a few moments she felt quite awkward, being with him. She'd not expected him to come to her door, but he was most certainly a gentleman and clearly he didn't want an unescorted lady arriving at the ball. He was wearing some kind of scent that was playing havoc with her olfactory senses, so she tried a bit of mouth-breathing to try and calm them down.

'How many people are going to be there?'

'A few hundred.'

A few *hundred…*

‘Where is the ball being held?’

‘In the White Room.’

‘I don’t think I’ve been there.’

‘We use it only for the most special of occasions.’

She nodded, walking alongside him, trying not to think that this might be the last time they’d be together. Trying not to think of how much she liked him. How much he might think that she was running away. Because she didn’t like to think that she was.

‘Will Mara and Alex be there? So I can say goodbye?’

‘Of course.’

‘Great. That’s…great.’ She didn’t *feel* great. She felt sad. But she had to do the right thing.

A few hundred.

He stopped suddenly. ‘I think I should leave you here. If we arrived together it would send out the wrong message.’

‘Maybe you’re right.’

She was wrong for him. He was trying to tell her that. The kiss in the pool had been a blip on both their parts. They couldn’t be anything more. It had just been physical.

She nodded. ‘I’d rather everyone assumed I was just a normal guest. Nothing to do with you.’

Which I’m not.

He removed his arm from hers and straightened his jacket. ‘And of course I’d hate to throw you to the wolves. The press,’ he explained.

‘Exactly. I’d rather stay out of the papers.’ Though that was the least of her worries. She’d rather stay as far away from him as she could because she just didn’t trust her physical reactions to him.

He smiled ruefully. ‘You promise not to leave without saying goodbye?’

‘I promise,’ she said, hating every word, knowing that deep in her heart she longed to be in his arms and held by him, pressed close, cherished and adored. Their kiss in the pool might have been the biggest mistake she'd ever made, but it had felt so good! And that was why it was so confusing.

'I don't want you to leave without a chance to…'

She got sucked into the hypnotic gaze of his eyes. 'Chance to what?'

She saw the hesitation in his eyes. The fight within him. And then he was stepping close.

He reached up to stroke the side of her face. 'I feel like I know who you are. And that I'll never meet anyone else like you again. I'm not sure I want to lose you.'

Krystiana sucked in a breath, trying to steady her racing heart. 'I…'

'You feel it, too.'

'Matteo…'

And suddenly his mouth was on hers.

She closed her eyes in ecstasy. Giving herself one more moment of bliss. A single moment in which she'd allow herself to take what he could give.

Her hands lay upon his chest and she could feel his heart pounding, the muscles beneath his skin, the way he wrapped himself around her as he pulled her closer still.

Her logical mind was screaming at her to stop, but she couldn't. She silenced the voice. No, that was wrong. The voice disappeared. Because all she wanted to experience was the feeling of his lips upon hers. Her body pressed against his. The fire building in her soul. The heat that was searing her skin, making every nerve-ending electric.

She'd never felt this before. Never been like this with anyone before. Not like this. There'd been awkward fumbles and kisses from guys she'd not felt such attraction for, and with Adamo it had been good, but with Matteo it was a fierce thing—a force that powered through her like a hurricane. Unstoppable and unrelenting.

As the kiss deepened and her tongue entwined with his she groaned in delight, cradling his face in her hands, feeling the soft bristles of his beard beneath her skin. She knew she wanted more. Oh, so much more… But…

They broke apart and stared at each other, both surprised, both overwhelmed by what had just happened. Stunned.

Her fear at what would happen when she had to leave had just been made worse! Kissing him had just made it a lot harder.

Why am I doing this to myself? What on earth is going on?

Krystiana looked up and down the palace corridors but no one was around. This was just between her and Matteo.

'I'm sorry. We…er…shouldn't have done that.'

'No.'

'But we keep doing it.'

'Yes.'

'Why? Why would we punish ourselves like this?' She was almost in tears. Could hear it in her voice.

He took a step back. 'I'm sorry. I don't mean to. It's just that when I'm with you…'

'What?' She needed to know what was driving him. What was causing him to keep kissing her. Because then it might make sense to her why she kept kissing *him*.

He frowned and took a step towards her, his gaze dropping to her mouth before he looked back up at her eyes.

'I'll see you in the ballroom.'

The White Room was exactly that. White walls and ceiling. A white marble floor. Columns thick as tree trunks like silver birches, pulling the gaze upwards towards numerous crystal chandeliers. Huge gold vases held swathes of white lilies, roses and jasmine.

As she descended the steps towards the milling crowds,

accepting a flute of champagne from a server, Krystiana hoped she could lose herself in the crowd. Even if she *did* feel there was a huge neon arrow above her head, lit up with the message *I just kissed your prince!*

She felt torn. And exhilarated. Confused and trapped. Could the whole world see the imprint of his lips on hers? Was it written all over her face? Heat and lust and secrets?

I should have known better!

She was muddled in her thinking. Being with Matteo stopped her brain from working properly. She really felt something for him, and it wasn't just attraction—it was something more than that. Krystiana had never wanted to be with a guy as much as she wanted to be with him. She had never felt more attracted to someone in her life.

This was new territory for her! Uncharted, dangerous territory, with someone who was forbidden!

Or was he?

Now that she'd kissed him, now that she'd tasted a little of what he had to offer, a new voice was suggesting that maybe she should enjoy it. Maybe it was all right. Maybe, just maybe, he *was* the man for her…

Perhaps that was why it was so confusing—because she was fighting something that she should just accept. But how would she know for sure? How would she know she was safe giving him her heart? It had never worked before when she had done that. She couldn't think of one relationship in her life that worked well. Well, except for with Dr Bonetti. They loved one another. But they were from the same world.

Krystiana took a sip of her champagne, intending only to take a small swallow, but downing the whole thing in one. Surprised, she passed her empty glass to another server and took another full glass, determined to go slower with this one.

If two people were attracted to one another then why

shouldn't they make something of it? Why shouldn't they act on their attraction? They were grown adults. They could make their own decisions.

He'd been through the same things as her. The same scares, the same terrors, the same fears. He knew how she felt and she him. Where would she find *that* again?

Sighing, she sipped her champagne, stopping only to turn at the fanfare of trumpets as an official announced the entry of His Majesty King Alberto and his son, Crown Prince Matteo.

She stared up at him from her place in the crowd and could see the certainty and assuredness on Matteo's face, trapped within a practised smile. She saw the way his gaze coasted all around him, oozing authority and power as he descended the steps into the room, and how he stayed a few steps behind his father, honouring royal etiquette.

She glanced at Alberto. The King she'd met just once. A tall, proud man, he was greeting a long line of people, smiling and shaking hands. He looked a little more drawn than before. A bit grey… He carried a heavy weight upon his shoulders—perhaps it was that?

He was soon to abdicate. And happily, by all accounts. Krystiana had no doubt that Matteo would make a fabulous king. He was strong and steady. Overflowing with charitable, selfless acts that his people adored him for.

As do I.

Matteo would make an excellent leader for his country. All that he had been through had only served to make him stronger.

The King got to the end of his long line of meet-and-greet people and stepped up to a white podium which was adorned with the Romano royal coat of arms—a gold shield, with a sword at its centre, flanked by a lion on one side and a unicorn on the other, both rearing up as if honouring the sword.

The room went quiet.

The King looked about him, waiting for his moment. The ultimate public speaker. 'Ladies and gentlemen of the court, nothing makes me happier than to see you all here—though my happiness is tinged with a little sadness that this will be the final ball I will host as King. But my successor is one you all know, love and respect, and I know that he will follow the honour, tradition and heritage of this fine land. My only son—Matteo.'

The crowd clapped, smiling broadly.

'We all know his story. For those of us left behind it was an unsettling time. We were cast adrift, uncertain, unknowing. We tried what we could to ensure his safe return, but each time—as you know—the guerrillas who held him proved not to be reputable people and they kept him from us. Matteo did not get to see the birth of his daughter. He did not get to see her early years or experience the joy that we did as she began to sit up, then crawl, then walk. Nor did he hear her first word, but I'm sure he was very pleased to hear it was "Papà".'

He smiled at his son, who stood proudly by his side.

'But we did get him back, and he has proved his strength and fortitude. Returning strong and unhurt by his time away, for which we are very grateful. Tonight I would like to name this ball in his honour, and also to announce some incredible news.'

The crowd inched forward, eager to hear it.

Behind the King, Krystiana saw Matteo's smile falter somewhat as he turned his gaze to his father. Clearly Matteo did not know what the King was about to say.

'It has been decided that in anticipation of Matteo taking the throne next year, he will go on a six-week tour of the kingdom of Tamoura, visiting every major city and every urban centre, meeting the people and showing the world that no one can beat down the strength and courage that my son has. He will be a *strong* king! A king committed to the welfare of his people. Hopefully, he will meet as many of them as he can. His full itinerary will be posted tomorrow at the royal court and the tour will begin in one week's time!'

Matteo's smile broadened, as if he'd already known this would be the King's proclamation, but she knew better. She could see the surprise in his eyes.

He didn't know about this.

She was shocked, too. He was leaving the palace. Perhaps it was a good thing that she was packing up tomorrow, because if she'd stayed her heart would have been broken anyway. He would be leaving on a tour of the isle. No doubt with a jam-packed itinerary. He would be returning to the world where he lived and she… She would be returning to hers. She had patients. He had subjects.

The bubble was popping. She'd always known that it would. She would have popped it herself tomorrow. This would push him. Prepare him for kingship. It would be a good thing for him. Good for her, too. Because if he was leaving in just one week, then she could leave knowing that his mind would not be on her departure, but on his travelling arrangements.

You see? We never would have had a chance. I was right to stop this.

She tried to make herself feel happy about that, but she was struggling.

The King stepped back to hold out a hand to his son and Matteo stepped forward to take it. As he clasped his son's hand and pulled him into a hug the crowd began to cheer and applaud.

But their cries of joy quickly changed to cries of shock as King Alberto slumped in his son's arms, his face pale and sweaty, and Matteo had to lower him gently to the ground…

* * *

'Call for an ambulance!'

Matteo couldn't believe that this was happening. What was wrong with his father?

Holding his father fast, he stared at his slack face. 'Papà, hang on—don't you die on me!'

Behind him, he heard a commotion as someone pushed their way through the crowd and he heard her voice.

'Excuse me! Excuse me—please, make way…'

And then there she was. Krystiana. Kneeling down on the floor beside his father, a pool of grey silk around her as she assessed the situation, her fingers at his neck, assessing for a pulse.

'Okay, he's breathing—that's good.' She quickly unbuttoned the King's jacket and laid her ear against his chest and listened. 'Does someone have a watch? With a second hand?'

A man Matteo didn't know offered one and he passed it to Krystiana, who kept her gaze on it as she listened to the King's chest once again.

'He has tachycardia.'

Matteo frowned. 'What?'

'A fast heartbeat. Too fast. We need to get him to hospital, where they can give him some drugs or a shock to bring it back down.'

Servants arrived in droves to usher the guests into another room so that the paramedics could come in, get the King on a trolley and attach electrodes to his chest to monitor his heartbeat. It was one hundred and fifty-two beats per minute.

'Papà, you're going to be all right.'

The King took his son's hand in his. 'I'm okay…'

The paramedics looked to Matteo. 'Are you coming in the ambulance?'

He nodded. 'Yes. So is she.' He pointed at Krystiana, who looked shocked to be included.

'Then, let's go!'

Matteo and Krystiana followed the paramedics down the long palatial corridors and out to the ambulance. Thankfully their arrival had been through the rear gates, so hopefully there wouldn't be too much about this in the press the next day. Besides, it was just a fast heartbeat. He wasn't having a heart attack or anything. They'd get him sorted out at the hospital.

As they got on board Krystiana looked at the ECG tracing. 'It looks like he has atrial fibrillation.'

'What does that mean?' Matteo asked, needing to know everything that was going on.

'It's the upper chambers of the heart. The atria. They're creating irregular impulses that are rapid and uncoordinated.'

'What does that mean for my father?'

She shrugged. 'It could be a temporary thing and stop on its own, but he might need assistance to stop it.'

'How?'

'Drugs. A shock to the heart.'

'An electric shock? But why now? What's caused it?'

'I don't know, Matteo. I don't know your father's health history. Does he have high blood pressure?'

'I don't think so. He hasn't mentioned anything.'

'Heart disease?'

'No. Papà, how do you feel?'

'Like something is trying to jump out of my chest.'

'Are you in pain?'

'No, it just feels…*weird*.'

'We're nearly there. Hang on.'

He felt Krystiana lay a reassuring hand upon his shoulder.

The paramedics kept on observing the trace, monitoring

his father's blood pressure and pulse rate, and Krystiana had placed an oxygen mask over the King's face, murmuring to him to try and control his breathing, to remain as calm as he could. Before he knew what was happening they were pulling up at the private entrance the royals used at the hospital.

They wheeled his father in and got him hooked up to another heart machine as the paramedics relayed what had happened to the attending physician.

The doctor told the King that they would give him a beta-blocker to try and get his heart-rate below ninety beats per minute.

'You might feel some tiredness, and your hands and feet may get cold. We'll monitor your blood pressure continuously and see how you get on.'

'Grazie.'

'You must just rest for a while.'

'Si.'

Matteo had expected more action. This was his father's *heart*! Could he die?

'Why aren't you doing more?' he asked the doctor.

'We're doing what we can. We have to see if the medication will bring down the heart-rate.'

'And if it doesn't? How long do we leave it?'

'Matteo, give them time,' Krystiana said, her voice soothing and calm.

He glanced at her, saw the concern on her face and knew instinctively that she was right. They didn't need him interfering and asking too many questions or getting in the way. This was their territory. They were the ones who knew best.

'Matteo…?' His father held out his hand to him.

'*Si*, Papà?'

'I think I might have to hand over to you earlier than suspected.' He smiled, his eyes sad.

What? No! That wasn't what Matteo wanted to hear. Become King? *No.* His father still had years left in him. Didn't he?

'No, you won't. This is just a blip, Papà. You'll be back home tomorrow—just you wait and see.'

'No, I fear not. There may be some things I have kept from you…'

Matteo frowned.

'Dr Szenac? Would you mind if I spoke to my son alone?' his father asked.

Krystiana nodded and stood up. 'Of course. Take all the time you need.' And she stepped out of the private room, closing the door quietly behind her.

Matteo turned back to his father, apprehension and fear filling his heart. 'What is it?'

'I wasn't sure when would be the best time to tell you… but…when you were away I got ill. The cardio doctors believed it was stress brought on by your kidnapping.'

Cardio. The heart. An ice-cold lump settled in his stomach.

'What happened?'

'I had a heart attack.'

He stood up in shock. *'What?'*

'It was minor, Matteo, but I needed bypass surgery. You see this scar line?'

Matteo frowned as he stared at his father's chest. His father was quite hairy, and he almost couldn't see it. The scar that ran from just below the dip in his throat down to the bottom of the sternum.

'Why didn't you tell me?'

His father shrugged. 'I was always going to abdicate when I turned seventy—you know that. When you were taken I had no idea where you were. My only son. My only child. The stress of everything… The day you were returned to us was the greatest in my entire life! For a moment, I thought Alexandra would have to take the throne!'

He tried to laugh. But it fell flat in the small room.

Matteo stared at the scar. A mark that showed his father to be frailer than he'd realised. Not the invincible, strong man he'd believed him to be but human, just like the rest of them.

'You should have told me. How did you manage to keep this from me?'

'I swore everyone to secrecy. Why upset you? You had just come home, learned that your mother was dead and your marriage was over! I couldn't tell you about this, too! I was protecting you, believing I would last until your coronation anyway. Honestly, I thought you would never have to find out. And I'm sorry that you have.'

Above his father's head, the machine beeped out the fast heartbeat. The drugs didn't seem to be working. Matteo felt doubt and fear. He couldn't lose his father.

'*Ti amo*, Papà.'

'I love you, too. Now, let me rest awhile.'

'All right. I'll just be outside—but buzz if you need *anything*. Okay?'

'I will. Go now.'

He kissed his father on the cheek and left the room. As soon as he saw Krystiana all the emotion he had been feeling came to the fore and he felt tears burning his eyes. He went straight into her outstretched arms.

Being held by her, being close to her, made him feel comforted. She was warm and loving and he knew that she cared for him. She *had* to. Ever since that kiss they'd shared… It hadn't been one-sided. She'd responded too. And now she was the one to comfort him, to make him feel safe. He'd always felt safe with her, and *safe* was a good thing after two years of never knowing if you'd get to see tomorrow's sunrise.

She sat him down. 'Are you all right?'

He told her everything his father had said about his prior heart condition. The heart attack. The bypass.

She sat listening, nodding occasionally. 'That makes sense. Fibrillation like that can often be caused if there's a prior heart condition.'

'Will he be all right, do you think?'

'It's a long time since I worked on a cardiac ward, Matteo. I'd hate to say the wrong thing. But what we *do* know is that he's in the safest place he can be. Where his heart-rate will be continually monitored.'

'When should the drugs take effect? The rate was still high.'

'They should have worked by now, really. He might need shocking. They might give him amiodarone… I'm not sure.'

He took her hand in his. 'I'm glad you're here.'

She smiled back uncertainly. 'I'll stay for as long as you need me.'

He was glad to hear it. His foundations had been rocked and he needed an anchor. He didn't know what it was that was flooding through him, these feelings for her—feelings that he'd never expected to have again. But the thought of losing her whilst his father teetered on the edge of an abyss… *No*. It would be too much.

He reached forward to stroke the side of her face. 'Thank you. There's something about you, Krystiana… I don't know what it is, but…'

She was looking deeply into his eyes, their souls connecting. 'Don't say any more.'

He nodded. 'Thank you.'

He narrowed the distance between them and felt his lips connect with hers. He'd craved her ever since he'd last kissed her, but that kiss had been different. This one was gentle and slow, savouring every moment, every movement. She tasted of champagne, and her honeyed scent stimulated his senses into overdrive. He wanted so much more…

He barely knew what was happening in his world right now. But he was looking for comfort.

Matteo's father was sitting upright in his bed, looking nervous. The doctors had placed pads on his chest and were going to try and shock his rhythm back to normality.

'Will it hurt?'

'Yes, but not for long. And if it works you'll feel much better almost instantly.'

'Good. All right. Go ahead.'

He laid his head back and the doctor pressed a button that lowered the pillow end of the bed. He had to be flat for this.

Once he was lying flat, the doctor looked about him. 'Charging…stand clear…*shocking*.'

King Alberto's body flinched violently and then he groaned, relaxing back onto the sheets.

Krystiana looked at the heart monitor, but his heart-rate remained high. She felt for the King. This couldn't be good at all.

'Charging. Stand clear. *Shocking*.'

Again the King's body went into violent spasm and then collapsed again, but this time the heart-rate began to drop and finally went down to eighty-four beats per minute.

The cardio doctor smiled at Matteo. 'We have sinus rhythm.'

Matteo reached for his father's hand. 'It's done, Papà, you're going to be okay.'

Alberto smiled wearily at his son. *'Grazie a Dio!'*

'We'll keep monitoring your father overnight, but if he maintains his rhythm I see no reason why he can't be up and about tomorrow.'

The cardio doctor shook Matteo's hand, smiled at Krystiana and then left the room.

Krystiana sat down in the chair opposite Matteo and smiled, happy for him and his father. She knew how much he needed his dad. Knew that connection. She missed her own—or she missed the father she'd *believed* she'd had before he took her. That father—pre-kidnapping—had been someone she'd idolised.

Afterwards…after all she'd been through…their relationship had been spoiled. She'd had no father to come home to. And every time she'd turned on the television she'd seen her father's face. Every time she'd opened a newspaper there had seemed to be a new story about him and his 'unstable mind-set', according to ex-girlfriends and old enemies who had all earned a few *zloty* selling their stories.

When she'd gone back to school everyone had treated her differently. Even the teachers. All she'd wanted was normality. To be treated as she had always been treated. But all the kids had suddenly wanted to be her friend. To be invited back to her house so they could examine the home that had once belonged to Piotr Szenac.

Even her own mother had begun acting strangely, and she'd felt a distance between them. A distance that had puzzled her—because surely her mother had wanted her back? She'd fought for custody of Krystiana.

And then she'd died. Less than a year after Krystiana had come home Nikola Szenac had been hit by a bus. Krystiana had been fetched from her school lessons to be told by the headmistress. And then she'd been alone in the world, struggling to understand all that had happened, until Aunt Carolina had reached out to save her.

And now here she sat, an orphaned girl from Poland, beside the bed of the King of Isla Tamoura.

'We should get something to eat. It's late.' Matteo stood

up and kissed his father's cheek. 'Is there anything you want me to bring tomorrow?'

Alberto smiled. 'Some decent pyjamas would be good. These hospital gowns are a bit itchy.'

'Nonsense! I'm sure they are the finest cotton.'

'Hmm… You're not wearing one, though, are you?'

'Fair point. Goodnight, Papà. Krystiana and I will be back in the morning.'

Alberto turned to look at her curiously. 'I must thank you, Dr Szenac, for saving my life.'

She shook her head. 'I didn't do anything. Not really.'

'You looked after me *and* my son. I am grateful you were with us.'

She smiled. He was a good old man. A good father. 'I'm glad you're feeling better, Your Majesty.'

'Call me Alberto.'

She blushed. That didn't seem right. He was the King of Isla Tamoura! Calling him by his first name was intimate. For friends and family. She wasn't family—so did he consider her a friend?

'Thank you, Your Majesty.'

He smiled. 'Go and get some sleep. It's been a long day.'

'It has. Yes. You too—sleep well.'

'I'm sure I will. Now you go and do the same.'

CHAPTER TEN

ONCE THEY WERE back in the palace Matteo couldn't help but pull her close, savouring the feel of her in his arms. He'd nearly lost his father. But she was still here and he needed her closeness and comfort.

'You were my rock tonight. I don't know how I would have got through it without you.'

'You'd have survived. You'd have had no choice.'

'I guess not.' He looked at her and stroked her hair. It was so soft.

'You need to get some sleep,' she said.

'Are you prescribing that?'

She smiled. 'I am.'

'Perhaps you could help me sleep tonight?' he asked, with intent.

She knew exactly what he meant. But was he suggesting it for the right reasons?

Laughing, she pushed him away, pretending that she had misunderstood. 'I could prescribe you a sleeping tablet.'

'You're not my doctor, though.'

She smiled. 'No. I'm not. All right, why don't you have a mug of warm milk? A warm bath?'

He considered both options. 'I've never enjoyed warm milk, and I take a shower first thing in the morning.' He raised an eyebrow. 'There is another way that you could help me sleep...'

Krystiana could only imagine how wonderful that might be, but someone had to be sensible here. 'And what would that be?'

'You could come with me to my quarters and make sure I get into bed on time?'

She tilted her head to one side, considering it. Trying her hardest not to laugh.

Oh, she wanted to. She could feel her body saying *yes*. 'Perhaps.'

'You could lie in my arms and stroke my hair until I fall asleep.'

She smiled. 'I could.'

'There are many things we could do. I keep fighting this…but I want you in my arms so much, you have no idea.'

She had a very clear idea. She could feel his arousal pressed against her.

He kissed her lips. Then her neck, trailing his mouth delicately down the long, smooth stretch of skin, drinking up her little moan of pleasure. 'I hear that orgasm is a wonderful precursor to a good night's sleep…'

He heard her throaty chuckle and raised his head to look into her eyes, a dreamy smile upon his face.

'Prolactin levels *do* make men sleepy. As does oxytocin and vasopressin—all produced by the brain after sex.'

'I love it when you talk dirty to me.'

She laughed, but then her face grew serious. 'You know, wanting sex is a classic response after someone has experienced the shock of feeling their mortality.'

He raised an eyebrow. 'Is that right?'

'Yes. People want to prove they're vital. What better way of cheating death than to do the very thing that creates life?'

He cocked his head to one side. 'Is that a bad response?'

'Not necessarily. But a woman likes to know that her

man wants her because he wants *her* and no other reason—not just because he wants to prove how full of life he is.'

He looked her directly in the eye, so that she was not mistaken. 'I want to be with *you*. Because you've been driving me wild for days and I've not been able to do anything about it. Because I've been fighting it. Telling myself it was the wrong thing to do. But right now I'm not sure I believe any of that. What happened tonight proves that life is short. I want your lips, your kisses, your arms around me. I want your body pressed into mine and to hell with everything else! I might have had a shock tonight, but that shock has taught me that life is meant to be lived—and why should we deny ourselves what we want in life more than anything?'

She smiled.

The press of her curves against his body was almost driving him insane! To hell with tradition and law and being careful! He'd done that for so long, and since coming back from the mountains he had kept a tight control on so much of his feelings and emotions. But he couldn't do that with her. She changed him. Made him want. And need.

And right now he needed her in his arms and in his bed.

She kissed him on the lips. 'Then I'm yours.'

What the hell am I doing?

Acting recklessly. Giving in to her temptations. Not thinking.

Despite everything—despite the fact that he could have anyone he wanted—he wanted *her*, and that knowledge was strangely exciting and powerful. It gave her a thrill. Her heart pounded and her blood hummed with an inner energy that she couldn't explain when she was with him.

As she slipped out of the grey dress lent to her by Mara she looked at herself in the bathroom mirror and wondered briefly who this woman was. She felt as if so much had changed since she had come here.

Krystiana removed her earrings, her necklace, slipped her feet out of her heels and removed the last of her underwear. On the back of the bathroom door was a robe and she pulled it on, checking her reflection.

I'm ready.

Sucking in a deep breath, she opened the bathroom door and leaned against the doorjamb as she gazed at Matteo, who stood waiting for her beside his bed.

'Are we sure about this?'

'Do we have to be?' he asked, before making his way over to her, his hands cupping her face and pulling her lips towards his once more…

'Good morning.'

'Buongiorno!'

She kissed him, inhaling his lovely male scent of soap and sandalwood. 'Any news from the hospital?'

'He had a restful night.'

'That's great!' she said, even though she knew that the quicker King Alberto recovered, the faster everything would change, throwing them into turmoil once again. But that was for later. For a time she wasn't ready to think about.

He must have seen the hesitation in her features. 'What's wrong?'

'Nothing. Honestly, I'm happy for your father.'

'But?'

'But nothing.' How could she tell him? It was incredibly selfish! What did she want? For his father to be ill a lot longer?

He smiled and pulled her close for a kiss.

It was heaven. Being kissed by him. Being held by him. In his arms she just felt so…*adored.* It was an addictive state, and Krystiana knew all about addictions, having looked after many addicts in her time. They constantly craved that high. That feel-good moment when every worry and concern just melted away because they were in a state of bliss. She could understand it a little more, experiencing this. The high she got being with him.

'Are you going to the hospital this morning?'

'I thought we could go after breakfast?'

'You want me to come with you?'

'I'm taking Alex to see her grandfather. Mara's staying here, as she has a business meeting, and I thought Alex might cheer him up.'

She nodded. Alex brightened everyone's lives. She was such a cutie. And she would grow up to be a stunner, she had no doubt. If Krystiana was going to get to know Matteo, perhaps she ought to get to know his daughter better, too?

'All right. But are you sure you need me in the way? It seems like a family moment.'

He took her hand and squeezed it. 'I want you with me. Now, let's eat. Out on the terrace—it's a wonderful morning.'

Sergio—who appeared to be totally unruffled to find her in Matteo's bedchamber this morning—served them dark, strong espresso, sour cherry *crostatas*, custard-filled *ciambellas* and some *strudel di mele*, alongside a selection of fresh fruits and juices.

'I can feel myself putting on the pounds just looking at this.' Krystiana smiled.

Matteo smiled back at her and reached for her hand, bringing the back of it to his sugared lips and kissing it. 'Eat.'

Mara brought Alex to them, greeting Matteo by kissing both his cheeks and doing the same to Krystiana.

'Give your father all the best from me and tell him I'll be in this afternoon.'

'I will.'

Matteo crouched down to look at his daughter, who smiled at him from behind her mother's legs, holding a bedraggled teddy.

'Hey, Alex! Are you ready to come with me and see Nonno?'

Alex nodded. Smiling, Matteo reached out for her hand and then scooped her up into his arms.

'Saluta tua madre.'

Alex gave her mother a smile and Mara bent down for a kiss. 'You be good for your father.'

Alex nodded, hugging her teddy.

Mara smiled too, and then her eyes narrowed with amusement as she looked at the two of them. 'Something's changed…'

Matteo smiled. 'Just pleased to be with my daughter again, in the knowledge that my father will be back pounding the hallways before we know it.'

'Okay…' But Mara seemed to suspect there was something else. She looked at Krystiana and seemed to come to some conclusion. She raised an eyebrow. 'You're *happy*.'

He laughed. 'Is that so wrong?'

Mara smiled 'Being happy? No. Not at all. Remember to say hi to your father for me.'

'I will.'

She kissed her daughter and walked away.

Today was going to be a *good* day. He was going to see his father and then, when he got back, he was going to think about what was happening between him and Krystiana.

It was all moving so fast. And he had done something he'd told himself not to do. He'd given in to his physical desires and slept with her, and it had been wonderful, mind-blowing, and everything he'd suspected it would be. But where did it leave them? It could never be serious between them. That was against the law—they couldn't marry. And he'd never thought he'd be the type to have a fling, so…

Whatever happened, he wanted to do the right thing. He didn't want to upset Krystiana. He didn't want to confuse Alex about who was in her life and who wasn't. And nor did he want to cause pain to himself.

He strongly suspected he might do that anyway. Either way, whatever it was that they had could not continue for any length of time. The time would come when it would have to end.

The question was, could he end it without hurting her?

Matteo and Alex walked hand in hand into King Alberto's room, Krystiana following dutifully behind.

'Papà! How are you?' Matteo kissed his father on both cheeks.

'Much better, today, Matteo. Now! Do I see a tiny little princess who needs a big hug from her *nonno*?'

He reached out for Alex and the little girl let go of her father's hand and jumped up into Alberto's grasp.

'Careful, Papà. You're meant to be resting.'

'Holding my granddaughter will do me *good*, Matteo.' Alberto kissed Alex and gave her a little tickle, and her wonderful bright laughter filled the room. 'Oh, and Dr Szenac! You are here, too! Hello! How is my son behaving himself without me there to keep an eye on him?'

Krystiana smiled. 'He's being good.'

'I'm glad to hear it. Though I'm surprised to see you here today. You doctors just can't stay away! You're like vultures!' he said with a laugh.

Krystiana felt her heart pound with nerves as Alberto sat Alex on the bed and passed her a small wrapped gift. 'Here, I got you something. Open it!'

Alex tore through the paper and beamed when she saw a book covered in bright animals. She lay back against her grandfather and began to turn the pages.

'Alex, what do you say to Nonno?'

'Grazie.' Alex smiled shyly at her grandfather.

'Good girl.' Matteo ruffled her hair, smiling at the cute response. 'How on earth did you get her a present?' he asked his father. 'I thought you were on bed rest?'

'One of the perks of being a king, Matteo, and I needn't tell you, is that I have servants to do my bidding.'

His son smiled. 'Ah… Have the doctors been in to see you yet?'

Alberto nodded. 'Yes. They've checked me out and told me I need to take it easy. Take it *easy*? I run a country, I told them. That's no easy feat.'

Matteo smiled. 'And you do it very well. If I'm half the King that you are then I will consider myself to be lucky.'

'Well, you're going to get the chance earlier than you suspected.'

Krystiana felt her heart miss a beat. Matteo? King? That was *very* different from just having a romance with a prince.

Matteo frowned. 'What? No. You're as fit as a fiddle.'

'That's just it, Matteo. I'm *not*. I wish I were—I do. I know you need more time to get used to the idea, but you've had a whole lifetime waiting for this day. I'd hoped that a grand tour of Tamoura would be a gradual introduction to your new duties, but I'm having to face facts. My heart has given me a second warning now. If I want to be around to see this beautiful little one grow up and walk down the aisle one day, then I've got to take a step back earlier than I expected.'

Matteo glanced at Krystiana. 'What does that mean?'

'I'm going to abdicate *now*. The press have been notified already, and told that it's my recommendation that you are crowned as soon as it is possible.'

Matteo shook his head. 'Papà, *no*!'

Alberto reached out to take his hand. 'Matteo… No one *ever* feels ready. Do you think I was? Do you think I knew what I was doing when the crown was placed on my head? No. But it's how you act when it is. How you learn and grow to become the man you need to be to carry the country forward.'

'But…'

Matteo seemed lost for words, and almost on the verge of having to sit down. Instead he reached out for Krystiana's hand and squeezed it, not noticing the King's raised eyebrows as he did so, nor his questioning look at Krystiana.

'You still have months left before you said you'd abdicate. Take that time—a final farewell to the people. I—'

Alberto held up his hand for silence, his face stony. 'I was a new father when I took the throne. You were three weeks old. I was sleep-deprived, stressed and worn out. I'd just finished a world tour, had a new baby son… Life *happens*, Matteo. There will never be a perfect time. Dr Szenac, *you* seem to know my son well. You think he's ready, do you not?'

Krystiana swallowed, her mouth suddenly dry. She looked at Matteo, knowing he wanted her to say something that would support Alberto's carrying on for a bit longer. But she couldn't. She had to answer the King honestly.

'He's more than ready.'

Alberto smiled. 'You see? Everyone else knows you can do it.'

Matteo would make a great king. He was kind and caring, considerate and thoughtful. Yes, he had been through a great ordeal, but it had only served to make him stronger. More resolute.

But what did that mean for *them*? She had *slept* with him!

Alberto smiled. 'You will take the throne, Matteo.'

She saw Matteo glance at her with uncertainty, and in that glance so many things were conveyed. Doubt. Fear. Hesitation.

They were at the beginning of a relationship that could be something amazing. But she had no idea of how it was to be with someone like him! He was a *prince*. About to become a *king*. And she was just a normal girl from Poland. A doctor.

This acceleration of events was terrifying. What *was* she to him? Would it become serious? Was it casual? Would she be discarded and left behind?

'Are we going to talk about what happened today?' Matteo threw his jacket to one side as he walked into his quarters, Krystiana following slowly behind.

'Okay…'

'My father wants me to become King! I thought I had more time. I thought that…' he turned to look at her, saw the concern on her face '…that *we* had time.'

'We do. Don't we?'

'If my father has already alerted the press, then the focus of the whole country will be upon me. And also on *you*.'

She remembered what media attention felt like. It had been awful. Terrifying at times. But she had survived it. 'They would only be focused on me if we were together.'

He stopped pacing to face her. 'I guess that's the big question, isn't it?'

She gave a single nod. 'It is. What *am* I to you, Matteo?'

It was a terrifying question to ask. It would put him on

the spot. But it was an answer she needed to hear, because she needed to know. Needed to prepare herself for whatever onslaught was coming.

'Honestly? I don't know.'

That wasn't good. A small part of her had wanted him to say she was his everything. That he couldn't get enough of her. That he couldn't bear to be without her. But he wasn't saying any of those things.

'I don't want to hurt you. I know that. This situation is complex and extreme, and I can't assume that you'd want to be a part of this mad world that I live in.'

She said nothing. No, she didn't want to be hurt either. But she had a feeling she would be.

Krystiana sank down into a chair. 'Perhaps us being together is a bad idea? I get the feeling your father would not approve.'

Matteo looked down and away, as if he was weary.

'You're going to become *King*, Matteo. Sooner than you thought. Perhaps you and I ought to back off from one another for a while until all of that is done?'

Part of her thought that if they did back away from one another they would each have breathing space. This all seemed to be moving so fast! He was going to wear the crown! Perhaps with time apart he would begin to see that they weren't best suited, and by then she would have prepared herself for the inevitable and her heart would not be as broken as she suspected it might be.

Matteo sighed. 'You might be right.'

She'd suggested it, but it was still a shock that he accepted it so readily. Perhaps he'd meant more to her than she to him?

Krystiana swallowed, her mouth dry, trying her hardest to stop the tears from burning the backs of her eyes, trying to be brave. They'd had one great night and it had been the most amazing night of her life. And to wake this morning, in his arms… She couldn't remember ever feeling so happy. But she'd always suspected that if they were to have any type of relationship it would be a brief one, and now it was looking more than likely that that was true.

It didn't make it any easier to know that he could happily discard her so quickly.

After Krystiana had gone Matteo stepped out onto his sun terrace and looked out over the hillsides. He knew he had to give them both space, but in his heart of hearts he also knew that, if he was being honest, nothing could ever have come from their relationship. He'd been an absolute fool to allow his desire and his lust for her to overcome every iota of common sense and logic he possessed!

His father had announced to the press that he was abdicating and that his son would be crowned King as soon as it was possible. The media was in a frenzy, as was to be expected, and he… He was apprehensive.

He should be thinking of his country. How the small kingdom of Isla Tamoura needed him to be a strong leader. And yet all he could think of was Krystiana.

Things had happened between them so quickly. And he suspected he knew why. They could both connect on something that not many people got to experience—thankfully. Their kidnapping. He couldn't imagine what it must have been like to have been taken by her own father. He tried to imagine his father doing such a thing. Locking him into a hole in the ground. His mind just couldn't compute it. Krystiana's father must have been so desperate after he lost his custody battle… He knew how crazy *he'd* almost gone, thinking he would never see his own child.

Krystiana had told him, hadn't she? That she didn't want a proper relationship. That she couldn't foresee having one. So really maybe he was doing her a favour? She didn't want this either!

His pathetic attempt to convince himself that he was doing this for *her* made him feel slightly ill.

He got up and began to pace once again—back and forth, back and forth. He caught a glimpse of his reflection in the mirror and stopped to stare at himself, trying to work out when it was that he had changed from being a man determined never to get involved with anyone again into a man who had barely been able to keep his emotions and desires in check around Krystiana.

He'd never wanted to feel loss again and yet he'd got involved with a woman he knew he could never have!

How on earth had he ever allowed it to happen?

She found herself standing outside Mara's office, holding the grey dress she'd borrowed draped over one arm. She knocked.

Mara opened her door. 'Krystiana! Come on in!' She stepped back to allow her entrance.

'I thought I'd better bring back your dress. It's been cleaned. I think one of the servants spirited it away when I was at the hospital this morning.'

Mara smiled, taking the dress from her. 'Thank you. But you could have kept it, you know?'

Krystiana shook her head. 'Oh, no! It must have cost a fortune. I couldn't do that.'

Mara gazed at her for a moment, obviously sensing her nerves and anxiety. 'What's wrong? Come on—sit down. Tell me what's going on.'

And suddenly the tears were falling. She couldn't help it. It was almost as if Mara's empathy and kindness had just opened up the dam and it had all come pouring out.

Mara, bless her, sat next to her with an arm around her shoulders. Just being there. Just waiting for when she was ready to talk.

'Matteo and I…' Krystiana sniffed, dabbing at her eyes

with the tissue that Mara offered her. 'We've been…er…' How to say it? This was his ex-wife! But she was also his best friend, so…

'You've been…courting?'

She knew? 'Not really. Not *dating*, as such. Just… I'm not sure how it happened, really, but…'

Mara waited.

'We slept together.' She felt awful telling Mara this.

'And now it's complicated?'

Krystiana nodded. 'It always was.'

'I understand. Matteo and I, even though we knew our future, were caught up in an extraordinary situation. And now the man that you…you have feelings for is about to be King, and that's not a normal thing at all for anyone to have to face.'

'No one would approve of us.'

'You don't know that.'

Krystiana didn't have to think for too long. 'I do. Matteo held my hand in front of his father and I could see he wasn't pleased about it.'

'The world is complicated, Krystiana. Nothing is always simple or as it seems. Sometimes all you can do is go with what your heart tells you.'

'It's telling me so many things.'

'Then perhaps you should ask it a question? How would you feel never to have Matteo in your life ever again?'

She couldn't imagine what that would be like. To only see him on the television… In the newspapers… Online… 'It would be awful.'

Mara smiled. 'But you would survive it?'

'I've already survived so much. Had my heart broken too many times. I'm not sure I want to go through that again.'

'Sometimes we have no choice about our battles.'

Krystiana smiled ruefully. 'You sound like you're trying to tell me to prepare myself. That there is no future for us.'

Mara looked away. 'I like you, Krystiana. I think you and Matteo could be amazing together. You'd make each other happy.'

'But…?'

'But if you want to be with him then you need to talk to him.'

'About what?'

Mara smiled. 'About everything.'

CHAPTER ELEVEN

MATTEO OPENED THE door to his quarters to see Krystiana standing there, looking apprehensive and nervous. Smiling, he welcomed her in, dropping a kiss on her cheek. She looked so beautiful, her eyes bright and kind, her smile full and wide. He felt his heart lift at seeing her, even though he felt depressed.

'Hi,' he said.

'Hi. I wonder if you have a minute to talk?'

'Sure. Can I get you a drink?'

'No, it's all right. I just want to say this whilst I have the nerve to and then I'll go.'

Oh. That didn't sound good. But, then again, she was smiling—so what did that mean? Had she made a decision?

'I'm all ears.'

'Yes.'

He narrowed his eyes. 'Yes…?'

She laughed. 'Yes! To you. To *us*. One of us has to say it! I want us to try to be together. Despite all that's going on, despite you becoming King, and despite other people's disapproval—when there is any, which I'm expecting there to be. I'm just a doctor, after all, and—'

'Hang on—let me get this straight. You want us to be a…a couple?'

His heart soared. Not for one moment had he thought

she would come to such a conclusion, but she had, and it was wonderful, and despite all his fears he wanted this one moment when he did something for *him*. Because his life was about to spiral madly out of control when he became King. He knew he was throwing caution to the wind, despite the rules, but surely he could worry about those at a later time?

'Come here.' He pulled her into his arms, his lips meeting hers, and he kissed her as he'd never kissed her before!

He knew what this had cost her. He knew how terrified she must have been to say it. And it felt *so right*. This was the woman he'd been waiting for his entire life. She was perfect. Intelligent, kind, loving, beautiful. And she understood him. Understood more than anyone else ever could. Because she'd been through it, too.

And when his father had collapsed he'd felt *safe*, knowing she was with him. He'd felt loved, knowing that she was thinking about *him*, that he was thinking about *her*.

She was his strength. His heart. His life. And though he was worried about what the future might entail for them, his fear was not as strong as his love. His need. That was a bridge they could cross later. Surely there was a way?

'I love you so much, Krystiana Szenac!'

She smiled back. 'And I love *you*!'

They kissed. Unable to get enough of each other. He had no doubt that he would have taken her to his bed right there and then, if he'd been able to, but he had people coming. Delegates. Business meetings.

'Let's celebrate! Just you and me. Away from here. I could get us reservations at Jacaranda. Very discreet.'

'Go out with you in public?' Her face was flushed with excitement and nerves and apprehension.

He nodded. 'We need to get away from this place. Just be *us*.'

Krystiana nodded and gave him a quick kiss before she headed back to the door. 'Dress code?'

He gave it some thought. 'You'd look beautiful in anything.'

She laughed. '*Formal* would have done nicely.'

'Formal, it is.'

'Right. Then I'm off to get ready.'

He checked his watch. 'It's two-thirty in the afternoon.'

'A girl needs time to look her best, Matteo.'

'You're already perfect.'

She smiled and blew him a kiss. 'Good answer. But I'm still going to have a bath and do my hair.'

She began to close the doors behind her.

'Wait!' he called, sliding over to the door in his socks, skidding to a halt in front of her. 'One last kiss?'

She pressed her mouth to his and he savoured the taste of her.

'Not the last, Matteo. But the first of *many*.'

She'd needed to be brave many times in her life, but going to see Matteo and admitting what she wanted, to be in a relationship with him, was probably one of the bravest things she had ever done. She had put herself *out there.* As if she was on a precipice and he had the ability to knock her off, to send her crashing to her doom.

She'd given him that power and he hadn't let her down at all. Her gut instinct had been *right*! He wanted to be with her as much as she wanted to be with him!

And she was quickly learning that one of the advantages of living in a palace was that there seemed to be a hairdresser, stylist and make-up artist always on site. Apparently Giulia was there mostly for Mara and Alex's sake, but she was thrilled to get her hands on someone new and decide what to do with her.

'Your hair is just *bellissimo*! Thick and long.' Giulia

was running her fingers through it, admiring it, trying it this way, then that. 'I think we need a messy up-do. Like this—see? But if we leave these strands here and here we can make tiny plaits and twist them through…like this. *Si?*'

Krystiana had never done more than put her hair in a thick plait. 'Whatever you think is right will be fine.'

'We can tousle it, tease it, and if we are careful we can use jewelled slides here and there. Let me do it and I'll show you—I promise you'll love it.'

'Okay.'

'And what were you thinking for make-up?' Giulia looked at her carefully in the mirror. 'Such expressive eyes… You need more than mascara on those. How about a deep, dark smoky eye? A nude lip? Earrings to match the jewels in your hair?'

Krystiana frowned. 'You're the expert. How long will all that take?'

'A couple of hours. We have plenty of time and then we can take a look at your wardrobe.'

'My wardrobe…?'

She didn't really have much in there. It wasn't as if she had loads to choose from. She'd mostly got ordinary work clothes with her. Suits… Dresses fit for being in her practice office—not a romantic soirée.

'Some things have been sent over for you.'

She turned in her seat. 'Oh? From whom?'

'The Crown Prince.'

'Matteo?'

'Well, he had a little help from me. I went shopping at his request.'

'When?'

'When you first arrived at the palace. He wasn't sure how much we would be able to rescue from your home, so he sent me out to fetch you a range of outfits.'

'Oh. But you don't know my sizes.'

'Stylists can *tell.* Just by looking. Trust me—I have picked you out some wonderful things.'

Krystiana smiled at her reflection as Giulia set to work with her hair. She quite liked it that he'd wanted to get some clothes for her, and she wasn't at all upset that he might have been a bit presumptuous in assuming that she was staying.

If he hadn't done it then she'd be knocking on Mara's door again, raiding *her* wardrobe! And there was something wrong about wearing the clothes of a man's ex-wife to make him fall for her! She was looking forward to searching through the boxes and bags that were now on the bed to see what there was.

She'd never been treated in such a way! Had always been careful with money, even though her job paid well. Growing up in a household where her mother had scrimped and saved every *zloty* had clearly rubbed off on her.

With her hair looking exquisite and her face made up by the talented Giulia, who could do things with a blender brush that Krystiana had no idea how to replicate, she set to going through the new outfits.

There were trouser suits and tailored dresses, flowing skirts and perfect heels. Linen trousers...even a couple of swimsuits! But in the end they both agreed that a duck-egg-blue dress, that skimmed over her hips and flared out just above the knee would be perfect.

Krystiana tried it on, twirling and twisting in front of the full-length mirror to check how it looked. 'This is so pretty, Giulia! Did you choose it?'

'Matteo chose this one. He said it would match your eyes and it does.'

Krystiana smiled. 'Good. Then I shall definitely wear it. Are we all done?'

Giulia tapped her lips as she assessed her. 'It needs one more thing... Here.' And she pulled from one of the bags a small box, cracking it open for Krystiana to see the jewelled bracelet inside.

It glittered and caught the light and it was the most beautiful thing she had ever seen. 'Oh, my word! He bought me *that*?'

'Yes.'

'It must have cost a fortune! I can't wear that! I'll be afraid of losing it all night.'

'It has a safety chain. Try it.'

Giulia clipped it around her wrist and she felt the weight of it on her arm. Just enough to notice. If it *did* fall off she would know instantly.

'So… I'm ready?'

'Yes, you are. I'll gather my things together and then I'll go.'

'Thank you, Giulia. You're a miracle-worker!'

'It was my pleasure. Have a good night.'

There was a gentle knock at her door and Krystiana opened it.

Matteo stood there, looking handsome in a smart suit, his white shirt crisp and clean, open at the collar. He looked like a handsome spy, set to seduce.

'You look…' He looked her up and down, his eyes appreciative. 'Amazing!'

She blushed. 'Thank you! So do you.'

'May I escort you down to the car?'

He held out his arm and she slipped hers through it, smiling. 'Thank you! You may.'

Together they walked through the palace corridors, past various members of staff going about their duties. They all looked up and smiled at the two of them and Krystiana felt admired and adored. Clearly they were a handsome couple.

In the car, they were driven slowly through the grounds of the palace and out through the gates, then down towards the bustling capital city of Ventura. Before she knew it they were pulling up outside a smart restaurant, set back from the road. Either side of the doors were railings behind which had gathered a bunch of people with cameras.

She felt her heart begin to race. 'Are they paparazzi?'

'Looks like it.'

'How did they know we were coming here?'

'I don't know. Someone must have let something slip. Shall we go back? We don't have to go out there.'

Her heart was racing and she felt a little clammy. Back in the palace she'd been sheltered from this, and though she knew she'd agreed to this, now that the moment was here it still felt a little…frightening.

'Just stay by my side—all right?' she said.

He nodded. 'Keep your eyes on me. When we're out of the vehicle we'll give them one moment when we stand together, give a quick smile, and then we'll be indoors. I promise you they can't see inside, and they can't step through the door. We'll have privacy for our meal. All right?'

She nodded, not sure she could speak.

'Okay. Deep breath and then one, two, three…'

Matteo opened the car door and suddenly a barrage of flashing lights assaulted her, blinding her slightly. She could hear clicks and whirrs and felt the flashes blinding her, leaving imprints on her retinas. She had to fight the urge to hold her hand in front of her face and run inside.

Instead, she gripped his arm, feeding on his sure strength and composure, and when she looked up at him he was smiling down at her with such ease that she couldn't help but smile back. And then they gave the press what they wanted. A quick pose. A quick smile. A small wave and then they were inside the restaurant.

She let out a heavy breath and looked to Matteo with relief. He was smiling at her and he kissed her gently on the lips. 'You did great.'

'It all happened so fast.'

'We all learn how to work the press. Give them enough to keep them fed and watered, but always leave them hanging on for more. And always be polite.'

'It almost feels like a game.'

'It is. They're all in competition with one another for the best shot, the best photo, the best smile. Because that's what sells.'

'I guess tomorrow everyone will know who I am?'

He nodded. 'They won't know for sure, though. It will all be speculation.'

So he can deny us later?

She hated it that the thought flittered through her brain, and she dismissed it. If he'd not wanted anyone to know about them then he would have ordered the driver to bring them here. He wouldn't have got out of the car with her. She was just being ridiculous and nervous because she was putting herself out there, on the line. Of course she could trust him.

The maître d' met them and escorted them to a small private booth at the back of the restaurant. A piano played softly in the background, and she quickly realised it wasn't being piped through speakers but was an actual pianist sitting at the instrument.

Candles lit the restaurant, alongside wall sconces and chandeliers, creating an intimate mood, and she sat at the table, suddenly feeling hungry. The nerves from facing the press had emptied her stomach.

A server draped her serviette over her lap and poured water into their glasses. 'Would you like to see the menu?'

'Thank you,' she said.

The server bowed and presented them each with a leather-bound menu. 'The special today is venison, which has been marinated in juniper, served with a parsnip *velouté* and a wild mushroom sauce.'

'Thank you,' she said again, and smiled shyly at the server and watched him walk away. 'This place is beautiful.'

'It's a favourite of mine. The chef is very good.'

She smiled. 'Did you come here with Mara?' she asked. She didn't want to think that this was where Matteo had brought *all* the women he'd wanted to impress in his past.

'No. I didn't. I only found this place after Mara and I had split.'

She smiled shyly. Thankful.

'So, what do you fancy?'

Krystiana beamed and reached across the table to take his hand. 'You.'

'Tell me what you were like as a little boy.'

She couldn't imagine what he must have been like. *Her* only recollections of growing up in Poland seemed to be around her own kidnapping, and then afterwards moving to Isla Tamoura. Adapting to a new way of life and thinking how strange it was. Surely his childhood had been a lot more sturdy.

He smiled. 'My father would tell you that I got into all types of mischief.'

'And what would *you* tell me?'

Matteo laughed. 'That he was right! There was this one time he was having an official meeting. Very important. Children not allowed. I can remember being fascinated about why all these important-looking people were allowed into this room and I wasn't! Was there some treasure there they were all looking at? Were they eating fabulous food? Did they have great computer games? I felt sure I was missing out on something, so I crept in and hid behind a drape at the back of my father's chair. I listened and listened, absolutely sure that I'd hear something secret or amazing. But they were droning on about olive yields and crop rotations and it was the most boring thing I'd ever heard—so I thought I'd liven things up.'

'What did you do?'

'I jumped out from behind the curtain and made the loudest and best dinosaur noise that I could possibly make.'

She laughed, imagining it. 'What happened?'

'My father turned in his seat and gave me *"the look"*. I knew then I was in trouble. I was escorted out, and about an hour later he came and told me off—said that as punishment I had to help the gardener for the afternoon.'

'Wow.'

'And of course you know how *that* turned out. I ended up designing nearly all of it.'

'It sounds like you were a very happy young boy.'

'I was. I *was* lucky.' He looked at her. 'How about you? There must be something from your childhood that's a good memory?'

She had to think about it. But then she remembered. 'My father once promised me a pony. He said that one day that I would have the best pony in the world! He got me a poster for my room, and a small cuddly toy that was a horse, but he said that one day I'd ride a pony that was all mine. I never got to do it, but I remember how hard he tried to give me what I wanted. He wasn't always a bad man.'

'Matilde could be yours.'

She looked at him. Was he serious? 'What…?'

'She could! You on Matilde, myself on Galileo—we could have many happy rides together.'

'You see a future for us, then?' she asked, her heart beating merrily. She was testing him gently. Needing the reassurance of his words.

He sipped his water. 'Of course.'

Later, Matteo walked her back to her rooms in the palace. Once inside the doors of his family home she had pulled off her heels, and she padded barefoot through the corridors, her head leaning against his arm.

She'd had such a wonderful evening with him. Listening to his stories and tales, laughing at his anecdotes, of which he had many, and just enjoying listening to him speak.

She realised just how long it had been since she'd been able to do that. Her whole adult life had been filled with patients—sitting and listening, assessing, analysing, looking for clues to their physical or mental state, considering diagnoses, selecting help methods and suggesting therapies and strategies they could use to get better.

But tonight she had just *enjoyed*. And she had told him a few tales of her own. Not having to be guarded about what she said, knowing that he would enjoy whatever it was and really listen to it.

She'd felt so good with him. So natural. And as she'd looked into his eyes over the table, as they'd eaten delicious food that had tasted as good as it looked, she'd just known that she could fall for this man hugely. If she hadn't already.

At her door, she turned to face him, pulling him towards her for a kiss. His lips on hers felt magical. This truly was blissful! To have such joy and happiness after all that they had both gone through. It almost felt as if it were a dream. And to think she had nearly denied herself such happiness…

'I want you to stay with me tonight,' she said boldly, looking deep into his eyes, telling him with her gaze exactly what she wanted.

He kissed her again, and then she took his hand and led him inside…

'Could you undo the zip?'

Krystiana turned away from him, to present him with her back. He gazed at the soft slope of her shoulders, at the gentle curls of honey hair at the nape of her neck and at the long zip that trailed the length of her spine. He took hold of the zipper and slowly lowered it, leaning in to kiss her soft skin as he did so.

She leaned back against him, gasping softly as his lips trailed feather touches and his hands slipped under the dress at each shoulder and slid the fabric to the floor.

Turning again, she faced him with a smile and he took in everything about her. The softness of her skin, the gentle swell of her breasts, her narrow waist, the feminine curve of her lips.

'You're so beautiful,' he whispered, reaching for her mouth with his own, sliding his hands down her sides, curving them over her buttocks and pulling her against him. Against his hardness. Wanting her to know how much he wanted her.

'Matteo!' She gasped his name as his hands cupped her breasts, and then again as his tongue found her nipples, delicately licking and teasing each tip. He worked lower, down to her belly, hooking his thumbs under her panties and slowly, slowly pulling them down.

He wanted to lose himself in her, but a loud voice in the back of his mind was yelling at him, telling him that this was *wrong*. That nothing could come of it. He would have to let her go and he was being a terrible man—keeping up the façade that everything was fine. Soon he would have to tell her the truth, and that would tear her apart. He didn't want to be just another man who would break her heart, so he kept putting it off and putting it off—and now look at where they were.

She thought they were making love.

But he knew he was saying goodbye.

She woke in his arms. A lazy smile was upon her face. Her body was still tingling, comforted by the feel of Matteo spooning her from behind.

Last night had been everything she had ever dreamed of, and she knew that out in the wider world the people of Isla Tamoura would be waking up to newspaper reports of the coronation and the Crown Prince's new beau. They would have the rest of their lives to enjoy each other. They'd made it official last night, with that public appearance. Now everyone would know.

Briefly she wondered if she ought to call the practice and make arrangements for her patients to be taken on by Dr Bonetti for a short while. Later on she could decide about when she'd return. It had been so long since she'd taken any time off she felt sure Dr Bonetti wouldn't mind, and she'd just covered for him, so…

There's plenty of time before I have to do that, though.

Getting out of bed, she pulled on her robe and opened up the double doors that led outside, closing her eyes to the wonderful warmth of the early-morning sun.

This would be her life from now on. This wonder. This joy. Living in the palace with the man of her dreams, the love of her life. Yes, she knew she loved him. Everything would be different now.

She glanced back at Matteo, still blissfully asleep in her bed, his face relaxed, and realised they'd both got through the night without a night-light. It was as if the love they had between them was what they needed to be strong enough to fight off the fears that plagued them.

Was that all it took? A loving pair of arms?

Whatever it was, she didn't mind. She was happy. And in love. Probably for the first time in her life. She had fallen for him deeply.

His eyes blinked open and as soon as he saw her he smiled. *'Buongiorno.'*

'Buongiorno.'

'You're up already.'

'Ready to face the world!'

He groaned. 'No. Not yet. Let's just stay here and pretend the rest of the world doesn't exist. Come back to bed.'

She smiled coyly at him and padded back towards him, disrobing and falling into his arms, feeling his lips on hers and delightful sensations rippling through her once again.

'Aren't you tired?'

'Of this? *Never.*'

Krystiana laughed. 'Don't you have to go to the hospital this morning?'

Matteo groaned and rolled over to check his watch, blinking at the time. 'Yes. Of course. You're right. Five minutes…then I'll get dressed.'

'Five minutes?' She bit her lip and looked at him questioningly.

He laughed, unable to help himself. 'I can do a lot in five minutes.'

And then he disappeared under the bed sheet and she felt his mouth trail down her skin, lower and lower, until she gasped with surprise and delight.

She'd wanted to capture the moment of Alex playing in Matteo's beloved flower garden. She'd thought it would be a wonderful gift for him. So as Alex frolicked amongst the blooms, trying to catch butterflies with a gauzy net, Krystiana stood back, splashing colour onto canvas.

She'd show him when he got back from seeing his father! He would love it. It would be unique. It would be put in pride of place in his quarters. The lush greens of all the foliage, the spots of gold, bronze, cherry-red, fuchsia-pink and lapis-blue flowers, and amongst it all a beautiful little girl, her long ebony locks flowing behind her, her net held high, ready to swoop.

'Look at me, Krissy—look!'

She was so beautiful, Matteo's daughter, and it was

important to Krystiana that they got along. She wanted to create a happy painting. Made with love.

Just as she was adding the finishing touches she felt a prickle on the back of her neck. The sensation of being watched.

She turned to see who it might be.

It was Matteo. Up on his sun terrace, looking down at them. He was far enough away not to be able to see the painting, but there was something about his stance that made her think he was upset.

She put down her brushes and wiped her hands on a soft cloth. 'Alex? Let the painting dry, won't you? Don't touch it. I'm just going to see if your father is all right.'

Her first thought was that maybe something had happened with his father. Had King Alberto deteriorated? Perhaps he'd had a heart attack in the night?

Oh, please don't let him be dead!

She hated to think of Matteo being hurt in such a way. Going through the loss of his last remaining parent…

The thought made her steps slow, and for a moment she stopped still completely, just to breathe. To gather herself—strengthen herself for whatever revelation was about to come. It had to be something bad, didn't it? Otherwise Matteo would have come down to see her in the gardens with Alex.

Everything had been going so well since last night. They'd both finally found happiness. Was the beginning of their love going to be marred by death? She sincerely hoped not…

Krystiana didn't knock as she entered his quarters. She knew he would still be out on the sun terrace and he was—standing with his back to her, ramrod-straight. There was a sternness to the set of his shoulders, to the upright nature of his posture—as if he was holding himself so as not to break.

'Matteo?'

He didn't answer her. Or turn around. And that alarmed her. She walked to his side so that she could see his face. It was cold and stony. Like a statue.

She reached out to touch his hand with hers. 'Matteo? Are you all right? What's happened?'

He said nothing for a while, then he blinked and squeezed her fingers tightly, before responding, 'I went to see my father.'

She felt as if a cold, dead lump was weighting down her stomach. 'Is he all right?'

'Fine. Well, health-wise, he is. The doctors think he can come home.'

She felt a wave of relief surge over her. 'But that's *great* news!'

He nodded. 'It is.'

'So…why aren't you happy? You look…stressed.'

And that was when she noticed that in his other hand he held a small glass of whisky. He lifted it to his mouth and sank the drink in one gulp. Wasn't it a little early for hard liquor?

'Matteo? You're scaring me. Tell me what's going on. *Now.*'

He turned to look at her and she could see that he had been crying. His eyes were red and puffy.

'My father saw the newspapers this morning. He was not pleased that he had to learn about us through a third party.'

She sucked in a breath. 'Okay…' That was acceptable. They should apologise for that. King Alberto should have been told by them. They'd got that bit wrong. 'Does he not like me?'

'He does. But…' He glanced at his glass and saw that it was empty. Scowling, he placed it down on the balcony edge. 'He reminded me of a certain unpalatable truth.'

She blinked, not understanding. 'What truth?'

Matteo turned away, as if unable to look her in the eyes. And that scared her.

'The law of my country states that those first in line to the throne can only marry another of royal blood.'

What? No. That couldn't be right!

But the more she thought about what that meant, the more she knew something like this had always been going to happen. It had all been going too well.

The tears escaped. Trickling down her cheeks. 'Royal blood?'

He could only marry a princess? Or a duchess? Something like that? Well, she wasn't either of those things! She was just a girl from Poland who'd once lived in a giant block of flats. A girl from a poor family whose father had hunted rabbit and pigeon to feed his family meat. A girl who had fled to this island seeking a better life than the one she'd had to leave behind.

They were worlds apart. The only way she'd have royal blood would be if she stole it from someone and kept it in a small vial!

'This is ridiculous! It's got to be wrong!'

'It's not wrong. It's an archaic law of my land and has been for hundreds of years.'

Her eyes widened as her brain scrambled to find some way out of this. 'But if we didn't know, surely it isn't our fault?'

He turned and walked over to the liquor cabinet. Without a word he refilled his glass and knocked back the whisky again, his gaze downcast to the floor.

And suddenly she knew. She tried to make him look at her. 'You *did* know. You knew and yet you slept with me anyway. You made me think that we could be together! How could you? How could you treat me like this? Like a…a plaything. A toy! What did you think I was? Some kind of casual fling?'

'Krystiana—'

But she didn't want to hear it. She'd told him she'd been hurt before, and how much it would cost her to trust someone again, and what had he done? He'd lied. He'd kept secrets. He'd used her. For his own gratification!

He was worse than Adamo.

Overcome with tears and humiliation, she fled from his room.

Matteo winced as his door slammed behind her and felt sick to his stomach. The visit with his father had been a lost battle before he'd even entered the room—and now this. Surely there must have been another way he could have done this? Another way he could have gently explained how they could never be more than what they were now.

But his father had forced his hand. He had told him that he needed to tell her the truth or that he, Alberto himself, would have the royal chamberlain inform her of the rules by the end of the day. Tell her that she would have to give up her claim on the King's son because he could never be hers.

'Why are you doing this?' he'd asked his father.

'I'm trying to stop it before either of you get hurt.'

But it was already too late. His father didn't know the depth of his feelings for Krystiana. Or hers for him. And he hated it that he had trampled all over her heart with his dirty shoes.

But, hell, she'd not wanted a relationship either—so what the hell was *she* doing, allowing them to get into such a situation? He'd thought they'd both be safe. Neither of them had wanted it and yet somehow, in some way, they had been unable to stay away from each other.

And now he was faced with another loss. Another heartbreak. Was he doomed to suffer? He should never have got involved, he told himself once again, as he slammed his hand against the wall in frustration and upset, and he would never allow himself to get into a situation like this ever again.

His heart would be off-limits.

Access granted only to his daughter.

Krystiana refused to pack the clothes that had been bought for her. Or the jewellery. Or any of the gifts she'd been given during her time in the palace. If she took any of it all it would do, when she got home, would be to remind her of what might have been, and her heart was instinctively telling her that if she wanted to get over this then she had to leave it all behind. Then she could almost pretend that it had never happened. Like she had when she'd left Krakow. All she'd taken with her then had been some clothes in a small suitcase and a solitary doll with only one arm.

She'd seen plenty of patients in her time who had used denial as an effective tool to pretend that bad stuff hadn't happened. And right now she thought it was a damned good strategy! Though she'd suggested that they might do better by facing the bad stuff, so that they could heal, right now she wanted to wholeheartedly embrace the concept.

Angrily she went from drawer to drawer, grabbing her clothes roughly and shoving them into her suitcase, throwing in her shoes. She didn't even bother to wrap her paints and spare canvases separately.

Who cares if I get paint over everything?

She didn't. Her heart had been broken the instant she'd realised that Matteo had lied to her, and she knew she couldn't stay a moment longer. She couldn't believe the mess she had got herself into!

I fought against this attraction. I should have listened to myself.

If she had, then none of this would have happened and she'd already be out of here. She should never have stayed for that ball. She should have gone.

But it had been impossible. Her desire for him had been plain fact. There'd been no way to walk away from her love. Her soul mate. The man she'd seen herself with all the way into the future.

How gullible she must have seemed for him to use her likc that, knowing how she'd been treated in the past. He'd known what it had taken for her to open to him like that, to put herself out there, and he'd—

She cried out loud as pain ripped through her chest and hiccupped her way through her final packing. Bruno sat in the corner, his head tilted as he watched her frantic movements, trying to work out what was going on.

His father must have delighted in forcing Matteo to tell her the truth. Or perhaps she should *thank* the King? She'd seen it in his face, that time Matteo had clutched Krystiana's hand for support in the hospital. The way his eyes had narrowed… She should have questioned it then.

Behind her, the doors to her apartment opened.

'You're leaving?'

Mara stared at her, her face a mask of shock and concern.

Krystiana wiped at her eyes, determined to stop crying once and for all! 'I have no choice!'

'There must be something you can do…'

'There isn't, so…' She turned to Mara and pulled her towards her for a hug. 'Thank you for being my friend here. It could have been awkward between us, but you made it so easy. Thank you.'

Mara hugged her back. 'Are you kidding me? It's so obvious that what you and Matteo have is real. You look at each other the way Philippe and I do.'

Krystiana sniffed. 'It was never real. Matteo *knew* I couldn't be with him.'

Mara looked away.

Krystiana stared at her. 'You did too?' she asked with incredulity.

'I'm sorry. But I couldn't be the one to tell you. To break your heart.'

Krystiana slammed down the clips on her suitcase. 'A heads-up might have been nice!'

'I tried! I told you to talk to him!'

But she didn't want to hear any more. Did *everyone* lie? 'I've got to go. Say goodbye to Alex for me?'

'Where are you going?'

She shrugged. 'A hotel somewhere? A bed and breakfast?' She looked at Bruno. 'One that takes dogs...'

'Will I ever see you again?'

'Do you read the *Lancet*?' Krystiana smiled, trying to crack a joke in the midst of her trauma.

'No.'

'Then I guess not.'

'I'll talk to Matteo.'

'There's no point. I wouldn't have any more to do with him if he was the last man alive.'

'Krystiana, please! Promise me you'll wait here until I get back?'

She nodded, knowing she was going to break her promise. But what did she owe Mara, if anything? Mara had been complicit in this lie, too. Mara whom she'd thought was a friend.

After Matteo's ex-wife had left Krystiana took one last look around the place and then left, trailing her little suitcase behind her.

'Come on, Bruno. Let's go.'

CHAPTER TWELVE

SHE'D NOT BEEN lying when she'd told Mara she'd stay at a hotel or a bed and breakfast. She just hadn't said it would be in Rome.

Isla Tamoura was not a place she could be right now. Everyone would know her—know her face. She wouldn't be able to find refuge at work either. People would show up just to gawp at her and ask questions. To see the royal fool. She needed to go somewhere no one would find her.

She'd dropped Bruno off at her aunt's place. Thankfully she'd been out, so she'd left her aunt a note on the counter. Bruno would be fine with her—she knew that.

At the airport, the first thing she spotted was her face on the front of a newspaper. She was standing next to Matteo outside the restaurant last night. Smiling. Looking nervous, but happy.

Feeling sick, she fumbled in her handbag for a pair of large sunglasses and let her long hair down loose. She didn't want anyone spotting her. Didn't want anyone recognising who she was.

She sneaked into the women's toilet and splashed her face with cold water, staring at her reflection, trying to equate the drawn-looking woman in the mirror with the one who had just this very morning woken up in the arms of the man she loved. A woman who had believed that her worst problem at the time was whether she'd have time for a quick shower before breakfast.

How was she here? Why had he lied? When he knew that the truth was the most important thing he could have told her?

Sliding the sunglasses back onto her face, she headed out of the bathroom and went to the customer service desk.

'Are there any flights to Rome soon?' she asked the perfectly groomed woman behind the desk.

The woman, whose name tag read *Leonora*, tapped at her keyboard, reading the screen in front of her. 'Yes, ma'am, there's a flight at three this afternoon.'

'Any seats available?'

'Yes, ma'am. Window and aisle.'

'Okay. Who do I need to see to book that?'

Leonora told her where to go, and before she knew it Krystiana had a plane ticket and had checked her luggage. Only an hour until her flight time. What to do to pass the time?

She saw a coffee shop and felt the need for a huge slug of caffeine, and maybe some restorative chocolate, despite the feeling in her stomach.

She sat down at a small table, trying not to be noticed. Opposite her, a man sat with a woman whom she supposed to be his wife. They were discussing her picture on the front page of the newspaper. Wondering whether they were serious? Whether they were in love?

She tried to sink down in her seat, hoping no one would notice her.

I should have bought a paper to hide behind.

She looked about her and saw a discarded one on the table next to her. She picked it up and shook it open, hiding her face from the crowds.

One hour to go and she could be out of here!

* * *

Matteo stared at the empty apartment. 'She's really gone.' He felt guilty. Angry. It had all come crashing down around his ears so quickly. Such intense happiness, contentment and love, and now this.

He was feeling empty. Stunned.

Heartbroken.

The thought that he might never see her again almost crushed him into inertia. It was like being back in that cave, wondering if he'd ever see his loved ones again?

Mara laid a friendly hand upon his arm, her face filled with sympathy. 'She told me she'd wait.'

'She didn't want to get involved with me. *Told* me she didn't want a relationship. That she didn't want to be that vulnerable.'

'She loved you, though. You can't help who you fall in love with.'

'Like you and Philippe?' It was a cheap shot, and it was out of his bitter mouth before he could reel it back in. He was hurting and wanted to lash out, but he should never have lashed out at his best friend. 'I'm sorry. Forget that.'

'No, you're right. I gave up on you. I left you behind.'

'You thought I was dead. It's hardly the same.'

'But I still must have hurt you.'

'I thought I'd never love again. I was determined that no one, anywhere, would open me up to loss. Ever.'

'Krystiana left because she couldn't be with you in the way that she needed.'

'She left because I *lied*. I hurt her. Whatever must she think of me?'

'She'll be okay. She's strong.'

'She shouldn't *have* to be okay. Shouldn't have to be strong. She deserved the truth, but I never told her any of it because I knew how deep I was already in!' He'd never felt so frustrated in all his life. 'I thought I could bury my head in the sand. I thought I could find a way around it.'

'I'm sorry, Matteo.'

'I need to speak with my father.'

'He's resting. He needs to take it easy. You can't go in there, all guns blazing.'

'So what do I do?'

'I don't know. Maybe you should just accept the fact that you got this wrong?'

Matteo sank onto the end of the bed. 'In the worst way possible…'

'You don't know that for sure.'

He looked at her with resignation. 'Yes, I do.'

On arrival in Rome, Krystiana headed straight to the nearest information desk and looked for hotel and bed and breakfast listings. She didn't want anywhere in the main city, but something on the periphery. Somewhere a bit more remote.

She found a perfect place called the Catalina that belonged to an elderly couple. Their bed and breakfast was on the outskirts of Rome, in Lazio, and her bedroom windows looked out over the countryside that formed part of the Riserva Naturale di Decima-Malafede. A nature reserve that was meant to host a population of wild boar.

After the hustle and bustle of life in the palace and work in Ventura, it felt good to be looking out at trees and grassland. Anything that didn't remind her of life at the palace was absolutely fine by her.

She checked in under a made-up name, wearing the floppy sunhat she'd bought in duty-free and the large sunglasses that covered half her face. And then she sat in her room, dwelling on all that had passed.

* * *

Krystiana was doing what she always did in times of trauma—she was painting. Her room was beginning to fill with some pretty dark canvases now that she'd been here a week. It stank of paint and turpentine. She hadn't eaten much and seemed to be existing on coffee. Espresso.

She refused to do anything else. Hadn't turned on the television or read the news. She didn't want to hear anything about what might be happening on Isla Tamoura. Didn't want to think about Matteo in his garden, or playing with Alex, or eating breakfast on his sun terrace. To wonder whether he was being groomed to meet up with women who were more *suitable*. With *royal* blood. As opposed to the normal red stuff that ran in *her* veins.

He hadn't tried to contact her—which she was pleased about. It was what they both needed. No contact. Otherwise it might be too painful.

I've been a fool!

She'd spent her entire life telling herself that she was worth something. That she wasn't damaged goods and that she deserved the truth. And even though she'd thought she'd found it in Matteo, clearly she'd been wrong. He'd been forced to reveal his lies. The way Adamo had. Her mind reeled as to how she could have been so misled. She'd believed so much that he felt the same about her.

He was a good actor. Perhaps it was something they taught young royals on Isla Tamoura. Always to seem confident and believable. There were all those speeches they had to make—that had to be part of it, didn't it? Because being a good, strong king was something he wanted to present himself as. He was practised.

I never stood a chance.

And now, just as she'd known she couldn't dig her way out of that hole in the ground when she was six, she knew that the situation she was in was just as futile. It was almost a special skill she'd developed—acknowledging when something was a hopeless case—and there were only two things you could do when you had no power at all: accept it, or suffer trying to fight back.

She'd had enough suffering in her life. And though she knew it was going to hurt, walking away from the man she loved, she knew she had no choice. She was resigning herself to the fact that she'd been right. People were weak and they let you down. Love saved no one.

She hoped she would learn something from this experience. Learn that she could only ever depend upon herself, as she'd always suspected. That at the end of the day, no matter how many people you had around you, it was down to you and you alone to survive.

'What about Katherine? She seemed very interested in you.'

Alberto sat across the breakfast table from Matteo, who was nonchalantly tearing pastries apart, but only nibbling tiny parts of them.

He sighed. 'She was very nice. Clever conversation…'

'And *pretty*!' His father laughed. 'She would provide you with some beautiful children.'

Matteo smiled. 'I already have a beautiful child.'

'Your coronation is in one month. Are you going to be ascending the throne with a fiancée?'

'I don't think so, Papà. A relationship takes time to build. I can't make a decision like that after only spending one evening with someone.'

'Of course not. But it would be nice for the country to have another happy celebration to look forward to after the coronation.'

Was that all that mattered? All that *should* matter? His *country*? What of his own life? Did that not matter at all any more? 'I won't be marrying anyone, Papà. I dined with Katherine because she was a guest here. No other reason. Not because the country needs a pick-me-up. I've already sacrificed so much—don't ask me for any more.'

Alberto held up his hands in supplication. 'Fair enough. I won't push. Now, are you bringing me my granddaughter later today? I haven't seen Alexandra for an age.'

'She'll be here later. Mara is bringing her over with Philippe.'

'He's a good man for her.'

'Yes, he is. Better than I ever was.'

His father looked at him, considering him. 'And…the doctor? You haven't heard from her?'

'No.'

Matteo did his best not to think of her too much. It hurt. It was too painful when he considered what he had done. It had never been her fault. It had always been his. He'd known the rules from the beginning and he'd thought he could do his own thing anyway.

'Good. You need to move on. More important things are coming up.'

He nodded. But he knew he would *never* forget her. How could he?

'You've got your robe fitting today, yes?'

The coronation robes needed adjusting for Matteo's broad form. 'Yes.'

'I might come along. It's been a long time since I saw those robes. My own coronation, in fact. That was a great day. Great memories. It'll be the same for you.'

'I'm sure it will.'

'You're sure you're all right? You seem very…*absent*.'

'Fine.'

'You'd tell me if there was something bothering you?'

'Of course!'

'Good. I'd hate to think you were keeping something from me, like before.'

'We never *kept* it from you, Papà. It was something new for both of us. We were trying to work it out for ourselves first.'

The King nodded as he hauled himself up from the table and then surprised his son by saying, 'Dr Szenac did seem a very nice woman. I'm sorry I had to force your hand, but I had to do it before you got in too deep. I couldn't bear the idea that you were going to get hurt further down the road, and neither was it very fair to her, when *you* knew the situation. I was surprised at you, son.'

Matteo stared at his father. 'We were already in too deep. We got hurt anyway.'

'I know what it's like to lose a loved one, Matteo. When I lost your mother, I…' He shook his head, clearing away the thought. 'Anyway, I did what I thought was best. For you. I only want the best for you.'

'*She* was the best, Papà. And I ruined it.'

Alberto nodded. 'I'm sorry.'

And he left his son sitting at the breakfast table, surrounded by a litter of pastry crumbs.

She'd been spending a lot of time in the nature reserve. It was just so peaceful out there and she'd managed to complete quite a few new paintings—including one of a sunset over the lake that had been astoundingly beautiful.

Decima-Malafede had been a comfort to her torn and broken soul, but after she'd packed the last of her canvases, checking out her room for one last time, Krystiana went downstairs, hugged the proprietors of the bed and breakfast, who had become good friends, and bade them goodbye.

It was time to go home.

Aunt Carolina had called with the news that repairs to her villa were complete and it was liveable again.

The news had been a nice surprise, but she'd felt a wave of sadness wash over her. Matteo had done that for her. Sorted out the villa. She'd kind of imagined, not too long ago, that they would both drive back there in one of the palace cars and look around the rebuild together. She'd briefly imagined putting the place up for sale, seeing as her new life was going to be based in the Grand Palace, the House of Romano.

None of that was to be. *What a fool!*

But she couldn't stay here, hiding away from life. Enough time had passed for her to be able to return, and hopefully the media would have moved on. Surely Matteo would have told them their relationship was over?

'They might still try to talk to you. Get the inside story on Matteo,' Aunt Carolina had warned.

But how could she stay away? She needed to return to work, and she needed, more than anything, to find her old routine. Her routine had kept her safe and secure. Unknown and unloved. That was the best way.

Handing over her key, she gave the owners a sad smile, thanked them for their care, their consideration and their silence, and then she walked out through the front door.

Wondering just what she might be walking back to.

Her villa felt strange. Hers, but not quite hers. Maybe because Bruno wasn't with her? She needed to collect him.

Krystiana set her bags down and slumped onto the sofa, feeling apprehensive at being back. There'd been no press on her doorstep. Had they given up? Figured she was gone? She hoped so.

With nothing better to do, she reached for the remote and switched on the television. As it came to life she heard the voice of the newscaster mentioning that the Crown

Prince of Isla Tamoura was now King Matteo Romano, after his coronation earlier that day.

No wonder there aren't any press at my door.

She stared at the images of him on the throne, red ermine-trimmed robes around him, as he held the sceptre and orb, a crown of gold and jewels upon his head.

He looked very regal. And handsome.

She sucked in a sudden breath, the loss almost too much to bear.

She didn't know how to feel. Her heart was breaking so painfully. How was it still so raw?

She grabbed the remote and turned off the television, trying to wipe the images from her brain as she began to cry, holding a cushion in front of her as if its very presence might somehow cushion the force of the pain racing through her once again.

It was like a thorn in her side. A pain twisting deep in her heart.

He'd moved on.

Without her.

Clearly he had accepted the duty he was meant for and she wanted to be happy for him. But…

It hurt. More than she'd believed possible.

Krystiana cried herself to sleep, still holding the cushion like a shield.

'You thought I wouldn't find out?'

'Find out what?' Matteo sipped calmly from his espresso.

'Don't be coy with me, Matteo. You *know* what I'm talking about! The law that now allows you to marry a commoner!'

Matteo wiped his mouth with a napkin as he shook his head. He'd thought about this a lot. Thought about what was right. And what he knew was this—he loved Krystiana. He would never find such a connection again. His entire happiness had been destroyed by a law that was archaic and out of date, and he'd been determined that his first order of business as King was to get it changed.

His entire life had been empty since she'd left and his heart had *ached.* He had fought against himself more than anyone else, in deciding to do this. Nothing might come of it—she might never forgive him—but he had to try.

'You want me to be a king who leads his country into the future, yes?' he said now.

'Of course!'

'Well, in that case I take it upon myself to change a few things. Make this a new, modern monarchy. We need to move with the times if we want our people to relate to us and respect us.'

'Are you going after her?'

Matteo stared at his father. Wasn't it obvious?

'Yes. If she'll have me.'

He expected his father to rant and rave, to argue that a king should never debase himself by begging for a woman's affections, but surprisingly he did not.

Instead, his voice was low and gentle. 'She means this much to you?'

'I love her and I've been miserable without her here. Couldn't you tell?'

His father nodded. 'Yes. I could.'

'You lost Mamma years ago. But if you could have a chance to get her back wouldn't you take it?'

His father stared at him, his eyes softening, welling up with tears. 'Yes.'

'Well, then… Would you deny me the love of my life? Knowing how it feels to be lost without her?'

'No. I would not deny you. You must love her very much to have done this.'

'I do.'

He stepped forward to clasp his son and pat him on the back. 'Then you have my blessing.'

Matteo was surprised. 'Really?'

'I've seen how you've been since she's been gone, and quite frankly you're almost back to how you were after you first came home after the kidnapping. You have no life in you. No joy. The only time I see you happy is when you are with Alex. I wasn't the right king to challenge the rules, but you *are*. Like you say—it's the future.'

'Thank you,' he said, feeling emotional. 'That means more than I can say.'

'Do you think you can bring her back?'

'I don't know. But it was never about the law keeping us apart. It was about me not telling her the truth. I'll need her to put her trust in me and I'm not sure if she will.'

'Well, call me when you know for sure.'

'I will. Thank you, Papà.'

'Good luck, son.'

CHAPTER THIRTEEN

AFTER A LONG day at work—and it had been a *long* day—there was nothing Krystiana loved more than to walk along the beach, barefoot, watching Bruno frolic in the sea. There was peace out here, freedom. *Anonymity.*

She'd spent the last few weeks fielding questions from her patients, trying to move them back to the topic of themselves rather than her and her fleeting romance with their King. It had been hard denying that there was anything going on, and every time someone questioned her about it it was like being stabbed in the heart again as she told them that, no, she and the King were not together. That it had simply been a friendly meal together and the press had misconstrued it.

It was exhausting, quite frankly—so much so that she was even considering moving elsewhere. Maybe starting her own medical practice…perhaps in Rome or Florence? Somewhere far away from here.

But she'd already fled from one home. She didn't want to have to flee another. She loved this island so much.

Bruno yapped with happiness as he brought her over a ball he'd found and dropped it at her feet. She picked it up and threw it as far as she could, smiling as he chased after it. She couldn't take him away from this, either.

She looked out to sea, watching a white yacht in the

distance. It looked so calm and peaceful. So pretty. Almost worth painting.

But she didn't have her easel or paints. It was just herself and her dog.

And that's all it's ever going to be.

Matteo's anxiety levels soared once he got into the car that would take him to Krystiana's villa. He knew she was back. He'd been notified the second she came back, her ID having flagged up a special program in the airport.

When his secretary had told him he'd had to fight the urge to go after her straight away, knowing there was no point in doing so until the new law had been passed. He wanted to present it as a *fait accompli.*

He'd missed her so much, and when he'd learnt that she had flown to Rome he'd wondered if she was ever going to come back. But she had, and he had taken some comfort in knowing that she was back on the island. He had stood each evening on his balcony, looking out towards where he knew her villa was, imagining that she was looking at the palace on the hill so far away…

It was a romantic notion, he knew, and probably a bit silly, but it was because he was heartsick, missing her like crazy. He knew that once he saw her again he would be able to tell her everything he had been doing. He would apologise profusely and hopefully—*hopefully*—she would take him back.

But she might not. He'd hurt her—he knew that—and she might not want to risk that again. Plus there'd be the whole thing of being back in the public eye again. He'd already ordered the press to stay away from her villa and her place of work, to give her some chance of returning to normal. He'd even taken one newspaper to court, taken legal action against them harassing her, and thankfully they'd obeyed the order.

Everyone missed her. Mara wanted her back. Alex talked about her. Well, mostly it was about Bruno, but still…

As the sleek, dark vehicle pulled to a halt outside her refurbished villa he felt the butterflies in his stomach all launch into flight at once. His heart pounded, his mouth and throat went very dry, and it took him a few moments to get out of the car. When he did, his legs felt as if they would go out from under him.

He was met with a flashback of what the place had looked like after the crash. The debris, the rubble… The accident that had caused their love to happen.

It was weird how life worked. If there'd been no accident she wouldn't have stayed at the palace and he wouldn't have got to know her, to fall in love with her.

He glanced at the windows. Had she seen him yet?

Straightening his jacket, he walked up to the door and knocked, his heart hammering, sweat beading his armpits.

There was no answer. So he knocked again.

A silver-haired head popped up over the fence next door. 'Hello? Are you after Krystiana? Oh, my God! It's *you*!' The head disappeared as the woman next door curtsied. 'Your Majesty!'

'Has she gone out?'

'She doesn't get back until late these days.'

'Where is she? Work?'

'No, no. She goes down to the beach with the dog.'

He turned to look down at the long sweep of golden sand far in the distance. 'That beach?'

'I guess so. I'm not sure.'

'Thank you. What's your name?'

'Anna.'

'Thank you, Anna. I would be grateful if you didn't mention this visit to anyone just yet.'

'Of course not.' She made a zipping motion across her lips and smiled.

He smiled his thanks. A reprieve. A moment or two in which he could gather himself some more.

He got back into the car and gave the order to his driver. 'Take me to the beach.'

'Yes, sir.' And the driver fired the engine.

Sitting on the sand, looking out to sea, as she often did, she thought about all that had happened in her life to bring her to this spot. The quirks of fate. The actions of others and how they could impact on your own life and the choices you had to make.

If she'd not been part of Dr Bonetti's practice… If her Aunt Carolina had lived somewhere else… If her parents hadn't divorced…

No wonder she wanted as much control over her own life as she could get.

She was sitting there, drizzling sand through her fingers, when she felt a prickling on the back of her neck. As if she was being watched.

Krystiana turned around…curious, cautious…her heartbeat increasing slightly, searching for a pair of eyes, hoping to brush it off as a flight of fancy, or that perhaps it was just another dogwalker, or a fisherman come down to the coast.

But it wasn't a dogwalker or a fisherman.

It was a king.

Matteo stood tall and proud, his dark form silhouetted against the sun as he walked across the sand directly towards her. She scrambled to her feet, dusting off the sand from her clothes, her heart thudding away like a jackhammer.

Why was he here? After all this time?

What was left for them to say to each other?

Far behind him, blocking access to the beach, were security guards so they could have privacy. She saw their dark-suited forms, the sun glancing off their sunglasses.

She fought the need to run towards him, to fall into his arms. But her love for him had almost broken her so she held firm, letting him come to *her*. If he was here to make an apology, then he could do all the work.

He looked as handsome as ever. Maybe even more so. Was he taller? Or was it just a different bearing he had? That somehow becoming King had changed him?

'*Buonasera*, Matteo.'

'*Dobyr wieczór*, Krystiana.'

She was surprised to hear her own language. 'You learned Polish?'

'A little.'

'That's good.' She sucked in a huge breath. 'What brings you here?'

'I came to ask for your forgiveness.'

Forgiveness?

Krystiana's heart almost leapt from her chest. 'Why?'

'Because I love you and I can't live without you.'

Her cheeks flushed with heat at his words. Words she'd longed to hear him say, but words that put daggers into her heart. Why was he doing this? They couldn't be together! It was torture.

She looked down and away. 'Let's not go through this again.'

'I want you to come back with me, Krystiana,' he said.

No! Please don't say that to me! I can't go through this heartbreak!

'Matteo, no—'

'I changed the law.'

She looked up at him, shocked, her heart thudding. 'What?'

'I changed the law about kings not being allowed to

marry who they wish. And even if it had been impossible for me to change it I would have come and fetched you anyway. We could have lived in sin.' He smiled.

She stared at him, open-mouthed. Surely he was joking? He'd changed something that had been practically written in stone since his country had begun writing its history? For *her*?

But it didn't matter what he'd done. The law wasn't the point. His lying to her was what had been the fault.

'But…'

'I'm sorry. So, so sorry! For hurting you. For making you think that I had lied to you.'

'You did.'

'But I didn't mean to! I was confused. Torn by everything that I was feeling for you. I kept trying to fight it, but I couldn't, and before I knew what was happening we were getting serious and—'

'Are you blaming *me* for this?'

'No! Absolutely not! You're blameless. I tried to make it feel as if it was your fault, but no, it was all mine. I knew what it would do to you and yet I still did it. I should have thought about how much you needed me to show you that I could be trusted, that I could be relied upon and I can be all those things! Because I'm thinking more clearly now than I have in my entire life!' He paused to gather himself again. 'I love you and I want to show the world that, and I want you to see that I also acted from a place of fear. Something I found hard to admit to myself. I'm a king. I was a prince. I never thought I'd want anyone ever again after my kidnapping and then you walked into my life. I tried to fight it. I did. I think you did, too. But something kept pulling us together and I'd already been through so much, I thought to myself that I could allow myself this brief moment of happiness and to hell with the consequences! I thought we could deal with them later.'

'Until your hand was forced.'

He nodded. 'I don't expect you to forgive me. Or to trust me. Not at first. But I am begging you and I will get on my hands and knees to ask you to give me the chance, again, to show you who I really am.'

'Who are you?' she asked, her voice almost trembling.

'A man who loves you. Who wants to marry you and keep you in my life for ever, until death do us part.'

It was everything she wanted to hear. And she wanted to trust him, so much!

'Your father hates me, we—'

'My father doesn't hate you. He was trying to protect me from getting hurt further down the line. Not realising how much we were already in love! But now he knows and he has given us his blessing.'

She was in shock. Not sure what to say. 'He has?'

'Yes. I'm sorry, Krystiana. Sorry I wasn't strong enough to do this in the first place. To have fought for you. But I couldn't do anything to change the law until I became King myself. Then I could put forward a new decree. These things take time, needing approval from my parliament, all that nonsense, and I couldn't tell you what I was doing, because I didn't want to give you false hope if I failed.'

He stepped forward, tucked a windblown tress of hair behind her ear. 'There could never be anyone else but you. It's always been you, Krystiana. Let me show you the truth of my love. The truth of my heart. That you can put your life and your heart into my hands and I will keep them safe. That I will cherish you and adore you for evermore.' And he made to kiss her.

She thought for just a moment. Hesitated, but then she closed her eyes in ecstasy as his lips touched hers and somehow, before she knew it, her arms were around his neck and she was pulling him close, revelling in being with him, kissing him, holding him, once again.

He had changed the law for her. And he was trying so hard to explain why he had acted the way that he had. And she could forgive him for that, because she'd known he'd been just as confused as she.

They could be together! She melted into the kiss, sinking against him.

'Are you sure you want me?' she asked him breathlessly. 'I'm complicated and I have faults and I get mad quickly and I—'

He smiled, laughing. 'I do.' And then he let her go, so that he could get down on one knee.

Reaching into his pocket, he pulled out a small red box, something that he had bought a long time ago, but had never had the chance to use. Opening it, he revealed a beautiful diamond solitaire ring, that winked and glittered in the low evening sun. Bruno dropped his ball, as if sensing the moment and came to sit by Matteo's side, looking questioningly at them both.

'Krystiana Szenac. You brought light into my life. Gave me hope where there was none and I cannot live without you. I love you so much! Will you do me the honour of becoming my Queen?'

Krystiana gasped, laughing.

He was looking up at her, smiling, hope in his eyes and she knew instantly where she wanted to be.

At his side.

'Yes! I will!' She held out her hand so that he could slide on the ring and it fitted perfectly! She gazed at it in awe, then she pulled him to his feet and kissed him.

The beach melted away, her sorrow melted away. Perhaps happiness did eventually come to those that waited?

She'd never thought so much joy could come from so much heartbreak.

Never thought that that amount of joy, could ever be hers.

EPILOGUE

'IS THIS ALL RIGHT?' Krystiana tried to speak without breaking her smile as she gave her newly learned royal wave from the car touring through Tamoura.

Matteo glanced at her and smiled. 'It's perfect. As are you.'

They were travelling in a convoy of security, in front and behind of their car were mounted soldiers in their finery, the horses' hooves clip-clopping along the roads as Matteo and Krystiana and Alex were driven through streets filled with adoring, cheering crowds.

In front of them, Alex waved madly from a window, enjoying being the centre of attention, but after a mile or so of doing the same thing, the little girl got a bit bored and she sat beside Krystiana and laid a hand on her stepmother's barely swollen belly.

'When is the baby coming?' she asked. 'Today?'

Krystiana smiled at her stepdaughter and stroked her cheek lovingly. 'Not today, darling. Many more sleeps before the baby arrives.'

Alex sat back in her seat. 'I want a girl.'

'Do you? We'll have to wait and see. It could be a boy *or* a girl. Now, wave, *mio caro.* The people want to see you.'

She smiled at Matteo and clutched his hand with her own, squeezing it tightly. It had been almost two years since Matteo had arrived on that beach to ask for her hand in marriage and since then so much had happened. So much had changed!

They'd got married in a beautiful cathedral, with the ceremony nationally televised. They'd honeymooned in the Caribbean, and when they'd returned home to begin their royal duties together Krystiana had discovered that she was pregnant with his child.

And life as *Queen* was everything she had hoped it would be. She wasn't just a figurehead. She wasn't just her husband's wife. She was a pioneer, bringing her work and experience to the forefront, opening up clinics and bringing awareness for those who had been abused, held hostage or kept as slaves. The press loved her and she made sure she used every public opportunity that she could to help those that were less fortunate.

She was still doing good.

Still helping.

And her heart was filled with love and hope for the future.

She wasn't alone any more.

The darkness and the fear were gone.

And love and light filled her heart every day.

* * * * *

THE PRINCE'S CINDERELLA BRIDE

AMALIE BERLIN

Hina Tabassum: Your enthusiasm for my books is something I return to on hard days. Thank you for that. And for your smart reviews. Always a good day when one pops up!

Laura McCallen: Thank you for two years of hard work, dedication and enthusiasm. You will be missed.

CHAPTER ONE

It was a strange sort of medical facility, but the changes made to Almsford Castle since ex-Princess Anais Corlow's last visit made it seem almost like a new place. Or at least like an alternate version of reality that she could pretend she'd never been to, and never run away from…

Sometimes for several seconds at a time.

Dr. Anna Kincaid—as she was now known—checked her watch. Twenty minutes left in her lunch hour, right on schedule. She climbed onto the gym's treadmill closest to the exit. She could run for fifteen minutes, shower like lightning, and be back in time for her first patient of the afternoon, same as yesterday.

As soon as she got the belt moving, she increased the speed until she had to push herself to keep up. Not a sensible way to exercise but, no matter how determined she was to remain in the new job that allowed her to stay in Corrachlean with her mother and the quiet life they'd built, every minute she was at Almsford she felt the need to run. It built over the day, faster when she wasn't busy helping patients than when she sat alone in her office with just her memories.

Anais had more or less died the moment she'd left Prince Charming, Quinton Corlow, second son of Corrachlean. Without her husband, she'd had no title—something she'd never cared to have anyway—but she'd also lost her country, her home, for the last seven years.

Almsford Rehabilitation Center now belonged to Corrachlean's soldiers, people who wanted her there. People who welcomed her, maybe in even greater proportion to how unwelcome she'd been the last time around. The people made it possible for her to set foot in the grounds. The physical changes to the building made it possible for her to stay, but running in one place kept her from running away.

Protective sheeting covered the stained-glass window running along the top half of the twenty-foot western wall in the ballroom-turned-gymnasium, adding another little barrier to her past, to keep those soul-crushing memories from overwhelming her.

To let her—almost—put it all away.

Laughter, warm and masculine, danced up the corridor that branched off the gymnasium to the first-floor patient rooms.

A sparkling sensation, like the meeting of a million tiny kisses, sprung to life at the top of her head and spilled in a cascade down her back, tickling across her neck and over her shoulders, all the way to her thighs, effectively wiping every thought from her head.

Everything but the thrill, everything but the smile she felt over the thrum of her muscles and the murmur of the machine.

Somewhere inside, part of her soul sat up, and a surge of excitement blossomed in her belly. Images of silk sheets and a field of daisies filled her mind, the brush of green leaves tickled her bare calves as she half ran, half danced through them…

She knew that laugh.

Oh, God.

She stumbled and would've fallen off the treadmill if not for the safety bars.

Not him. Not here.

She wrenched herself from the machine and careened backwards, her legs boneless and quaking.

Quinn's voice came from some distance away, but he might've been walking down the corridor towards her. She could poke her head out to check and smack straight into those famed dimples.

Which way? Gardens?

Too exposed.

How awkward would it be if Corrachlean's beloved, rascally soldier Prince came waltzing down the hallway and saw her there after seven years of self-imposed exile? She'd done her best to change her appearance, even beyond the ways the world and their divorce had changed her. Maybe he wouldn't recognize her, at least long enough for her to skirt past him?

The patients hadn't recognized her, and she'd stayed away from anyone who'd known her except for Mom.

He wasn't supposed to even be in the country—the last she'd heard he was still on tour. At the very least, he should be in another country, castle, the palace or somewhere, with a svelte model on his arm, if gossip rags were to be believed… And why wouldn't they be? They'd been right about their marriage spiraling down the drain, no matter how painful and horrible it had been for them to publicize it in increasingly callous ways.

She'd been back four weeks. It might be a small island nation, but she should've been able to avoid him for a year at least. But one month? Four weeks? Thirty measly days?

Anna shouldn't have any feelings about Prince Captain Quinton Corlow one way or another. Maybe—if she followed the pattern of most of the heterosexual women who encountered the caramel-haired devil—she should swoon at his movie-star looks if he happened by. Swooning involved paling, so that could seem legit.

But she definitely should not be breaking out in a cold sweat and considering whether her heart rate had reached a fast enough pace to require cardioversion.

Before she could muster the courage for a mad dash to

her office, another blast of his voice ricocheted up the corridor, cutting escape from her mind.

Not laughter.

Not words spoken with joy. His voice trembled with alarm and the hoarse expletive that followed either shook her or the building.

A breath later came a terrible bellow for help.

"Quinn..."

Her heart lurched, and by the time her thoughts caught up with her body she was running again, down the long hallway.

He'd sounded far away, but she couldn't tell how far. As she pounded past each open door, she slowed down to peek inside for signs of distress, then spent time dodging people as they limped and rolled out of their rooms.

The residents turned further down the hallway, and she relied on their reactions to direct her.

Three rooms from the far end on the right-hand side, a door stood open and people were gathering around it, forcing her to wiggle through.

"Sorry. Sorry..." she said in passing, and didn't stop until she was through the door.

Even from behind, even despite the changes seven years as a soldier had made to the breadth of his shoulders, every atom in her body recognized him, crouched over someone on the floor.

Her Quinn. Her husband.

No. Once, maybe. Not anymore. As she absorbed his presence, the rest of the room came into focus.

The bed sat upended and had a raggedly cut bed sheet tied to the bars of the headboard.

Hanging.

She moved around Quinn and crouched over the patient on the floor. His skin was still tinged cyanotic.

"Lieutenant Nettle?" She said his name and reached to

check the pulse of his carotid, narrowing her focus to the most urgent place: her patient, not her ex-husband.

Before she could count ten seconds, a large hand clamped onto her wrist, yanking her gaze from her watch's face to Quinn's.

The shock of recognition blazed across his heartbreakingly handsome features, made only more devastating by the years that had passed. His caramel hair, once short and smart, had begun to grow out, but it was his stormy gray eyes that slapped her like an accusation.

She forced her gaze away, down at the patient, mentally scrambling for what she should be doing.

"Don't." She said the only word she could wrench from her mind and, seeing pink returning to Nettle's face, pulled her arm away and stood back up. "I want him off the floor."

"I want his neck stabilized first," Quinn bit back, but the incredulous way he looked at her said he was having as hard a time navigating this sudden overlap of two realities as she was.

But he was handling it better. Of course Nettle should be stabilized first. "I'll…I'll get a brace."

In contrast to the way her body had responded to his laughter, what dug its talons into her now was far darker even than that rise of panic that had bid her run.

Guilt. Sorrow. Anger. Fear.

Nasty beasts that tore at her competence, her professionalism.

The familiar tang of fear and rage settled like rot at the back of Quinn's throat.

Prior to his tours, that acrid combination had hit so infrequently he couldn't have named the emotions without examination. Now he knew them the second they descended. The only thing he didn't know was which person before him had summoned them this time—the best friend he'd found dangling by his neck, or the ex-wife who'd abandoned him.

He knew one thing: Anais didn't deserve the space in his head right now, even if she well deserved his rage. Ben was the one who mattered.

"Be still, man," he said, as Ben struggled beneath his hands, then looked at Anais. She could come back into his life as quickly as she'd left it, but that slapdash, incompetent disguise wouldn't fool anyone.

She stood still, staring at him as if she'd lost all her sense.

"Collar," he repeated to break through her shocked expression.

Don't think about her shock. It couldn't be anything more than fear that he'd yell at her—out her, maybe—but right now she only mattered inasmuch as she could help Ben.

He quickly smoothed his hands down his thighs, drying the suddenly sweaty palms, and then fixing them around Ben's head to keep him from moving it as she finally broke into motion out of the room.

Discipline had been drilled into him after the King had ordered Quinn's divorce and enlistment. He'd learned to follow their orders and he'd taught his body to follow his own. Self-discipline would see him through this, no matter how wrong it had been to see Ben hanging there, no matter how wrong it was for him to finally see Anais again like this, no matter how wrong it was that she'd changed so much. Falsely brown hair, eyes, tanned skin… Wrong. All of it.

The resolve to speak evenly was all that let him banish his anger as he turned his attention to Ben—who obviously didn't know who she was. "What's the doctor's name?"

"Anna," Ben answered.

A brown name for a bizarrely brown makeover.

Grasping for the only way he knew how to face such a situation, he attempted some levity to try and take the bleakness out of his friend's eyes. "The good news is, your arms still work great. I'm fairly certain I'll have a black eye later."

"You should've left me be," Ben said, his voice a painful-sounding rasp that could only come from an injured throat.

"I don't think so," Quinn muttered and then looked at the door. "Rosalie would be doomed to treason if I had, after she'd murdered me slowly in retribution."

Where the hell had Anais gone to get the brace—across town?

"What are you even doing here, Doc?"

"You've been avoiding my calls worse than my ex-wife," he said just as Anais came back into the room, the sounds of tearing straps accompanying her ripping the collar open, and perfectly complementing the color draining from her face. She'd heard him. Good.

He focused back on Ben, and that anger instantly diminished. "I came to see you, idiot."

Quinn accepted the collar and fitted it around Ben's neck for stability. Only when it was in place did he help Ben into the wheelchair.

Having tasks to do helped. Not looking at Anais helped. If he looked at her, the way his heart thundered in his ears, he'd say or do the wrong thing. That was something about the military that had worked for him—he'd never had to worry about how to say something, just whether he should say it or not. Soldiers appreciated blunt honesty more than diplomats. Something his brother Philip would remember after Quinn's first royal function.

"You should've let me hang," Ben said again, the words sinking into the middle of Quinn's stomach.

He shook his head. "I came to see you before I met with the King, which should give you some idea of my priorities right now. You're the last person in this room I'd let hang."

She'd hear that too. And she'd hear this… "Maybe even the last person in the world, though I might have to make an exception for any of *GQ*'s cover models. Even May's, and you know how that ended."

Petty. But it felt good to be just a little bit mean. Not that it could be all *that* mean—she was the one who'd left. And it made Ben almost smile, even the slight quirk of his lips was better than the desolation he'd seen in his friend's eyes.

"You're going to have to suffer me checking you over."

She'd returned with a bag, wearing a white jacket over what he could only classify as workout clothes, the shoulder of the jacket embroidered with the lie that she claimed as her name. Dr. Anna Kincaid.

Kincaid. Family name. Just not her maiden name. Or *his* name.

From the bag, she produced a stethoscope and handed it to him without his asking, but not without her hand trembling.

Afraid? Maybe she trembled with sympathy or worry for her patient, if she could even feel those human emotions.

He snatched the device, fitted it in his ears, and went about his job. His former job. He wasn't a medic anymore; yesterday had been his last day as a soldier.

Concentrating on the fast but steady thudding he heard through the ear pieces took more willpower than he'd have thought he had to spare. The urge to throw Anais over his shoulder like a caveman and take her somewhere to make her give him answers was just as strong. Maybe stronger. He'd been waiting seven bloody years for answers, and he'd never gotten a satisfactory one. He'd wait until he'd helped his friend, because today his luck had changed. She was here; answers were a matter of time.

Breaths sounded ragged but normal, all things considered.

"Let's get out of here. I think we could use some fresh air."

"Qui— Prince… Captain? There is a protocol…" Anais said from behind him.

He turned and looked pointedly at her embroidered shoulder. "I'm sure there is. Send whoever will be coming out to the garden, Anna."

"Yes, sir." She didn't flinch, though he noticed she also didn't look him in the eye.

Grabbing the handles of Ben's chair, he maneuvered them both right out the door and down the hallway. He knew the way to the garden.

He'd loved a girl in those gardens. A girl who apparently no longer existed.

How the hell had she managed to sneak back into the country under a different name, and start practicing medicine at a government facility, of all things?

Once they wheeled out into the fresh air, Quinn angled them to a bench so he could sit and be on eye level with the person he'd actually come to see. The one who obviously needed to talk.

Parked in a patch of summer sunshine, he waited. It wasn't the time for pushing. It wasn't the time to tell Ben he should want to live, or to tell him anything about his own condition. He'd listen. And he'd talk about other things. Be a friend. Be present.

Call Ben's fiancée and family as soon as he left.

Leave this Anais nonsense to figure out later. It wasn't really important. There was nothing she could say to him to make any of what had gone on between them better.

I never loved you.

I stopped loving you.

You were never that important to me...

What could she really say to explain leaving?

The desire to know was just a natural reaction to seeing her again, a summoning of that anguish he'd moved past at least a few years ago.

It didn't really matter. She didn't matter anymore.

Three hours and at least a hundred self-reminders not to think about Anais later, Quinn found himself outside the shut door to Dr. Anna Kincaid's office.

Anna Kincaid. Anna. Kincaid. The name summoned bile

to his throat. Seven years might as well have been seven minutes for the crush of desperation that had him wanting to claw through the door to reach her.

He'd managed to shove her to the back of his mind—for part of the time—and been present for his best friend, but it wasn't good enough. He'd heard the sparse number of words Ben had been able to speak, but in the long silences she'd filled his head again and again. When the psychiatrist had found them he'd been allowed to stay, but he hadn't learned much more about what had driven the attempt. All he really knew was what his eyes could tell him, and the memory of the strangeness he'd felt when he'd lost comparatively insignificant pieces of his own body to service. Some days still, he was shocked when he looked down at his hand and saw that not only the fingers but his wedding ring were gone. Some days, he still expected to find her beside him in the morning when he woke.

What he should be doing right now was making calls and going to the palace—where they'd expected him a few hours ago. Instead, he stood at her shut door. He couldn't hear her inside, but he could feel her in there, like heat on his skin.

If he felt like admitting it to anyone else—he barely felt like admitting it to himself—he'd felt her at the old family castle the moment he'd stepped into the building. At the time, he'd put it down to memories haunting him more than something in the present. But, standing there, he didn't even have to touch the door to feel her on the other side. His mangled hand hovered over the knob, and it heated his palm like light…

His hand wavered; he had to pull back from the knob. His arm felt seconds from a cramp, riddled with tension.

He didn't know which was worse—not knowing still, or that he could be so daft to even think for a fleeting second that anything about her could still warm him. The heat was long-simmering rage and pain. Nothing light about it.

If anyone noticed him standing here, feeling the energy emanating from her door when any rational person would just go inside…the psychiatrist would want to spend some time alone with him next.

He opened the door and it slammed directly into something, halting his forward march.

She stumbled out from behind the door, looking disoriented, but her stagger gave him room to enter and he took advantage of it, shutting the door directly behind him.

“Why were you standing there?”

“I was thinking about locking the door,” she said without preamble. Then, redirecting his question, “Why were you standing outside the door?”

“Anais, I’ve had a hell of a day. I paused because I wanted to make sure I had control of myself and didn’t come right in here and shake you hard enough to knock the brown off of you. What the hell are you playing at with this drab makeover and the name-change? Are you in the country illegally?”

She flinched, then shrugged back from him across the distance of her tiny office. He’d struck another nerve. That shouldn’t please him, but the pink that flashed in her artificially tanned cheeks and the way she smoothed her hair down felt almost like satisfaction. He had seven years of jabs in reserve and, by the look of things, it wasn’t going to get boring anytime soon.

“Of course I’m not here illegally. I had my name changed. Legally. Then I changed my appearance. My mother is getting older—she’s got diabetes and had a heart scare last summer, not that I should have to explain myself. This is my country too, and I shouldn’t have to lose it forever because I married poorly when I was young and naïve.”

A tic in his right eyelid flickered at her return volley.

Definitely different from the Anais he'd known.

"How…?"

"Your brother changed my name for me quietly." She rubbed her cheek and he knew where the door had clocked her, but she stayed standing there, close enough—only because of the wall behind her—that he could reach out and touch her if he wanted to.

He did want to, so he shoved his hands into the well-worn fatigues he preferred these days, comfortable clothing he'd soon lose as he picked up a new mantle of duty.

"I went with Anna because it's close enough to Anais for me to still save myself if I start to say my old name. Kincaid is my grandmother's maiden name, so I have some attachment to it. Doctor, however, is legitimately mine."

Softness had always abounded in Anais. Tender heart. Soft, free-flowing wavy strawberry-blonde hair. Curves that bewitched him. Gentle aqua eyes. Youthfully plump cheeks and lips… Soft.

A red mark darkened that formerly plump cheek, outside the blush that had already faded. She'd had her ear to the door listening when he'd slammed it open. Not locking it. Or maybe not locking it yet, whatever she'd claimed.

She made herself sound even harder than she appeared. That physical angularity was by far the biggest change, and the one that had momentarily thrown him when she'd come into Ben's quarters. Not her hair color, her eye color, the glasses, or that suspicious tan… It was how square her jaw seemed now, the gauntness of her cheeks, and the now slender but apparently strong body supporting it all. Anna Kincaid was hard.

He didn't know what else to say.

For seven years, he'd had a million questions for her—mostly in the first couple of years when everything was hardest. But now, standing here, he didn't want to ask her why she'd gone. Those old wounds could pop back open with the slightest prod. His chest already ached just looking at this shadow of his brightly colored Anais.

"Are you living back in Easton?"

"No. Are you still at the penthouse?"

"Yes," he answered. Why it had been so important to him to come find her after speaking with Ben? "Is there something you want to say to me?"

Like *I'm sorry*?

She shook her head, then seemed to change her mind as the shaking turned into a nod, her voice going quieter. "How do you know Lieutenant Nettle?"

"Served together. First tour," Quinn answered again. Did she feel anything for him anymore? Besides anger? Somehow, *he'd* earned *her* anger? Her anger, and the fact that she wanted him gone was all he could make out. Her eyes used to sparkle when she saw him, even the last time she'd seen him—which she'd no doubt known would be the last time—they'd still sparkled. But with them hidden under those unremarkable brown contacts, he couldn't see it. Or it wasn't there. A wife who had feelings for her husband…her ex-husband even…wouldn't look so hard when he'd never wronged her. Never done anything wrong but love her. Even a friend would look kindly upon a soldier returning home after seven years in a war zone, but she just wanted him gone.

Over the course of his tours, he'd learned to fight his way out of dodgy situations. Fight and survive first, complete the mission second. He couldn't fight his way out of this. He didn't even know where to start.

He could make her feel anger, maybe some polite curiosity, but nothing else. Touching her would just hurt him; there was no Braille hidden on her flesh that would tell him the truth, or what he wanted to hear: that she regretted leaving, that she'd suffered because of it, that she was sorry.

He forced his arms to relax, then thought better of it and

wrenched his mangled left hand from his pocket to present to her.

"Ben was there to help when my fingers were shot off." Seeing her blanch only emboldened him. With as much detail as he could summon from that day, he described the way the wedding band he'd still worn had become platinum shrapnel Ben had to pull from the remains of his palm. The way Ben had to cut away his dangling finger. "And that still hurt less than you."

Her eyes went round, with his hand held up for her inspection, and her breathing increased in speed and force; soon the heated air fanned his hand across the distance. The two fingers, thumb, and partial palm felt the flutter like the barest breeze.

"Get used to seeing me around here. I'll try to keep the cameras away, for Ben's sake."

Her open-mouthed breathing turned to choking, and he realized she was going to be sick a half-second before she turned and flung herself over her office trash bin and retched. Her whole body convulsed with the force of each spasm.

His stomach lurched too.

Damn.

They'd both changed. The last vestiges of the man who'd married her, who'd loved her, felt sick too, wanted to look away.

But the realist he'd had to become couldn't feel too badly. What had even made her sick? Hearing how he'd lost his fingers, or the idea the cameras that invariably ended up following him might catch sight of her?

As if it mattered. He should leave her there, let her get on with it, savor the little thrill of revenge that had run through him at her visceral reaction.

He wouldn't pull her hair aside and soothe her back. He wouldn't apologize for not softening the brutality of that situation for her, the way he'd softened it for his family.

She wasn't his family anymore. She'd been the one to leave. And he'd never gotten to say anything to her about it, since his family had shipped him off to boot camp directly afterward.

What was a little vomiting in that context?

CHAPTER TWO

NEVER BEFORE IN his homeland had Quinn felt so tense while riding in the back of a car. Every prior leave, he'd been able to disconnect that hyper-alert state traveling in a Humvee usually triggered while on duty.

First Ben, then Anais—both wrecked him. But going home for real—not just another leave—was the cherry on top of a terrible day.

Despite his late arrival—and he hadn't missed the fact that it had grown dark—Quinn had been requested to arrive by the main entrance. Usually he'd have gone around to a smaller, more private entrance.

It was showtime for the press.

But it looked relatively empty now, only a few cameras lingering to the side.

If he had to climb the grand entrance to go inside, he'd let himself out of the car. Quinn jumped from the back as soon as it stopped, thanking the driver over the seats, closed the door and jogged up, waving in passing at the few tenacious photographers who'd waited. No talking. No posing. He barely smiled.

Once inside, he bypassed servants, ignoring the familiar opulence he'd been raised in, and hurried across the foyer to the King's wing. Within two minutes, he knocked and opened the door to the King's study, but found Philip sitting behind the desk.

"You're not the King," Quinn murmured, making sure to gently close that door too.

His youthful habit had always been to bound through doors and expect them to close behind him—the same tactic he'd used with nearly everything: bound through, expect it to get sorted out in his wake. A tactic his family had spent years trying to talk him out of, and which his divorce and sudden soldier status had actually accomplished. Now he paid attention to doors. It was something small he could always control, and doors often presented a hazard or added protection. Doors now mattered.

Philip rose, checking his watch, but smiling anyway. "And you're not here at noon."

"No, I'm not." He should try to be amiable, but at that precise moment all he could hear was Anais's confession that Philip had changed her name. "Why didn't you tell me Anais was back in the country?"

He tried to sound calm, but even a dead man would've heard the bitterness in his voice.

Philip had rounded the desk, hand out to shake Quinn's, but he dropped it to his side with the question. "I was going to tell you when you got here. It seemed like an in-person kind of conversation to have. You've seen her already?"

"She's working at Almsford Castle with amputees. I went there to visit my friend, Ben Nettle; I told you about him. And that's…a story I really would rather not get into right now. But you know she's not fooling anyone by dipping herself in brown dye."

"She fooled me." Philip shrugged, and then reached out to grab Quinn by the back of the neck and pull him into a hug.

"That's because you're an idiot." It didn't feel like a time for hugging to Quinn, but he went along with it. A little brotherly ribbing was as playful as he could get right now. Clapping one another on the back a few times, they both retreated and Quinn went to help himself to a Scotch.

"She's changed more than that. I was surprised when she told me where she was going to work. I don't think she realized that the new facility was at Almsford Castle," Philip said, returning to his seat. "How was it to see her?"

Quinn eyeballed three fingers of booze since he had two fingers on that hand to measure with, and took it to the front of the desk to sit. "I don't know. Unpleasant. I guess. I don't want to talk about Anais."

"You brought her up."

"I did. Now I'm bringing up Grandfather. Is he here or did he go off on vacation for his rest?"

"He's here." Philip sat up straighter suddenly, his voice growing suspiciously softer.

The hairs on the back of Quinn's neck rose. This apprehension was more than he'd felt when deciding he needed to start serving the family and the people again as a prince. Something was wrong. "Where is he?"

"Sleeping. He spends most of the time sleeping now."

Those words had never fit their grandfather. Despite his advancing age, he was a vibrant man, always on the move. But the sober tones in which Philip delivered the news gave them weight, gave them truth. And gave him that feeling in the pit of his stomach for the third time that day.

The heat returned and he knew it for what it was: *helpless anger.*

"Was that something else you wanted to tell me in person?" He truly hadn't come home to fight with anyone, but it seemed to be all he'd been doing since he'd stepped foot into Almsford Castle.

The grimace that crossed Philip's face confirmed his suspicions.

"He didn't want you worrying when you were away," Philip admitted, his voice trailing off.

Quinn noticed for the first time the three-day growth of beard his always immaculately groomed brother now wore.

"He has good days and bad days, but is usually awake for a few hours in the late morning, early afternoon."

When Quinn had been supposed to come earlier.

"What's wrong with him?"

"He's an old man, Quinn. Time catches up to everyone."

He felt his head shaking before words—demands—began pouring out. "How, specifically, has it caught up with him? Heart failure? Some kind of cancer? Stroke? What's wrong? What happened?"

"Kidney failure is the big one right now. There are other more minor diagnoses, but his kidneys are the biggest worry. He's on dialysis, but he's too old for a transplant, and his body isn't holding up well to dialysis."

Quinn took a deep pull on the drink, considered draining it, then carefully placed it upon the desk.

"What does that mean?" He'd had training as an EMT in the military—hence Ben calling him Doc—but he wasn't actually a doctor. He hadn't dealt with dialysis in combat situations, so he didn't know anything about it. If he'd never gone into the military, he would've been better equipped to understand, assuming he'd gotten into medical school as he'd—as they'd both—planned.

Another life. He'd enjoyed his life as a soldier; it was his life as a prince that was stressing him out.

"Some people live a lot of years on dialysis, but his body just isn't strong enough. He's had the access port moved twice now. Keeps getting infected and he's running out of places to put it or the will to let them try another location. He's already said he won't be having another one placed." Philip headed for the decanter and poured his own drink.

After their parents' unexpected deaths when they were children, Grandfather had stepped up to fill the father role—even when he was busy running the country. Quinn just didn't know how to process this information. One more thing. A third person to save.

Well, second. Ben and Grandfather. He wasn't trying

to save Anais, and what could he even save her from? Another bad spray tan?

"Not to put pressure on you, but I'm hoping that having you around will give him the urge to fight a little longer," Philip muttered. "Then I wonder if that's selfish of me, but I can't help it. It's not looking good. I'm glad you're home. We need you. I need you here."

"I want to see him," he said, redirecting his thoughts to what mattered at this precise moment. He could only deal with what was before him.

"He's sleeping."

"And I want to see him. I can sit quietly at his bedside, Philip. I will be here tomorrow when he wakes, but I want to see him now. Let me prepare myself so I don't go in looking at him like he's a dying man when he sees me for the first time." He added, more quietly, "Let my first shock be when he can't see it. I've already had two shocks since I got home. I don't think I can look a third person I love in the eye like that."

A third person he loved. God help him, he'd done it again.

"Loved. Someone I loved. You know what I mean."

"Who was the second?"

Not Anais.

"Ben. I should feel bad that I didn't come here first and see Grandfather, but if I had Ben would be dead. He tried to hang himself in his room this afternoon, and I got there in time to stop him, get help, get him cut down… Which is why I have to see Anais again tomorrow, because I need to go back for Ben."

And he needed to make those calls still. God, this day really sucked.

His brother nodded to the nearly empty second tumbler. "Drink the rest first. Sounds like you're going to need it. Will you be staying here tonight?"

"No," he said first and then, after finishing his drink,

shrugged. "I don't know. Should I? I was going to go to my flat. Unless you think I should stay to see when he wakes?"

Philip shook his head. "You don't need to stay, but you look rough, Quinn. Your room is prepared if you want to stay. Might do you good."

Sleep would do him good. He stood again, but it took all the strength in him to follow his brother down the hallways to the King's suite.

Before they'd even entered, he heard the soft hums and beeps of life-saving equipment and knew Philip had been trying to soften the blow.

But Quinn smelled death. He knew the scent of it by now.

Anais stood at her favorite treadmill—the one she hadn't been on since Quinn's terrible cry for help had shattered her will to hide and sent her running toward him for the first time in years.

Her work day had ended over an hour ago, and Quinn was still on site, still with Benjamin Nettle as far as she knew—as far as everyone knew. A prince couldn't spend hours a day for three days straight in the building without word getting around.

What she didn't want to get around? That she'd been waiting for him today. Was still waiting for him. That knowledge would trigger too many questions and the conclusions she needed no one to reach if she wanted to stay. And she had to stay. Her departure from Corrachlean had meant leaving Mom, and they'd spent seven years apart. Visits had been impossible before Anna Kincaid had been born.

Quinn hated her Anna look—she could tell by the way he'd looked at her, as if she'd sprouted some horrifying, self-induced deformity. But she liked it in a way. It made her feel invisible. After fitting in—which she'd never truly done anywhere—being invisible was the next best thing.

But he hated more than her new look. He hated *her*.

And, really, what could she expect? Aside from expecting to not see him for a long, long time—or ever, if she'd had her way.

The treadmill whirred beneath her feet, and she took one of the safety bars to steady herself as she inched up the speed and the incline. Maybe exercise could wipe her mind, help her zone out and forget she was waiting for him.

The only way she'd kept going after they'd fallen apart was to practice willful amnesia. Not letting herself wonder about him or how he was doing, never thinking about how he felt or if he ever thought of her. She couldn't do that and keep going. Which probably made her the second person who hadn't been thinking about how Quinn felt—he never dwelt on anything that hurt. Not for himself. Not for her. Not for anyone, at least when they'd been married. She'd spent darned near a year trying to work him out, and all she had was: he liked sex with her and hated responsibility.

Then, two days ago, she'd learned something else—something that took her breath every time it replayed in her head, hundreds of times per day: losing his fingers hurt him less than she had.

Was he still suffering in the way she never let herself wonder if he was suffering?

She didn't want to believe it was true. His hatred was real, and he'd definitely wanted to hurt her, so it would be better if she could stop lingering over it. No matter what, her leaving had been kinder to both of them in the long run. If she'd stayed with Quinn until Wayne had followed through with his threats, Corrachlean's people wouldn't have been the only ones to think terribly of her; Quinn's opinion would've plummeted into earth too. At least he hated her now for something that was ultimately kinder. Even if she never wanted him to know that.

Maybe that was why, despite knowing he'd been at the facility the past two days, she hadn't been able to drag herself to Ben's room to ask him to speak with her. Or maybe it was something more cowardly. Maybe she was afraid that Ben would know who she was now, and she couldn't blame Quinn if he'd told him. He'd never promised to keep her secrets, and what loyalty did he owe her? Sharing something that was going on in your own life could be a kind of currency to get your friends to talk when they needed to.

"You're leaving notes for me now?" Quinn's voice cut across the cavernous ballroom-gymnasium, jolting her from her thoughts so that she had to grab the safety bars again to steady herself.

Would his voice always jolt her?

Heart hammering, she shut off the machine. At least she had the exercise to blame for the way her words came out, breathy and with effort. "I waited for an hour in the foyer, long past the time it started to look weird that I waited for you. Then I decided to write a note. The envelope was sealed, the front was as formal as could be."

Grabbing a towel, she dried herself off as she walked to meet him, pretending her legs wobbled because of the running too.

"I noticed." Quinn thrust the envelope back at her, and looked around the ballroom to make certain they were alone. The last thing he needed this week was to have to explain why he was ogling the doctor or being overly familiar. "And I'm here. What do you want?"

The nod to revenge he'd felt on leaving her there bent over the trash bin hadn't even lasted until he'd gotten out the door—and that hadn't even been a version of Anais who looked like his wife. While her hair and eyes remained the wrong color, her glasses were now gone and the hair pulled back from her face let him almost see her. Almost.

Her hand shook a touch when she took the envelope, and he swallowed the urge to lash out at her again, to shock her with some other brutality from the frontline—he had a thousand such story grenades to hurl.

"I just want to talk to you about something. Will you come to my office?"

"Why not here?"

"It's private."

Their last conversation had been on repeat in his head since it had ended. While he'd met with his brother. While he'd found out the new family secret: the King was dying. Even sitting by his grandfather's bed, he'd had her on repeat, enough to riddle out what had set her off.

She'd paled before he'd even mentioned the cameras. She'd been sick about him, not about herself. She still felt something, no matter what she pretended.

It would've been so easy to tell her to go to hell, ignore her, as he'd been more or less doing since that first day. To come when she was at lunch, leave when she'd gone home, and continue driving Ben up the wall by refusing to leave him alone in his misery.

But she wanted to talk. And, God help him, he still wanted to talk to her. Maybe this was his opening. Apologies started with regret and, whether she'd admit it or not, he could see she had regrets.

Quinn waved a hand for her to lead the way, and the relief on her face notched his hope higher. He had to pick up his usual leisurely pace to keep up with her and, directly in her wake, her scent channeled to him.

Sweaty, but she still smelled fantastic. Clean, but sweet. Sexy.

Her long, heavy locks had been pulled up high on her head, and the straightening she'd inflicted on it had come undone in the dampness. Waves stretched up from the bottom, where the mass had brushed against her bare back, gathering sweat. A shiver racked his body, raising chills all over him, and Quinn had to thank fate he was walking behind her rather than in her line of sight.

Getting wrapped up in hormones wasn't the right tack for this conversation—whatever it was going to be about.

Before she'd left him, he could've easily made any private conversation with her about what his body wanted.

He pulled his gaze to her feet, which seemed safest. Only feet attached to slender ankles, and then his eyes tracked up over the soft skin covering the newly acquired definition in her calves. Her thighs. Her rear…

The shorts she wore clung in a fantastically distracting manner and, just below, he could see the dark little mole that always wanted to be kissed, peeking and retreating from the hem of her shorts on the right as her clothing moved with each step.

By the time they reached her office he had to keep reminding himself of the objective, but every reminder was a little quieter than the hunger for her that had him shaking.

"It's hot in here," he muttered, dragging his jacket off and tossing it onto the back of one of the guest chairs.

"It gets warmer in here at night. Sorry. Would you like something to drink first?"

"I'm fine." He dragged the chair back and sat down, nodding for her to do the same. Hopefully outside of his reach. "But take out the contacts first."

"What?" She stilled, her expression shifting to something uncomfortably close to fear. "Why?"

As if she had anything to fear from him. Aside from something he might say to upset her…

"You want to talk to me? Great. I don't want to talk to Anna. I want to talk to Anais. When you've got them in, it's like I can't see you, but you can still see me. You want me to stay? Take them out."

"Anna wants to talk to you."

Anna. Right. This wasn't about them. This was about work.

Grabbing his jacket again, he rose and headed toward the door. Only a romantic idiot would've gotten his hopes up. It angered him that he'd gotten them up without even realizing it. She'd been gone for seven years, now she suddenly wanted to reconnect? Sure. *Dumbass.*

He'd reached the knob before she cracked. "Wait."

The sound of rustling came from behind him: drawers opening, things being dropped on the desk top. When he looked back, she had a contacts case and some fluid on the desk. Half a minute later, she had the contacts out and a tissue blotting her eyes.

"Still not used to them?"

"They're fine." She dropped the tissue on the desk, squared her shoulders, and came back around to sit as he'd done, chair turned, facing him. When she finally looked at him, his chest squeezed. Blue-green, like the southern seas on sunny white sand. Even with all the other changes, she was truly his wife in that moment. His eyes burned at the thought and he let his head bow forward until the burning passed, needing to get on with things, to keep from reaching for her, his tropical songbird masquerading as a pigeon.

And with the door closed, he couldn't smell anything but her.

God, this was a mistake.

"What did you want?"

Don't touch her.

Don't touch her. Don't touch her.

"I wanted to talk to you about Lieutenant Nettle."

Ben. Right. Good. He'd spent all that time at the facility for Ben, and she was one of his doctors. Made sense, if someone had a functioning brain.

Rather than saying anything else, he nodded. The sooner he let her get on with it, the sooner he could leave.

"I think it's been really great for him to have you here. I'm glad you keep coming back. Not just because you averted disaster; he wouldn't see anyone but staff otherwise. But now he's talking a little, mostly to you, I think. But he's having you stick around when the therapist comes, right?"

"Right," he said, then added, "What does Ben need? Just spit it out."

She shifted, tried to sit up straighter, but her shoulders already nearly reached her ears because of her stiff posture.

"It's not my place to say this—it has nothing to do with his limbs. I treat bone injury, not…soft tissue. But, since he's allowed you to become part of his care, I'm taking the liberty on the chance that you can help him."

Anais waited for his nod of understanding, and swallowed past the lump of fear in her throat. Since her mad scramble out of the country, she'd made a point of being good at eye contact. When you looked someone in the eye it established a connection that usually helped you in some fashion—intimidating muggers, letting professors know you meant business, letting patients know you were there and cared about what happened to them. Helpful.

Looking Quinn in the eye, she felt small. And hideous. The contacts didn't change her vision in any way, but they made her feel hidden, and unseen was safe. Now she had to dig deep for the courage she hadn't even glimpsed since she'd seen him.

One piece chipped free from her Anna armor, and she was stuttering with tears burning.

"He's got more damage than just his legs." Her voice was too high, too shaky.

Quinn's stormy eyes lifted to hers again, narrowed. "I haven't seen his chart and getting him to talk about his injuries is almost impossible. Was he shot? I know about the IED. They throw off shrapnel."

"He wasn't shot. There were a few abdominal wounds from shrapnel, but most have healed nicely." She should've rehearsed this. The words didn't even want to move through her throat. "He lost one testicle."

Anna would be stronger. She'd look him in the eye again.

It took force, and strength she didn't really have at the

time, but she met his gaze. The description of damage took the disappointment out of his eyes; he'd focused on Ben, just as she'd hoped.

"They were able to restore urinary function. But there's more…" She saw understanding dawn on his face and, the second it came, she wished she hadn't needed to tell him.

CHAPTER THREE

"MORE TO RESTORE?" Quinn's words came slow and low, as if tension and gravity made him pause for a breath after each word.

"Repairing areas with vascular damage." She clarified, "They did what they could the first time, but it didn't heal properly. The surgeon is confident he can restore full function, but Nettle—Ben—won't talk to anyone about it. I even tried once, early on, because the staff GP said he'd gotten nowhere either. The psychiatrist also had no luck. He shut me down really quickly."

Quinn took it in dead silence.

Was he getting it? She couldn't tell if it was his usual tactic—letting the bad wash over him like water off a duck's back—or if he was processing. There was concern on his face, but his silence didn't give any hint to his thoughts. She'd have to put it to him straight.

"I think if you talk to him about the procedure and why he should have it, he might listen…"

He reached behind him and rubbed the back of his neck, finally pulling his gaze away from her for a moment. "He's talking a little, but I don't want to push him. It's a delicate balance, right now."

Like Quinn was talking a little. It was only an opening, but one she'd never got before. Talking about problems, at least his friend's problems, might be within his capabilities. He hadn't said no. He just needed convincing.

Anais stood and dragged her chair closer to him, close enough that their knees almost touched.

"He's got a chance at a normal life if he has the procedure. I doubt he feels like getting married knowing he won't be able to father children, or…be…with his wife." Don't linger on the sex, even if she knew Quinn would definitely get that rationale. "I think that particular injury is an even bigger one mentally to him than his legs. It's the reason for how you found him, I'm sure of it."

Quinn's expression hadn't changed—concerned, maybe a little out of his depth and horrified at the idea of talking to his friend about something so personal. But what got more personal than asking your friend to cut your dangling fingers off?

She kept going. "With the surgery, he could have a normal life. We can work with him on his mobility— his life won't ever be entirely normal because he's a double amputee, but he could have a family."

A family. Something she'd wanted with Quinn. Something she still wanted, but had never been able to picture with anyone else. The word had become like a weapon, a word that could hurt them both. But if she couldn't reach Nettle, she had to reach the person who could.

Whatever it took.

Before she could think too much about it, she took his left hand, forcing him to look at her again.

"What are you doing?" he asked, his stormy gray eyes sliding from their hands to her eyes, but lingering heavily over her mouth.

He started to pull away.

"Wait!" She transferred his hand to lie on her palm and traced the jagged edge left after the blast. "If you could have back these parts that were taken from you, if you could have them, fully functional, wouldn't you want it? I know this was terrible for you, and I haven't—" she swallowed "—I can't close my eyes without seeing it."

Her throat squeezed so hard she could barely breathe, let alone talk. Blessedly. Those weren't the words she'd needed to say. This wasn't about her. It was about him. About Ben.

"Imagine you could have a place for your wedding ring, the next time you married." She felt tears slip as she said the words. "Wouldn't you want that? I know…it didn't…go the way…either of us hoped it would, but sometimes…"

"I have no desire to get married again." The words dropped like lead.

A sharp jerk pulled his hand from hers and she lifted her eyes to his, not even trying to hide the tears quivering in her vision.

She'd messed it up, yet more proof they never knew how to talk to one another. This wasn't supposed to be about them. How had it become about them?

Pressure on her neck made her lift her head, and the next instant his mouth covered hers. The moment stretched out and she measured it in breaths and heartbeats. One breath she was in her chair, the next she was in his lap, her sluggish mind struggling to catch up.

All she knew in that moment was an ache that seared into her. His mouth, hot and desperate, on hers echoed the frenzied need crouching in her own breast since the moment she'd heard his laugh. She was a silly, naïve twenty-year-old again, starved for his kisses, for his touch, for the heat of him against her.

When she opened her eyes, it hurt to see him. His brows were wrenched, as if touching her hurt more than helped. As if he tortured himself with every kiss, but couldn't stop.

She didn't want to stop. She didn't want to feel him shaking or the mingling of pleasure and bitter need that twisted her insides. But she couldn't stop.

Her arms came around his shoulders, pulling him close, reveling in his solidity, the breadth of him. His face had matured; his body had as well. He was a new man, but still the same.

His arms around her waist bent her toward the floor, and he paused only long enough to shove chairs violently away, making a space for them.

There was no way for reason to intervene, not when his unfamiliar and heady mass pressed her into the cold wood floor, and his hands began frantically pulling at the material separating them.

Her tank top came up and her front-clasp bra popped open at his insistence. He only took his mouth from hers to turn his attention to her breasts.

Her breath left her and she moaned so loudly that he lunged back over her, covering her mouth again with his own, absorbing every tortured gasp he ripped from her.

Before she registered movement, he'd stripped her from the waist down. She could only hold his mouth to hers, needing his kisses to continue blocking out the world. Needing to fill her lungs with him.

Tenacious, unhesitating, he pulled her legs around his hips, and launched himself into her.

Dizzy and breathless, only his mouth kept the broken sobs of her regret and need from echoing through the whole facility.

Like a wild thing, he set a thundering pace, hollowing her out and tearing down those carefully constructed walls of protection. Anna was gone. Anais was too. All thoughts gone. Nothing left but this need to get closer, to wrap her legs around him and pretend that the years in between never happened. Forget the bad times. Forget the end. Even forget the wedding. Pretend she didn't know it was only lust and anger driving him. This was hate sex for him. That horrible need to be closer. They might never be cured of it but it had been twisted by her leaving, and by his never showing up to begin with.

Still, she hung in that heartbeat where she'd still believed they could have that future she'd so desperately wanted. With this man—the only man who could bullhead through her reservations and convince her to act against her best interests.

He was with her, connected, inside her, but leaned away until it was his idea to return for another desperate, suffocating kiss. That frequent distance kept her from reaching for him until he deigned to return to her.

The last time she'd held him, he'd still been a boy. A decidedly handsome, sexy boy, but now, broad-shouldered and deliciously heavier than he'd been, he still felt like hers. Angry, but hers. Wanting to punish her, but still part of her.

It was wrong. All of it. The sex. Wanting to see him. Wanting to know him… Wrong. Stupid and wrong.

Stretched too taut, the thread of her pleasure snapped, and the first wave of her climax blasted through her, but she was too far gone for moans or any sound. It was all she could do to keep breathing.

When he stiffened and jerked, his broken breaths told her he'd come with her, and there had been no barriers in those few moments. Not even the sort that would prevent pregnancy.

Pretend it was still then. Back when they'd had a future. When she'd have felt only bliss at the idea of having his child. Before she'd learned how much to value a quiet life.

Quinn relaxed against her, his stubble-roughened cheek to her shoulder, rapid breath fanning her hair.

What were they doing? Why had she kissed him back?

Her hands ached to smooth over his back, to relearn the body she'd once known. To comb through his hair, trace his jaw and feel the rasp of his whiskers against her fingertips. She wanted to luxuriate in the tactile experience his body could bring. Just hold on and pretend for a little longer.

Instead, she curled her fingers to her palms to keep from stroking his skin. As soon as she got control of her thoughts, of her mouth—as soon as she could stand the idea of him looking at her again—she'd push him away. Off her, out of her…

No words came from her, not out loud, but it was as if he heard her anyway. Quinn lifted himself, off and away from her, severing their connection before he'd even gotten control of his heart.

On his knees between her legs, still mostly dressed, he rested and silently looked over her naked body. A heated look, at least. He still wanted her. This could be the first in a long, tangled back and forth—something she wouldn't be strong enough to withstand. Or it could be another sign that it was once again time to run.

She pulled her tank top down to cover her breasts, and scooted back to sit up, legs together. As if that would make her less bare to him.

What could be more heady than knowing how little effort it had taken to have her? A kiss. Just one kiss. And she'd practically begged him.

"I need my shorts." She didn't want to crawl past him to reach them, but she would if she had to.

Without a word, he shoved the crumpled garment at her, and climbed to his feet, righting himself. Tucking in. Zipping up.

"If you're wondering, that was goodbye," he announced as he bent to look under the desk for his shoe. "That's all."

The goodbye she'd denied him.

"Right," she managed, no words coming to mind that would provide her with the same emotional distance. He'd just announced the end of whatever they'd had, as if it hadn't ended once already. That was what he'd been doing—ending things?

He'd had a goal, but why had she gone along with it?

Because…chemistry.

Because she was still vulnerable to chemistry. Because in some ways she'd be forever stupid.

It had blinded her before. Blinded him too. They'd tried

to build a marriage on chemistry—the height of bad reasons to get married.

If he'd loved her, if he'd ever felt anything for her besides lust, he would've listened when she'd tried to tell him about the photos, her blackmailer. He would've helped her. Helped them. He would've cared what was happening to her. But he hadn't. Everything always just magically worked out in Quinn Land. Fate was kinder to him than it had ever been to her, and he took it for granted.

One last anger-filled time was his version of goodbye. There weren't feelings attached. For either of them. She had regret, and chemistry, and that was plenty. How much worse would it be to still love him and have him never able to feel the same?

Even weakness and chemistry-fueled unprotected sex on her office floor was better than that.

Snagging the shoe, he straightened his sock and crammed the shoe back on.

Following his lead, she shimmied into her underthings and stood.

"Are you going to talk to Nettle?" There. Those were words. The thing she'd actually wanted to talk to him about before all this insanity happened.

"I'll talk to him."

She turned to grab her shoe and heard the door close.

Whatever. She sat down and put the shoe on.

Showering, changing, and going home would help. Get the scent of him off her. Clothe her far too bare form. Drink tea while not letting on to Mom that anything was wrong. And sleep…

Leaning over the desk to get her bag, she noticed the large envelope she'd prepared for this talk.

He'd left without the literature. *Of course he had.*

Snatching the envelope from her desk, she ran out after him.

Just before he got to his car, she made her way through

the door at the front of the building. “Quinn… Prince Quinton.”

Get it together.

He turned and looked at her, left the car door standing open and met her halfway. “What else?”

“You forgot this.” She pushed the envelope into his hand—the lights in front of the building harsh against the falling darkness.

No contacts. No freaking real clothes. Hair back. Proof yet again that fate refused to do her any favors.

Except one thing: no one was really about to notice her eye color, or how closely she resembled the former Princess. No one outside his employ, at least. Five cars parked in front of and behind his. How much security did he need to come to a rehabilitation center for soldiers?

“It's literature on the procedure. How it's done. Case studies. So you can prepare your talk.”

With Nettle. It was on the tip of her tongue to call the soldier by his last name again—it was a distance tactic she'd been relying on, and had noticed it bothered Quinn—but she couldn't take a single drop more drama and hostility between them. Not until she had time to think. Until she had time to prepare for the possibility that she could've just irresponsibly conceived with her ex.

Once his hand closed on the envelope, she spun and headed back inside. Shower. Shower first stop. Then get the hell out of there.

When Quinn had agreed to come home, he'd thought it would go a little differently.

Summer had arrived, so naturally he'd assumed there would be loads of parties to attend where he would meet women. Drinks. Philip would fill his schedule with meetings, dinners, and appearances, telling him what to do, when, where, and what was expected of him. All that.

All he had so far was news of his grandfather's terminal

illness, a friend who'd tried to kill himself, an ex-wife he couldn't keep his mind or his damned hands off, and now a tricky emotional situation he was utterly unequipped to deal with.

And a distinct lack of drinks.

Slamming the door to his penthouse, Quinn tossed the envelope Anais has shoved at him onto the counter, and made a beeline for the fridge.

He grabbed a tumbler, threw some ice into it, and turned toward the liquor cabinet, only to stop. That route out of his kitchen had been blocked by large lidded plastic crates. Stuff he was supposed to deal with too. Seven years' worth of junk that people had just been sticking into crates for him…and he'd been ignoring for every leave.

But it was better duty than that penis conversation.

He backtracked and went the other way around the kitchen to reach for the rum, which would at least get the taste of her out of his mouth.

Instead of kissing her, he should've asked how to start this conversation.

He drained the glass entirely, felt his stomach lurch, and put the glass back down.

The man knew what parts were malfunctioning. It was his body. They'd told him that he could probably get it fixed. He knew these things already.

How would Philip handle this task?

Something heartfelt. Make an appeal to his better nature—whatever that would amount to.

He poured himself another glass and took another pull on the rum, and put the tumbler down.

Anais had never approved of drinking, for any reason. No wine with dinner. No beer after an arduous exam. Strip poker was fine, but not with shots. Not for her. And when she'd gone he'd thrown himself into spirits whenever the opportunity presented itself. Boot camp and deployment had probably saved him from becoming an alcoholic that first year.

He should watch the drinking since she'd strayed back into his life.

He turned his attention to the first crate, lifting the lid and riffling through its contents.

At the bottom of the stack of papers requiring his attention was a large yellow envelope, crammed with documents.

He flipped it over and read: *Divorce of Prince Quinton Corlow and Princess Anais Corlow née Hayes.*

Right. Bloody timely. He flung the packet over his shoulder in the vague direction of the sofa, and went back to the crate.

Gifts.

Books.

Things to be looked at later, when he'd not drunk enough rum to make his eyes go blurry.

A photo album filled with pictures taken during their whirlwind marriage.

Half a crate's worth of quasi-attentive sorting painful garbage was enough for one night. There really wasn't enough rum in his place for further torture.

Flopping one leg over the edge of the crate, he pushed the remaining material to the far end to make room for what he had to put back in.

A white-handled gift bag tumbled out of the moving pile of stuff, hit the bottom of the crate and spilled a small unopened package wrapped in pale blue paper and a silver bow onto the floor.

His heart stopped the moment he saw it.

It must've been the first crate the palace staff started packing for him. Copies of divorce papers. The gift he'd bought Anais for their first anniversary—the one they hadn't made it to—an engagement ring she'd never gotten before the wedding because they'd impetuously eloped.

He swallowed, then kicked the small box back to the

side. Stuffed into a crate by someone who didn't know its value. He put it right back there, suddenly too bitter to care about the small fortune buried under papers by his boot.

Enough of that.

He began dumping the bits he'd sorted out right back into the crate. Too much. All too much to deal with tonight, when all he really wanted was a shower and some sleep.

CHAPTER FOUR

STILL MARRIED.

The words rattled around in Quinn's head, as they'd been doing since he'd seen the morning news.

Sitting across from his ranting brother on the naughty schoolboy side of the King's desk at least made the news feel real, if still unpleasant. He'd never inspired his brother to rant before. Father, Mother, even Grandmother, God rest them. The King never ranted, though that sad, disapproving shake of his head always hit harder.

But, as he watched his brother pace and growl at him, he fully realized how things had changed.

Grandfather was dying. Philip now worried about these things, and felt as if he'd inherited a problem.

Quinn had always done his best to care when he was being lectured, but he never really had. Things always worked out, somehow.

Well, except for his marriage.

His day had started with a phone call and a number of emails, all directing him to programs and pages with the kind of annoying news reports they'd always lobbed at Anais, whether she deserved them or not.

They had always been big on inappropriate sex and full of tales of devious female conniving. And big on underestimating him—though they weren't wrong about him having wildly inappropriate…

Who was he kidding?

It was appropriate.

It felt appropriate.

It felt like a damn lightning bolt—illuminating to the point of scorching.

One enterprising journalist had caught a picture of them together and had gone off to investigate the court records of their divorce. Although apparently there were no court records. It must be a mix-up. It *had* to be a mix-up.

"Are you listening, Quinn?"

"Yeah, I hear you. You're angry. You don't know how it could have happened. I wish I had the answer for you."

Philip sat back down and stared hard at the photo of Quinn and Anais. "What's she wearing?"

"Workout clothes. She…runs. Or maybe boxes. I don't know. She works at the rehabilitation facility. She probably exercises all the time. It wasn't some kind of cheap ploy to get my attention."

Even though it had gotten his attention, or just focused his attention.

"When did you start defending her? You never…"

"You never attacked like this before. I know you're stressed out, but she literally did nothing wrong." Nothing that was caught on camera, he prayed. "She'd been working out when I left Ben for the evening, and since she wanted to talk to me about his care, I went to speak with her. The documents she's handing me in that photo are something to do with the medical care. I haven't read them yet."

"Great."

"Yeah. So calm down. I saw the envelope of official divorce documents last night when I was going through the big crates of rubbish accumulated for me since I enlisted. I'll go home, find the papers, and you can show them to the press. Then all this goes away." Those words should've been easier to say. Shouldn't be making his stomach churn.

"Except that she's here, and now the people *know* she's

here." Philip rubbed both hands over his face. "Her name change means nothing. It'll probably be used as evidence of more crimes they can attribute to her. I tried to warn her this could happen."

Because, no matter how horrified Philip had been by their inappropriate and spontaneous marriage, he'd always liked Anais. He still did, Quinn could see. This didn't only upset him because it was bad publicity, no matter how inopportune the timing.

"Doesn't matter. She can't win in this situation anyway, Philip. She was reviled as my wife, and then crucified when she left me. One or the other scenario should've made the people happy, but it didn't. This is just melodrama to sell papers."

"You always say that."

"It always goes away," Quinn tried again.

"No, someone always makes it go away. But I'm not doing that this time. You show the papers to the press. This is your first official royal duty: cleaning up your own mess. I have actual things to do that don't involve monitoring or refereeing your love life."

"How is this my mess? I was away in freaking boot camp when the divorce was arranged." Quinn couldn't help but complain a little; he was being blamed for not knowing exactly what a divorce by royal decree entailed? "I'll handle it. But I didn't leave her. I didn't ask to go into the military or to be divorced. I went where I was told, and did what I was told."

He'd never wanted to go into the military, but had ended up there because he couldn't think straight enough after she'd gone to make a counter offer, or even string together an argument. She'd gone, then it'd felt as if his family had given up on him too—shipped him off to be someone else's problem.

"You did," Philip said, anger dispelled with the quiet words. "And we're all proud of you for the sacrifices you made for your country, and the man you've become. But now that man can handle..."

"I said I'd take care of it." Quinn cut him off. Philip might be the heir to the eternal throne, but he wasn't wearing the crown yet. "Don't be too proud. I did what I had to do in the military—made a new family, found a way to fit and belong. Then I was told to come home and give that new family up, so I have. I'll sort this out, as you've ordered. My love life is fully off your plate."

Philip didn't argue further; he didn't look as if he knew quite what to think or say in that moment.

"Is he having a good day?" Quinn changed the subject as he rose and gestured to the door leading to the King's wing.

"He was doing well when I saw him before you arrived."

"Has he seen the papers?"

"Yes."

"Then I'll go and reassure him now."

As Quinn strode from the room, he heard Philip swearing under his breath behind him.

Upset a little? Seemed to be his habit, upsetting everyone. Including himself.

A good brother wouldn't have admitted feeling abandoned by his family in his hour of need. He'd have sucked it up and let them continue in blissful ignorance, just happy he'd turned his pathetic life around. But that was something he'd learned from the military: bluntness had its advantages.

A soft knock on the ornate carved door to his grandfather's bedchamber, and he opened it enough to peek inside.

Awake.

Sitting by the window in the sun, book in hand.

"Come." The once robust voice sounded brittle and diminished. Whatever reserve of righteous anger Quinn had built up likewise diminished.

"It's Quinn," he said then let himself in, paying mind to the gentle closing of the door. "I just wanted to reassure you that the situation with Anais will be sorted out."

"Oh? Well, that's good then. I'm sure you and Philip can handle it."

Yes. Philip could handle it, Grandfather would take comfort in that, so Quinn didn't correct him. "Don't worry yourself over it."

"She looks strange with her hair dark. Does it look better in person?" Grandfather gestured to a newspaper on the table beside him.

"Not particularly," Quinn admitted, grinning despite the subject as he moved another stately wingback closer to where the King sat. "She looks like she's playing dress-up in someone else's skin too."

"Left a mark on her too, I think."

Their divorce.

Quinn couldn't find words for that. He nodded, and turned as another knock came, followed by the sound of a trolley being pushed into the room. "Lunch or tea?"

"Lunch," the King's valet answered, stopping nearby and settling a tray across the King's lap to begin serving.

"I'm not hungry right now, Henry. Perhaps just tea."

Quinn gently dismissed Henry and headed to the cart to pour two cups, then peeked beneath the cover on the delivered plate and announced it cod, beans, cheese, good bread. The King didn't get excited about food like a soldier did. Or even a former soldier. Anything that looked this good? Definitely worth being excited over. Unless you were terribly ill.

"I could send for some soup, not so heavy?" Carefully, he transported the cups along with a small plate of cookies. Maybe he could tempt him there at least.

"Have I told you how much you remind me of your father, Quinton?"

"No. If you had, I would've said you were lying." It took effort to fake this upbeat air, but it would be less upsetting to both of them if he did. At least he could pretend things were normal, as he'd been doing with Ben, he realized. He'd been pretending with everyone but Anais, and just now, Philip. "I remember my father well, and Philip is the one who is like him."

"Later on. When he was a young man, he was like you. Bold. Carefree. Full of energy."

He wanted to talk, so Quinn would listen even if the words made no sense. And when his energy had depleted, Quinn would go home and read those damned papers and maybe call Ben, see what had been going on at the center today, as the press went into full-blown attack mode.

By the end of her workday, between watching the gathering throng of reporters forced to stay outside the Almsford gates, and the many worried calls from Mom to hear about the same at home, Anais had worked up a head filled with lightning.

They followed her from the castle to Quinn's penthouse, but knew enough to stop in the lobby while she stormed on through the shining white marble of her former home, past the familiar gray-haired guard at the reception desk, and straight for the elevator.

"Miss?"

When she pressed the button and the doors slid open, only then did she look back and saw the shock of recognition on his weathered face. "Haven't you heard, Alvin? Quinton and I are still married."

Before he could say anything else, she stepped inside and pressed the button for the top floor, sending the box rushing toward the heavens. Or, more probably, elevated Hell.

One of the world's fastest, finest elevators rocketed her straight to some kind of elevated perdition framed in gleaming marble and modern lines.

Contemporary in every way, the building had always driven home just how badly she fit there. She'd been a long-term visitor there, nothing more. It had never been her home any more than the place where she'd grown up had been. She hadn't missed it for a second when she'd gone, even when she'd missed Quinn so badly she could only go through the motions of everyday life—excelling where she was supposed to excel, but it had all been a way of getting her from her morning bed to her bed at night, and the blessed oblivion of sleep.

When she'd done her rotations in the psychiatric wards during medical school, she'd understood how people ended up addicted to drugs, or addicted to anything that took them out of their lives. She'd felt addicted to sleep, though came to realize it was depression muted to the world by an overachieving personality.

Reaching Quinn's door, she pounded without stopping until, wild-eyed, he swung it open. "Please, do come add to my terrible day. If you're here to yell at me too, stow it. I don't know what's going on any more than you do."

"You didn't call your army of lawyers?"

"Not yet." He left her at the door and went back to digging in one of three massive crates taking up the largest part of the living room—at least the parts not covered by furniture or clutter. "I thought I'd start by digging up the divorce papers."

"And they're in those crates?"

"I saw a marked envelope in one of them the other night while self-medicating with rum," he practically sneered. "But these things are full of junk and I can't remember what I did with the packet."

He dove back in, snatched up a packet of something, examined it, then chucked it over his shoulder before diving back in.

"What did the papers say?" Since she was there, she'd darned well help. The sooner the papers were found, the sooner the press would lose interest in her. She tossed her bag onto the counter and dumped another onto the floor, then sat in the middle to start sorting. The one good thing about being super angry while being around him? There wasn't anything endearing about the man right now. Or sexy. All she felt was alternating waves of anger and terror, back and forth like a pendulum. None of that was sexy, which was the one part of it she could be thankful for.

"I didn't open it. Why on earth would anyone open divorce documents to read them? They weren't written by John Grisham." He copied her method and resumed sorting. "Wait, you're annoyingly organized. Where are your copies of the papers?"

Her copies! She could almost laugh, "That's adorable. You think I was included in things. No. I went to the States, and no one bothered to look up my address, I guess. I signed the papers before I left. I don't even know what happens after a royal divorce, but I signed the bloody papers."

"Yeah, I—" His pause bid her look at him again.

Uneasiness crept up her spine. "You what?"

"I don't really remember any of that." He looked genuinely confused—not a trace of sarcasm there, just befuddlement.

"You don't remember signing your divorce papers?"

He shook his head, brows pinched above eyes tracked to the side, as if searching his memory.

"Didn't that strike you as odd?"

That question earned her all his attention.

"Odd? What struck me as odd was that my wife had just left me. That I was suddenly enlisted in the military. That medical school was permanently off the table. Those things struck me as odd. Shocking and odd."

Anais had been biting her tongue since she'd arrived, mostly trying to be more civil than the crackling in her ears demanded, but this quintessential Quinn manner of conflict resolution had her working not to shout at him.

"You want to do this now?"

"No, I wanted to do this seven years ago. I'm through waiting."

She could tell by his tone that he had worked up a lungful. And she'd be damned if she cowered behind his rage.

"Fine. Now it is. But back then? If you'd been paying any attention, you would've seen it coming. I didn't leave you spontaneously. It happened over months. I needed your help—I needed more than your arrogant certainty that things would just work out, and you shut me down every time I reached out to you." Anais climbed to her feet. At least she could run if she needed to; sitting on the floor made her feel even more vulnerable than this conversation.

He snorted, "When did I shut you down?"

Before answering, and because she wanted to scream, Anais looked around the room for the envelope while taking deep, slow breaths.

"There was your answer for everything: sex. Or telling me my concerns weren't important and that I should forget about them. *Don't worry, don't worry, don't worry. Everything will be fine.*" She flipped open the next crate, somehow doing all the talking. "Except that's not how life works. Things weren't fine. The people hated the idea that I was married to you, and every day it got worse. And guess what? They still hate it! I'm not allowed to go back to work until we get this sorted out, so help me find the papers. What color was the envelope?"

"Yellow. Large. Big black type on a white sticker. *Divorce of Prince Quinton Corlow and Princess Anais Corlow née Hayes.*" He answered that first, then looked back. "And why would you get fired? Anais Hayes doesn't even work at the clinic. Dr. Anna Kincaid works there. She might have a passing resemblance to Anais, but there's little else of Anais there."

"You're right. Anais died seven years ago." The words ripped out of her before she had a chance to consider them, hot on the edge of tears. She continued working through the things in the second crate, picking up every item only long enough to verify it wasn't a yellow envelope.

"You started this insane self-coloring program then? But Philip only changed your name this year."

She ignored the question, pushing back where she felt least exposed. "Please, let's talk about how, in order to come home, I had to engage the help of the Crown Prince to change my name without the public finding out. Having to rely on royal favors to live a life that those same royals wanted nowhere near them? Made my life *perfect*."

Quinn pushed a full crate out of the way. "Because it was so perfect after you left? Great. Good to know you didn't suffer for a second after going. I always wondered. You went to Shangri-La. I went to a war zone."

Another shot that sailed straight and struck her right in the *subgenual cingulate cortex*—aka Guiltville, Her Brain.

"Don't even pull that with me." She grabbed a stuffed animal and winged it at his head. "I didn't say that at all. And you didn't care the whole time we were married. I needed you and you didn't give a damn, so why would you care after I left? You wouldn't. You didn't. I will concede that you went somewhere awful afterward. I went to a shoddy walk-up in a shoddier neighborhood in the Rust Belt—which might as well have been a war zone."

"So, you felt right at home?"

Right where she belonged. She couldn't even argue with that, but he'd share his load of the blame.

"I guess. But, since we're on the subject, I know all this bluster was just you not wanting to admit that my leaving was not all me. It was you. And you don't want to talk to me about something that hurt and scared me. Still. It's easier to hurl blame." She gave up on the second crate and headed to the one he'd already searched, and turned it over again.

She needed this to be done before Wayne came back out of the woodwork with a barrel of shame and denigration in tow.

* * *

Quinn couldn't do this, not with her refusing to look at him. The papers could wait, but he was through waiting. He prowled over to her, took her elbow, and turned her to face him.

"I don't know what you're talking about. You mean I didn't want to spend all our time together fixating on the media? Yes. That's right. It did no good for anyone; it just made you more upset. That doesn't mean I didn't care. I cared. I cared about you more than anyone."

"I was looking for solutions!" She jerked away. "You remember those. That's what you're looking for with Ben. Who, by the way, I love that you're helping. Talking to him and seeing him through this. But it only goes to show how little you did that with me—to show that you were never mine, not really. We had chemistry. We had wild chemistry, and that was all you needed or wanted."

She spun away, her arms folding over her head in a cage, her fingers fisting in her own hair. The hopelessness of her action silenced him.

Her version of the downfall of their marriage didn't at all match his. Their problem was…well, he still didn't know, but it wasn't stupid rumors and paparazzi. Although anger that she couldn't see past that problem when it had become so present today wouldn't help him understand what had really happened back then.

What had she said? She'd needed him and she'd been scared.

The word sucked the anger out of him. "What were you scared of?"

"Does it suddenly matter?" She returned to the crate, back to sorting through the stuffed animals and cards, back to not cooperating. A few minutes ago she'd wanted to talk; now she didn't?

He needed a freaking compass to keep up.

"You said you were scared and that I was avoiding talking to you about it. So, what were you scared of?"

She pushed back from the last crate and gestured around the room, "Where were you when you last saw the envelope?"

Still not answering. Not looking at him. Not hearing him?

This whole conversation had been too heated, too angry, not something to inspire sharing of confidences. With a sigh, he dragged a chair over, gesturing for her to take it, and asked more gently, "What were you scared of?"

Anais sat in the chair and leaned forward, putting her elbows on her knees—the way he often sat when angry or stressed—and then systemically turned her head and scanned every inch of the room, still not answering him.

Something inside him didn't want to accept that she'd been scared. The word rankled.

He understood fear now, really understood it. He hadn't then; nothing in his life had ever been so bad that he couldn't face it before his first tour. But Anais had grown up differently than he had. She'd come from a poor urban area, she'd worked hard to get scholarships and the best grades she could, but her life before university—and anytime she'd gone home on holidays—was anything but safe and comforting. She'd been acquainted with real fear long before he had. And the idea that he'd left her alone with that fear curdled his stomach.

"Anais?" He said her name softly as he dropped into a crouch before her, eye-to-eye with her where she leaned in his favorite position. She bolted back, ramrod straight, wariness darkening her unnaturally brown eyes.

"Can we take out the contacts for good now? The cat is out of the bag, Princess. Brown contacts aren't going to hide you anymore."

Reflexively, she rubbed the base of her throat, then

twisted her hands in her lap. "I guess they weren't as effective as I'd hoped."

"Didn't work on me." He smiled, tired but willing to let go of his anger to get through to her.

It worked. She reached up and plucked the contacts from her eyes, and when she focused on him again those blue-green eyes warmed him like a hand reaching out from the past to pull him back to her. As if the past seven years had never happened. But then he remembered it had. And he remembered why he'd crouched before her.

"Thank you." He tried again, "What scared you? Please tell me."

"Something happened that I didn't want anyone to know about. It would've ruined…everything." She gestured helplessly, and looked back toward the kitchen. "I need to throw these away."

When she looked back at him, she squinted over his shoulder and leaned forward slightly, staring across the room. "I think it's under the sofa."

A secret. She'd tried to share a secret with him, to ask for his help, and he'd not listened to her? The idea was so unthinkable that when her digression came he was thankful to turn his attention to the sofa.

He'd thrown it. The memory swam back through the rum-soaked haze that had separated him from it, and he rose to go fetch the documents.

A moment later he had the envelope. Anais joined him, sitting a seat away on the other side of the sofa, and leaning toward him just enough to see the documents he withdrew. There was a note inside stating that the documents would be filed as soon as he signed, and several places flagged throughout where he'd need to put his name.

"Damn," she muttered and then scrubbed both hands over her face. "Is there an expiration time on those kinds of documents? If you sign now can they still be filed or do we have to have solicitors redraft the whole business and start over?"

Start over.

He had no idea what the answer to her question was, but he knew the answer he wanted. Start over. With her. They weren't divorced. They weren't the same people. Things could be different this time…

CHAPTER FIVE

"WHAT HAPPENED IN your past that you didn't want people to find out about?"

"Quinn, focus on the papers."

"I am."

"No, you're focusing on things that only mattered when we had a marriage to save. And you said you didn't want to get married again." She went to finally toss the contacts, but he'd swear it was to shut down the conversation.

And that was too bad. He wasn't ready; he'd waited years so she could give him more than a few minutes. "I don't. I married you. Yeah, you left, and we both thought we were divorced..."

"We are divorced."

"Until I put my name on these documents, we're still married." Quinn dropped them onto the coffee table and turned to face her, ignoring the hitch in his chest that came from her words. "Marrying you wasn't the wrong decision. Maybe I failed at being a husband in every regard, but marrying you wasn't wrong. You feel it too, or you and I would not have ended up on the floor together within seconds of being alone in a room. You still want me."

"Chemistry. As I said. And you said that was a goodbye or did you forget that too?"

"We have chemistry and a legally binding marriage. Unless you want to take it to court and let them decide." He couldn't focus on the goodbye bit. He'd said it at the time more from anger than because he'd thought it through.

"What could you possibly say in court to make people believe this is a real marriage? You and I haven't had a scrap of communication in years. You didn't know where I worked, you didn't know about my name change, you didn't even know I was back in the country." She flung her hands up, as if those sad facts won the argument and he was too simple to see it.

So quiet he could barely hear himself over his own pounding heart, Quinn answered, "I'd say I still love you."

For a second, he thought she was going to slug him. His words hung there in the air as those blue-green eyes narrowed and her nostrils flared.

Definitely going to do something to him.

Quinn waited, holding her gaze…

"Well, that's just perfect!" she finally shouted, throwing her arms toward the ceiling, her voice rising with every word. "You still love me. Great. That's *great.* Because it worked out so well last time. Not that I believe you. You've tarted your way across at least four continents on your leave over the last few years. Because it gets around, you know. News. Playboy Prince back at it, once unsaddled from his horrible bride. Of course, I'm sure you were thinking of me the whole time!"

"I'm not making excuses for seven years of perceived bachelorhood. You don't need to explain how you've spent that time either—and, for both our sakes, I beg you not to. It doesn't matter now." He said the words quietly enough that she had to stop her tirade to hear him. "You should know better than to believe everything you read in the gossip rags."

"So those pictures were just faked? No cover models?"

Words he'd said just to upset her on that first day had apparently hit their target. He gritted his teeth. *Stay on track.* What good could come from making her believe the worst of him when it wasn't true? "There's never been anyone else. Not in any way that counted. Not in any way that couldn't happen in public."

Her head fell back, eyes swiveled to the ceiling as she breathed out. It only lasted long enough to name it: relief. Long enough for her too, by the tension rocketing through her.

Relief to rage.

Her still lovely features twisted and, with a sound caught somewhere between a scream and a sob, she took three wide steps across the room and returned with the wrought iron poker which had been leaning beside the fireplace.

He tensed, ready to defend himself, even if the very idea that she'd actually attack him was so alien it made the world tilt.

She lifted the thing and brought it down with all her might on the glass-topped table where the unsigned divorce documents rested. Once. Twice. Again. Again. Punctuating each swing with a word either grunted or screamed. "I. Hate. This. *Table*."

White spots in the shape of the poker appeared with each swing until finally a resounding crack announced a split in the top. He flinched and leaned back as she brought the iron rod down again.

Another smash shattered it, leaving the documents lying amongst the broken shards.

He made it up and around the table's remains as she shifted her attention to the metal base and brought the weapon down again. "I. Hate. This. Table. Hate. Hate. *Hate*."

When she changed her swing, Quinn took the opening and shot out his left damaged hand, stopping her swing. The force of the impact sent a spike of pain spreading through what remained of his palm and up his arm.

The shock of hitting something living made her let go, and she froze on the spot, looking at him, looking at his hand. He flung the rod down and then swept her up in his still aching arms to track away from the coffee table carnage.

"What are you doing? Put me down!" She squirmed until he released her across the room, away from any shattered glass spray. Before she could get any distance, he locked his good hand around her wrist, and felt her fist ball.

The pit that had opened in him as he saw her destroy the coffee table began to make his guts swirl. "More violence? This is not you."

Anais was gentle. Tender-hearted. She didn't go on destructive rampages when upset. She got very quiet, she spent time alone. Sometimes she cried. She didn't break things.

At least this smashing spree was easier on his equilibrium than watching her cry had ever been, but he still felt the need to stop it. He raised his voice. "Stop fighting. I'm no danger."

"Every second I'm with you I'm in danger!"

Reactive words to make him back off. Part of him even wanted to, but the biggest thoughts echoing in his mind refused to let him leave.

She hadn't broken them. She'd just been the one to walk away from his mess.

"I could never be a danger to you," he said softly, holding her gaze, praying she actually heard him. He'd heard her—even if it'd taken nearly eight years if he counted their marriage.

He'd always known they'd been in trouble, but he'd also thought they'd have more time. He'd thought he'd be able to get her to stay until the tide turned, that something would happen, that opinions would change. Because they had been in trouble, but he'd still wanted her with every piece of him.

He still did. Yes, they'd changed. She was a doctor now. He was a man, not just walking around in a man's body. Surely the people wouldn't see them the same way.

"Let me go."

The demand came, and neither of them pretended it didn't mean more than a simple request to release her wrist.

"No," he said, keeping eye contact and his hold on her arm. "It was a mistake last time."

"I don't want to be your wife."

"I didn't want to go into the military. Or get divorced. Amazingly, both of those things worked out well for me. I'm not the same man I was, Anais. Tell me what you were afraid of."

"That's nothing you need to know anymore," she said through gritted teeth. "What I'm currently afraid of? Staying married to you. I don't want to be part of the PR parade that is being a princess. I hated it the first time, and this time it will only be worse."

She swung her arm up to her face and, with her free arm, grabbed his wrist in return. Without missing a beat, she turned out to the side, twisting his arm at the shoulder.

He wasn't ready for it, and the twist and sharp stab of pain made him let go of her wrist. Just as she'd wanted.

"I never fit. I could never fit or be accepted—it was futile. All I ever was, all I could ever be, was a stain on you and your family. That's still what I'd be."

Stepping away from him, she grabbed her bag and swung it over her shoulder, but paused when she looked at him, at the shock he could feel written on his face. She'd easily slipped his hold and, more importantly—she could've really hurt him if she'd wanted to. Did *Gray's Anatomy* include a section on self-defense and the best way to dislocate a shoulder? What, in God's name, had she been up in the States?

"You never fought for us, Quinn," she said, plucking his thoughts in his face. "You never fought for me. You never even met me on the damned battlefield. After you, I had to learn to fight for myself."

She was nearly at the door. Leaving a conversation she didn't want to be part of—something she'd probably learned from him. Fighting might make her stay. "Looks to me like you learned to hide yourself."

"I did that too." She swung the door open and looked back at him. "Do yourself and your whole family a favor. Sign the papers."

She didn't blink, and there was a warning in her stare: *get ready for a fight.*

"What are we doing here, Doc?" Ben asked, sounding tired already even though Quinn knew this was the first time during his stay at Almsford that he'd been to the gym. Physical therapists were required to ask every day but, since his attempted hanging, they hadn't been pushing anything. Not that he couldn't still be tired; emotional exhaustion was more insidious than the physical variety.

"What do you think we're doing?"

"Some kind of lesson on perseverance, I guess." The disgruntled tone at least sounded a little more energetic than it had seconds before.

Quinn parked the wheelchair where they could both watch an amputee patient using the parallel bars for stability while he walked on a new prosthesis under direction from a physical therapist.

"Nailed it," Quinn said.

"Not exactly the same situation," Ben said after spending a few brief seconds watching the man. "He's still got a functioning leg. I'm missing two."

"One and a half," Quinn corrected, fetched himself a chair and sat down beside Ben. "With a prosthetic on your longer leg, you could use crutches and get out of this chair. Then, after you got used to one, you could go for the other."

"Your wife feed you that line?"

"Gave me the literature. Why? Would you be more willing to hear it if it came from Rosalie? I'm sure she'd tell you the same, if you'd see her."

Ben eyed him sideways, "Don't make this harder. She deserves better and you'd feel the same way."

He was talking about his other injury, the one he didn't discuss directly. And, since he didn't, Quinn didn't tackle it head-on either. In a way, this not talking felt productive and safe, but he could see it being too indirect to deliver any results either. "There's a fix for everything, brother."

"You tell that whopper to your wife too?"

He didn't really want to talk about Anais, but Ben had brought her up twice. "Haven't exactly. Woman damned near broke my hand, and then my arm last night. Right after she obliterated my coffee table with a fireplace poker."

Ben's brows shot up. "Guess I'm lucky she didn't have a weapon handy yesterday when I called her a bad princess."

There was no containing his wince. "She wasn't a bad princess. She just never had a chance. Starting to think it was my fault too. Philip told me to clean it up. He meant to settle the divorce, make it official, but I don't want to."

"Because she didn't have a chance?"

"No. I don't know. I just can't wrap my head around the idea of letting her get away a second time." If they were doing this about Anais, he wasn't backing off Rosalie. "I never could let her go. Neither will Rosalie. If you keep on, you're sentencing her to a half-life. She'll never get over you, and you know it."

"She's stronger than you."

"Tell yourself lies, if that's what you've got to do," Quinn muttered. "She said I never fought for her. Don't know what irritates me more—the idea of it, or that she's right. I'm not making that same mistake again."

"Helen's going to be so happy to see us. You should've heard her when I called to say we were coming."

Anais checked the rearview as Mom spoke, noting the long string of cars still following all the way from her townhouse to the main street in Easton.

Security? Media? She didn't know who they were, just took a small amount of comfort in the distance between her back bumper and their front. All the while trying not to let on to Mom how nervous they made her. "It's good of her to be willing to open the shop on her day off."

"Are you worried about coming?"

Of course she'd noticed. Even with seven years of ocean between them, Mom had been able to read her through nothing but a phone line. Sometimes less. Sometimes she'd known when to call.

This was supposed to be a happy visit for Mom, and Anais didn't want to ruin it. "I'm glad we decided to come. It'll be nice to see everyone, and maybe Aunt Helen can help me peel away another layer of Anna and look more myself. It'll be nice to see me when I look in the mirror."

"That won't be a problem. At least with your hair. I don't know about your skin, though."

"She might have some tricks. People will have come to her about an overly orange experience before. But I'll exfoliate later. Always makes it fade faster."

Anna's look no longer served her, and might never serve her again—even if she truly needed it. If she couldn't get this marriage situation smoothly and quickly sorted out, she might need to run again. The thought shot a pang through her belly. What could she do then? Cut her hair off? Gain weight? Plastic surgery? Would Mom come too next time? Anais couldn't leave her behind again. Not now.

The small inner-city salon came into view; directly in front of the building was an empty parking place. Anais darted into it and parked before looking up and down the street to take inventory.

Cars lined both sides of the street, nowhere else to park. Maybe that would work in their favor—deter some of the vehicles following them.

They bundled out of the car and Anais waited for her mother to go into the salon ahead of her, then turned to track the progress of the vehicles, making mental note of the makes and colors.

One of them squeezed into a spot just after another car pulled out, but the other four picked up speed and headed uptown.

"Must have found a better headline than *Princess Visits Salon*," Mom said from beside her, arm coming around her waist. "Well, most of them. That one black car probably hasn't heard about whatever is happening yet."

She was trying to help, and that defeated the whole point of Anais's plan to give her mother a good day with her sister and friends, since moving in with Anais had separated them. To take her mind off their uncertain future, and how that might increase the distance between them if they were forced to leave. "Go say hi to Aunt Helen. She's probably about to explode in a shower of fabulous glitter by now."

They'd no sooner stepped inside and away from the door than Anais heard a click behind her and a spike of fear had her spinning to face the danger. A pink-smocked woman she didn't recognize had locked the door. "To keep them cameras out, Princess."

The uniform marked her as an employee, which abated Anais's alarm a little. She really had to do better if she wanted Mom to have a good day. "Thank you, that's a good idea. Don't… I'm not really a princess. It's all a mistake. Please call me Anais."

She'd pretend the door locking would keep everyone out, not just the lawful people who wouldn't break through the wide picture window upon which the salon name had been painted.

Anais focused again through the window on the black sedan that had followed them; the window was rolled down, and she half expected to see Quinn sitting there, but she saw a man in a black suit instead, with an earpiece. He nodded once to her across the way, and the darkened window rolled back up.

Royal Security.

Great. Now the King had gotten involved. Was that better than cameras or worse?

Worse, she decided. It validated the situation somehow. Made Quinn's cooperation seem less likely.

A flurry of greetings broke in on her thoughts and before long she'd been ushered out of her jacket, into hugs, and finally a spinning chair, and some nice person muted the still running television on the wall behind her. Although Easton had never fit her either, there was a homey feeling to her aunt's salon—somewhere she'd safely spent hours with her nose in books and where no one had made fun or bullied the local Poindexter.

Work, card games with her friends; Mom was there so much that Anais was practically related to their core group—they all thought she was brilliant, and had been proud of her marriage. People she'd let down in many ways—some they still didn't know about and wouldn't, so long as those pictures stayed private.

She almost felt as if she belonged there, a feeling she'd been looking for when she'd set her sights and non-existent seduction skills on Wayne Ratliffe. The idea had been: community acceptance through the coolest guy in the neighborhood. Get him to like her; the rest would fall in line.

It was everything past the idea that had gone wrong. Her teenage brain had no execution skills. Pretending to be cool meant drinking the alcohol he'd given her. Two drinks in, making out sounded like winning. Three drinks in, he'd convinced her that girls who took pride in their bodies shared them with boyfriends… And then the pictures…

She should be paying attention to what they were saying.

She felt Mom's gaze before she saw it as Mom launched in with the talking Anais was failing to do. "Strip out the brunette…dye the proper shade back if needed…blah-blah-blah…spray tan removal…"

Their excitement redirected easily enough, Anais settled in, with tired but genuine smiles dutifully mustered.

Helen spun her so that she could watch the window through the mirror in front of her, and got to work, whisking a protective cape around her and snagging a bowl of foul-smelling chemicals with an applicator.

No book today; she could either fixate on her past stupidity, stare paranoid out the window or listen.

Or she could think about Quinn, since they were chatting about him now.

It had been two days since she'd seen him and Hulk-smashed his coffee table. The urge to break it, or throw it off the perfect balcony, had been with her every day, starting about the fourth month of their marriage—when they'd been gifted with the keys. Prior to that, they'd lived in a small flat near the country's best university—and social strata—a scholarship had granted her access to, and had come to the capital on the weekends to try and get his family used to her and for her to take some solace with her mom.

Someone else had bought the penthouse.

Someone else had decorated it.

Someone who probably thought a microbiology major would want obsessively modern tastes, which had instead shocked her system. But their whole marriage had been a shock to her system. And they'd spent so much time in the bedroom, she'd convinced herself that the rest of the apartment didn't matter. Just like she'd originally bought Quinn's notion that the rest of the world didn't matter. Until it began to matter. Until she'd started seeing glimpses of Wayne. Until Wayne had made clear it was still true—that she'd never belong with Quinn any more than she'd belonged in Easton.

She still didn't know whether or not she'd actually seen him early on, or if it had just been her subconscious worrying her about that part of her past she'd been ignoring, that part which would come up and derail them. Corrachlean had remained a monarchy, steeped in traditional values through the centuries. It was a quaint culture that embraced certain modern notions—like equality—while still clinging to old values. A super-common princess raised by a single, never-married woman, who hadn't even a father named on her birth certificate, was impossible to accept, even without adding low-class nudies.

And Anais couldn't even make an excuse for it—at least not one that made her seem less pathetic.

They could never accept her and she still so desperately wanted them to.

Even Quinn wouldn't if he found out. He accepted her as she was, or as he thought her to be: sensible, with good judgment, highly intelligent—*brutally intelligent,* he'd once called her as a compliment. He loved that about her. Her act of extreme stupidity would counter that argument very effectively, even without introducing jealousy into the mix.

"Anais…"

Her mother's voice broke in as her chair began to spin, and soon she was looking at Quinn in full regalia on the television while one of the women scrambled to find the remote they'd just had moments ago, and a chill shot through her.

"Is he doing it?" Mom asked just as the volume returned and TV Quinn stopped nodding and waving and started to speak.

"I don't know. I hope so."

"Ladies and gentlemen, thank you for coming today."

Quinn stood at a podium in front of a sea of reporters, cameras rolling and, with a patience she couldn't believe he possessed, waited for them to get serious footage. She'd seen nothing of him on film—nothing past the grainy night shot of her giving him the documents for Ben.

He wore such a grave expression; for a moment she thought he was going to announce something serious about the King. The royals were always loved by the media—

except for her—but she hadn't seen any recent footage of the King, come to think of it.

But the Playboy Prince wasn't smiling. Not joking. Not charming them into letting him get away with murder.

"Today I want to speak to you about my wife, Dr. Anais Hayes or, as she's been known since returning to Corrachlean, Dr. Anna Kincaid. I know you're shocked, and really we were both surprised to find out the dissolution of our marriage had never been finalized. But it was a happy surprise."

Her anxiety beast reared up in her belly and started chewing.

"Oh, sweet mercy, don't do this, Quinn," Anais whispered, and only remembered she stood in public with foil in her hair when Mom's hand found hers and made her fingers release the knot she'd twisted her protective cape into.

"What's he doing?" Mom asked, the question whispered.

"He's..." Public. They were in public. Even if it were just Mom, Aunt Helen, and a couple of Mom's friends. She could trust family to keep things quiet, but maybe spilling any secrets in front of friends—no matter how close—wasn't the best idea.

She tried to force a placid air. "I don't know what he's doing. He didn't tell me he was having a press conference."

"Since we last saw Anais she's been in the United States. She took all the pain that came from our parting and channeled it. Made it through medical school with astounding grades—in keeping with the way she tackled university—and over the course of her training specialized in helping those who have served our country and paid the price with their bodies. I can't think of a more honorable, a more noble mission to dedicate her life to. I'm very proud of her."

Dammit.

"He's right," Aunt Helen said, and Anais couldn't argue because...what could she say? *I made a series of decisions that led to him losing his fingers; the least I could do was help others who suffered a similar fate?*

Over the years, his official royal uniform had been remade to fit his broadening frame, and in that time he'd really learned how to wear it. He looked more comfortable in it than she remembered and, even without the decorative epaulettes, his shoulders were broad and square beneath the tailored lines.

"I want to be clear now. The divorce was never finalized because of my inaction. She signed where she was told to sign, and I assumed that someone took care of those things for me and never checked in when I was home on leave. We've never had a divorce, and we're not going to have one now. I'm asking you to give us the space we need to fit our lives back together. I'll do whatever I need to protect her. I came home to fulfill my duty to my family, and she is *my family, so I'm starting with my wife. If we have to leave Corrachlean to have any kind of peace together, to have the family we were always meant to have, we'll leave. I don't want that to happen."*

"Did he just threaten to abdicate?" Mom asked, alarm evident, and three other sets of eyes swiveled to Anais.

"He's not going to be King," Anais murmured, even though she heard his intention as clearly. "He can't abdicate, but I think maybe he threatened to renounce his title."

Why in the name of heaven would he do that?

He seemed done talking, and once again stood stoically for the cameras, waiting.

Then the questions began…

CHAPTER SIX

AFTER THE PRESS conference Quinn changed and nicked a car from the palace garage. Forgoing a driver, he followed his GPS to Anais's town home.

Nice, quiet, upper middle class neighborhood. The late summer sunshine filtered through the leaves on the tree-lined street, one broad beam of light illuminating a parking place directly in front of her home. His opening gambit in the fight she'd threatened had felt right at the time but, going to face her now, his mind seemed some insane cocktail of worry, pessimism, and straight-up giddiness.

Fortune favored the brave, but he had no idea what it did with the inappropriately giddy. No man should be excited to fight with the woman he loved, but the other evening he'd felt closer to Anais than he had during their whole marriage. It was hard not to look forward to that kind of fire.

He parked the understated black sedan and hurried to her door. The street was quiet and more or less empty, aside from a woman walking her dog down the opposite side. The press seemed to have listened to his request—at least for now. No cars had followed him and he could see no cameras camped at her door.

He rang the bell and slipped a hand into his pocket, feeling the weight of the velvet box he'd retrieved from the crate tucked in there.

The ring she might not accept.

Probably wouldn't accept.

Might even smash with whatever weapon she had handy…

His pulse increased the longer he stood there. Just stick to the plan. Tell her they were staying married. Explain his plan to seduce the press. Tell her…

Still no one answered the door. He pressed the bell again.

Maybe she'd gone. Fled the country already. Had she had time for that since his announcement?

As he reached for the bell again, the door cracked open. Eyes that had once no doubt been the exact blue-green shade of Anais's found him, paler but distinctive enough to recognize the mother-in-law he hadn't seen in years.

"Sharon. Hello. Is…she here?"

"She's upstairs." No greeting, but she did let him inside. "She went to bed with a headache, but said to send you up if you came by."

Expecting him. Perhaps lying in wait with a fireplace poker…

The door closed behind him and she took a moment to engage the locks, something he was thankful to hear as he'd already started up the stairs.

"Last door," Sharon called after him. "Don't drive her away again, Quinton Corlow. She needs a home. She was happy here the past month."

He stopped midflight and looked back down at her, nodding because he didn't know what to say. But she had already turned and picked up a book she'd obviously been reading before he rang the bell, and sat on one end of the sofa.

From his position, he could see downstairs well enough to realize the stark difference in style between it and the penthouse. Bookshelves everywhere, loaded sometimes two rows deep with books. Furniture he could best describe as fluffy. Comfortable and welcoming, and…not why he was there. Later. He'd keep it in mind later when they looked for alternate housing to the penthouse. Or maybe just lived here… He wanted her to be happy in her home, and the penthouse had obviously failed in that.

Last door upstairs, he reminded himself, and completed the climb.

Stick to the plan.

The white panel door stood silently where indicated, no signs of movement beyond. No light below the door, and it was still daylight. But she was in there. He could feel her inside.

Taking a chance, he bypassed knocking, and instead peeked inside as quietly as the door would allow. Anais lay atop the blankets, eyes closed. Asleep?

The creak of the door opening brought Anais fully awake, "Mom?" The word came out before she'd even gotten her eyes fully open.

Quinn slipped into the room and faced her. Since his press conference, he'd changed back into the fatigues he'd been wearing most of the time when not in full royal regalia. "Sharon said you weren't feeling well. Has your head improved?"

"Not entirely. But it doesn't feel like my skull is being cleaved in two right now. Are you going to make it worse?" She stood up; it felt like the kind of conversation she'd be better able to handle on her feet, and with some light. She switched on the bedside lamp.

"Your hair…"

The wonder in his voice had her looking at him again. As she'd turned to the lamp, he'd crossed to her and now stood less than a foot away, his broken hand suddenly cupping her jaw. While she'd expected him to come by, she'd been unable to come up with a way to handle this thing he'd thrown at her. Now, with his hand on her face and the way his eyes searched her every feature, the pull of him further scrambled her thoughts.

"It's you. Finally." He swallowed hard, brows pressed too sharply together; he almost looked in pain, as if he'd just lost her, as if he couldn't bear to blink and risk her disappearing. The hand cupping her jaw stayed, but his free hand slid into her hair and smoothed the locks between his fingers. He finally looked from her face to the strand to watch the play of the color in the light. "It's really close. A little lighter than normal, like you've been at the beach."

The words, so at odds with the reverence and pain in his face, yanked her back into herself. "Aunt Helen stripped out the brunette today. Probably took a little extra color with it..."

"You're beautiful." A reverent whisper. The heat from his hand on her cheek left a fiery trail down her neck and over the skin bared by the strappy tank top she'd worn for sleep. His eyes followed his hand over her shoulder, then over her chest, concealed by the thin material she wore.

Beautiful, he'd said—the word, his voice, and his eyes said the same. He looked at her with an intensity and longing that twisted at her insides. She drew closer.

"Your skin is so soft."

Her palms ached and she rested them against his chest, felt the muscle bunch and tighten under her touch, and slid them higher toward his neck, just to feel his skin under her aching hands.

Sweet mercy, what was she doing?

She should move away right now. Take him to another room. She'd just wanted some privacy to talk when she'd told Mom to send him up, to keep her from being dragged further into this mess.

"In the desert, in the heat, everything felt sharp." He still stroked up and down her arms, speaking so quietly she wasn't even sure he knew he was speaking. "The wind would come and the sand felt like a million tiny knives. I liked to think about soft things, soothe myself with memories..."

In the wake of his hands, that dizzying tingle returned,

following his fingers and spreading out from them like an epicenter for some heart earthquake. Head sparkles and feet like lead came from the worshipful things he said.

"I could never remember anything softer than your skin. Could spend infinity stroking your skin."

He leaned forward and she lost all will to resist as his lips touched her shoulder—softness framed by the delicious scrape of the day's beard, scrubbing her mind.

He didn't kiss—there was no kissing—time stretched out as he simply stroked his warm, full lips feather-light over her shoulder, into the curve of her neck, then up into the hair behind her ear.

"You belong with me," he murmured, arms sliding around to bring her fully against him. "And I belong with you."

Yes.

Warmth rolled through her. It was like a drug. He was like a drug.

Her cheek rested against the center of his chest and she leaned against him as he stayed, head curled down, so that his every word was spoken into her skin, like a brand she'd never be able to scrub off.

"I know how to make it work this time. I know how to make them listen, make them love you too. I have a plan."

If he'd thrown her into Arctic tides off the northern coast he couldn't have surpassed the shock that lanced through her.

He was doing it again! Distraction. Distraction and sex and sweet words, and she fell for it every cursed time.

She jolted back, an accusing finger jabbing his way to convey the words stuck in her throat.

"Easy now."

"I'm not a horse!" she blurted out, possibly the dumbest thing she'd ever said in anger. Which was *his* fault too. Touching him never did anything good for her cognition. "Is this part of your plan? *Oh, Anais, you're so beautiful...*"

Two more big steps backward gave her more room to breathe, to think, but Quinn seemed to be amused more than anything. Amused and…exhilarated.

But it passed quickly.

"No." With the one word, the silk fell from his tone, along with the excited light in his eyes. "I have a publicity plan. They listened today. They're not loitering at your door. They didn't follow me here. They're listening. Our situation has changed."

Now she remembered what she'd gone to sleep to try and forget—his ridiculous press conference where he'd tried to make the people like her by telling them she was a doctor. "You threatened to renounce your title. That's why they're listening. They have to see how serious you are before calling your bluff. That'll take them at least a day. A week if you're lucky."

"You say that like it was an empty threat."

"You know it was empty. You're not going to follow through on that. You want to be here or you'd still be serving. Whatever you just said about soothing memories of softness. You didn't leave the military after your injury, and I know they would have offered it to you."

"We could argue this all day and you'd still be wrong." He waved a hand. "That's not what I was talking about. Our situation is different because you're different. You're accomplished, not just a common girl the daft Prince fell for. And there's nothing people like better than a fairy tale. All we have to do is give them the fairy tale, Cinderella. Do some appearances…"

"Some appearances? You're talking about more than appearances!"

"We'll go through with The Sip; I've already got someone organizing the invitation lottery on that since the people complained about missing it the first time. They'll eat it up."

"Of course they complained. It's Corrachlean's centuries-old royal engagement traditional party, and everyone loves free-flowing mead and bad decision-making." She grunted when her head throbbed again.

"Not you."

"No, not me," she replied.

"And then we'll have the lavish wedding every Cinderella would dream of." He crossed to her again and leaned past her to pick up a bottle of pain relievers. "When did you last take one?"

"Too recently, even though they're clearly worthless." She took a breath, smelled only him, and then took another couple of steps away from him in the other direction so she could try and maintain some semblance of sense. "I don't want this."

"And I don't want a divorce. Besides, I don't believe you. You were right there with me moments ago. You were right there with me on your office floor. It's still there. We're not going to be the first divorce in the history of the royal family. You wanted me to fight for you? This is me fighting for you."

Her cheeks burned—like she needed to be reminded how easy he could have her. She stammered, "It's too late for grand gestures."

"I don't accept that."

"Because you say it's not? I can't go back to that unforgiving spotlight. I don't want to be a freaking princess—"

"What's the alternative?" he cut in. "Tell me what your plan was after our faulty divorce was discovered. Just to wait for the fervor to die down? I tried that once; you lost your mind. You already are *a freaking* princess, in the most literal sense. Right now. That's who you are. Princess Anais Corlow, not Hayes, and sure as hell not Kincaid."

"Legally, I'm Dr. Anna Kincaid."

"Actually, you're not. Philip doesn't have the authority to unilaterally rename a princess and strip her of her title. It's invalid, like those unsigned divorce documents."

Shock that she hadn't considered that sent her scrambling. "Fine! Whatever. I don't have a plan for any of this. You just threw it at me on live TV. I've been trying to figure out how to make this go away; you're just making it worse."

"I could make it much worse."

The quietly delivered statement made her breath catch. That was a threat. By this point in her life she knew a threat when she heard one, and that was a threat. She didn't even have to take the coldness of his tone into consideration, or the way his deep gray eyes hardened over like ice sheets blowing in from the North Sea. "What are you saying?"

"I'm saying the press listened to me today. We can give them the fairy tale, or I can give them my heartbreak. How long do you think it will take to die down if I tell them I came home from a war zone to this, that you led me on then broke my heart again?"

She wobbled and staggered backwards until the wall stopped her. Quinn reached for her, but she'd stopped before he could cross the distance to her.

"That's you fighting for me, or just with me? I think I like the old Quinn better; at least he wasn't…horrible." Old Quinn joked, used happy distractions, in retrospect. This Quinn? She didn't know him.

"I am fighting for us."

"By lying and manipulating people? You know that's not what happened."

"I just told them we weren't getting divorced and how happy that made me. Two true things."

"You're blackmailing me now? I already have one blackmailer; I don't need two!"

A flash of fire in his eyes alerted her to the words that had flown from her mouth. His long stride ate up the distance between them and his hands on her shoulders kept her facing him, fingers biting into her shoulders enough to trigger an ache, which should've blocked out that damnable tingling, but didn't. "You have a blackmailer?"

She shook her head immediately, desperate for some

way to rewind that accidental confession. "No. Kind of. I did have."

"You had a blackmailer?"

"And, you know, I could have two if you're joining the ranks." She laughed bitterly as she sifted through anything she could say to salvage this.

Nothing could put that genie back into the bottle. But maybe it would tell him exactly how unacceptable she'd be as a royal if the pictures were ever leaked.

"Blackmailed over what, Anais? By whom?" The way he looked at her made it impossible to look away.

"I have nude photos. Out there. Someone else…has them." The words came out broken, and just having to say them made her feel broken. "You can't have those and be a princess without getting a blackmailer. That's just a little fact of life I learned about ten months after we eloped. There's no way to spin that into a fairy tale. Cinderella only had to overcome being the help. Not being incredibly stupid one regrettable night."

"Ten months?" he repeated, his brow pinching as the cogs started clicking into place.

"Yes. Ten months. And for a whole month I tried." The air had gone thin; she breathed too hard and had to swivel her eyes upward to keep the stinging tears from falling. "Never mind. Just accept that I have this, and he will come back. Now that you've done this, he'll come back. He's… He's coming back."

"Someone you were dating?" He wasn't backing off.

"No. Kind of. I was a teenager. He was just a guy in my neighborhood."

That answer took away some of the tension from his frame. "And?"

"And what?" She ducked from beneath his clamping hands, and darted across the room again. "He found me after we were married and demanded money or he'd sell the photos; he carried a huge grudge over some other things, and I didn't know how to make him go away. At first I told him it would take me a while to get the money—and, considering the amount he wanted, he accepted that. I tried to work out how to fix it, and how to tell you, and I tried so many times, but it never worked. So, I left. Okay? I removed myself so at least if he did come out with them you'd be blameless. Because what could you do then? I'd already be gone and my leaving would've been good news to the people."

Despite the wild look in his eyes, Quinn didn't chase her this time—her first nod to hope. He got it, or he was getting it. "You never told me any of this."

"I tried. Every time I brought up the terrible public outcry against my very existence, you'd change the subject or we'd end up naked."

"Quinn, I'm being blackmailed," he said. "That's all you had to say to stop my coping mechanisms."

"Oh, sure." She stilled, the spike drilling down into the top of her head jabbing again. "Because that's the way to make your new husband eager to feel helpful and protective. We *didn't talk* about things. We didn't. We played, we flirted, we teased, and we spent more time naked than we spent clothed together."

"That's an exaggeration."

"It doesn't feel like one."

He stopped the question with a wave of his hand. "Just give me his name. Where does he live?"

"Like we've been pen pals all this time? I don't know where he is and won't until he comes at me again. I don't even know why he never sold the photos after I left without paying him. That whole first year away, I expected it to show up on my Internet alerts but it never did."

Quinn crossed to her desk, picked up a pad and pen from the tidy top, and handed it to her. "Write down his name, approximate age, where he used to live, whatever you remember."

"What are you going to do?" She took the pad, but didn't yet start writing.

"I'm going to fight for my wife. You don't need details, unless you're worried I might hurt him."

"I don't care if you hurt him." She wrote Wayne Ratliffe's name, the address of his former dingy apartment around the corner to where she'd grown up, lingered briefly over the five-year age difference between them... Then handed the pad back to Quinn, unsure how to feel about it. He hadn't gotten it yet; maybe he still needed to work through it. Until then, Quinn had access to people to handle these sorts of situations, she didn't, and it would serve him and the family if this didn't come out.

Even if those weren't legit reasons to accept his help, it would do her sanity good—that prickling feeling that Wayne was waiting just around every corner had resurfaced the instant she'd learned they were still married and the world knew it.

Quinn ripped the top sheet off and set the pad back on the desk, then fished a small box from his pocket and set it on top of the paper.

Without asking or opening the box, she knew.

Engagement ring.

Another sinking in her stomach she'd have to ignore.

CHAPTER SEVEN

"ANAIS, HONEY, HE'S HERE, and he's brought the whole brigade with him."

Anais sucked in a deep breath and rose from the least comfortable and least wrinkle-inducing chair in her living room, and smoothed her hands over the pretty white eyelet lace dress she'd purchased yesterday for today's outing with Quinn. "Do I look okay? I feel silly, wearing such a dress for a walk in the park."

"You always look beautiful, and the sandals make it a little more sensible."

"All that's missing is a big floppy hat and oversized glasses," she joked and leaned over to hug the worry out of her mother.

The squeeze she got in return bolstered her courage. It had only taken three days of constantly weighing Quinn's proposal to decide there were more pros than cons. Mom's worry was what finally made her come around. She couldn't run again. Mom deserved to have her and her sister in her life. If the heart condition had frightened Anais enough to go to Philip for help, she'd find the courage to do whatever she had to do to stay.

"You don't have to do anything you don't want to do. We can leave. Any country would be lucky to have a talented, caring doctor come to them."

"I know, Mom." She kissed her mother's cheek, glad

she'd kept her big list of reasons to herself. Mom's heart reacted badly to stress; the situation already worried her enough she'd been popping in and out of rhythm since the press first showed up on their doorstep.

It would all be worth it to stay and keep her healthy; no matter what Mom said about leaving together, this was her home.

As long as Quinn could take care of Wayne.

"It's going to be okay. Things might still change, but you know Quinn's never been cruel to me. I'm going to play it by ear. You're not going to have to leave home or Aunt Helen. Try not to worry, okay?"

She made some sound that both affirmed her intention to not worry while highlighting her disbelief that Anais thought it was possible not to.

The bell rang, Anais smoothed her hands over the cheerful princess dress again, and paused by the entrance table to eye the velvet box there. She still hadn't opened it, and couldn't even say why. After grabbing a small matching handbag, she carefully picked up the box as if it were rigged to explode, put it into her bag, and stepped out of the house and into Quinn.

Without missing a beat, he kissed her cheek and took her hand in his left, the usual way they'd held hands. "You look beautiful. I think I'm underdressed."

Threats last time, charm today. And she'd ignore the heart flip that happened when he'd kissed her. The threat didn't need to be forgotten; it was a reminder why she had to go with the flow until he caught up with her on the only sensible, peaceful way their lives could go. The one where *he* dumped *her* this time, and the media lost interest.

She stepped back far enough to get a look at him. The gray slacks he wore were obviously made for the man, crisp and lightweight but still tailored. His white button-down sat open at the collar, revealing the thick masculine neck that...said as much about his transition from boy to man as anything could. He'd gone from slim and lithe to broad and strong, and the definition in his neck made it clear to her how the rest of his body would reflect this strength.

"You look great." She didn't comment on his freshly shaved jaw, the curls starting in the thick brown hair that had grown out of the neat military cut he would have worn since enlisting. Ignore that too; she didn't need reminding of the boyish, carefree fop she'd always delighted in running her fingers through.

"Somehow that didn't sound like a compliment," he murmured, then looked at their joined hands, paused a beat, a measuring slant to his brow, then let go with his damaged hand and switched sides to link five fingers with her own.

"Why did you just switch sides?"

He squeezed her fingers with his whole hand and gave a little tug toward the cars, answering quietly. "It looks better, draws attention away from the imperfect, messy parts. And I thought you might prefer it."

"You seriously think I feel revulsion for your injury?" She could buy him wanting things to appear perfect—a walk through the city's largest green space on a sunny summer afternoon would yield photos of some kind—but his suggestion she'd feel disdain over his missing fingers made her stomach turn heavy and she couldn't keep the annoyance at bay. "I work with amputees—"

"I didn't soften the situation for you when I told you," he cut in, his voice staying low despite there being no one near enough to hear them. She had to remind herself he'd probably never considered how she'd faced his injury. He continued when they'd settled in the back seat, "I did for everyone else. Only you, me and Ben know how that went. The rest of the world, including the current and future king, believe the fingers cleanly came off and we just had to bandage it up and carry on."

Talking about it hurt. So did thinking about it.

Unable to stop herself, Anais reached for his left hand

and clasped it in both of hers, suddenly needing him to really know that the only negative she felt about it was that he'd gone through it and that her ring had probably made it worse. "You don't trust me, so why did you tell me a truth you don't want known?"

"Anger." He turned his hand in hers and gripped, strong but not hard, dexterous control as good as she could hope for anyone. "You were too calm, and inside I was boiling."

She'd looked calm? Every part of her had been shaking, but maybe fear and regret could be hidden better than rage. Arguing her state at the time wouldn't do anything for them, so she just let silence fall as he gave orders to the driver and the black sedan entourage pulled onto the quiet street.

He'd hurt, and he'd wanted to hurt her too so he'd lashed out, lending weight to the notion he could strike at her again if she refused him now.

Where could this kind of marriage leave them in ten years? After children? After their volatile passion had run its course?

There'd been no one since him, and he'd said the same. Seven years of celibacy was a long time. Felt like some version of love, maybe…if he truly could become involved, if he was going to help with Wayne because he wanted her safe more than the idea of it ruining his plan to undo that black mark that divorce left on his royal record.

She retrieved the ring from her handbag and handed the box to him. "Should I wear this?"

"Do you like it?" Quinn asked, a tone in his voice hinting how important it was for her to say yes. "If you'd prefer a different ring…we can make that happen."

"I haven't looked at it," she admitted, keeping her hand flat for him with the box sitting on her palm until he took it.

Whatever he thought about that, he opened the box and presented the ring to her.

Anais had expected ostentatious, to feel self-conscious about the size of the stone—Quinn's way always involved big gestures—but she hadn't expected to *feel*. Or the way the air became so thin.

She hadn't expected a blue-green stone, hadn't even known such a stone existed. Large, yes, but not horrifying. And there were two additional but smaller princess-cut diamonds flanking it in a platinum band so delicate it didn't look strong enough to support the gems.

Heartbreakingly beautiful.

"It matches your eyes," he offered softly, and the ring bomb went off as he plucked it from the velvet pillows and slid it onto her finger.

Eyes burning, she took a slow breath then clamped her mouth shut to stop her lower lip trembling.

A beautiful ring shouldn't make this harder; she wasn't that person. She'd never cared about that stuff.

Another breath as she felt her hand fist, keeping the ring from moving, keeping her from gazing at it as if she were star-struck. "Sapphire?"

Please be a sapphire.

"Alexandrite."

A stone she hadn't even heard of. Probably magnificently rare and jimmied off some ancient crown or necklace, one bit of the family jewels to show how serious he was.

"New?"

"Seven years old." He turned her chin toward him, leaned in and kissed her mouth lightly; again her lip trembled. "Can I infer you like it?"

"Seven years?"

"It was an anniversary present."

Pow.

"It's beautiful." She swallowed, cursing herself for how dejected she sounded over being given a magnificent ring.

He'd kept it the whole time. He'd picked it out when they were still together. An engagement ring, for the engagement they'd never had.

Damn him.

The weight of it all drowned out everything ricocheting through her mind, and Quinn let her drift into silence until they got to the park. He kept her hand; his thumb brushed her finger, slightly moving the ring this way and that, playing havoc with her emotions.

No threats, just charm, sweetness and romance. She'd almost prefer the angry man who'd trapped her into this arrangement to this shimmer of who she'd fallen so hard for that she'd let herself live in the fantasy that she could ever fit into his world. She'd found a place in the medical world, more than she'd ever found anywhere, including where she'd grown up and those first seventeen years of never fitting in.

The car pulled into the park and Quinn helped her from the back. Taking his place again on her left where he could hold her ringed hand in his whole hand, guiding her down a cobblestone path through the trees ringing a large meadow and central pond.

The security detail walked several meters behind, close enough to respond quickly in case of emergency, but far enough for a modicum of privacy. About the same distance ahead of them, another couple walked, blissfully unaware through the cool afternoon shade of the silver birch trees.

"Have you had any luck tracking down Wayne?" She opted for a shorthand, normalized manner to ask about the bane of her adult existence. The horrified delight she still felt from the ring needed countering.

"Yes, but I haven't met with him yet," Quinn answered, his voice so quiet and sedate she had to look at him to work out whether to attach positive or negative meaning to his words.

Nothing. Just calm.

"Have you contacted him?"

"Not yet." He released her hand, stepped around to the side he preferred and wrapped his arm around her waist instead, anchoring her to him.

In the cool shade, his body pressed heat against her skin.

No, not heat. Warmth. A sense of security despite the lack of movement on Wayne. "Why not?"

"He's not in a position to cause damage right now. We have some time."

"How do you know?"

"He's incarcerated," Quinn answered, the calm in his voice fracturing briefly with a note of disdain. "Solitary confinement for another few days. He attacked a guard."

Jail? That shouldn't shock her. Blackmail wasn't the man's only crime. "What did the police get him for?"

Giving a minor alcohol?

Inappropriate contact with a minor?

Talking a drunken teen into nudie shots?

Even though Anais knew she was smart, she'd still had her thinking corrupted by the desire to belong somewhere… to someone. So her crime was worse than other girls he'd just tricked. She'd known better and done it anyway.

"I'm having his record sent over tonight but, with what I've learned, he sounds like a great guy. Do me a favor and don't tell me how you ever dated with someone like that."

Dated. They'd never dated. The implication caused her to bristle, even though she was supposed to want Quinn to be coming to exactly this kind of conclusion—the one that would lead to him thinking her not suitable for the royal family.

This was her opening to tell him the truth—pathetic and tired after a childhood of bullying and verbal abuse, she'd walked herself right off the cliff and was still falling. To point out the way it mirrored her decision-making when she and Quinn had eloped. Willful ignorance, ridiculous self-deception.

"We've all been stupid teenagers once."

The words refused to come.

"Once I know what he's been convicted of, and if there has been any previous incarceration, I'll know how to approach him."

All sensible. And surprisingly proactive, but too new a character trait to trust. "Please keep me in the loop. I need to be involved in this. To know what's going on."

"I'm handling it." He didn't sound angry, even leaned over to brush his lips against her temple. The couple ahead of them had finally noticed who walked behind them and now had a cellphone out. "You wanted me to help with it before."

"I did. I do," she whispered, smiling at the couple, still several meters away, then leaned up to kiss his cheek in return. Because it felt as if he'd kissed her head as part of his PR thing. "I trust you to handle it. It's just been eating at me for so long; being afraid of it, of him, is hard-wired."

The quiet confession earned her a longer look, a spike of irritation in his eyes. "I'll fix it. I'm used to storming barriers." This should be seen as a romantic walk with sweet touches, and she really hoped the cameras didn't pick up the quiet, tense conversation. All they needed was a video to deal with.

Another group of people approached from the park's other path, and the couple who'd been filming stepped to the side to allow them to pass.

With the path about to become narrower, Anais pressed against him, trying to edge Quinn off the walk with her to make way, but his arm firmed at her waist and he held her to the center.

"We need to move," she whispered, and he shook his head, lifting the whole hand he'd earlier freed and waved at the people.

The group stepped off the path, and Quinn continued forward. "People are used to a kind of deference, and even if it feels strange to me too it's tradition and I try to keep it up. You'll have to get used to things again."

"It feels rude," she muttered, her smile faltering for the first time since they'd reached the wide open public space. "I'm no different to them. I think putting myself into that false headspace is part of why I struggled so much with the title. I hate being called Princess."

"Next time we'll move to the side, and you'll see what happens. The smoothest way of handling things is the traditional route here, doing what people expect. Like this. Courting. The Sip. The wedding."

"It's not really a wedding. We're still married."

"But we never had a proper wedding. This will be a fresh start for us. Starting over, and doing it how we should've before. It's a wedding."

Pick your battles, dummy.

As the path opened to a wide meadow, he steered them to the east where she now saw a small table and servers hovered nearby. Lunch in the park. Let it never be said he didn't know how to put on a show. Maybe he was right.

"Shouldn't fairy tales have picnics on the ground with red gingham blankets?"

"We can sit on the ground if you want, but you're the one in the white dress." The charm and smile returned. "Ben met with the designers for a prosthesis this week. Even met with the vascular surgeon. Hasn't agreed to surgery, but he's listening."

"How did you manage it?" She went with the subject change. Ben was her patient too and she'd been failing to get him to consider a prosthesis for a month. "Did he hit you with RoboCop jokes?"

He pulled out her chair. "He hit me with much worse. I just have better ammunition to fight back."

The afternoon sun warmed her shoulders and she let her eyes track over the park as he settled opposite her and the servers began to fuss, filling glasses with juice and water, presenting dishes of fruit, cheese, and little meat pastries. No wine. He remembered that too.

More sweetness and consideration. Fighting for Ben. Fighting for her?

Looking at him got hard.

She shifted her gaze toward the pond and, set against the green water, maybe thirty meters from where they sat, he stood.

A shock of ice shot through her and she heard Quinn urgently saying her name.

Lanky, tall, gaunt of face, shaggy brown hair, and a deep corded scar across his right cheek.

It was happening.

A glass of water shot off the table and Anais saw it, but barely had enough control of her shaking hands to latch on to Quinn's closest arm. "It's him."

Quinn let her glass fall, gaze fixed on Anais's bloodless face. Even her forever pink lips looked like chalk, but the violent tremble in her hands on his arm just made it worse.

Her fear summoned his; needles of awareness assaulted the back of his neck and he felt himself tensing, readying for a fight.

She'd said *him.*

"Him?" he echoed, following her gaze to a man loitering some distance away.

Ratliffe?

Couldn't be. He was rotting in solitary in prison an hour from the capital as of two hours ago.

Quinn forced himself to relax and waved off the approaching security team. He didn't even know what Ratliffe looked like yet but, even if he had, he was too distant to see much aside from generalities. Tall. Overly thin. In need of a haircut, a shave, and a tee shirt without a hole in it.

"It's him," she said again, then looked at him, then back at the security people. Quinn shook his head at them again. "How did he know we'd be here?"

"It's not him, Anais." Shifting from fighting mode to being gently protective, he disengaged her clutching hands to take them both in his own. "He's in solitary, remember? That's not him."

"It's him."

The fear rolling off her made him doubt for a few seconds but, unless the man was an escape artist, it wasn't him. "I'll go see."

"No!" She squawked the word, causing people nearby to look in their direction. Even someone who didn't know her wouldn't be able to mistake her panic.

"I'll take Mr. Potts with me." He gestured toward the leader of his security detail and, after rising, obstructed her view of the man until she looked up at him.

She'd said she hated it when he distracted her from her fears, but it was the only way he knew how to divert her when she got overwhelmed. But it also helped him.

He tilted her chin up and brushed his lips over hers, increasing the strength of his kiss until she kissed him back, even just briefly. "I'll just double-check, okay? You stay here. If it's him, I'll handle it. I promise."

It wasn't him, but he needed her to calm down. Talking about the man who'd tormented and blackmailed her had just made this fear materialize with the first person who looked passingly similar from a distance. Once he'd made sure she'd feel better.

He just wouldn't tell her he hadn't seen Ratliffe's photo yet.

By the end of the weekend, Quinn had come to understand the depth of Anais's fear over the photos and how the specter of Wayne haunted her.

Their outing in the park had generated the photos and videos online he'd hoped for, but his quiet, but admittedly strange, conversation with the man she'd mistaken for Ratliffe overshadowed their success. He'd been cordial and, despite his confusion, had produced identification when requested. He'd even been polite when Quinn had brought him to Anais for introductions, and through the embarrassment that had brought color back to her cheeks and sent her apologizing profusely—something she hadn't yet done with *him*.

At the charity brunch they'd attended late the following morning, he hadn't even needed to question the server she'd also mistakenly thought was Ratliffe. By then, he'd seen the man's file and had his mugshot on his phone to show her quietly, without causing a scene.

The most important thing for him to do with regard to their relationship had been to sort this situation out before anything else.

So now, nearing midnight on Tuesday evening, he knocked on Anais's door.

"What happened?" she whispered the second she opened the door, one hand shooting out to grab his arm and drag him inside before locking up.

She'd been asleep when he'd called to tell her he was coming, and her hair was delightfully messed up, but the pink silky gown and robe she wore took the majority of his attention. The low light in the room only accentuated the way the silk draped from her breasts and skimmed her waist. God, she looked good in it. He'd had a mission…

"I wanted to tell you tonight, as soon as it was done."

"So, tell me." She kept her voice low, pulled the short silky robe tighter around her, and went to perch on the sofa. "Stop dragging it out. Did something happen?"

He followed the conversation better once she stopped moving around and stopped jiggling. "I got the…"

The word *video* almost flew, but he checked himself in time. She'd never once mentioned a video to him—just pictures—and they scared her beyond reason alone. If she found out there was actual footage…

"You got the pictures?" she filled in, still speaking in low, but now frenzied tones.

"Yes." He cleared his throat. "And he's gone."

"What do you mean, he's gone?" She kept her voice low. "Is he dead?"

He finally found the wherewithal to look the room over and make sure his mother-in-law wasn't downstairs with them, and her question solidified. *Dead?*

"For God's sake, I didn't kill him."

The sudden exasperation in Quinn's voice had Anais flipping on the table lamp to better see him.

Lines she'd never noticed creased between his brows, evidence of a great deal of recent scowling. He looked tired. Exhausted, really. She patted the sofa cushion beside her and looked up at him. "Sit with me. I'll stop interrupting so you can tell me."

He more fell into the sofa than sat and, as soon as he'd settled, reached for her and tugged until she rested against his side. "I arranged early release from his grand larceny sentence; he was escorted with guards to the palace for a long talk, and made a deal that ended with me having the blackmail material, him without access to retrieve any copies and then out of the country with a tidy sum of money."

Before his words had a chance to settle, he'd upped the ante by dragging her into his lap.

Intimate and gentle despite his haggard appearance, he wrapped one arm around her waist and rested the other hand on her bare knee, thumb stroking in a leisurely way.

Distracting.

He sounded so certain that Wayne was out of their lives—that it was over. "What…?"

"I've spent the whole day with a loathsome man for you; do I not deserve a little bit of cuddling?"

The cheeky tone and lopsided grin were impossible not to return, and Anais felt herself smiling despite the subject of only seconds before. She propped her elbow on his shoulder and let her fingers scratch through the short, thick curling hair atop his head. "Is that how it works?"

He tilted his head into her hand and closed his eyes, but his hand stroked up her thigh and back, leaving those happy tingles racing over her skin. But his certainty was convincing, especially when it became clear how much he'd actually done.

"I don't know what to say," she whispered, feeling relief so palpable that this whole endeavor suddenly seemed possible. Or at least less terrifying. "You look tired."

"Long day," he confirmed, and opened his eyes, his hand still stroking up and down her thigh. He wanted to stay.

More. She wanted it too. "You could sleep here."

It took a lot to make the offer, so when he removed her hand from his hair and sketched a rueful smile she'd already started bracing herself for rejection.

"The sofa looks comfortable, but I'd rather a bed."

Since they'd met again, there had been kisses of all description—angry, overwhelming, gentle, sweet, tender—and all initiated by him. But she wanted to kiss him, even if it might not convince him she meant him to stay for more than sleep. She wanted her mouth tender from the day's growth of scratchy beard; she wanted that delicious burn all over her. She wanted to finally see the man's body that time and service had given him. He'd somehow managed to stay dressed that time in her office.

He hadn't stopped touching her, so she followed the will of her pounding heart and brushed her lips lightly against his. "I meant upstairs."

The way his fingers curled into her thigh and the uptick in his breathing said he wanted that too, but, as she tilted her head to deepen the kiss, he pulled back, regret in his eyes. "Is this gratitude?"

"Grat—?" She stopped and shook her head, leaning back to look at him. "No. It's not gratitude."

"Did you finally accept that I love you?" he asked, then flopped his head back, eyes closing. "Please say that's it, because I want to stay."

He couldn't be happy with progress; he wanted everything when he wanted it.

She didn't want to talk about this, not right now. "I know you care, but why does this have to be about love? It wasn't about love in my office. That was hate sex."

"That wasn't hate sex." He lifted his head sharply, instantly annoyed, but his hands stayed gentle, as if he'd willed them to be so, even while putting her off his lap.

His reaction shocked her almost as much as the grief she felt at losing the cage of his arms and the solid heat beneath her. But when he scooted an entire cushion away, that shock turned into grief. "What else would you call it?"

"Years of agony."

His bitter, disbelieving laugh robbed her of anything else to say. It took everything to keep the burning in her eyes from pouring salty rivers.

"What's it going to take? Do you think I half-violated a citizen's rights and kicked him out of the country because I just kind of like you and really like what's between your legs?"

Still no words came, even when he rose and stomped for the door.

"So that you can't be further confused, I'll make it clear. When you accept why I'm doing all this, I'll go upstairs with you. That's it."

Love. She knew what he meant.

If she said what he wanted to hear, it would just be because she wanted him to stay and stop looking at her like that.

Even if it was exactly how he should look at her—shock and bitterness that meant he was reconsidering this foolish idea.

"Did you look at the photos?"

"That's what you want to know?" He shook his head, jaw gritted as he closed his eyes for long, stuttering heartbeats. "I saw enough to confirm it was you. That's it."

Which should've made her feel a little better, but didn't. "Where are they?"

"Penthouse safe. You can have them after the wedding." The smile he gave her was all teeth, sharp and unhappy. "Think of it as the world's most messed-up wedding gift."

"More blackmail to marry you? Is *that* an act of love?"

"Collateral," he corrected. "If you love someone, set them free? I'm supposed to just let you go? Because you said you wanted me to fight for you. You can't have it both ways."

CHAPTER EIGHT

ANAIS WALKED THE LONG, winding corridors of Sisters of Grace Hospital, her hand tucked into Quinn's. From the dampness of his palm, she knew he was worried. Not that anyone else could see it—the military bearing seemed marrow-deep now, to the point that he practically marched and she had to jog to keep up.

Ben's surgery started in an hour, having been scheduled with remarkable speed during the few days she'd been away from Almsford—something Quinn finessed.

"He'll be all right," she whispered to him, but he gave no sign he'd heard her until the door to their private waiting room finally swung shut behind them.

It had barely clicked closed before he tugged her into his arms and seemed to deflate a little until his chin rested on her shoulder.

She said it again, no matter how close it felt to the kind of assurances she'd been trained to never give. For him she'd forget that training. "It's going to work. He'll do great."

He released her and pushed a white handled shopping bag into her hands—the one she'd thought carried a gift for his friend. "I asked if, as one of Ben's doctors, you could pop in and out of the surgery to keep us updated on how everything was going. Would you?"

Ben was still pre-op, with a long surgery ahead, and Quinn was already a breath away from completely wrecked.

A peek into the bag confirmed her suspicions: scrubs.

Aside from demanding she marry him, Quinn had asked very little from her so far; really nothing compared to all she'd asked of him. Wear this gorgeous ring, go for a walk and picnic in the park, attend tonight's Independence Day party at the American Embassy… All requests made in service to his Make People Like Anais campaign. This was the first thing he'd asked for himself.

As awkward as it was to barge into another surgeon's OR, she didn't want to say no. She remembered clinging to her computer for any news she could scavenge in the days after Quinn had been injured.

Waiting when the life of someone you loved hung by a thread was absolute torture.

"If they'll allow it," she ventured. "I don't have privileges at this hospital."

"I cleared it all. Thank you." He breathed out slowly, a small amount of tension ebbing from his worried brow. "Rosalie's in with him right now, but she's going to be in here with us, waiting. I'm sure she'll appreciate updates too."

"I'll do whatever I can. Is there somewhere I can change?" She'd thrown herself—quite unsuccessfully—at the man only days ago. It'd be pointless to get weird about changing her clothes in front of him now. "Or can you stand against the door? I'll be quick."

His brows popped up, but he nodded and went to plant his shoulder against the only exit. "Want me to turn around?"

Just a polite question; the man already looked like he had no intention of moving, the confidence she'd been missing immediately returned.

"You've seen it all. Your body's the mystery here."

"How's my body a mystery?" Quinn asked, his eyes tracking each button's release down her front.

The weight of his gaze on her, changing in a hospital waiting room, shouldn't have brought back that maddening tingle—a feeling she was starting to make peace with and maybe even enjoy a little. Aside from him touching her, it was the next best thing. Even when it started feeling more like a striptease than a simple matter of necessity.

Her blouse fell open, and Anais had never been so happy to have selected a pretty white lace panty set over her usual combination of whatever she'd blindly grabbed from the underwear drawer. The pressure of looming princesshood made her feel the need to dress in her best, and that even included the bits no one would see unless she was in a tragic accident. Under Quinn's plan, she now felt obligated to wear pretty, matching underwear.

"Your body's different." She tried to sound unaffected, but she might've turned so that her underthings were displayed anyway. *He'd* turned her down, after all. By his heavy-lidded stare, he was at least distracted. "I bet you're at least thirty-five pounds heavier than when I last saw you undressed."

He'd not undressed for the office sex that Quinn's vehemence troubled her ability to categorize. She'd been the only one naked for that.

She shimmied out of the baby-blue pencil skirt and retrieved the scrubs.

"Your body is different too," he said thickly. Then, with way more energy, he added, "You got a tattoo!"

Before she could say anything about it, her door guard left his post and crossed to her.

"Quinn!" she squawked, grabbed the scrubs top and darted around him to block the door herself. "You are supposed to be blocking the door with your extra pounds!"

"Hold still. Infinity symbol… Tiny writing." He fell to one knee, grabbed her by the hips and spun her around to get a better look at the slender ribbon of script circling back on itself. *"Today's courage is tomorrow's peace."*

The words had his brows pinching and he looked up at her, working on the meaning in relation to her.

"I know what you're thinking." She tugged the top on and carefully stepped around him. "Stay at the door this time. I need the bottoms."

"That's not what I was thinking."

"No. You're thinking, with a motto like that I should've handled Wayne on my own."

"Wrong again."

Of course she was. People didn't get tattoos to remind them of things they'd like to forget. She'd made the mark on her flesh in the hopes of getting it off her heart.

*Leave today, have peace tomorrow...*only it hadn't happened that quickly. But she didn't want to talk about it right then. "Okay, maybe I don't know then."

She tugged on the bottoms and, after her usually nimble fingers refused to tie the drawstring, gave up and just stuffed her utterly impractical and improper kitten-heeled feet into the shoe covers from the bottom of the bag.

He was still watching her; she could feel it, vibrating the air, bringing on another round of tingles and an accelerated heartbeat that could either be desire or the sick feeling this conversation summoned.

Let it drop. Today was already too emotionally fraught for him to engage in this.

"Do you want to know?" He obviously didn't feel the desire to let go, but the low rumble his voice developed echoed other desires.

Ignore those other desires too; he'd made clear the price and she wasn't willing to pay. "Will it bring me peace tomorrow?"

The laugh she got in return eased her a little, another form of distraction.

"You're kind of hit and miss on the application of this motto."

"I'm a work in progress. It's there to remind me."

"That change takes courage and an act of will?"

She nodded, her throat suddenly unwilling to let sound through.

Please, stop there.

“Did it work with me?”

When he said those things, it always made her feel as if the ground were falling away from under her.

It would do her no good to deflect again; that his question knocked the air out of her answered well enough. “I don’t know how to answer that.”

“Truth is always appreciated.”

Not true. He wouldn’t want her if he knew the truth about her lackluster judgment, morals…the battered self-esteem she fought against all the time. “In a way, it did. In other ways, it didn’t.”

He nodded in a slow, measuring way. “How did it make things…not better?”

“You know how,” she said, but couldn’t find any strength to make her words more than a ghost of the feeling she’d wallowed in for years after leaving.

“Tell me anyway.” He was near her now, near enough to touch, near enough his whispered command felt like a warm request.

“I missed you.” Because she’d already admitted she’d left for his good once, not because she’d wanted to. “But I stopped being so afraid all the time. If you’re angry about that, I get it—I sacrificed *us* to save *me*. And you. Your family. It was the only thing I could do.”

“And now?”

He wanted her admission—and Anais could only pretend to herself that she didn’t love him when he wasn’t with her—but she didn’t want to accept that he still loved her. Or had ever loved her. It meant taking all the blame for their marital failure; it meant saying his emotional distance would’ve made no difference. That was something she wasn’t even able to consider.

If only she’d known how to make him listen back then.

If only she'd tried harder.

If only she'd been stronger for them both.

The limousine stopped outside the American embassy in the heart of the capital, Anais and Quinn in the back. A red, white and blue awning, patriotic sashes, flowers and decorations lent color to the gray stone nineteenth-century building, honoring the country's Independence Day celebrations.

Anais smoothed her hands over the sleek up-do Aunt Helen had wrestled her frequently frizzy waves into. Still intact. A quick inventory of her sapphire dress reassured her further. Unrumpled, at least from the front.

"You look gorgeous," Quinn said beside her, capturing one of her fussing hands along with her attention, but making no move to exit the car yet. "Did you know they do this at almost all their embassies? Even the American Embassy in London."

"I wondered," she admitted, going with his efforts to distract her, even if he'd not really picked a subject that could do anything to take her attention from the knot in her middle or a curiously jelly-like weakness in her arms she'd bet would worsen when she had to teeter her way up the red-carpeted entrance where all the cameras could legitimately film them tonight without violating Quinn's request for space.

Quinn's car door swung open, a smartly suited young man holding it for them, but Quinn leaned closer to her, a soft chuckle announcing the joking tone that had always delighted her but which she'd only heard a handful of times since coming home. "I always wondered if it was considered rude. It seems kind of rude."

Good mood undamped since Ben's successful surgery hours earlier. She shared his relief and happiness for his best friend—and, having watched him with Ben's fiancée the whole day, fully understood what the couple meant to

Quinn, which invested her even more in their now hope-filled future.

But the prospect of an official diplomatic function in formal attire? Yeah, that put a damper on her glee.

She made herself come up with words; talking about anything was better than silently worrying about how she'd perform tonight.

"I don't know. I guess I never thought about it. I wasn't even aware they celebrated it here. Growing up, anytime I saw random fireworks displays in the city, I'd watch, wonder briefly what they were about, then go back to whatever I was doing—reading, most likely." At home, the salon or the library—the extents of her teenage territory.

Her knees wobbled as he led her up the carpet, but the long gown hid that manifestation of fear turning her bones to cartilage.

Quinn didn't miss it. He closed his free hand over hers and continued in low, conspiratorial murmurings as flashes went off on either side of them, which she'd darned well smile for over the butterfly tornados in her belly. "Like going to your ex's house to throw a *Remember-When-I-Threw-All-Your-Things-On-The-Lawn* party."

She smiled for real, despite her nervousness. "Actually, it's considered American soil. Not sure about the skies above, but this ground is theirs. So, welcome to the USA on Independence Day."

It made her feel a little better, talking with him, or maybe just doing anything with him that could distract her from the worry that had knotted her up in one form or another all day.

And maybe it also helped to get to be a wee smarty-pants. Quinn had always appreciated that about her—she got to be something besides a jabbering idiot once tonight before she did something stupid and laughter chased her from the party.

"Been studying?"

"Yes. And it's probably against some custom, making fun of a nation's favorite holiday. Although, having been to a number of Fourth of July celebrations in the States, some sort of ruckus wouldn't be out of line, though my previous experiences might clash with tonight's festivities."

"Which would be…?"

"A barbecue, copious amounts of beer, ill-advised and inebriated handling of barely regulated explosives, a possible trip to the Emergency Department, and prayers for a nearby fire extinguisher."

"Definitely at odds with a black-tie dress code."

They breezed through a decorated lobby with security checking invitations. Open double doors led into a wide, expansive room probably only for entertaining, and which made her double down on her nerves.

Quinn steered her towards official-looking people and made greetings and introductions. She had to release his arm to shake hands or risk looking even more like the lot of them terrified her, but regretted it immediately. His hand had steadied her a little; without it her smile trembled in a way that couldn't be missed.

By the time she'd gotten through her third set of introductions, Quinn steered her to a corner and turned her to face him.

Standing so close, when she met his gaze, the gathering party faded a little behind him. When he cupped her cheeks and planted a sweet, chaste kiss on her lips, the din faded even more in a wash of warmth and a strange peace. Their first kiss since the fight.

"Do I have your attention now?" The teasing note in his voice softened the criticism she always felt too vulnerable to in this kind of situation. "You have to stop fidgeting."

Her grimace couldn't be thwarted.

"Everyone's looking at me," she tried to explain, and immediately heard how ridiculous it sounded. Right behind that, she actually processed his words and felt herself twisting the engagement ring around her finger. "I didn't realize I was fidgeting."

His thumbs began stroking lightly over her cheeks and he kissed her again, this time well enough to send shivers to her belly and the tingles she'd developed a begrudging love of to the rest of her. This was what she'd always found so addictive about the man; he could pour molten desire into her by simply touching her face. A few seconds of kissing sky-rocketed the effect.

When her heart pounded enough to jiggle her chest, he lifted his head again. The playful spark had vanished, and now his heavily lidded eyes told her he was regretting that sexual détente he'd issued.

"People are looking at you because you're beautiful and elegant. And because we're news—more than usual because we asked not to be news. They're not watching because you're messing up."

"Except fidgeting and having attention issues."

His response was a gentle smile, then a brief brush of his lips on her forehead. "We don't have long before they call us to dinner. I rang ahead to confirm we'd be seated together. Relax. Be yourself. What do you think they see when they look at you that's so objectionable?"

"I don't know."

His raised brows bid her try again; he wasn't going to let her blow the question off. Releasing her cheeks, he took her hands and waited.

"They see uncultured riff-raff. Or a devious, low-born she-wolf who tricked you into marriage—"

"No. I didn't ask what they *said* about you," Quinn interrupted, "or do you *believe* you tricked me into marriage with your magic vagina?"

The words *magic vagina* were like a tiny hammer to her knee, and her foot sprang forward before she could think it through. Her toes bounced off his shin hard enough for him to wince, but it conveyed how seriously she'd always taken that particular slight…

"I think they'll see me kick someone important," she

grunted. "Or make some other mistake in protocol or manners. It doesn't matter that yesterday I downloaded instructions for American diplomats on how to behave at social functions. I read it three times, but I might miss something small, or do something dumb and..."

"They'll think you're an idiot?"

She felt heat rush into her face and she forced herself to nod. "My intelligence is the only acceptable thing about me. Even when the country was at the height of their hatred and disapproval, that was the one back-handed compliment I got. *How could someone so intelligent think an illegitimate commoner eloping with a prince could ever be acceptable?*"

He leaned in again as if to kiss her and she pulled back.

"If I mess up or do something stupid I'm nothing special at all." The words came in a rush, but heated up a little at the end as she whisper-hissed, "I don't even have a magic vagina."

"Oh, yes, you do." He laughed at that. "But, more importantly, one mistake doesn't make anyone into an irredeemable idiot."

"We have this thing called the Internet—and yes, it does. Mistakes live forever online. Ask celebrities with their awkward school pictures everywhere."

He looked briefly pained and out of his depth, but a slow breath and a shake of his head released it. "I'm not going to talk you out of this tonight. But you just smiled a little. Why did you smile?"

She'd smiled? A quick inventory of her face confirmed it. Her cheeks did feel recently bunched. "I'm not sure. I guess somewhere in that I stopped feeling so afraid. Maybe even felt a little good?" No wonder he liked to use distraction on her. "Or maybe I felt better because I kicked you."

"Do you want to kick me again? I'm here to be supportive."

The offer made her cheeks start to bunch again, so she leaned up to give him the kiss she'd dodged.

"Or that. Kicks, kisses, groping behind Old Glory over there, I'm good for all of that. In the name of being a supportive husband."

"Okay, enough with the husband business, support man," she said but didn't step away from him.

"Enough with the husband business *for now*," he agreed, then jerked his head toward the party. "You ready to go back in?"

And…smile gone. She forced a fake one that was at least steadier now.

"Follow my lead and remember they're our allies; this isn't some tense diplomatic situation. You lived there for years; you *have* things to talk about."

She wouldn't turn down a little pep-talk. The talking was what helped.

"I do think you should reconsider your position on alcohol. It helps sometimes."

That she would turn down.

They returned to circulating and she took every spare second he was in conversation to examine others in attendance and mentally compare herself before switching up her posture to mimic the most graceful she noticed.

By the time dinner had been rung, she'd nearly gotten control of her worrying. No matter what Quinn thought about her alcohol prohibition, she had hard evidence and personal experience on how stupid she could be when her self-esteem and inadequacies collided with booze. She might end up topless, giving the ambassador a lap dance. And the ambassador was a long-married grandmother.

As soon as they sat, Quinn snagged her closest hand and kept hold of her between courses—sometimes beneath the table, sometimes on top. Even when he'd half turned away from her to engage in conversation with his neighbors.

It helped, but her table neighbors' social graces made up the difference, not hers. They drew her into conversation so subtly she didn't even realize the subject had turned to her until she'd answered several questions.

How was it to be home?

What State had she lived in?

Was she excited about the wedding?

These were easy to answer, mostly. The wedding talk? At least she knew what she was expected to say and fell into that narrative well enough.

"How did you choose your specialty?"

The steak she'd been enjoying seemed to transform, from charred delight to a ten-ton boulder in her belly.

The woman who'd asked probably thought it a completely innocent question, but easy answers came to an end and she had to put her fork and knife down before she dropped them.

She could give the standard response she'd used—a patient during her rotations had captured her heart. It was touching, and complete fiction.

The truth would maintain Quinn's narrative, but…

Quinn taking her hand beneath the table again made her aware of how long she'd taken to start answering. She glanced his way to find him watching her, interested brows up, no censure there.

She wasn't sure whether to say it, or even *how* to say it. How she should even feel? Would someone secure in her relationship feel that old pain, or the shame the admission would still trigger? Would a normal person have gotten past it all? Would she own it, flaws and all? Would she feel the aching sense of exposure Anais still had to swallow past?

She didn't know where the decision came from, only that Quinn's hand in hers gave her the strength to say it.

With a steadying breath, she started to speak.

"I was a first-year general surgery fellow when I changed to orthopedics. When Quinn was injured." She stopped. Having never heard him speak of his injury in public added another layer of hesitation. Would he mind? Truth, he'd claimed, was always appreciated. A quick glance showed no dismay, just sharpening interest.

"Like everyone else, I'd heard he'd been shot, but not where, or how seriously for a couple of very long days."

The hand holding hers lifted their joined hands back to the table top; she took the silent encouragement.

As soon as she'd heard he was all right, she'd walled those toxic feelings off—spent no time thinking of the days and the hurt she'd buried behind them. Those days had been so packed with terror, guilt, and worry worse even than when she'd left him. Self-preservation demanded zero reflection. So there was no practiced, logical story to tell, just a rush of words and emotions, unfiltered, unordered, far too revealing.

"By the time his injury and amputation were announced, I was a mess. Happy he was alive, so relieved that I felt guilty over effectively being happy he'd lost his fingers." Her throat thickened. She reached for her water. Over her glass, she saw the number of eyes focused on her, heard the silence that had fallen, and felt the scorching tears gathering.

It was too much. She was saying too much. Every part of her wanted to make an excuse, to flee the table. Except the hand tucked into his, and the part of her that wanted him to know that, although she'd left, she'd still been with him in her heart through those dark, dreadful days.

But she couldn't look at him.

"I changed my track the day I heard. I guess I wanted to help people who were going through the same thing he was going through."

His quickened breathing told her he'd been affected, as did the slight tremble of his wine glass she saw in her peripheral vision.

Was that enough? She lowered her head to dab at her eyes, praying for the topic to shift.

"You wanted to help him, but you couldn't," the woman

summarized for her, and Anais could only nod, mouth twisting to control her trembling lower lip.

Quinn lifted her hand. The brush of his lips across her knuckles pulled her watery gaze sideways to him. If she looked at him fully, she'd lose her mind and control of the unpredictable sobbing that had carried her through those days.

CHAPTER NINE

WAIT STAFF CIRCLED the table, placing dessert plates before each guest—something fruity in red, white and blue. Quinn couldn't focus on it. If he could harness the current coming through Anais's hand now *gripping* his, he could power the capital.

He turned more to face her, pretending it was to share a dessert with her when really every ounce of his willpower was engaged in fighting his instinct to spirit her away. Just to hold her. Just to put his arms around her and rock through the pain he still felt vibrating through her.

He felt the weight of everyone's gaze now—everyone but her—but he couldn't blame them. Or her. But he needed to look at her as desperately as her grip said she needed to keep hold of him.

Mechanically, she went about a few bites of the berry concoction. She ate, but didn't taste it; her half-bowed head and blank eyes made it clear.

Before they'd made a dent in the dessert the fireworks display was announced, and guests departed the table for the veranda to the rear gardens. She started too, but Quinn tugged her close enough to wrap an arm around her waist and steer her to the dance floor instead. His obligation to remain through the fireworks display was the only thing keeping him from taking her away with him.

The lights in the great room fell, to minimize the distraction through the wide veranda windows separating them from the guests outside watching the sky, but the dark also made it feel secluded, almost private.

"We're not going out?" she whispered, but turned into his arms as he steered her around the floor.

"I can see from here," he said, not wanting to break the spell between them and what it told him.

She loved him. She'd never stopped loving him. But it felt as if a stiff breeze could blow her away, so he folded her into his arms and rested his cheek against her temple.

Tilting her head, she whispered by his ear, "Are you okay?"

Worried about him. More proof.

"A little overwhelmed," he admitted, unable to summon a better answer, unable to make a clever or cajoling response, the words aching in his chest. "I didn't know that about your specialty. I'd wondered, but I should've asked. I should've sat down with you and just talked, not about all this…just to know. What I missed. We should've found time to sit down."

He felt her nodding, felt her pull him a little tighter, even felt the regret rolling off her.

"We've never really done much of that. Only when we were dating."

The softly spoken words burned. He tried to think about times after they'd eloped when they'd just sat and talked about anything for longer than a few minutes, but he couldn't. In that moment, swallowing past the lump in his throat, he was glad for the dark, even glad for the way his lungs refused to draw a complete breath—it drove home the part he'd played in the downfall of their marriage—she hadn't ducked out of conversations he'd started, not once.

"We'll do better this time."

Her nod expressed her hesitation as much as it could be agreement.

Yes, she still loved him, but that hadn't stopped her from leaving the first time. He had to do better.

"I think you could've talked to me about Ratliffe if we'd had that kind of marriage. A relationship you felt safe in."

"Maybe." Her hand slid to the back of his neck and she kneaded as she gave him that single word.

No matter how long ago it had been, she was still raw. He felt it too, but that same wound had started to heal in him the day he'd found her again, when it started to feel like something he could control.

"We've got a good forty-five minutes right now." He kissed the side of her neck just as the first flash of sparkling light illuminated the dark room and the music erupted with the loud, alarming bang.

"Quinn?" She leaned back and the fireworks illuminated her face; eyes wide with concern broke through the wariness that had grabbed him.

"I'm fine," he said quickly, then forced himself to relax. "Just startled me."

"I didn't think about the fireworks. Are you sure? We can go. I can…" She paused, her eyes swiveled toward the ceiling as she tried to scheme. "I could faint or something as a cover?"

Her comical attempt at subterfuge relaxed him further. "I'm really all right. I don't have PTSD. Just a bit of…inattention to anything that isn't you right now."

Even in the green glow of the skies, he saw her blush. Then he saw her focus on his mouth with a kind of intention that might as well be invitation. Quinn took it, pulling her closer again and brushing his lips over hers. The lingering strawberry from dessert only magnified her natural sweetness, and the sweet ache that had been growing in his chest since her story.

She'd given them an out and he could happily sink into her kisses, into the soft sighs she rewarded him with as he deepened the exploration of her mouth. When she stroked her tongue past his lips, he tumbled into the mind-blanking bliss that always came when touching her—but this time it came with a little needle of loss.

They'd been talking. He wanted to talk to her right now more than he wanted to kiss her, even if only just.

The music accompanying the thundering explosions shifted into loud, enthusiastic twentieth-century rock'n'roll, and he went with it—sealing the deep, toe-curling kisses with a slow, tender one.

She smiled even before her eyes opened back up and, with it, the heaviness that had crept over them lifted.

They were still on the dance floor, and he actually felt like dancing.

He started her swaying, in the way of two people who couldn't let go of one another and couldn't spare enough attention to pick their feet off the floor. "Tell me about medical school."

"That'll take much longer than forty-five minutes, unless you narrow it down."

"Good point." He squeezed her again and reformulated the first question. Then, as soon as she'd given a brief answer, he asked another, shooting forward another and another, gathering facts and amusing her by making her slow dance sway through "God Bless America" and "Born in the USA"…

The fireworks display passed in a heartbeat, long before Quinn was done asking questions, the lights inside had come back up and guests once more invaded the alone time he'd had with his wife.

Faster than could've ever been considered diplomatically acceptable, Quinn had whisked Anais to the US Ambassador and made their farewells to a knowing smile blessedly free of rancor for the representative of their host nation who'd failed entirely in all things diplomatic since dessert.

In the limo on the way to her house, their conversation turned to him. Even though the greed he felt to know more about her railed against it, he fought the desire to redirect—she needed to understand him if she would ever trust him enough to stay.

They talked about his adventures with Ben, things she'd heard about him via the media through the years, she even had him telling her a childhood story she'd heard before but which still made her laugh.

"I feel a bit silly offering tea in my living room while we're both in formalwear," she said, locking her front door behind them. She hadn't asked whether he intended to stay the night, and he was glad for it. If he had to make the call right now, he'd say he was staying, and that would force a different conversation. Knowing she still loved him, he could wait for other admissions.

She kicked off her shoes, getting comfortable.

"If it helps, I'd be happy to strip down to my skivvies and drink tea. So long as Sharon won't come downstairs and be horrified to find me in my boxers."

One corner of her mouth lifted in tandem with her hand, a half-shrug and a half-grin to his silly offer. "Mom's gone to Aunt Helen's for the night to play cards. If she'd been here alone all evening waiting for me, she'd just have worried herself sick. Her heart tends to go out of rhythm when her blood pressure rises."

She'd mentioned her mother's illness a few times, but he'd never asked for specifics. That seemed like something else he should remedy.

"Is it bad?" He took her hand, even though knowing would make it harder to force Anais's hand with the wedding—a threat that already felt inconceivable to carry out.

"It could be much worse than it is," she said, stepping a little closer so that their arms weren't stretched to the limit across the space between them, still happy to touch him, something he felt pathetically grateful for. "I'm hopeful that by the time surgery becomes imperative, the procedure will be safer. It's pretty safe now, but there's one sneaky, deadly, irreversible complication that hits about one percent of patients, and by the time it's detected it's almost always too late. As long as the condition is livable with medication and lifestyle management, I don't want her to risk it."

He could understand that. He'd take that situation with his grandfather in a heartbeat, but getting the old man to come around to the same way of thinking hadn't yet worked for him. "Sneaky, deadly, irreversible…words you never want associated with a heart procedure."

"No."

He stepped closer so that she tilted her head back to look up at him. "I didn't mean to turn the conversation to sad subjects, but I guess we do need to learn how to discuss painful topics too."

She nodded, but the frown that crept over her face let him know the instant her thoughts drifted to some other painful subject, and hung there.

"A kiss for your thoughts," he prodded.

"Not money?"

"Are you kidding? My kisses are far more valuable than money." To prove it, he dropped his lips to her mouth—fleeting affection. "Play along. I've got a fragile ego."

"Not unless you're collecting other people's egos as pets," she snorted and then reached for his other hand—the one that she always insisted on holding, even when he tried to maneuver her to his right. Still she didn't give voice to what was on her mind, just stroked his hand for a moment then, just as quickly, dropped it, freeing hers to slide under his lapels and over his shoulders, easing the jacket down his arms and off.

Waiting for her to talk was horrible. Especially when, in exchange, he had small delicate hands on his chest, burning through the thin barriers of his clothing. Focus diminishing…

"The suspense is killing me. I gave you the kiss; you're supposed to pay up with words now."

"I'm helping you get comfortable," she argued, folding the jacket over one of her arms then reaching for the ridiculous American flag bow tie he'd gotten only for the flamboyant party.

"I can't multi-task. I'm either all in this conversation or I'm going to want to enjoy being undressed. That's it."

"Okay," she said slowly. "I've been avoiding asking you about your tours. I don't know if you need to talk about them, or if you want to, or if talking would do anything good for either of us."

Good for either of us. That part was what stuck out to him. She was a little afraid to ask, but felt compelled nevertheless.

"I can talk about my tours in a far more civilized manner than when I told you about my hand." Recalling that conversation put tonight's revelation in an even harsher light. Guilt bit even through the feel of her gentle touches, and lingered as she hung the jacket in the coat closet.

He wouldn't apologize for it again; that would turn the conversation, make it harder for her.

"Ask, love. Ask me anything."

She closed the door and leaned against it, compelling him to come to her when she didn't return. He could control his need to touch her, but not if she felt far away, if he couldn't feel her heat and wrap himself in her scent.

"Why didn't you come home after you were wounded? I know it was offered, automatic, expected even. You had to fight to remain." She'd been serving wounded soldiers long enough to have wondered, but he didn't even have to ask to know she'd had that question in her heart for years.

It was right there in her furrowed brows—old pain, worry she'd sunk into years ago, something he couldn't even blame her for anymore.

He couldn't blame her, and he didn't want her to blame herself. She would if he answered.

After he'd decided to return to active duty, he'd allowed

himself to fantasize that she was worrying about him. Pretended she was suffering over him. Even sometimes in the hospital during his recovery, when he recalled the deaths of so many friends and how easily it could've been him, he'd pictured her mourning him if it had. All immature ways to handle his grief over losing her, but it had all come from a deep-seated belief that she'd never feel those things, even if the worst had come to pass.

Knowing it would've been all he'd imagined and more made it even harder to say the words.

"Ask anything except that?" she ventured when he failed to find words.

"I don't want us to stop talking."

"It's a conversation-stopper?"

"Feels like it."

The worry was still in her eyes, but she kept on. "We need to learn to discuss painful subjects."

His words from only moments before jostled his conscience, despite her not giving them even a hint of mockery.

"It's not that I don't want it to hurt *me*." It was the only way he knew to put it.

Her slow nod and pained expression hit him harder than her silence.

Continue or not? He couldn't always trust his instincts when it came to Anais.

"I'm going to put the kettle on and change. You think about a way to say it," she directed then just left the room, as if words were so easy. She knew better.

Though, to be fair, he was probably the one hiding the most right now. She still thought Ratliffe had just taken photos of her—she didn't have any idea about the video. But this conversation wasn't that one. Focus on one trauma at a time.

Quinn undid the top few buttons of his shirt, then rolled up his sleeves to the elbow and sat on the sofa, but he couldn't make himself comfortable. If they'd sorted out their relationship already, he'd rip off the formalwear and get comfortable. Hell, he'd rip off all the formalwear, carry her upstairs and kiss every inch of her—especially the inches that made her writhe and moan.

Where they stood now, stripping down for comfort would be even weirder than late night tea in a tuxedo in her living room.

And thinking about how uncomfortable he felt was kind of a dodge for thinking about the subject that made him even more uncomfortable.

He puffed a breath and laid his head back on the sofa cushions.

There was no gentle, non-accusatory way to put it, which meant it could only end one of two ways: by starting a fight with her, or with her just taking more blame onto herself.

She wafted back down the stairs in pajamas that looked equal parts comfortable and silly—littered with hearts and, inexplicably, cartoon monkeys. Somehow the baggy tee and shorts made his modified formalwear look like the most ridiculous outfit in the room.

It was a quick trip to the kitchen and she returned with two steaming mugs and a package of cookies tucked under one arm, but he was still unprepared for the subject.

"Come up with the right words?" she asked, placing the lot on the table and sitting beside him crossways, giving him no gentle lead-in.

"No."

"Then just say it. However it comes out, that's how you need to say it. I didn't have the luxury of rehearsing a painful subject at dinner. It didn't shut down conversation, but seems to have started it."

Just say something.

He couldn't stop his hands scrubbing over his face. He hated feeling helpless. "I went back because I thought I'd be going to a new unit with Ben."

"You didn't think he'd want you to be safe, away from the fighting?"

"I knew he would've, but I wasn't so wounded as to be incapable of service. Leaving would've been selfish."

Dangerous word…

He stared at the ceiling but there weren't any answers there, just an expanse of white. And a tiny spider, which he could probably point out and distract her from this conversation…

"Why would that hurt me?" she asked, not raising her voice—still calm, but too perceptive to be dodged. "What aren't you saying?"

His head throbbed behind one eye and he mashed his palm against it.

Didn't help.

Touching her would help. He caught her closest hand again and worked his thick, clumsy-feeling fingers between her slender digits. Her thumb stroked his skin, helping more with that connective current still buzzing between them.

"Because it felt like I'd be abandoning them. Him. It wasn't some kind of respect for duty or the honor for service that got me back in a forward area. When my grandfather sent me into the military I had to make a new family, and I couldn't abandon them."

Like everyone here abandoned me.

He didn't need to say the words; he could already hear them echoing in her mind.

Her thumb stopped stroking and silence fell as she digested it. Even without looking at her, he felt her staring at his hand, and impulse confirmed it as he gave in to the need to see her.

But it was the distinct lack of yelling that spoke the loudest. She was taking it onto herself.

"It wasn't just you," he said softly. "It felt that way with my family too."

"Because of me."

"Because of *me*." He leaned on the word. "If it had just been a failed marriage, everything would've gone differently. Seven years of service has given me a different perspective. I know I was spoiled—I always thought of my wants first. I wanted you—I made it happen. Like everything else in my life. I don't begrudge them my military service—I came to love it pretty quickly. I would've easily been a lifer if I hadn't been called home."

She nodded at appropriate intervals, assuring him that she'd at least heard him, but when she slipped her hand free and roughly shoved the rolled cuff up to bare his left arm—specifically the scar peeking below the cuff at his elbow—he wondered if she'd heard him after all.

"You went through another attack?"

Redirects were better than wallowing in what he'd laid out.

"That happens in a war zone, but I'm going to assume you're asking if I was wounded in another attack. And, yes, I've picked up a few non-life-threatening wounds here and there."

"A few?" Her voice rose sharply and she climbed over to straddle his lap while her fingers tore through the buttons on his shirt, her face a picture of such horror he was almost afraid to say anything else.

"Non-lethal," he said slowly, but leaned forward as she shoved the shirt off his shoulders, then attacked the tee shirt beneath.

The word hadn't penetrated; she searched him as if he carried live explosives.

"No one reported other wounds. It wasn't in the news or in the papers. Mom would've told me if she'd heard anything like that, and I had alerts. I had alerts, Quinn. I had Internet alerts to tell me when anything happened with you. There wasn't anything reported!" She leaned back enough to look at his chest, and found both scars at once.

"I didn't report them. They were nothing…"

"Dammit, Quinton Corlow! What else?"

"Should I just list any wound I've had since I saw you? These are nothing."

"Was this another bullet?"

"No," he answered as her gentle fingers stroked over a puckered scar on his right flank. "That was a little piece of shrapnel. Again, it was nothing. It barely got past the body armor."

"And this?" She gingerly touched a three-inch slice of a scar on his other side.

"That was a bullet. Grazed me."

"Any other places hidden by your clothes?"

He tried not to look at the scar on his left arm, the one she'd initially spotted but had gotten so carried away in searching she seemed to have forgotten. He'd like her to keep forgetting it; he'd like her to forget anything to do with *that* injury. "Just what you've seen."

Nothing more to see. Move along...

"None of these required surgical intervention?" She caught his face and those gorgeous blue-green eyes drilled into him.

He wanted to be annoyed, but he had a seven-year void to fill where he would've killed for her attention and concern. "The bullet didn't lodge in me. The shrapnel was so shallow I grabbed it with tweezers. Only needed antibiotics and butterfly strips."

"And this one?" She let go of his cheek and reached for his left arm, his heart plummeting as she lifted it to examine the scar. "A fourth attack?"

"No."

"Two at once?"

He nodded and, for all his talk of openness and learning to discuss painful things, he let instinct take over—to protect her from further gory details as he protected family. She was family again. Gripping her hips, he tugged her forward until that hot little mound of flesh between her thighs ground into him.

Pressed against him, it wasn't even a stretch to trace kisses along the side of her neck, to nose into the strawberry locks she'd let down when she'd gone upstairs to change.

Anais's breath caught at the pressure of his rapidly responding body between her legs. The treacherously light brush of his lips along the tender, sensitive skin below her ear brought a melting heaviness that demanded more.

He'd survived—the living heat of him rocked beneath her, urging her fully against him, compelling her arms to slide around the wide breadth of his shoulders. He was safe now. It might feel urgent to know, but so did the desire to be closer.

His arms around her, his hands beneath her pants squeezing bare flesh as he ground her purposefully against him… made his intentions completely clear.

"Let's go upstairs," he murmured against her ear between kisses, and the words somehow brought their situation back into hazy focus.

He'd said *no* on Tuesday. Not without words from her.

Slowly, understanding began to seep back in.

They'd been talking and he'd suddenly shifted direction.

She knew that pattern.

She pushed against his shoulders to open enough space to look at him.

"Why now? You've changed your mind about sleeping with me?"

The sigh that burst from him accompanied by those previously heavily lidded eyes snapping closed answered even before he flopped his head back against the cushioned seat-back.

No words. No denial. No agreement.

He *was* distracting her.

"You ass!" She shoved herself off his lap hard and didn't stop until she was a good meter away.

"See? I knew this would lead to a fight."

"You tell me about that scar right now!" She ran back through the conversation. He thought knowing would hurt her. "That happened when your hand was shot? A second bullet?"

He hadn't lifted his head or opened his eyes. She'd have wondered if he'd fallen asleep if not for the vein pulsing wildly in his throat.

"No."

"Shrapnel?"

"Yes."

His flat answers made it worse—as if she was going to hear he'd been injured by friendly fire, or while hammering on a live bullet in some suicide attempt.

The ring...

"I thought you said it was stuck into your palm." She meant to shout. She meant to scream. But the words were just above a whisper.

Enough to hear her, he opened his eyes but there still was no life in his words. "Not the ring."

"No?"

He shook his head and a pleading look descended over him.

"Worse than the ring?"

What could be worse than the ring?

"Any additional information about that is going to make it worse. Just let it go."

"Please tell me."

"Bone."

One word dropped and her body went haywire, like every possible sensation fighting for control of the nerves in her skin. Cold. Burning. Tingling. Jolting pain. Her hands flew to cover her face, as if that could protect her from it.

The darkness behind her eyes filled with terrible visuals to accompany the words. A slow motion track of a bullet striking his hand, then a spray of flesh, bone and platinum.

The first time her mind had conjured the images of what

had happened, his fingers had come off intact…after dangling by skin. Now they exploded, flesh, blood, and pieces of his own bone lodging in distant parts of his body.

By the time heavy rolling nausea replaced the sensation short-circuit Quinn's hands closed on her shoulders to shake her out of it.

"This is why I didn't want to tell you." He demanded, "Are you sick?"

Demanded.

"Yes!" she barked in return, flinging her hands free of her face and his off her in a spike of adrenalin she'd never been so thankful for.

Anger with herself wasn't the only emotion she had a right to in this moment. He'd earned her anger too. "What else are you hiding about that?"

"Nothing."

"You know what? I don't care. I don't care. You have to go now. I want you to go. You go home." She knew she was muttering. She knew she was ranting. She became aware she was also ripping through the closet when she snatched up his jacket and slammed the door. "Clothes. You have clothes. Put on your clothes."

He took the jacket, but eyed her with such calm she wanted to hit him.

"Clothes in case the cameras followed us home. And I hope the car waited so you don't have to call a cab or hitchhike!"

"Anais…" The way he said her name proclaimed her the unreasonable one. "I didn't want to make it worse. I was cruel when I told you about it the first time."

Grabbing both shirts from the sofa, she pushed them into his arms too. "No, rather than just telling me, you did what you always do. Distracting me with sex from something you didn't want to talk about. You said we'd do better this time, but you're *still* doing it."

The difference was she wouldn't let him get away with it this time.

"We have done better. It's a process. You don't fix things overnight. Yeah, okay, maybe I screwed up, but you didn't see your face at dinner when you talked about my hand. And when I told you the first time…"

When he started pulling his shirts on, she pushed past him to head up the stairs.

"This isn't done. Be angry. That's fine. I'm not exactly happy either right now, but we'll talk tomorrow."

Rolling her eyes, she called over her shoulder to lock the door behind him, too weary from the dreadfully long day to even keep fighting about it.

CHAPTER TEN

QUINN GAVE ANAIS three days to get over being angry with him. No calling. No texting. No standing outside her house with a stereo blaring some sappy love song…

He tried to wait and be patient, and that lasted until Wednesday. The Sip was coming up and he needed this sorted out before they had to make their biggest public appearance before the wedding the following weekend.

Which was how he found himself knocking at her office door after Ben had alerted him to her presence at the facility for the first time since their divorce failure had been made public.

This time, he didn't wait or second guess, just knocked and went inside.

She sat at her desk, dressed in her uniform, a prosthetic limb on the desk and a pair of calipers in hand, checking measurements. When he closed the door, she looked up as if she'd expected him. "Hi."

"You're back at work?"

"I'm here two days this week only. They needed me to fill a couple shifts while they're scrambling to hire someone to cover my patient list until we know whether I'll be able to come back full-time." She gestured to a chair opposite her desk. "I was going to call later."

"You were?" He sat. It all seemed too easy. There wasn't that fizzing crackle about her that announced her anger today and, with the transparency of emotion in her eyes these days, that was something to take comfort in.

She gestured again with the calipers to a newspaper on the corner of her desk. "Story about the embassy party and The Sip."

"I've seen a few photos of us from that night, but no articles yet." He opened it where she directed him to read the story while she finished up with the prosthetic.

"It's pretty positive," she said and began packing up the limb.

The writer reported mundane facts about the party and general impressions of those in attendance, but finished with a quote from an unnamed source about the royal couple.

"'Princess Anais choked up when describing the harrowing days after the Prince Captain's injury and how it changed her heart...'" Quinn read out loud, then looked at her, the words leaving a bad taste in his mouth. "That's not exactly accurate. You said it changed your specialty, but this makes it sound like you heard I was hurt, realized you loved me and then magically became a good person."

For once when talking about the media, she chuckled, rising to round the desk so she could lean against it before him. "But it doesn't say I did something bad."

"You think it's positive?" He chucked the paper onto the floor and wiped his hands on his trousers, just to get that slick newspaper feel off his skin.

"It's more positive than anything else they ever wrote about me. About us."

Hearing her say *us* after a tense few post-fighting days helped a little. "I suppose. But I still don't like it. Someone putting it like that when it was personal and heartfelt. It wasn't a show. I don't like the way it's being twisted."

He was so turned inward, trying to match the words he'd read with the speaking voices of those who'd been sitting near them, he didn't notice her moving until she filled his vision and just sat across his lap.

That simple move summoned a smile he couldn't contain as their eyes met.

"You're not angry with me anymore?" he asked, holding off on wrapping his arms around her, on kissing her, until he was certain.

"I got over it last night. But I was still dreading this conversation. Be happy. The article did something else good for us besides not painting me as a horrible wretch." She wrapped one arm around his shoulders and leaned in, giving him an unspoken green light to do what his arms ached for.

"What's that?"

"Gave you the chance to say something wonderful, and complain about the press with enough heat to rival my old tirades."

He couldn't help pressing his luck. "If I write a strongly worded letter, you think you might feel moved to kiss me?"

Her answer was to press her soft lips to his, warm, lingering and loving. One kiss that lasted long enough to imprint the feel of her long after it ended and she'd leaned her forehead against his.

Cheekiness aside, he felt the words coming out before he even knew what they were going to be. "Are we okay?"

She nodded subtly. "Just don't do it again. I'd rather you hurt me than sweep everything under the rug. I get that you don't mean it that way, but it makes me feel like you don't care enough to make the effort."

"That's not—"

"I know."

He should tell her about the video. The one he hadn't watched. The one he really knew too little about to drop on her now.

She tilted her head to his shoulder and, instead of speaking, he held her closer.

He'd tell her.

After the wedding.

* * *

A wide valley ringed the base of Palace Peak, the land long devoted to sport or merrymaking related to various holidays and festivals.

In honor of The Sip—the big, traditional party given before royal weddings—massive colorful tents littered the valley in a zigzagging path toward the palace, each representing a different brand of mead made by his countrymen.

Quinn watched as, far below, people prowled from tent tavern to tent tavern, sampling each brand's mead en route to the large white pavilion at the back, where the revelers would cast their vote on the gender of their future child and await their King and his family.

He couldn't see the details from the high vantage point at the rear of the palace, but from a distance it looked like fun, like organized, colorful chaos.

Due to the popularity of the event, in his grandfather's time—when travel became much easier—it had been changed to an invitation only event rather than the free-for-all the old festival valley took years to recover from. For three generations now, a select few thousand guests were invited personally by the royal family, and a lottery system bestowed the remaining five thousand plus-one invitations, resulting in ten thousand more guests from the citizenry. Nearly fifteen thousand people waited for them below.

One big, ironically named open bar.

"Did the organizers provide safe, free transportation for our guests and extra security as I asked?"

Quinn turned at Anais's voice and felt a huge smile steal across his face. She hated the title, but in that dress...she was a princess. A princess dressed in a color he would never tire of. One sexy bared shoulder, then some manner of short, sheer blue and green ruffled silk that blended together but still hugged her slight curves.

"And food to lessen the possible drunken debauchery, Your Gorgeous Highness."

She scrunched her face at the title. “Don’t forget lessening the extent of the probable poor decision-making.”

How in the world had he fallen in love with a teetotaler?

“So, you’re saying you don’t want the gender of our first child being predicted by a bunch of lushes? Have you no respect for tradition?” He slammed his fist into the balcony balustrade to act out his faux outrage.

His antics were rewarded with a tiny smile.

“I’ll believe that when you show the science behind it.” She straightened his tie, his shoulders, then tugged on his tails to be certain he was ordered. “We should go down; the day’s almost done and I’d like to get seated before the crowds reach to the pavilion.”

She was not at all looking forward to the party. Even with the cheerful, spritely folk music dancing up from the valley below. He wouldn’t even mention the toasts—drunken and sober—that had become part of the tradition. She’d stopped indicating her displeasure at the idea of staying married, but he didn’t want to risk upsetting it more than tonight’s spectacle would.

“Are you looking forward to the dancing? I know you’ve been practicing, and your dress keeps your feet visible so every drunken reprobate can marvel at your fancy stomping.”

She snorted then but took his hand and tugged him back through the palace and into the carriage waiting for them.

In the light of the late afternoon, the ring on her finger shone blue-green—the perfect color, the color that had informed his decision to badger every jeweler in Europe until he’d gotten the stone he wanted of sufficient size for a proper engagement ring, but small enough she’d actually wear it.

She took his hand as she settled into the cushioned seat and the carriage started down towards the large tents.

Things had been calm between them since that day at Almsford and, as long as they got through tonight smoothly, everything would be all right. He could see the finish line; they just had to keep it together until they got there.

Hoofbeats on cobblestones announced them and the crowds parted, opening a path to the rear pavilion. She waved, as was expected, and he did as well though he kept an arm around her shoulders.

If he had any chance of giving her any ease tonight, it would be through contact. He shouldn't stop touching her. The connection helped them both, and even if he'd sworn off using distraction to soothe her, this wasn't using sex as a distraction. It didn't count.

Only when they were inside the white pavilion did Quinn's good mood falter. It was the throne that did it, the one that would stay empty tonight because the King was too ill to attend.

"What's wrong?" Anais asked from beside him at the high table. When he turned toward her, the grim and worried shadow had returned to her lovely eyes.

Don't trouble her with it yet.

Later.

"Philip's not here yet. But it's fine—he'll be in time for the toasts."

While the King wouldn't be attending at all. People would wonder why. She'd wonder why, might even take it personally—her relationship with Philip had always been good enough, but the King had kept her at a formal distance.

Telling her the truth now would just give her one more thing to be concerned about, when she should be looking like a happy bride.

"Should we have waited for him and the King to ride with us?"

The King...

He was saved from another lie by the sudden cacophony of Philip's arrival and a small army of guests behind him. "He came down earlier to try the meads and cast his vote. He's campaigning for the sweetest mead available. Although no one really believes it. Sweet meads never win the vote; everyone always thinks it should be a son born first and votes dry regardless."

"Wants a niece, does he?"

"That's what he said. What he actually said was: I'm so good at breaking traditions, I should have a girl to break the streak. Give the country a born princess to fuss over again."

There had been no daughters in the family at all since the late eighteenth century, helped by the custom of keeping families small to avoid a sprawling royal line and possible inheritance issues.

She accepted it with a little shake of her head, still untalkative. Where Philip was, order soon followed. As soon as he'd greeted them both, he took to the dais and began the formal festivities.

Toasts came—as much as they could be called toasts when it was far more like his cousins and extended family roasted him instead. By the time a lull came, the band at the far end began to play.

Anais's pointed looks toward the empty throne said more about her attention than words could have. He definitely had to tell her after the party. Truthfully, he couldn't think of why he hadn't told her before—sitting with his terminally ill grandfather had been part of his daily life since returning home.

Philip hand-delivered two tankards of the sweetest mead to them. Anais took a literal sip and went to cast her vote for the sweetest mead available.

When she returned, it was with a pallor so stark that when he saw her crossing back to him he was compelled to meet her and lead her back to her seat.

"It affected you that strongly?"

The confused look she gave him answered that question.

"That tiny sip?"

She swallowed visibly and shook her head, her gaze skating over the crowd to land on a lanky, dark-haired man.

Not again.

He'd taken care of Ratliffe. The man was out of the country and would be arrested if he returned without royal decree.

Her fear, which he'd once tried to ignore, was now like a foghorn to him. It made keeping quiet a massive undertaking.

Another drink of the mead held his tongue, but he struggled to mask his frustration while watching her go from visibly stricken to breathing more evenly, and finally to where some color returned to her cheeks.

Pale and terrified to quasi-normal.

She'd reasoned through without his help. That had to be an improvement. Public appearances must be triggering them; this was the third time it had happened.

With no other weapons in his publicly acceptable arsenal, he offered her his hand and stood. When she slowly mirrored his action, he led her onto the dance floor. Distraction was all he had right now.

Only one sighting of the specter of Wayne Ratliffe tonight. Anais still didn't know if that was because afterward she'd purposely avoided looking at many people, or because the jubilant mood of the people celebrating their engagement had washed those probable hallucinations away.

She'd like to think the latter, then she could tell herself that she was getting over it. She'd like to pretend that since Ben's surgery she hadn't seen Wayne everywhere.

Well, everywhere but the American Embassy. She couldn't make any more sense of that than she could the scores of waking nightmare visions clogging her days.

They plagued her so effectively she couldn't help jumping to that conclusion about the random daily calls and hang-ups happening since Quinn had removed Wayne from the country. Even though her numbers were unlisted and she couldn't conceive how he'd get them.

Anais took Quinn's hand as he helped her down from the carriage which had brought them back to the palace.

He was the only good part of her evening. Nothing terrible had happened at the party, but he had been a bubble of peace in the chaos.

She wanted to stay in the bubble with him tonight. Pretend this was going to work out as much as she could no longer deny she ached for it to.

As soon as her feet settled firmly on the ground, she stepped against him and reached for him, rising on tiptoe as her arms crept around his shoulders and urged his mouth to hers. Not an ounce of resistance held him from her, his wonderful mouth pressed to hers, and soon he had his arms tight around her waist, his head tilting to deepen the kiss that had become her unspoken plea to stay.

Late in the evening, late in their relationship, and late with admissions she'd known the truth of for weeks, Anais leaned her head back just enough to give it words. She whispered against his lips, "I believe you."

The sharp intake of his breath made her open her eyes, and the intensity of the emotion she saw made her throat constrict. He nodded, accepting her words, and then immediately swept her into motion with him. One arm released her, but the other stayed around her waist as he hurried her up the long stairs through the public entrance of the palace and across the brilliantly ornate and decorated foyer to the private wing.

Practically running, his feet didn't slow until he had her alone in his suite and the door closed. With a twirl, her back touched the door and his mouth fell on hers again, the hunger of his kiss sparking over every inch of her. She even felt it in the arches of her feet.

She had questions and fears, and darkness hovered on the horizon. The country might accept her now, but once Wayne returned for real—and he would—it would come undone. But that wasn't tonight, and she needed to be close to Quinn, to soothe away the worry she'd seen on his too handsome face every time he had looked toward the empty throne. She needed to see the rest of him, the body she'd known and which was at once strange and familiar to her wandering hands.

Finding the front of his collar, she fumbled with the black bow tie until the feat of continuing to be kissed senseless while trying to untie anything became too much and she broke the kiss, tilting her head to see his tie enough to get it open, and the buttons beneath it.

Quinn shrugged out of the formal tails, tossed them onto a couch and then pulled her back into his arms.

He'd never been in bad shape, but now the man's shoulders could've been used to model anatomy for biology classes. She felt his hands wrestling with the numerous buttons up the back of her bodice, and her hands were pulled from their appreciative exploration as he spun her to face the door so he could attack the fastenings from the back.

A button or two, and he'd kiss the back of her neck, nip, bite and suck at the skin he could get at, then struggle to unwrap more of her.

Sometimes he brushed his lips so lightly over her skin goosebumps rose over her entire body.

In seven years he hadn't forgotten one thing about touching her. Even during the frenzied sex on her office floor, he couldn't help himself angling his thrusts just the right way, assaulting the most tender parts of her neck and shoulders with kisses that defined every type of kiss possible, leaving light marks on her chest for days after.

The emotion flowing off him now echoed that fervor, but was as far from that dark need as she'd been from home and from him for so many years.

When her dress finally came open and he could tug it down and off, he gave a triumphant laugh and within seconds the long-line bra she'd worn popped off too.

Only then did he let her turn back to him to resume her quest to get him out of his clothes.

"Bed this time," he croaked and she nodded, so starved for the feel of his chest she had to stop with his shirt half undone when she caught the gentle whorls of dark hair and pressed her lips to the center, then nibbled and licked her way up to his collarbone. His stuttering breaths and gasps sounded like music.

Her dress was abandoned several steps back. Panties and shoes weren't much of a barrier, so Quinn joined her fumbling efforts to tear through his clothes, and soon the shirt was gone. Her eyes went to those scars again, but this time her mouth followed—kissing each puckered ridge.

Every brush of her lips had him twisting, his breaths coming in stuttering gasps.

At the bed, he tossed her back and kicked off the rest of his clothes in mere heartbeats.

His body felt strong enough to put her faith in. Tempted her to compare that strength to his loyalty and love. But that put him out of reach; she couldn't have anything that beautiful.

He looked like a man who'd earned his strength through labor and toil, through hardship. But hardship didn't always build emotional character the way it could knit muscle.

"Any mystery left?" he asked, a flirting light in his eyes, his breathless smile brightening the need that had been roaring between them both.

Too much.

Thinking about it would ruin everything.

"Unraveling," she said instead, then laughed as he grabbed her feet and chucked her shoes over his shoulders.

By the time he'd stripped her bare patience had long been abandoned by them both, and she couldn't tell which of them was shaking hardest as he sank into her. All she knew was an exquisite ache in her chest, and the certainty that no one could ever replace him.

Fiery passion, pleasure so acute it was almost pain and raw sweetness she couldn't remember ever fully appreciating, but which she knew she didn't deserve.

At the height of it, when she'd shattered and he'd put her fragments back together again, she tugged his head onto her breast and smoothed back the damp, curling brown hair, stubbornly refusing to let those thoughts reform that had only amplified since he'd slid that beautiful ring onto her finger.

"I know you're not ready to say it," he murmured when his breaths had stopped coming in gulps, and lifted over her to look into her eyes. "But I need to say it."

Chewing her upper lip in an effort to hold back the tide building behind her eyes, she nodded and held his gaze as he said the words to her again, words she'd admitted she now believed. She still didn't deserve them, but she wanted them. Oh, how she wanted him.

A nod was the answer she could give and when he gently thumbed tears from her lashes and laid his head back down, she returned to petting his hair, knowing clearly this time that the shaking was hers.

The sweeter he was, the more certain she became he'd be snatched away from her and that she should run now, as fast and hard as her feet would carry her. The sweeter he was, the more she came to suspect she'd just had sex without barriers again because she wanted pregnancy to blame for being stupid this time. Pregnancy would make it understandable, maybe even forgivable, to stay until she was so consumed by him that his turning from her would destroy her.

But betrayal always came when least expected. He should know that almost as well as she did.

CHAPTER ELEVEN

"WAKE UP, SLEEPY."

His voice, warm and happy, broke through Anais's lazy morning sleep like a blast from the past, announcing Quinn's intention to get her up by any means necessary.

She had to work to keep the instinctive smile off her face.

"Nope."

Even as she said the word and tried to calm her cheeks, Anais felt her body tensing, readying for his attack.

It was an old game. She couldn't remember a day he hadn't woken up in a good mood—something she'd have sworn she hated before Quinn. But somehow, even when she wasn't legitimately reluctant to rise, she found herself playing along, which always improved her natural morning crankiness. Quinn's improvised wake-up techniques were more effective than coffee, both for her alertness level and her mood.

Sweet kisses.

Ear-nibbling.

Forehead-licking…

He'd even bitten her toes a time or two.

Once, he'd bitten her bum and turned his wake-up call into the best morning sex in history.

"Get up. Get up," he chanted, bouncing the bed a couple of times so that she jiggled in the covers. Then stopped.

Was that it?

She squeezed her eyes tighter shut, conscious now of the distinct possibility that, good mood or not, he just didn't *do* that anymore. In which case…yeah, she'd just be lying there, looking like a childish, lazy moron.

He'd stopped talking. She didn't hear moving either… Had he gone? Had he gone and she'd missed it?

The instant she opened her eyes to check he pounced, ripping the bedclothes back until she was bared to the hips. Then he loosed a battle cry, hands lifting with fingers curled in a classic *Gotcha!* position.

He. Was. Going. To. Tickle. Her.

Tickling. Morning tickling?

Before she could process it, he took a breath deep enough to puff his cheeks and launched himself at her belly.

One arm clamped over her thighs, the other wrapped over her chest to lock her arm down. Secured, he pressed his mouth to her belly and blew hard, unleashing the loudest, rudest noises into the room and sending those deep tissue vibrations through her.

Anais yelped, tried not to laugh, and did the only thing she could: squirm hard to get free.

But it didn't matter how hard she tried not to laugh or get away, she soon shook with the kind of crippling, uncontainable laughter that rendered her body useless.

When every breath sounded like a tortured asthmatic's he'd stop and let her get a lungful. Or maybe he just stopped to refill his own lungs, needing the air to continue his onslaught.

One of her wild bucks managed to free an arm, and she shoved at his head while helplessly laughing, yelling, *"Stop!"* and turning it into a seventeen-syllable word.

He did. Just backed right off, as if he'd marked a task off his morning to-do list. "Morning," he greeted, as if none of that had just happened, and leaned down to kiss her while brushing her thoroughly messy hair from her face.

Gentle. Tender. Loving. Addictive. Especially to someone like her who'd never belonged anywhere. But she felt as if she belonged with him. When they were alone, she felt as if she belonged with him, even *to* him in a primitive way that offended her feminist sensibilities. It was just the rest of his world she couldn't even imagine fitting into.

"The sunlight gave it away." Her voice came out far huskier than she could've done on purpose. She cleared her throat and asked, "How many cups of coffee have you had?"

Even if her role required her to be the reasonable one, she couldn't keep herself from petting him while she reasserted some reason into the morning. She loved raking her fingers through his messy curling hair.

"None."

"And not hungover, I see."

"Just on sweet, sweet lovin'."

She laughed again. "Perhaps still a little drunk."

"Just on sweet, sweet—"

Clapping a hand over his mouth was the only sensible way to stop this silliness, but nothing could stop her smiling. "Slept well then?"

Behind her hand, he nodded, his eyes merry.

"Have a plan for the day you're eager to get going with?"

Wrapping one hand around her wrist, he pulled her hand free. "Hungry. We're having breakfast in bed, but not until you're no longer naked."

Winking, he slid off her, leaving her aware that he was actually dressed—if pajama bottoms counted as dressed. He certainly wasn't naked.

She sat up and he tossed a tee shirt at her, which she dutifully whisked over her head and stuffed her arms into. "I wouldn't want to come between you and your oatmeal."

"Eggs. Bacon. Fruit. No oatmeal." He opened the door of the bedroom and gestured; she heard a rolling cart and tucked the blanket around her legs so she didn't look naked save for Quinn's desert camouflage tee.

"And after you eat?" She should bring up what she'd

meant to say last night before she'd ended up throwing herself at him in the courtyard.

He said quiet thanks to the lovely person who'd brought them food, then wheeled to the bed to join her. "After I eat, I'm going to sit with Grandfather."

She'd plucked up a slice of crisp bacon and had it to her mouth before his quiet words registered. *The subject.* With it came understanding, though she'd mostly worked it out last night. "How bad is it?"

"Ten." He lost the bright playful spark from only moments before, and his shoulders came down just a little. "Ten on a scale of ten."

"Is it…? Are you…?" The words refused to take shape. It seemed traitorous somehow to ask how long before the King died. Even phrasing it as grandfather to a grandson who loved him and couldn't be bearing up well against the coming end.

"He's stable right now, but his kidneys have failed and he's too old for a transplant." Over the next few minutes, and in as few words as he could get away with, Quinn outlined the severity of his grandfather's illness, the reason he'd not been at the party and how soon after the wedding they might be having a coronation.

"He's usually awake late morning, early afternoon, so I visit with him then and go to see Ben after."

"I'm so sorry." Pathetic words.

Corrachlean had been lucky with her monarchs; they'd had it good for so long that each new king came to the throne with the respect and love of his people as a starting position. No need to win the people over or prove himself. No matter how things had gone with her marriage, and they had never gone well, that loyal and even loving feeling for King Thomas had never left her. "You could've told me before now. You told me about Ben."

"At first I didn't because we were at odds. Then I didn't because you've already been stressed over our courtship.

Last night, I regretted not telling you before you were in a position to notice he wasn't around, but by then I didn't want to put a damper on an evening already filled with things you dislike: drinking and more drinking."

She looked at the plate she'd been munching from, but abandoned it in favor of a strong cup of tea. "Would you like me to come with you this morning? I brought a change of clothes with me. I could make myself presentable. But if he wouldn't want me to, please don't feel like you can't say no."

"He actually already asked to see you yesterday at our visit. I was working up to telling you." A tiny smile followed the admission.

She leaned over to kiss him, doing all she could to avoid bringing up their past relationship and trying not to think about how it would resume. "I probably won't say much; I don't want to interrupt your visit."

"No, I mean he wants to see you privately, love. I'll take you down, but after that I'm not invited."

"Why?"

"He said he wanted to talk about some things."

"That's not at all ominous…"

She liked that she didn't need to explain why it made her nervous.

"It'll be fine. You're not being called to task by the headmaster. He's not…" There, words seemed to fail him and he shook his head. "He's different. You'll see."

If things hadn't felt real at the party, standing with Quinn outside the King's private quarters did.

King Thomas had been the hardest sell to their marriage. Anais hadn't been so foolish as to be surprised by this, but she'd thought he'd come around when he saw how much she loved his grandson. He hadn't.

But, to be fair, he had an unruly, uncontrollable grandson whose behavior jeopardized royal stability, and she'd been a huge example of that.

He'd never been unkind exactly, but always disapproving. Disapproving enough to make it abundantly clear that she'd never fit into the family. Never be acceptable. Accepted. She'd even imagined him gleeful when he'd finally ordered their divorce.

Illness changed people, and Quinn had said as much. The best she could do would be to approach him as if she'd never known him, pretend there wasn't a difficult history there. Let him reject her afresh!

Holding Quinn's left hand, she walked behind him into the room after the little knock announced them.

"Grandfather?"

A stately leather wingback faced the morning sun streaming through open French windows, the only source of light in the quiet room. A hand lifted, indicating where he sat, right where Quinn apparently expected him to be—they were already heading in that direction.

"Good morning." Quinn took his grandfather's translucent hand and gave it a little loving jiggle before ushering her into his line of sight. "I brought her. Don't give her too much grief. I still have to get her to the altar. No scaring her off for another week."

He reserved a wink for her, driving home the notion that he was teasing, but he still kissed her cheek and all but put her into a chair opposite the King so she couldn't run away.

"Good morning, Your Highness." She never knew how to address the man. In her eleven-month marriage, she'd never made any attempt to come closer than formal titles.

Pale gray eyes met hers and she managed a smile, even as her training kicked in and she began taking inventory of his symptoms. It gave her a controlled center to start from when she didn't know what else was coming at her.

Flushed.

Weak.

Tired.

Quinn closed the door behind him, leaving her alone with her monarch.

"My son tells me you're to be wed at week's end. I regret that I won't be there to see either of my sons marry."

The words tilted in her mind a little. Quinn and Philip were his grandsons. Was that a symptom? Or was this a shorthand way of referring to the true state their relationship had grown into after the death of their father, the King's actual son?

"That's what I'm told too." She chuckled. "I've not been involved in any of the plans. Quinn said there are wedding planners who are seeing to everything, and they've had such short notice. I'm sure I'll be more than impressed with whatever they manage. The gown I know is far too beautiful for me to do justice."

"Nonsense, Mireille, I'm sure you'll look more beautiful than even Nicholas could imagine."

Mireille and Nicholas—Quinn's parents.

Symptom.

"I'll do my best and, if I fail, he'll still humor me." She stood up and slipped over to his side. "May I kiss your cheek, King Thomas?"

He tilted his head back, pale eyes smiling. Permission, even if he thought her someone else. Anais pressed her lips to his cheek and felt the heat that explained the flush and his confusion.

"You're warm," she said as clearly as she could, crouching down beside him in the light spilling through the windows. When she had his eye, she saw the instant the fog lifted and he recognized her. Right behind it, he realized his earlier confusion.

"Oh, dear, Anais, I thought..." His voice trailed off as his mind caught up.

She took his hand and smiled despite the tears she felt in her eyes again. "You have a fever, sir. You're not losing your senses. It's the fever. May I look at the port? I want to make sure it's not inflamed."

Although he would never have allowed such familiarity before, he squeezed her hand, then rolled up the long sleeve on his pajamas to reveal an AV graft in his upper arm. She didn't need the bright sunshine to see how red the skin was.

"Does it hurt right now, sir?"

"It's tender," he admitted and then laid his head back. "I asked you here to apologize for the way your marriage was received. You two acted on blind love, and I only saw breach of protocol and tradition, another instance where my grandson bent to impulse and whimsy. But once it was done..."

"You're not to blame for that."

"We're all to blame for it, I expect. That's how these things go. People don't fall from a single mistake; they fall from many." He reached up and patted her cheek and her heart fisted up, so tight she almost choked on it. Couldn't even name the flood of emotions that traveled with the tears in her eyes.

Sympathy? Worry for him? For Quinn? Gratitude at his sudden acceptance? All of it.

"He's going to need you, when the time comes."

Words that sounded like his blessing.

She twisted her mouth to the side, keeping it together long enough to offer words of comfort and gratitude, then a promise to look at his medical record and see what antibiotics would help.

No longer able to control the tears threatening, she kissed his cheek again and excused herself.

Quinn had told her what another infection would mean. And now she had to tell him.

Even had it been the longest hallway in the palace rather than the shortest, she couldn't have stopped crying before she got there.

* * *

"What do you mean he's in and out?" Quinn nearly shouted, then realized his volume. With a deep breath, he rolled his shoulders and eased down into the chair he'd abandoned with Philip on the business side of the King's desk.

Her red-rimmed eyes were clarification enough, but he couldn't accept it.

"He's experiencing moments of confusion," she said gently. "It's not dementia. It's probably the fever, but it's also possible he needs another round of dialysis sooner than expected. Toxins that build up in the blood can cause confusion. But he realized it; I didn't correct him when he called me Mireille and Quinn Nicholas. Then he recognized me."

"Mom?" Philip asked. He'd been looking far too calm for this conversation, but alarm edged into his voice upon hearing their grandfather had called his granddaughter-in-law by the name of his long-dead daughter-in-law.

"We'll just have to talk him into another placement," Quinn said. "Or will antibiotics clear it up?"

"I'm honestly not sure. I think once they get infected, it's hard to treat them without moving."

Her voice was so gentle it made it all worse. She was preparing him for the worst; every note of sympathy in her voice drove him that much closer to losing it.

"They've done three now?" she asked, looking at his grandfather's medical record. "Did they not want to try a fistula? They take a while to mature for use, but they don't get infected as often as grafts."

Philip reached for his phone. "They tried that initially, but it wasn't maturing as they needed it to."

"I don't know what that is." Quinn knew he should have learned everything about kidney failure too. He could've been reading that when he'd sat by hospital beds. And he'd do that after he put a stop to this. "I'm going to talk to him."

Anais stepped around the desk and clutched his arm to

stop him. "He needs to rest, Quinn. Go sit with him, but don't fight with him."

"That's all I've been doing since I got home, Anais. I've spent damned near a month trying, with varying degrees of success, to make two people I love want to live. Three, if you count you."

Quinn watched her retreat immediately, first the warmth he always needed from her, then her hands, finally her whole body—she stepped back from him and he didn't know if it was anger or hurt that propelled her.

He was being unreasonable, unfair even, to lump her in with Ben and Grandfather when her version of giving up on life was entirely metaphorical compared to theirs. But he couldn't apologize to soften his stance right now. Fire got things done.

Pounding back down the hallway with Philip on his heels, Quinn let himself into his grandfather's room. "You've got an infection, Grandfather. We're going to get the doctor here to schedule you for another graft. And antibiotics." He looked up at Philip. "You should go call the doctor."

"I did it while you were shouting at Anais," Philip muttered and then sat down opposite the King. "You're not going to feel better until the infection is taken care of. I think they can do another temporary site while this one heals…"

"No."

Until now, the King had been placidly listening to them both, but when Philip suggested treatment Quinn wasn't aware of—because he'd been in another damned country—it got a response, but not the right one.

What would get the right response? With Ben, he'd had Rosalie to use as a motivator, but their grandmother had long since passed away.

"Temporary access site sounds like a good thing." Quinn fumbled along to back Philip up. "Infections are a nasty way to die. I don't… I don't want you to die like that."

His throat closed on the words so that he had to take a few runs at it.

"I doubt any death is particularly pleasant, sweet boy. I'm just sorry I'm not going to be around for your wedding and to meet my first great-grandchild."

That sounded like goodbye. As if he were dying today. Or as if he needed to say things before the fever robbed him of his senses for good.

Quinn couldn't accept that. He'd never argued with his grandfather, or hadn't since his age had ended in *teen*, but he argued now. "You can be around for that."

"It's not your decision, Quinn." Philip's gentle rebuke set his hackles rising.

He stood and rounded on Philip, every instinct saying *fight*. "You're so ready for the crown you're ready to give up to a little infection?"

"That's not fair. I've been here…"

"And I've been somewhere I had to fight every day to keep people I love alive. I even had to fight to keep people I hated alive. You expect me to just sit back and let death take *him* when there are things we can do to prevent it?" He was yelling. He didn't mean to be yelling. Again. He'd just yelled at Anais…whom he couldn't find in the room. She hadn't come with them, wasn't there to see him losing it.

"Quinton."

His softly spoken name sucked the rage out of him and his strength with it. He felt it in the wobble of his knees and sat back down before they buckled. "Yes?"

"Philip hasn't given up at the first obstacle. He's been here through the other moves. That's nothing against you, but to you—who has just now been able to come home to us—this feels like the first."

He knew that. Logically, he knew it. But the idea of losing someone now that he'd finally gotten them back…

A dust mote swirled in a beam of sunshine from the open windows, and he just let himself watch. It was better than watching his grandfather giving up. It even felt kind of applicable—watching it drift into the shadow and invisibility that might as well be nothingness.

"I can give you one more move if you can give me something."

The words were the first iota of hope since he'd awakened with Anais's soft hair on his skin, and it yanked his attention back. "What can I give you?"

"Your word that with the next failure you will accept my decision."

He froze. Maybe the next time it would last longer. Long enough for Quinn to come up with an argument that would work. Hope was hope.

How long had the last move held? He should know that too. The King expected his infection to return soon, to not last as long as Quinn needed him to last.

"If I say no, you let yourself be eaten by this infection now?"

A nod was his answer.

There was no choice.

Despite the cold emptiness opening in his chest, Quinn nodded. It was still a win.

So why did it leave him feeling empty…and guilty?

Grandfather forcing bitter terms wasn't the same as him forcing Anais to say yes to the wedding. They would have a long, great, love-filled life together. Children. Unruly teenagers. Grandchildren. Maybe even great-grandchildren. Good things would come from *his* act of coercion.

It wasn't the same.

God, Anais hated the penthouse, but she'd had a last-minute dress fitting and it was the easiest place to do it.

Now done, Anais sat alone on his sofa, waiting for Quinn to get home. Her eyes kept skirting to the bedroom where the safe was. She couldn't remember the combination to the safe, probably the only reason she hadn't come for those pictures the day after he'd told her about them.

In days they were getting married, but she was rapidly unspooling. No work now; all she had to do was spend time at home, thinking of all the ways this could come undone. She stayed because she needed Quinn to help her shore up the crumbling walls around what remained of her sanity if they were going to make it to the church.

"Hey," Quinn said, drawing her attention away from the direction of the safe and alerting her to his arrival at once.

Before she could say anything the smile dropped from his handsome face. "What happened?"

Lots. Sort of.

"I need you to talk me through something," she said haltingly, because she'd just sat there when she should've been coming up with the best, most calm, rational way to start this conversation. Yet more proof she was losing her mind.

Quinn approached slowly; she must look as skittish as she felt. "Okay… What?"

"Your plans. Like 'Break in Case of Emergency' plans for the whole… Wayne comes back and shows his copies to everyone—including the King, who only just began accepting the idea of you marrying me a few days ago."

"Four days," Quinn said instead, settling carefully beside her. "You just have to make it four more days. Then things will calm down."

"That's not a plan." She laughed, too high and fast to sound like anything but panic. "You don't have an emergency plan, do you?"

"My plan is to keep tabs on him so he can't do anything like that, and it's working just fine."

"That's not a plan. That's hoping. Vigorous hoping maybe, but I'm talking about an evacuation plan for when the building catches on fire, and you're counting on the presence of a smoke detector to prevent fires from starting."

"What happened?" he asked again, his voice so calm it increased her alarm.

"I know you think you've taken care of Wayne." She felt her voice rising and tried to calm it, tried to speak more slowly. "It's been happening since the park. I know, or I think, and try to tell myself it's never him. How could it be him when I see him everywhere? That's not logical, and I remind myself of that, but I don't *know* that for sure. One of them could actually be him, but instead I convince myself ten times a day that I'm just losing my mind, which isn't helping either."

Not level. Not calm. One moment her voice was in the rafters, the next the bottom of the ocean…because she kept babbling. She hadn't meant to just subject him to a panic attack.

"Ten times a day?"

"I don't know, exactly. I don't keep count. I just see him. He might be in another country, but you can't be sure of that. He could still surface. He could have copies. He could wait years, wait until he runs out of money, then come back at us. How can we live with this and not have an emergency plan? What would you tell the King?"

As soon as it was out of her mouth, Anais knew she'd chosen the wrong example. The King wouldn't be here in years.

The grim line his mouth became confirmed the misstep.

"I'm sorry. I wasn't thinking." She tried to undo it before he got too upset about that to be logical about this. "It's just when I saw King Thomas, he made me feel like family for the first time. If just for a few minutes, it made me afraid to lose that. And, now that I say it out loud, I see it's not even about everyone else. It's you too. I'm going crazy because I'm afraid of losing you once you've seen them."

He scrubbed at his forehead. Didn't work, but his frustration with her couldn't be worse than the frustration she felt for herself.

"I'm not going to leave you over dirty pictures I already know exist."

"Knowing and seeing are different things. You can't know it won't change the way you see me." She felt her temperature rising and stood up; maybe moving would help. "It was over a decade ago and it still affects the way I see myself!"

"How much more than a decade?"

The slow tilt of his head with the lowering of his brows set off alarms in her chest.

When she didn't say anything, he tried again, and this time he did stand up. "How old were you, Anais?"

"Old enough to know better," she muttered. "Does it matter?"

"You're twenty-seven. Over a decade ago? Yeah, that damn well matters."

Not the point she was getting at. Anais wasn't even sure what her point had been before, but this conversation was doing nothing for that fear she'd been trying to ignore. "What matters is that I'm afraid all the time. It's not just my paranoid hallucinations… I'm getting calls. He calls, waits for me to answer, hangs up. Happens on my cell, at home too."

"That could be anyone. People just wanting to hear your voice."

"Or it could be *him*." Unraveling—the whole thing was unraveling, harder and faster, the more they talked. And it felt exactly like she'd imagined the Wayne blackmail conversation going seven years ago.

"Just listen," he said, making a clear effort to modulate his voice, even taking her hand, which usually helped. "I can come up with a plan, but it's not necessary right now. I didn't just remove him from the country under controlled custody. First, I had our cyber force search of his Internet footprint. Emails. Cloud storage. Everything. We did new passwords, wiped everything clean. Found nothing online, just what he'd stashed at his mother's place, and I took both of those cameras."

He said some other things… Anais could see Quinn's mouth moving, but a loud, persistent ringing in her ears covered the sounds coming out of his mouth.

Both cameras?

Two cameras.

Why would the cameras that took the pictures matter? Camera. It was one camera.

"It was just photos," she said, or tried to say. Her voice didn't even sound over the ringing in her ears. "What does the camera…? What do you mean?"

Still ringing. And her fingers went so cold they felt stiff. Stress was causing her to have a freaking stroke.

But her vision was crystal-clear. She must've managed the words, because she saw Quinn's face lose the angry color he'd built up, and his mouth stopped moving too.

It took him a while to start talking again, which was fine considering the state of her *stroke.*

Some deep breathing slowed her heart down enough for the ringing to decrease.

He'd started talking again. Something, something… *watched enough to confirm…*something.

Watched?

Watched.

"Video?" she asked, finally hearing her own voice over the ringing.

His slow, short nod came before more words, words of increasing clarity. "After the wedding. You can do whatever you want with it."

There was a video.

She scrambled to remember. How much had she drank?

A lot. More than she could handle, but Quinn had said he'd confirmed it was her…

"There wasn't a video. That's not me—it's someone else."

"It's you."

His quiet voice did more to convince her than anything in her memory could, but still her head kept shaking. *No.* Just no. Air was becoming an issue…she breathed faster, now through her mouth as her nose couldn't keep up with the demands her lungs made.

"You need to sit down before you faint," he said, and she couldn't argue with the diagnosis. She did feel faint, but she needed air.

Only after she got the balcony door open and the cool evening air blew in did she turn back to him, still panting.

In her wildest imaginings she'd always had that argument in the back of her mind. She'd thought she could say: *That's not me. Just some excellent photo editing...* It was done all the time for a reason, but video? Could video be edited like that?

Didn't seem like it.

"I can't do this." The words came out and she bent forward to brace her hands on her knees.

"You can. I have it. It's secure. No one will see it. But, even if someone did, it's not great, but it's not the end of the world. Everyone has sex. You may have picked horribly, but everyone will get over it. Including me."

"You're not listening." She went ahead and put her head between her knees, going silent as she focused on trying to control that part of her brain that shrieked: *Run!*

He was saying something but she couldn't listen and think, and she had to think. There had to be options. Some option that let her stay with him.

"Let's not get married!" she cried, standing up, feeling the panic again in eyes she could hardly even blink they were opened so wide. "Let's just finish the divorce and then…just stay together. I could live with that. It's unconventional but, as a princess, as a wife, they wouldn't ever let it go. But as a mistress? They'd practically expect me to have a sex tape or…whatever it is. I could live with just being together."

"I couldn't." He sprang from the sofa, but didn't chase after her. "I hate that this hurts you, hate that it scares you, but you're going to have to accept a minimal amount of risk in this. You have more chance of catastrophe by car than catastrophe by Ratliffe at this point. You're my wife. Even if you refuse the wedding. You were right; it's just a display—you're my wife already and that's not changing. All this will be easier once the ceremony is over."

"I'll never have another moment's peace if we go through with this."

"Do you think you will if you leave me again at this point? How will the media react to that? If he had copies—which I would bet the crown against—when would be a better time to come forward with them than when my threats could no longer be counted on?"

She shook so hard it even felt as if her eyes trembled. Why didn't he see it? And then she got angry, and it was so much better than the panic. "Why stop there? If you're going to threaten me, go on and threaten to give them the video yourself."

Quinn's head jerked back and, in that instant, she knew his threats had been empty this whole time. Funny, it didn't come as any sort of relief. The damage was done.

He wouldn't meet her in the middle still. He couldn't love her all that much. This wasn't killing *him.*

Twisting off her ring, she gingerly placed it onto the new coffee table.

Before he could lob another empty threat, she grabbed her handbag and hurried to the door.

She really hated his penthouse. Every time she came there, it felt more and more like a mausoleum.

CHAPTER TWELVE

THE DOOR CLOSED quietly behind Anais, and Quinn couldn't do anything but stand there and stare—first at the door, then at the engagement ring he'd so carefully picked out for her all those years ago, like another target on his new metal and stone coffee table.

Muscles across his shoulders and down his arms twitched with readiness, tempting him to attack it as she had the last one, but before he could cross the room for the weapon that burst of violent energy left him and he dropped to sit on the thing instead.

When he'd come into the room, he'd known it was about to go up in flames, but it had been his own frustration that had lit the spark. His mouth. Four more days and he could've handled this entirely differently. Everything would've been okay because he wouldn't have had to look for ways to relieve her fear *and* get her to the altar too. But tonight... he hadn't known which one to focus on. Looked like he'd picked wrong.

He needed solutions.

She loved him. She'd all but admitted it and, even if it would've been nice for her to say it once this whole time, he knew it without the words.

Rosalie had been the weapon to use on Ben, because he loved her.

His pain had worked on Grandfather, also based on love.

But not Anais. Why not her?

She'd been upset when she'd rung him earlier, asking to meet him, but, like a big dumb ostrich, he'd decided to assume she was just having another harmless Ratliffe episode and wanted to see him for comfort. He didn't even think breaking up had been on her mind until he'd let the video slip…after he'd failed once again to present solutions when she'd reached out to him.

When was he going to stop doing that?

He replayed the conversation in his mind, looking for something he might have missed. Tonight—he needed solutions tonight. Tomorrow she might speak to the press and the wedding really would be off.

His heart jerked and began to pound. With shaking hands, he grabbed the engagement ring off the table and slid it onto the upper segment of his left middle finger—the finger he'd intended to wear his wedding ring. It helped somehow. Not as much as her hand in his helped every other time he was upset, but…

She'd already been upset, but she must have thought there had to be a solution or she wouldn't have started the conversation.

Or maybe she'd just been imagining how it could go down from any destructive angle she could, dreaming up new ways to terrify herself. She hadn't yet had time to process the knowledge of the video. His chest squeezed as the ghostly image of her foundered around the living room. Even when she'd talked about his hand, she hadn't been that…broken by it.

What was on that video?

His gaze slid across the miles of white that seemed to stretch between him and the bedroom.

Not watching it, not looking at the pictures, had seemed like the respectful thing to do. That was what he'd told himself. Now it seemed like another instance of him ignoring problems so he didn't have to deal with them.

Even the thought of watching it made his skin crawl.

The video's very existence had annoyed him since he'd learned about it, and it had taken three shots of rum to soothe his rage after he'd watched only enough to verify that it had been Anais on the film.

Ten years ago, she'd have been seventeen, and he'd assumed she'd been that or older then. Over a decade? Best case scenario was sixteen. Sixteen.

Sending Ratliffe too far away for him to drive over and beat him to death tonight might have been the best decision he'd made since coming home.

With a churning stomach, he forced himself into the bedroom, and through the deafening clicks of the safe dial. Portable hard drive in hand, he loaded it on his computer.

The yellow indoor light on the dingy white walls in the video did nothing to detract attention from the girl drinking and grimacing from the tumbler of dark liquid in her hand. He'd hoped maybe she'd only been so recognizable because he'd been looking for her, and hyper-alert to the situation the first time he'd turned it on, but she was unmistakable.

"Is this alcohol?" she asked.

Ratliffe confirmed, while taunting her in the same breath. Would she prefer a kiddie cocktail? Chocolate milk maybe?

Damn, that was slick…

The look on her face as she stared at the drink, first weighing her options and then determined. The way she looked at him said she was on to him, but she still went along with it, drinking it and asking for another.

Why?

If she'd been sixteen, he'd be surprised. It felt wrong and dirty to watch it now, knowing that the evening had at least gone as far as nudity. His skin squeezed too tight for his body, almost as viciously as his stomach squeezed.

What was teenage Anais getting out of any of this?

Pausing the video, he went ahead to the bar and poured himself a rum. Was this how she'd used the drink, to deaden herself to whatever she'd been going to do? Had she come to the apartment just to take pictures?

He didn't want to watch it.

He took the bottle with him back to the desk, knowing it wouldn't be his last for the night. When he'd downed the shot, he sat and started the video again.

She talked very little, but Wayne went on about exploits he obviously thought would impress her. *Wrong.* That wasn't her impressed face.

The man refilled her glass when she asked, then trotted out a camera to show her.

Still staying…for some reason he couldn't understand. The more she drank, the less bored she looked, but she still didn't look as if she liked him at all, but she *did* fake it. She twirled her hair around one finger. Anais wasn't a hair-twirler.

Forced flirting. As if she'd read "twirl your hair" in a *How to Flirt* book.

Another surge of rage raised the hairs on the back of his neck and he took another drink of the rum, watching the scene unfold before him.

Over the next twenty minutes, she went from quiet kid with her first drink, to obviously drunk and *desperate* for Ratliffe's approval.

By the time the man joined her on the bed and Anais's clothes started coming off Quinn understood why it had happened. She'd said it to him a million times, but all those times it had sounded like such an inconsequential thing to him. Not something Anais, his strong, brilliant wife, could really be hurt by.

"I don't fit."

"They won't accept me."

"The only thing that's ever been acceptable about me is my intelligence."

"You can't know that it won't change the way you see

me. It was over a decade ago and it still affects the way I see myself!"

That one hurt the most because she was right; it did change things. Just not the way she thought.

It took an hour to speed through the rest, through rum and tears he grew too bereft to fight.

She'd posed while entirely nude, but was so innocent Ratliffe had to tell her how to show her body. He even arranged her on the bed at times. Eventually put the camera down and kissed her.

And she threw up immediately, all over the man's lap.

He almost smiled, but then she passed out and his gut returned to churning while he waited to see what Ratliffe would do. He wasn't that much older than her, but at that age…a few years made a big difference. He was more worldly, obviously. Seedier…

Quinn sped through, not relaxing at all until the man went to sleep beside her, and when she finally stirred Quinn choked on his own relief and slowed the video again.

She slid out of the bed, got up, got her clothes.

By the time Ratliffe woke and began making demands—talking about what she *owed* him—she was ready to go.

He blocked her path. Reached for her.

Quinn regretted the rum; his stomach lurched as he helplessly watched her scan the room for an escape.

It was just a room in a flat. Ratliffe blocked the only door.

She looked to the side, grabbed something and, without hesitation, smashed into his face.

The screen went strange and he realized his hands were latched onto the laptop, squeezing, as if he could reach in and grab her out.

What had she grabbed?

He forced his hands off the screen and the display smoothed back out.

Alcohol bottle—Quinn identified the weapon, then the transition. She'd gone from child to adult in that second.

Ratliffe staggered forward, his hands covering his cheek, blood running through his fingers, and she ran.

Not how he'd expected the video to end. Through his shock, he couldn't help but feel proud of her.

She'd given him that scar. The scar that people would ask him about for the rest of his miserable life.

Wasted booze. No sex. Puked on. And a lifelong scar? Yeah, that'd cause a wicked grudge. And Quinn hadn't known anything about their interactions when Ratliffe had come after her for money. In the retelling, she'd sanitized it, and he'd been so wrapped up in the revelation he hadn't asked. And he'd let him go. Sent him on his way with money, even—something else for him to fix.

The video told him something else. She had it in her to fight for them, but she'd spent so long fighting for herself she probably didn't know how to do anything but try and stay safe. Apply the lesson she'd learned.

Weight seemed to press down on the back of his neck and Quinn sagged into his chair as another realization hit him; he dropped his head into his hands.

He couldn't force or coerce her into this.

He had to sign the papers.

The clock had long past struck midnight by the time Quinn had stopped reeling enough to think straight and start moving again.

Detective called, reports—minimal as they were—gathered, Ratliffe was still in his new flat in his new country.

Though he'd been unable to even contemplate sleep, he had managed to stop drinking in time to be sober enough to drive by eight the next morning, the absolute latest minute he could wait to go to her.

Sharon answered the door almost as soon as he rang the bell, the first thing he'd been thankful for in nearly fourteen hours.

"Oh, no, Quinton Corlow. The last time you came, you

said you weren't going to upset her, but you did. If you want to talk to my daughter, you can do it through a lawyer."

She shoved at the door and he braced his shoulder against it. "Wait. I brought something Anais will want." He lifted the bedraggled yellow envelope and held it up to the narrow opening so Sharon could see it. Divorce papers.

Hope was the only thing keeping him upright—that and a plan only an idiot would take comfort in.

It took a few tense seconds, but she begrudgingly opened the door and let him inside, calling over her shoulder, "Anais, Prince Quinton is here."

Score one for Team Hope. Now just a few more…

Quinn followed the direction Sharon called and, to his surprise, Anais came around a corner from what he could only assume was the direction to the kitchen, considering the apron covering her torso and the flour dusting it.

"You're baking?" He couldn't help the question; he'd never really witnessed her doing much at all in the kitchen. She made an occasional burnt grilled cheese, but…

"I do that sometimes."

As she neared, he could see from the circles under her red puffy eyes that she'd not slept either.

Another spark of hope.

"Can we talk?"

He breathed as slowly as he could, and hoped he didn't pass out from lack of oxygen. She needed his confidence, even if it was a big fat lie right now.

She led the way up the stairs, another thing to be thankful for—this would be hard enough without his mother-in-law giving him the evil eye.

Once they'd stepped into her meticulously clean bedroom, he went to the desk, pulled out the chair and sat. Maybe that would help his agitated body need less oxygen. Also, his roiling stomach made it hard to keep steady on his feet.

Give her what she wants, then give her a reason to fight for them.

"You haven't gone to the press yet, have you?"

She stopped in the middle of the room and wrapped her arms around herself the way he itched to. "I assumed you'd want to do that."

Want to.

He sucked in a deep breath and felt his cheeks puff as he let it back out. "It's probably better if all marriage announcements come through the palace."

It was as diplomatic as he could be without lying to her, and he wasn't going to lie to her. Not today. No matter how much easier it would be to make up some story about Ratliffe meeting an untimely and wholly satisfying "accident."

She swayed on her feet, and he noticed she still wore yesterday's clothing. Another nod to hope.

Give her what she wants.

Opening the battered envelope, he extracted the documents he knew she'd recognize, and held them out to her. "I signed them and checked with the attorney to make sure they're still viable."

She watched with uneasiness and pain he'd give the rest of his hand for the opportunity to soothe away.

"When will you file them?"

Give her a reason to fight for them.

"I'm not," he said and, when she didn't take them, he laid them with the envelope on her desk and turned back to her. "I'm leaving them for you to file."

"Oh." She braced for the hit he had to throw.

He'd do it while looking her in the eye, but he wouldn't crowd her. He stood.

"I'm not doing this because I want a divorce. I don't ever want to be apart from you. You deserve more than some sketchy mistress situation. You *deserve* to be my wife, Anais. We *deserve* to have a family together. But I can't force you into this. Grandfather has my will held hostage by a promise, and it feels…"

"Bad," she softly supplied when his words faltered.

"And like he's not really living, even though the temporary port is fine until the new graft heals enough to use. Not living, just breathing. Existing. I don't want that for you. I don't want you afraid and unhappy, even if it means I get to have you with me."

She shifted on her feet, her arms staying around her body though her hands pulled away, flexing and rolling at the wrist. Tense. "Thank you. That's kinder than I deserve."

The words hurt. "No, baby." His voice broke and her eyes—those eyes he so loved—snapped to meet his, then widened at the tears he felt wetting his cheeks.

Make her fight for them.

Pulling the portable USB drive from his pocket, he let himself cross to her. Taking her hand almost broke him. It might be the last time she let him touch her, and he might be wasting it. Turning her hand over, he placed the storage device on her palm.

"The photos are in the envelope. I didn't look at them."

Her hand shook.

"But I did watch the video."

Color drained from her face and she stepped back. "Why?" She would've pulled away if he hadn't held fast, needing to keep the connection. It was the only thing that prevented that sharp knife he felt at his throat from carving into him.

"I needed to know what I was fighting. I've been doing what you and Philip both said I do—waiting for things to work out. You didn't know what to tell people—to tell our children—if it came to public scrutiny. I do now."

The short, soft, mirthless laugh said *nothing could excuse this.*

He tugged enough to get her closer so he could say words that should never be shouted.

"I'd say that feeling alone is terrible for anyone, let alone a child, but you were still strong enough to fight through it. I'd say an evil man hurt you, but you got away and never let it keep you from becoming the amazing woman you are. I'd say…we all make bad decisions when we're hurting, and that's the reason you can't let people stay alone. That's why we fight for people we love. That's why we fight for people who can't fight for themselves."

Her bitter, teary expression became wary again, then just closed.

"You need to watch it," he whispered through a tight throat and let go of her hand. "But not alone. I really don't want to see it again, but I'll watch it with you if you need me."

She'd heard him, because she looked at the drive as if to make sure it was still in her hand.

"I don't need to watch it. I remember everything."

"I don't think you do, or you're just holding that girl to impossible standards."

She closed her hand over the drive, her chin falling as she stared at it.

"How old were you?"

"It was the week of my sixteenth birthday," she answered, but didn't look like she knew why she had.

Days before the age of consent. It didn't really matter—there was no way for him to make that right, but it did ease him a tiny bit.

"Watch it with Sharon, okay?"

"Quinn…"

"Please. You need to see this. That girl made a mistake, and you don't deserve to spend the rest of your life afraid of a teenage error in judgment. Watch it; you'll understand."

He tried to be calm but heard the desperation in his own voice.

And he couldn't tell if he'd got through. Her head kept shaking. It didn't look like she was telling him no, more like she couldn't accept what she was hearing. It didn't jibe with what she thought she knew, so disbelief rattled her.

"If he tried to sell that video to any news organization, he would be lynched. He was an adult, which is a crime. It wouldn't matter if you'd been old enough in *hours*. Legally, he'd be screwed if he tried to show that video to anyone."

At this point, he wasn't sure she was hearing him. She didn't answer, but she had stopped shaking her head and seemed more together than he had been most of the night.

It felt as if he should stay with her, but he had to give her time to work through this and still squeeze in a trip down the aisle.

Which brought him to the last bit… The scariest bit.

"One more thing." His hands shook, so he stuffed them into his pockets, then thought better of that and hung his arms at his sides as still and casual as he could, but no amount of trying to slow his breathing would work. "I'm not calling off the wedding. I can't picture my life any other way than with you in it. If you come to the church on Saturday, I plan on making that life we'll share amazing. I'll always fight for you and for us, but I need you to fight too."

She looked at him again, still listening. "I don't understand."

"I'm leaving here and I'm going to talk to the press to make sure they don't blame you for this if you watch that video and decide you still can't be there. I'll do whatever I can to help you stay in the country, or go wherever you want to go if that's your decision."

His finger seemed to throb where the ring sat, the thing that had bolstered him through this. Quietly, he pulled it from his finger and placed it gently atop the divorce papers on her desk, framing her decision with two opposite choices.

With everything he'd thrown at her, there was no way for her to come to any decision right now. If she did, it'd still be *No* without watching the video, and she needed space to do that.

Quinn kissed her forehead, repeated the date, time and location of the wedding for her, asked she watch the video one more time and excused himself while his legs still held him.

All he could do now was wait. And pray…

Quinn had been gone for over an hour when Anais heard Mom gently tapping on her bedroom door.

"I'm okay," she called, hoping it was enough to get a little more quiet alone time to make sense of the things Quinn had said.

The one thing, mostly.

Signing the papers was an act of love. The rest of it… some kind of faith she couldn't even process.

On some level, she knew it was the kind of thing people—especially stupid people like her—would live their entire lives waiting to hear. The kind of words that should bring relief. But she felt nothing. Not even happy to know he hadn't been lying about the depth of his love.

How could she feel happy about that now?

Numb was at least okay enough to not be actively falling apart like she'd been all night.

"Did he take the papers to submit to court?" Still through the door.

The papers. From where she sat on the edge of the bed, she could only focus on that beautiful ring sitting on top of something so ugly.

"He left it up to me," she answered, then the door opened. With a deep, fortifying breath, she added, "I don't want you to worry about this. Stress kicks you out of rhythm, and I'm going to be fine. You don't need to worry."

"You don't look fine, baby girl. You have no color in your face, and you look like you've just witnessed a public execution."

Watch the video with Mom, he'd said. As if she could bear anyone else she loved to know such things, let alone witness them. Drinking. Making out. Nudity. Then the best part, where she smashed Ratliffe's face up with a bottle of cheap rum.

All that was her burden to bear. Consequences for bad judgment and immaturity. Life had handed her a lesson—or she'd grabbed it with both hands—and she'd learned from it.

"Sometimes I wish I'd never met him. Then I wouldn't have had to leave him, hurt him… Hurt me." The words came out and the numbness left in a blink. "But then maybe I'd be someone worse if things had gone another way. Or I guess maybe I'd be someone better too."

"Worse implies that you're bad now. You're not." Mom came fully inside and used the apron she wore to wipe the tears from Anais's cheeks.

"I feel like I am."

"What did Quinton say?"

She shook her head, sifting words for the ones she could share. "That he still wants me, but he won't force me because he needs me to fight for us too. I just don't think there can be a peaceful ride off into the sunset with him. There's just riding, and more riding, and no end to the riding. I'm not strong enough for this."

Quinn's summary didn't match what had happened, and the parts that did match weren't parts that made it any less shameful, pathetic, or stupid.

"You're strong when you need to be. We both are. We'll get through this, whatever you decide."

Support. The last thing she deserved. The trouble was she didn't know what the least selfish thing for her to do was. "I need to sleep. It's after ten a.m.; that's close enough to nap time."

If she gave up her alcohol abstinence, maybe she could sleep her way through the wedding day he refused to cancel.

CHAPTER THIRTEEN

COCOONED FROM THE WORLD, Anais passed the rest of the day and night alternating between sleep and staring at the small drive Quinn had left.

Morning came again, as it always did, and she considered ordering alcohol because now she missed the numbness she'd had in that first hour. Anything was better than this cycle of self-loathing and skepticism.

A knock at her door summoned her out of bed. A short conversation with Mom later, and Anais found herself on the sofa downstairs.

"I waited a whole day, and now you have to watch this."

"What is it?" Anais asked, focusing on the television.

Please God, not the video.

It wasn't. Whatever Mom had recorded started to play and she saw him. Quinn, but this time not in the formal attire he'd worn for his last press conference. He looked much as he'd done yesterday standing in her bedroom, making claims about the video that didn't stack up with the facts she knew to be as true as his hollow, haggard expression.

It hurt to see him. Would always hurt to see him but, after a while—a long while—it could scar over. It had last time. Kind of. It had become older pain, which was at least something peaceful. Something better than this place where her ribs felt as if they were broken and unable to generate the suction required to draw her next breath.

"Can you just summarize it for me? I can't watch him…"

Her broken sob stopped the words. The television clicked off and Mom laid her hand gently on Anais's head, then started smoothing her hair.

"He said, with the way things went for you during your marriage before—being attacked all the time in the media, and disparaged as not good enough for him—you're getting more and more afraid it will go back to that after the wedding."

Gritting her teeth, Anais tried to turn off her emotions again, but all she managed was to wring her hands until the skin burned, and slow, quiet tears.

"Okay," she said, but she still couldn't see how that would make things better. Maybe he was shifting the blame onto the press?

"And you might not be able to make that leap again. That you're afraid of your babies inheriting this stigma, but you haven't made up your mind yet. You're going to take all the time up to the wedding to decide, he said."

"That's not totally true," she said, needing Mom to know the truth, even if she couldn't tell anyone else. "But I guess I didn't say no when he pitched it. I didn't say much of anything."

Mom nodded, but in the morning light she didn't look as frail to Anais as she had since coming home. She looked like that woman who'd worked three jobs so they would stay afloat, refusing to let Anais get a job that would take her away from her studies and the better life Mom had wanted for her. Or maybe that was just what Anais needed her to be right now when her own strength was flagging.

"They're taking some of the blame for it."

"Who?"

"Everyone, I guess. People. Reporters. This morning, woven wedding crowns began appearing on the steps of the cathedral."

"Flowers?"

Mom nodded.

"I guess they really enjoyed The Sip." None of it made sense, especially the hope she felt fluttering in her belly.

"There's something you're not telling me, baby."

Yes.

She didn't want to lie to Mom. "I'm still trying to sort everything out."

"You know he's going to be dressed and at the wedding. People are still attending. It's not cancelled."

Breathe.

If things were as Mom reported, then he'd done what he'd promised—deflected blame. At least enough that she might be able to keep her home. Maybe even enough to work at Almsford again in a few months when the news died down.

There it was again, a lifting feeling that terrified her, that just left her with further to fall.

To hear Quinn talk, she'd been a victim, but really, she'd been stupid—the one thing she'd always had to cling to, cancelling the other things said about her, had been her intellect. But she'd been so stupid that night. Willfully stupid, not just naïve. Stupid and so hungry for attention and any small sense of belonging she'd drank his booze, and did other things.

Made terrible decisions. Got naked. Took photos. Made out. Blacked out…all with a man she wasn't even really attracted to.

None of that matched up with Quinn's victim hypothesis.

Then resolved it all with violence because she wasn't smart enough to handle things civilly.

The day before the wedding, her wedding dress, underthings and accessories came by courier in the morning.

At noon, a van and security men with a hand truck carrying a small safe arrived. The inventory listed the contents: tiara, necklace, earrings, worn by Lady Evelyn in her wedding to Prince Thomas in 1954.

A man with a large bouquet of flowers arrived as the jewelry delivery men left—but a small security detail stayed to provide security overnight.

Anais let them all in, because what else was she supposed to do? Just stood there, being an observer to her life because both choices paralyzed her.

She waved the flowers in, thanked the man, then spent some time staring at the roses, lilies and violets. Nestled in the blooms was a small envelope. A card.

She couldn't bring herself to look at the jewelry in the safe, but she fumbled the card out of the envelope and read Quinn's strong script:

Today's courage is tomorrow's JOY.

The words on her tattoo, but with Quinn's correction.

It struck her like a body blow, the simple word replacement. As did the words tucked beneath:

Watch the video. Please.

He thought she was aiming too low.

"What's it say?" Mom asked, coming down the stairs from her shower.

Anais handed the card over and took the bouquet to her refrigerator to spare the blossoms.

"What video?" Mom asked, following.

Deep breath.

"I need to tell you something."

Saturday morning broke bright and sunny after three days of rain and time that had crawled, maybe even stood still for black stretches of night, when Quinn struggled hardest.

Philip had to practically put him under palace arrest to

keep him from going to Anais's house, especially as days stacked up without word from her.

Now he stood at the altar in the beautifully decorated Romanesque cathedral where all the important family events had happened for centuries, wearing his finest, most stately regalia. And sweating buckets.

Every breath came with effort—not just for him. The entire congregation seemed to hold its breath at the slightest sound from the street beyond the ornately carved—and closed—doors at the far end of the nave.

He watched the door; everyone else watched him.

The place reeked of sweat and flowers, and he couldn't bear to look anyone in the eye for fear he'd see pity there, the certainty she wouldn't come. He especially avoided Philip's eye, and the King—who'd managed to come to the wedding and now sat in the first row.

Everyone who mattered to him was there except her.

She still had a few minutes. She'd come. He had to hold on to that if he wanted to keep from collapsing under the weight of his own decisions.

Ben, his best man, sat in his chair to his left.

Rosalie, who'd agreed to be Anais's maid of honor, waited alone on the bride's side of the altar.

It just wasn't enough time for her to work through it.

He should've postponed the wedding. Or stayed, watched with her, ignored her objections. Made her watch it.

The only thing three days had been enough for was to pull everyone else as far into his worry as he was.

It had been days of him seeing that same brave but stricken expression on every face, including the people lining the street outside the cathedral, waiting. So many clustered at the doors it might be hard for her to make it inside if…*when* she did come.

As if summoned under the weight of his stare and thoughts, the doors rattled and his heart, hammering hard enough to mold steel, fell into his shoes.

In unison, all the heads turned to the door. Breathless seconds passed.

Nothing.

Should he go check?

Could the doors have become locked somehow?

God, please...

His clenched gut answered him.

As coolly as he could, Quinn left the altar and jogged the length of the nave. When the doors opened enough to clear the frame, he closed them again.

Not locked.

She wasn't trying to get in.

She wasn't there.

Right.

He blew out a heavy breath and turned to walk, shoulders square with effort, head high with more effort, back to the altar.

Don't look at the clock.

His wrist felt heavy with the timepiece there. Everything felt heavy.

Everything to do with Anais was a gamble, not just whether or not she'd arrive—he was hanging by a slender thread of hope there—but whether she'd have the press after her and for how long if she didn't.

Should he still offer to renounce for her so they could leave the country together? Could he really abandon Philip to all this? Could he walk away from the last weeks or months he might have with Grandfather?

Yes.

He closed his eyes. Not even sure whether to be ashamed of that.

Anais's side of the cathedral was, ironically, the most packed. Everyone wanted to be seated as her guest, as if their bums on the pews could pull her in. Someone in the back was crying.

Sharon wasn't there either. Which should probably tell him something.

The doors rattled again.

God help him. He wouldn't go check.

He closed his eyes and forced his hands to unclench. His belly moved in and out, proof he was still breathing.

Doors again.

It wasn't until he heard the gasps that his eyes flew open.

She stood at the end of the nave, beautiful in her white dress, those strawberry waves flowing down her back, a bouquet dangling from her left hand.

Shaking, he gave up every pretext of keeping his composure. Some strangled sound of dismay and elation erupted from him.

The music started and she began walking to him.

He was supposed to wait.

The thought barely died before a more forceful one overrode it. To hell with propriety and tradition.

He *sprinted* down the center aisle to her.

"I'm sorry." She got exactly two words out before Quinn grabbed her by her wet cheeks and dragged her mouth to his.

He didn't need words. He only needed her. Her soft lips, her warmth, her grumpy mornings, her ravenous nights.

The kiss filled his chest after endless empty days.

She kissed him back with a frantic heat, grabbing at him—his waist, his hips, then his head, smashing flowers into his hair in desperation to get closer. Full of promises he didn't need spoken, echoing the explanations he didn't need.

Cheering started at some point, and he became aware that it had evolved to giggles and good-natured ribbing, but her arms around his neck and the flowers now smashing into both their faces hid tears he couldn't find a drop of shame for shedding.

"Prince Quinton."

The King's voice broke through and he pulled back from the kiss. They were supposed to get married now.

Her hands slid to his lapels and fisted there, not letting him go before she could whisper in his ear, the three words he'd already heard in her heart weeks ago, but which sounded more beautiful than anything he'd ever heard.

"I love you too." He looked deep into those blue-green eyes he loved, and though they were filled with happiness, hope, and regret, tears streamed down her cheeks.

"Forgive me?" she whispered again.

"After the wedding," he teased, too full of joy to care. On a whim, and because he couldn't even bear the idea of her being inches away from him after days of torture, he swept her up in his arms to carry her toward the altar.

People clapped again, but he had a mission to complete, and refused to put her back on her feet when they reached the priest.

Anais dropped the bouquet in her lap so she could have both her arms around his shoulders, and he didn't hear a word the priest said. All he heard was her, the promises in her eyes, and the future.

He let her down for the ring exchange, and their first official kiss that could've lasted forever as far as Quinn was concerned.

When Philip pelted them with rice ahead of schedule, Quinn reluctantly separated from his wife's sweet lips.

Her fingers stroked through the hair at the back of his head and the smile she gave him… He could finally breathe.

In the aftermath of the video, he knew there were still dark places they'd have to explore together, but if they hadn't stopped her from coming today he wouldn't let anything else stop them from taking those obstacles together. Fighting for each other, never against.

Today's courage for tomorrow's joy.

EPILOGUE

Fifteen months later...

ANAIS HELD PIPPA, her six-month-old daughter, to her chest as she stood beside King Philip behind a wide red ribbon spanning the entrance of Hero's Welcome, the project she and Quinn had dreamed up on their honeymoon and spent the months since building.

"Daddy and Be-Be are in trouble..." Anais murmured in sing-song fashion to Pippa and Philip, scanning the road behind them for signs of movement before she turned back to the crowd of citizens, soldiers and cameras there for the opening.

Life was so good she could hardly believe it from day to day, sometimes minute to minute. Even when her husband was late for their big dedication day.

"Where are they?" Philip muttered through his dutiful smiles.

"School..." Anais started to answer, but then she heard running behind her and turned to see Quinn and Ben Nettle racing toward them.

Even when irritated with him, her heart never failed to beat faster when she saw him.

"Sorry," Quinn panted, kissed her cheek, and then reached for his daughter. "Test ran late."

Pippa went eagerly into Quinn's arms, and Anais couldn't

blame her. Hands free, she fetched the oversized ceremonial scissors for Corrachlean's Bachelor King to use, if the autumn sky held back the rain until he'd finished the dedication speech.

Ben joined a pregnant Rosalie on the other side of the ribbon, still using his chair on university days. He'd gotten steady enough with both prosthetics to walk her back down the aisle last month, but it was still work for him to move around for long periods on them. He'd get there and, in the meanwhile, he and Quinn tackled university together.

Rejoining her perfect little family, Anais tucked in close to Quinn as Philip went over the assets of Hero's Welcome—the country's first specialized community for wounded veterans to assist them in readjusting to private life with their new challenges.

"How did you do?" she whispered to Quinn while Pippa alternated between shoving her fist into her own mouth and shoving into Daddy's.

"Goog…" he garbled around the slobbery baby fist, then pulled it from his mouth and made faces at her to keep their strong-willed baby from making her displeasure known about formal duties.

"Show me your grade later, and I'll give you a reward," she cooed in his ear. The man was a terrible influence on her, tempting her to goof off and flirt with him at their big opening.

Philip, who'd ascended about four months after the wedding, didn't mind so much when they goofed around. He was still getting used to the position, which he'd inherited unexpectedly when King Thomas, after a couple of months of relatively good health, didn't wake one morning.

"Dr. Anais Corlow will be operating the community clinic."

She stopped quietly misbehaving when she heard her name and waved briefly, smiling. Philip had stopped calling her *Princess* in favor of Doctor at her request, even if she was technically stuck with the title until Philip married and produced an heir. Something he'd better get on with if he didn't want her to start funneling women in his direction.

After talking about the clinic, Philip went down the list.

Mrs. Rosalie Nettle—Job Center Administrator
Lieutenant Benjamin Nettle—Counselor.

"Prince Quinton Corlow…in charge of making faces to amuse Princess Pippa, until he graduates, and then something with physical therapy."

Quinn had the grace to look fleetingly chagrined at his introduction, but rebounded with a quick smile.

He'd be a great part-time PT. He had other jobs that came first: devoted husband, delighted daddy, and sometimes reluctant but ever-faithful diplomat.

Philip left off the names of the operators for the community's amenities. Aunt Helen at the salon, Mom at the community center, and those operating the market, butcher, bakery, pharmacy, bank, and post office. But they had it all, a fully functioning community.

Philip cut the ribbon and, after the applause and photos, Quinn stopped goofing around with Pippa long enough to announce, "There's food and drink at the community center, and several of the differently equipped cottages are available for tours. Finally, Princess Pippa has graciously made herself available to drool on anyone who gets too close. At the community center. We're following the food."

He made her laugh every day. He never wavered when she got overwhelmed by some aspect of royal life, which blessedly was happening with less frequency.

She'd never felt she truly belonged anywhere, so they'd built a place where she unquestioningly belonged. They'd sold the penthouse and the townhouse, and built their new home within the community.

Wayne wasn't even a ghost on her horizon anymore. The

longer she spent with her new family, the better life got, and the less Wayne Ratliffe mattered at all.

Her family and her purpose gave her the kind of peace that came in second to the joy of Quinn's morning wake-up attacks, and Pippa's strawberry curls and stormy gray eyes.

* * * * *

COMING SOON!

We really hope you enjoyed reading this book.
If you're looking for more romance
be sure to head to the shops when
new books are available on

Thursday 22nd May

To see which titles are coming soon, please visit

millsandboon.co.uk/nextmonth

MILLS & BOON

Princess Brides: A Cinderella Story

MAISEY YATES

LOUISA HEATON

AMALIE BERLIN

MILLS & BOON

First Published in Great Britain 2025
by Mills & Boon, an imprint of HarperCollins*Publishers* Ltd
1 London Bridge Street, London, SE1 9GF

www.harpercollins.co.uk

HarperCollins*Publishers*
Macken House, 39/40 Mayor Street Upper,
Dublin 1, D01 C9W8, Ireland

ISBN: 978-0-263-41721-0

This book contains FSC™ certified paper and other controlled sources to ensure responsible forest management.

For more information visit: www.harpercollins.co.uk/green

Printed and Bound in the UK using 100% Renewable Electricity
at CPI Group (UK) Ltd, Croydon, CR0 4YY

HIS FORBIDDEN PREGNANT PRINCESS

MAISEY YATES

To Nicole Helm, ask and you shall receive. Dare and I shall deliver. Can I make a children's cartoon a romance novel? Yes. Yes I can.

CHAPTER ONE

SHE WAS BENEATH him in every way. From her common blood to her objectively plain appearance—that years of designer clothing, professional treatments from the finest aestheticians and beauticians and the work of the best makeup artists money could buy had failed to transform into true beauty—from the way she carried herself, to the way she spoke.

The stepsister he had always seen as a particularly drab blot on the otherwise extravagant tapestry of the royal family of San Gennaro.

The stepsister he could hardly bear to share the same airspace with, let alone the same palace.

The stepsister he was now tasked with finding a suitable husband for.

The stepsister he wanted more than his next breath.

She was beneath him in every way. Except for the way he desired most.

And she never would be.

There were a thousand reasons. From the darkness in him, to the common blood in her. But the only reason that truly mattered was that she was his stepsister, and he was a king.

"You requested my presence, Luca?" Sophia asked,

looking up at him with a dampened light in her blue eyes that suggested she was suppressing some emotion or other. In all probability a deep dislike for having to deal with him.

But the feeling was mutual. And if he could endure such an indignity then Sophia—in all her borrowed glory—certainly could.

"I did. As you know, it was my father's final wish that you be well cared for, along with your mother. He wrote it into law that you are part of this family and are to be treated as a daughter of his blood would be."

Sophia looked down, her lashes dark on her pale cheek. She had visible freckles that never failed to vex him. Because he wanted to count them. Because sometimes, he wanted to kiss each one.

She should cover them with makeup as most women of her status did. She should have some care for the fact she was a princess.

But she did not.

Today she wore a simple shift that made her bare legs seem far too long and slender. It was an ungainly thing. She also wore nothing at all to cover them. She had on flat shoes, and not a single piece of jewelry. Her dark hair hung limp around her shoulders.

He could only hope she had not gone out in public that way.

"Yes," she said, finally. Then those dark eyes connected with his and he felt it like a lightning bolt straight down to his stomach. He should not. For every reason cataloged in his mind only a moment before. She was not beautiful. Not when compared to the elegant women who had graced his bed before her. Not when compared to nearly any other princess the world over.

But she captivated him. Had done from the moment he had met her. At first it was nothing more than feeling at turns invaded and intrigued by this alien creature that had come into his life. She had been twelve to his seventeen when their parents had married.

Sophia had possessed a public school education, not a single hint of deportment training and no real understanding of the hierarchy of the palace.

She had a tendency to speak out of turn, to trip over her feet and to treat him in an overly familiar manner.

Her mother was a warm, vivacious woman who had done much to restore his father's life, life that had drained away after the loss of his first wife. She was also a quick study, and did credit to the position of Queen of San Gennaro.

Sophia, on the other hand, seemed to resist her new role, and her new life. She continued to do so now. In little ways. Her bare legs, and her bare face, as an example.

His irritation with her had taken a sharp turn, twisting into something much more disturbing around the time she turned sixteen. That sense of being captivated, in the way one might be by a spider that has invaded one's room, shifted and became much more focused.

And there had been a moment, when he had found her breathless from running out in the garden like a schoolgirl when she had been the advanced age of seventeen, that everything had locked into place. That it had occurred to him that if he could only capture that insolent mouth of hers with his own she would finally yield. And he would no longer feel so desperately beguiled by her.

It had only gotten worse as the years had progressed.

And the idea of kissing her had perverted yet further into doing much, much more.

But it was not to be. Not ever.

As he had just told her, his father had decreed that she was family. As much as if they were blood.

And so he was putting an end to this once and for all.

"He asked me to take care of you in a very specific fashion," Luca continued. "And I feel that now that it has been six months since his passing, it is time for me to see those requests honored."

A crease appeared between her brows. "What request?"

"Specifically? The matter of your marriage, *sorellina*." Little sister. He called her that to remind himself.

"My marriage? Shouldn't we see to the matter of me getting asked to the movies first, Luca?"

"There is no need for such things, obviously. A woman in your position is hardly going to go to the movies. Rather, I have been poring over a list of suitable men who might be able to be brought in for consideration."

"You're choosing my husband?" she asked, her tone incredulous.

"I intend to present you with a manageably sized selection. I am not so arrogant that I would make the final choice for you."

Sophia let out a sharp, inelegant laugh. "Oh, no. You're only so arrogant that you would inform me I'm getting married, and that you have already started taking steps toward planning the wedding. Tell me, Luca, have you picked out my dress, as well?"

Of course he would be involved in approving that selection; if she thought otherwise she was delusional. "Not as yet," he said crisply.

"What happens if I refuse you?"

"You won't," he said, certainty going as deep as his bones.

He was the king now, and she could not refuse him. She would not. He would not allow it.

"Why wouldn't I?"

"You are welcome, of course, to make a mockery of the generosity that my father has shown to your mother and yourself. You are welcome, of course, to cause a rift between the two of us."

She crossed her arms, cocking one hip out to the side. "I could hardly cause a rift between the two of us, Luca. No matter what you might say, you have never behaved as a loving older brother to me."

"Perhaps it is because you have never been a sister to me," he said, his voice hard.

She would not understand what that meant. She would not understand why he had said it.

And indeed, the confusion on her face spoke to that.

"I don't have to do what you tell me to." She shook her head, that dark, glossy hair swirling around her shoulders. "Your father would hardly have forced me into a marriage I didn't want. He loved me. He wanted what was best for me."

"This was what he thought was best," Luca said. "I have documentation saying such. If you need to see it, I will have it sent to your quarters. Quarters that you inhabit, by the way, because my father cared so much for you. Because my father took an exceptional and unheard-of step in this country and treated a child he did not father as his own. He is giving you what he would have given to a daughter. A daughter of his blood. Selecting your husband, ensuring it is a man of impeccable pedigree, is what he would have done for his child. You are welcome to reject it if you wish. But I would think very deeply about what that means."

Sophia didn't have to think deeply about what it meant. She could feel it. Her heart was pounding so hard she thought she might pass out; small tremors running beneath the surface of her skin. Heat and ice pricking at her cheeks.

Oh, she wasn't thinking of what this meant in the way that Luca had so imperiously demanded she do.

Luca.

Her beautiful, severe stepbrother who was much more king of a nation than he was family to her. Remote. Distant. His perfectly sculpted face only more desperately gorgeous to her now than it had been when she had met him at seventeen. He had been beautiful as a teenager. There was no question. But then, that angular bone structure had been overlaid by much softer skin, his coal-black eyes always formidable, but nothing quite so sharp as crushed obsidian as they were now. That soft skin, the skin of a boy, that was gone. Replaced by a more weathered texture. By rough, black whiskers that seemed ever present no matter how often he shaved his square jaw.

She had never in all of her life met a thing like him. A twelve-year-old girl, plucked up from obscurity, from a life of poverty and set down in this luxurious castle, had been utterly and completely at sea to begin with. And then there was *him*.

Everything in her had wanted to challenge him, to provoke a response from all of that granite strength, even then. Even before she had known why, or known what it meant that she craved his attention in whatever form it might come.

Gradually, it had all become clear.

And clearer still the first time she had gone to a ball and Luca had gone with another woman on his arm. That acrid, acidic curling sensation in her stomach could have only been one thing. Even at fourteen she had known that. Had known that the sweep of fever that had gone over her skin, that weak sensation that made it feel as though she was going to die, was jealousy. Jealousy because she wanted Luca to take her arm, wanted him to hold her close and dance with her.

Wanted to be the one he took back to his rooms and did all sorts of secret things with, things that she had not known about in great detail, but had yearned for all the same. Him. Everything to do with him.

As Luca had said not a moment before, he had never thought of her as a sister. He was never affectionate, never close or caring in a way that went beyond duty.

But she had never thought of him as a brother. She had thought of him in an entirely different fashion.

She *wanted* him.

And he was intent on marrying her off. As though it were nothing.

Not a single thing on earth could have spoken to the ambivalence that he felt toward her any stronger than this did.

He doesn't want you.

Of course he didn't. She wasn't a great beauty; she was well aware of that. She was also absolutely and completely wrong for him in every way.

She didn't excel at this royal existence the way that he did. He wore it just beneath his skin, as tailored and fitted to him as one of his bespoke suits. Born with it, as if his blood truly were a different color than that of the common people. As if he were a different creature entirely from the rest of the mere mortals.

She had done her best to put that royal mantle on, but much like every dress that had ever been made for her since coming to live at the palace, it wasn't quite right. Oh, they could measure it all to fit, but it was clear that she wasn't made for such things. That her exceedingly nonwaiflike figure was not for designer gowns and slinky handmade creations that would have hung fabulously off women who were more collar and hip bone than curves and love handles.

Oh, yes, she was well aware of how little she fit. And how impossible her feelings for Luca were.

And yet, they remained.

And knowing that nothing could ever happen with him, knowing it with deep certainty, had done nothing to excise it from her soul.

Did nothing to blunt the pain of this, of his words being ground into her chest like shards of glass.

Not only was he making it clear he didn't want her, he was also using the memory of his father—the only man she had ever known as a father—to entice her to agree.

He was right. King Magnus had given her everything. Had given her mother a new lease on life, a real life. Something beyond existence, beyond struggle, which they had been mired in for all of Sophia's life prior to her marriage to him.

He had met her when she was nothing more than a waitress at a royal event in the US, and had fallen deeply for her in the moment they met.

It was something out of a fairy tale, except there were two children to contend with. A child who had been terrified of being uprooted from her home in America and going to a foreign country to live in a fancy palace. And another child who had always clearly resented the invasion.

She had to give Luca credit for the fact that he seemed to have some measure of affection for her mother. He did not resent her presence in the way he resented Sophia's.

She had often thought that life for Luca would have been perfect if he would have gotten her mother and his father, and she had been left out of the equation entirely.

Well, he was trying to offload her now, so she supposed that was proven to be true enough.

"That isn't fair," she said, when she could finally regain her powers of speech.

Luca's impossibly dark eyes flickered up and met hers, and her stomach—traitorous fool—hollowed out in response. "It isn't fair? Sophia, I have always known that you were ungrateful for the position that you have found yourself in your life, but you have just confirmed it in a rather stunning way. You find it unfair that my father wished to see you cared for? You find it unfair that I wish to do the same?"

"You forget," she said, trying to regain her powers of thought. "I was not born into this life, Luca, I did not know people growing up who expected such things for their lives. I didn't expect such a thing for mine. I spent the first twelve years of my life in poverty. But with the idea that if I worked hard enough I might be able to make whatever I wanted of myself. And then we were sort of swept up in this tidal wave of luxury.

And strangely, I have found that though I have every resource at my disposal now, I cannot be what I want in the same way that I imagined I could when I was nothing but a poor child living in the United States."

"That's because you were a delusional child," Luca said, his tone not cruel in any way, but somehow all the more stinging for the calm with which he spoke. "You never had the power to be whatever you wanted back then, Sophia, because no one has that power. There are a certain number of things set out before you that you might accomplish. You certainly might have improved your station. I'm not denying that. But the sky was never the limit, sorely not. Neither is it now. However, your limit is much more comfortable, you will find, than it would have been then."

Her heart clenched tight, because she couldn't deny that what he was saying was true. Bastard. With the maturity of adulthood she could acknowledge that. That she had been naive at the time, and that she was, in fact, being ungrateful to a degree.

Hadn't her position in the palace provided her with the finest education she could have asked for? Hadn't she been given excellent opportunities? Chances to run charitable organizations that she believed in strongly, and that benefited all manner of children from different backgrounds.

No, as a princess, she would never truly have a profession, but with that came the release of pressure of earning money to pay bills.

Of figuring out where the road between what she dreamed of doing, and what would help her survive, met.

But the idea of marrying someone selected by her

stepbrother, who no more knew her than liked her, was not a simple thing.

And underneath that, the idea of marrying any man, touching any man, being intimate with any man, who wasn't Luca was an abomination unto her soul.

For it was only him. Luca and those eyes as hard as flint, that mouth that was often curled into a sneer in her direction, those large hands that were much rougher than any king's ever should have been. It was only him who made her want. Who made her ache with the deep well of unsatisfied desire. Only him.

Only ever him.

"I will be holding a ball," Luca said, his tone decisive. "And at that ball will be several men that I have personally curated for you."

"You make them sound like a collection of cheeses."

"Think of them however you like. If you prefer to think them as cheese, that's your own business."

Something burst inside her, some small portion of restraint that she had been only just barely holding on to since she had come into the throne room. "How do you know I like men, Luca? You've never asked."

Luca drew back slightly, a flicker in his dark eyes the only showing that she had surprised him at all.

"If it is not so," he said, his tone remote, "then I suggest you speak now."

"No," she responded, feeling deflated, as her momentary bit of rebellion fell flat on its face. "I'm not opposed to men."

"Well," he said, "one less bit of damage control I have to do."

"That would require damage control?"

"How many gay princesses do you know?" he asked.

"The upper echelons of society are ever conservative regardless of what they say. And here in this country it would be quite the scandal, I assure you. It is all fine to pay lip service to such things as equality, but appearances, tradition, are as important as ever."

"And I am already a break with tradition," she pointed out.

"Yes," he said, that tone heavy. "My father's actions in granting you the same rights as I have were unheard of. You are not his by blood, and in royal lines blood is everything. It is the only thing."

"I will go to the ball," she said, because there really was no point arguing with Luca once he had made pronouncements. But whatever happened after that… It would be her decision.

But she was too raw, too shocked, from this entire conversation to continue having a fight with him.

He wanted to marry her off to another man. He wanted her to be someone else's problem.

He felt nothing about doing it.

He did not want her.

He's your stepbrother, and even if he did he couldn't have you. As he just said, tradition is everything.

She squared her shoulders. "When is this blessed event?"

"In a couple weeks' time," he responded.

She blinked. "Oh. I'm not certain my mother will be back from France before then."

"She will be. I have already spoken with her."

That galled her. Like a lance through her chest. Her mother, of course, had no idea how Sophia felt about Luca. She told her mother everything. Everything except for that. Everything except for the completely forbidden lust she felt for her stepbrother. But even so, she couldn't believe that her mother had allowed Luca to have this conversation with her without at least giving her a call to warn her first.

"I told her not to tell you," Luca said as if he was reading her mind.

She sniffed. "Well. That is quite informative."

"Do not be indignant, *sorellina*," Luca said. "It is not becoming of a princess."

"Well, I've certainly never been overly becoming as princesses go," she said stiffly. "Why start now?"

"You had better start. You had better start so that all of this will work accordingly."

He looked her up and down. "We need to get you a new stylist."

"I use the same stylist as my mother," she said defensively.

"It doesn't work for you," he said, his tone cold.

And with a wave of his hand he dismissed her, and she was left somehow obeying him, her feet propelling her out of his royal chamber and into the hall.

She clutched her chest, gasping for breath, pain rolling through her.

The man she loved was going to marry her off to someone else. The man she loved was selecting from a pool of grooms for her to meet in two weeks' time.

The man she loved was her stepbrother. The man she loved was a king.

All of those things made it impossible for her to have him.

But she didn't have any idea how in the world she was supposed to stop wanting him.

CHAPTER TWO

"WHAT IS *THIS*?" The disdain in Sophia's tone when Luca presented her with a thick stack of files the following week was—in his estimation—a bit on the dramatic side.

"It is the list of possible husbands to invite to the upcoming ball. I feel strongly that an excess of five is just being spoiled for choice. Plus, you will not have time to dance with that many people. So I suggest you look it over, and find a way to pare them down."

"This is…" She looked up at him, her dark eyes furious. "These are dossiers of…*men*. Photos and personal profiles…"

"How else would you know if you're compatible?"

"Maybe meeting them and going out for dinner?" Sophia asked.

She crossed her arms, the motion pushing her rather abundant décolletage up over the neckline of the rather simple V-neck top she was wearing.

They really needed to get ahold of that new stylist and quickly. She was, as ever, a temptation to Luca, and to his sense of duty. But soon it would be over. Soon he would have his problematic stepsister married off, and then she would be safely out of his reach.

He could have found a woman to slake his lust on, and over the years he had done just that. After all, whatever was broken in him… Sophia should not have to suffer for it.

But during those time periods he had not been forced to cohabitate with Sophia. Always, when he had spent too much time with her, he had to detox, essentially. Find a slim blonde to remind himself that there were other sorts of women he found hot. Other women he might find desirable.

And then, when it was really bad, he gave up entirely on playing the opposite game and found himself a curvaceous brunette to pour his fantasies into. The end of that road was a morass of self-loathing and recrimination, but on many levels he was happy to end up there. He was comforted by it.

But this… Sharing space with her. As he had done since his father had died. No other woman would do. He couldn't find it in him to feel even a hint of desire for anyone else. And that was unacceptable. As all things to do with Sophia invariably were.

"You are not going on dinner dates," Luca said. "You are a princess. You are part of the royal family. And you are not setting up a Tinder profile in order to find yourself a husband."

"Why not?" she asked, her tone defiant. "Perhaps I want nothing more than to meet a very exciting IT guy who might swipe me right off my feet." He said nothing and she continued to stare at him. "Swipe. Swipe right. It's a dating app thing."

"That isn't funny in the least. As I said, you are part of this family." Perhaps if he repeated it enough, if he drilled it into both of them that they were family, his body would eventually begin to take it on board. "And as such, your standards of marriage must be the same as mine."

"Why aren't you looking for a wife yourself?" she asked.

"I will," Luca said. "In due time. But my father asked that I make your safety, your match, a priority."

He would marry, as duty required. But it would not be because of passion. And certainly not because of love. Duty was what drove him. The preservation of reputation, of the crown. If that crumbled, his whole life was nothing.

He would choose a suitable woman.

Sophia was far from suitable.

"What about the production of an heir?" Sophia lifted a brow. "Isn't that important?"

"Yes. But I am a man, and as such, I do not have the same issues with a biological clock your gender does."

"Right," she huffed. "Because men can continue to produce children up until the end of their days."

"Perhaps not without the aid of a blue pill, but certainly it is possible."

For a moment she only blinked up at him, a faint pink tinge coloring her cheeks. Then Sophia's lip curled. "I find this conversation distasteful."

"You brought up the production of heirs, not me."

She scowled, clearly having to take his point, and not liking it at all. "Well, let me look through the dossiers, then," she said, lifting her nose and peering at him down the slender ridge, perfecting that sort of lofty look that was nothing if not a put-on coming from Sophia.

Though, possibly not when directed at him.

"Erik Nilsson. Swedish nobility?"

"Yes," Luca responded. "He's very wealthy."

"How?"

"Family money, mostly. Though some of it is in sheep."

"His money is in sheep?" Sophia asked, her expression completely bland. "Well, that is interesting. And one would never want for sweaters."

"Indeed not," he said, a vicious turn of jealousy savaging his gut. Which was sadistic at best. To be jealous of a man whose fortune was tied up in sheep and who had the dubious honor of being a minor noble in some small village that wasn't part of the current century.

A man he had not expected his stepsister to show the slightest interest in. And yet, here she was.

"So he will have access to…wool. And such," Sophia said. "And…he's quite handsome. If you like tall and blond."

"Do you?" he asked.

"Very much," she said with a strange injection of conviction. "He's on the table." She set the folder aside. "Let us get on with the next candidate, shall we?"

"Here you are," he said, lifting up the next folder and holding it out toward her. "Ilya Kuznetsov."

She arched a brow. "Russian?"

He raised one in response. "Very."

Sophia wrinkled her nose. "Is his fortune in vodka and caviar?"

"I hate to disappoint you but it's in tech. So, quite close to that IT guy you were professing to have a burning desire for."

"I didn't say I had a burning desire for anyone," she pointed out, her delicate fingers tracing the edge of the file.

He couldn't help but imagine those same fingers stroking him.

If he believed in curses, he would believe he was under one.

"I don't know anything about computers," she continued, setting the folder off to the opposite side of the first one. "I prefer sheep."

She was infuriating. And baffling. "Not something you hear every day. Now, to the next one."

She set aside the next two. An Italian business mogul and a Greek tycoon. Neither one meeting up to some strange specification that she blathered on about in vague terms. Then she rejected an Argentine polo player, who was also nobility of some kind, on the basis of the fact that a quick Google search revealed him to be an inveterate womanizer.

"You're not much better," she said mournfully, looking up from her phone.

"Then it is a good thing that I am not in the files for consideration."

Something quite like shock flashed through her eyes, and her mouth dropped open. Color flooded her cheeks, irritation, anger.

"As if that would ever happen. As if I would *consider* you." She sniffed very loudly.

"As my sister, you could not," he bit out.

"Stepsister," she said, looking up at him from beneath her dark lashes.

His gut twisted, his body hardening for a moment before he gathered his control. The moment seemed to last an eternity. Stolen, removed from time. Nothing but those eyes boring holes through him, as though she could see right into him. As though she could see his every debauched thought.

Every dark, terrible thing in him.

But no, there was no way she could.

Or she would run and hide like a frightened mouse.

"In terms of legality, in terms of my father's will, you're my sister," he said. "Now, the next one."

She went through the folders until she had selected five, though she maintained that the Swedish candidate was top of her list.

It did not escape his notice that she had selected all men with lighter features. Diametrically opposed to his own rather dark appearance.

He should rejoice in that.

He found he did not.

"Then these are the invitations that will be sent out," he said. "And I will be reserving dances with each of the gentlemen."

"Dances?" She blinked. "Are we in a Regency romance novel? Am I going to have a card to keep track?"

"Don't be ridiculous. You can keep track of it in an app."

She barked out a laugh. "This is ridiculous. You're ridiculous."

"Perhaps," he said, "but if you can think of a better way to bring together the most eligible men in the world, I'm all ears."

"And what happens if I don't like any of them?"

"You're very excited about the sweaters."

"What if I don't like any of them?" she reiterated.

"I imagine something will work out."

"I'm serious," she said, her blue eyes blazing with

emotion. "I'm not marrying a man I don't like because you have some strange time frame you need to fulfill."

"Then we will keep looking."

"No," she said. "I promise that I will be fair, and I will give this a chance. But if it doesn't work, give me six months to make my own choice. If I can't find somebody that is suitable to me, and suitable to you, then I will let you choose."

"That was not part of the original bargain."

Six months more of her might just kill him.

"I don't care," Sophia said. "This isn't the Dark Ages, and you can't make me do what I don't want to. And you know it."

"Then you have a bargain. But you will have to put in serious effort. I am not wasting my time and resources."

"Well I'm not marrying a man just to suit you, Luca. I want to care for the man I marry. I want to like him, if I can't love him. I want to be able to talk to him. I want him to make me laugh."

Luca braced himself. Braced himself for her to start talking about passion. About wanting a man who would set her body on fire.

She didn't.

She had stopped at a man who made her laugh, and had not said she wanted a man who would make her come. He shouldn't think such thoughts. Shouldn't want to find out why that didn't seem to occur to her.

Why attraction didn't come into her lists of demands to be met.

It made him want to teach her. Didn't she understand? That physical desire *mattered*?

And if she didn't understand…

Some Swedish sheep farmer would be the one to teach her.

Luca gritted his teeth. “But do you need to want him, *sorellina*?”

He should not have asked the question. He shouldn’t entertain these thoughts, and he certainly shouldn’t give voice to them.

Cursed.

If he weren’t a logical man, he would swear it.

“Want him?” she asked, tilting her head to the side.

“Yes,” he bit out. “Want him. His hands on your body. His mouth on yours. Does it matter to you whether or not you want him inside you?”

He hadn’t realized it, but he’d moved closer to her with each sentence. And now he was so near her he could smell her. That delicate, citrus scent that always rose above the more cloying floral or vanilla perfumes the women around the palace typically favored. A scent he was always assured he could pick out, regardless of who else was around. Always Sophia, rising above the rest.

“I… I…” Her cheeks blushed crimson, and then she stood, her nose colliding with his cheek before she wobbled backward. “I’ve only ever wanted one man like that.” The words seemed to be stuck in her throat. “I never will again. I’m sure. And I refuse to discuss it. Least of all with you.”

And then she turned and ran from the room.

CHAPTER THREE

SINCE MAKING A fool out of herself in front of Luca days earlier, Sophia had done her best to avoid him. It wasn't that difficult. Luca was always busy with affairs of state, and it was actually for the best. The problem was that every time she heard heavy, authoritative footsteps on the marble floors of the palace, her heart caught, and held its position as if it was waiting, waiting to bow down to its king.

She did not want Luca to be the king of her heart. Being King of San Gennaro was quite enough power for one man. But her heart didn't listen. It beat for Luca, it stopped for Luca, tripped over itself for Luca.

It was starting to feel like she was running an obstacle course every time she made any movement in the palace. One wherein Luca was the obstacle that she was trying desperately to avoid.

But she wanted to see him, too. That was the real conundrum. The fact that she wanted to both avoid him and be with him all the time. Foolish, because he wasn't even nice to her. He never had been. But still, he captivated her in ways that went beyond sanity.

And today there would be no more avoiding him as he had engaged the services of a new stylist to help her prepare for the ball. The ball wherein she was supposed to choose a husband.

Luca and those dossiers had enraged her. She had picked every man who was completely opposite to him, to spite herself, mostly.

She highly doubted that she would marry any of these men. But one thing she knew for certain was that she would not marry a man who was simply a pale carbon copy of her stepbrother. She would not choose a man who was tall, dark and handsome, who had that kind of authority about him that Luca possessed. Because it would simply be an effort at giving her body a consolation prize. And that was far too tragic, even for her.

She shouldn't be tragic, she mused as she wandered down the labyrinthine hall toward the salon where she was meeting the new stylist. She had been a commoner, and she had been raised up to become the princess of a country. She had been adopted by a king. A man who had loved her, and had loved her mother. Who had shown them both the kind of life that neither of them had ever dreamed possible.

But Luca. Always Luca.

It was as though her heart was intent on not being happy. As though it wanted to be tragic. In the same way that it had determined that Luca would be its owner.

In a palace, a life of luxury, and with that came a fervent, painful love for the one man she could never have.

And, he didn't like her.

Star-crossed lovers they were not. Because Luca could hardly stand to share the same space as she did. He thought she was silly, that much was apparent from their exchange yesterday. They were from completely different worlds. The man couldn't understand why she found it off-putting to be looking through file folders filled with profiles of men she had never met, trying to work out which one of them she could see herself marrying.

Although she supposed it wasn't entirely different from online dating.

No. She refused to pretend that any of this was reasonable. It wasn't.

She wondered if she would ever find someone who just wanted *her.* These men, who had agreed to come to the palace, would never have done so if she wasn't a princess.

It was the only reason her biological father had ever spoken to her. After he'd seen her mother in the media, marrying King Magnus.

King Magnus had loved her. But…he had only strived to love her because of her mother.

And Luca…

Well, nothing seemed to make Luca like her at all. Not status, or herself.

He was consistent, at least.

She took a deep breath, bracing herself for the sight of him. That was another problem with Luca. Too much exposure to him and her poor heart couldn't recover between moments. Not enough, and it always flung itself against her breastbone as though it were trying to escape. Trying to go to him. To be with him.

Her heart was foolish. And the rest of her body was worse.

She gathered herself up, drew in the deepest breath possible, hoping that the burning in her lungs would offset the rest of her physical response. That it might drown out the erratic tripping of her pulse.

Then, she pushed the door open.

And all the breath left her body in a rush.

There was no preparing for him. No matter how familiar she was with his face, with that imposing, muscular physique of his, it was like a shock to her system every time. Those dark eyes, eyes that she sometimes thought might see straight through her, but they couldn't. Because if they did, then he would know. He would know that she was not indifferent to him. He would know that her feelings toward him were in no way familial.

He would be disgusted by her.

It took her a while to notice that there was a woman standing next to him. The new stylist, presumably. It took her a while, because as far as she was concerned when Luca was in the room it was difficult to tell if anyone else was there at all.

"You must be Princess Sophia," the woman said. "I'm Elizabeth."

"Nice to meet you." Belatedly, she decided that she should try and curtsy or something, so she grabbed the edge of her sundress and bent forward slightly. She looked up and saw that Luca was watching her with a disapproving expression on his handsome face.

If she bowed down and called him King of the Universe he would disapprove. He was impossible.

"She needs something suitable for an upcoming event," Luca said. "She must look the best she ever has."

"I am confident that I can accomplish such. It is simply a matter of knowing what sort of energy Sophia should be projecting. All these colors that she's wearing now are far too drab. And from what I have seen in pictures and publications over the years, her overall color palette doesn't suit her. I have plans."

Suddenly, Sophia felt very much like she was being stared down by a hungry spider. And she was a fly caught in the web.

"Just leave it to me," she said, shooing at Luca.

"I must approve the selection," he said. Obviously not taking kindly at all to being shown the door in his own palace.

"You will approve," Elizabeth said, her tone stubborn. "You will see soon."

The rest of the afternoon was spent styling and plucking and scrubbing.

Sophia felt as though she had been exfoliated over every part of her body. This woman did not try to have her hair completely straightened, but rather, styled it into soft waves, which seemed to frame her face better, and also—so she said—would not revert halfway over the course of the evening. Which was the problem that Sophia usually had with her hairstyles. Her hair wasn't curly, but it was not board-straight, either, and it could not hold such a severe style for hours on end. It became unruly when she got all sweaty. And she supposed it was not a good thing to sweat when you were a princess, but she did.

Then there was the matter of the gown she chose. None of the navy blue, black or mossy-green colors that her mother's stylist favored. No, this gown was a brilliant fuchsia, strapless with a sweetheart neckline that did nothing at all to cover her breasts. It draped down from there, skimming her waist, her full hips. Rather than making her look large like some of the high-necked gowns that had been chosen for her before, or blocky like the ones that hit her in strange places at the waist, she actually looked…curvy and feminine.

Typically, she didn't show this much skin, but she had to admit it was much more flattering when you could see that she had cleavage, rather than a misshapen mono breast.

Her lipstick matched the dress, and her eye makeup was simple, just black winged liner. Her cheeks were a very bright pink, much brighter than she would have normally done, but all of it created a very sophisticated effect. And for the first time she thought maybe she looked like she belonged. Like maybe she was a princess. Not a girl being shoved into a mold she resolutely could not fit into, but one who'd had a mold created just for her.

"He will approve of this," Elizabeth said.

"You know he is my stepbrother," Sophia pointed out. "He doesn't need to approve of it in that way."

The very idea made her face hot. And that she wanted him to…that she wanted him to want her was the worst humiliation of all.

"I know," the woman said, giving her a look that was far too incisive. "But you wouldn't mind if he did."

Sophia sputtered. "I… He can't."

"That has nothing to do with what you feel. Or what you want."

Sophia felt like she had been opened up and examined. Like her skin had been peeled away, revealing her deepest and most desperate secrets. She hated it. But she didn't have time to marinate in it because suddenly, the door was opening, and Luca had returned. Obviously, Elizabeth had texted him to say that Sophia was ready.

But she wasn't ready. She wasn't ready to face him, not with the woman next to her knowing full well how Sophia felt about Luca. Because now she felt like it was written across her skin, across her forehead, so that it could clearly be read by the man himself.

Her earlier confidence melted away, and her skin began to heat as Luca stopped, his dark eyes assessing her slowly.

Her body tingled, her breasts feeling heavy, her nipples going tight as though his fingertips were grazing her skin. As if he was doing more than simply looking.

"It will do," he said, his tone as hard as his features.

Her throat felt prickly, and she swallowed hard, feeling foolish, her heart fluttering like a caged bird trying to escape. How could she feel so much when he looked at her, while he felt nothing for her at all? While he clearly saw her as an annoyance.

He didn't look impressed; he didn't look awed or surprised with what she had felt was a total transformation.

"I am glad that I reach at least the bottom of your very lofty standards, Your Majesty," she said stiffly. "I can only hope that a certain Swedish noble has a slightly more enthusiastic response."

"I said that it will do," he reiterated. "And it will. What more do you want from me, *sorellina*?"

"I spent the entire day receiving a makeover. I would have thought it would garner a response. But it seems as if I am destined to remain little more than wallpaper. It is okay. Some women are never going to be beautiful."

She grasped the flowing skirt of her dress with her fists and pushed past Luca, running out of the room, down the hall, running until her lungs burned. The sound of the heels she was wearing on the floor drowned out the sound of anything else, so it wasn't until she stopped that she heard heavy footsteps behind her. And she was unprepared for the large, strong hand that wrapped around her arm and spun her in the opposite direction. It was then she found herself gazing up into Luca's impossibly dark and imposing eyes.

"What is it you want from me?" he asked, his voice low and hard. Shot through with an intensity she had never heard in his voice before. "What do you want me to give you? What reaction would have been sufficient? In the absence of the one man you have ever wanted, what is it you expected *me* to give you? Do you want me to tell you that you're beautiful? Do you want me to tell you the curves would drive any man to distraction? That every man in that ballroom is going to imagine himself holding you in his arms? Feeling those luscious breasts pressed against his chest? Kissing those lips. Driving himself inside you? Is that what you want to hear? I can give you those words, Sophia, but they are pointless. I could tell you that any man who doesn't want you was a fool, but what is the point in saying those words? What could they possibly mean between the two of us?" He released his hold on her, and she stumbled backward. "Nothing. They mean nothing coming from me. It will always be nothing. It must be."

"Luca…"

"Do not speak to me." He straightened then, his expression going blank, his posture rigid. "It will do, Sophia. You will wear that dress the night of the ball. And you will find yourself a husband. I will see to that."

It wasn't until Luca turned and walked away, wasn't until he was out of her sight, that she dropped to her knees, her entire body shaking, her brain unwilling to try and figure out what had just passed between them. What those words had meant.

He said it could be nothing. It was nothing. She curled her fingers into fists, her nails digging into her skin.

It was nothing. It always would be.

She repeated those words to herself over and over again, and forced herself not to cry.

CHAPTER FOUR

HE HAD ACTED a fool the day that Sophia had received her makeover. He had… He had allowed his facade to crack. He had allowed her to reach beneath that rock wall that he had erected between himself and anyone who might get too close.

He never acted a fool. And he resented the fact that Sophia possessed the power to make him do so.

His entire life was about the crown. The country.

His mother had driven the importance of those things home before she died. In an exacting and painful manner. One that had made it clear it was not Luca who mattered, but San Gennaro. The royal name over the royal himself.

He had shaped himself around that concept.

But Sophia had looked…

Thankfully, it was time. The guests had all arrived for the ball, with Sophia scheduled to arrive fashionably late so as to draw as much attention as possible.

His attention had been fixed on her far too much in the past few days. Sadly, everything his body had suspected about her beauty had been confirmed with this recent makeover. This stylist had managed to uncover and harness the feminine power that had always been there. And she had put it on brilliant display. Those curves, not covered anymore, but flaunted, served up as if they were a rare delicacy that he wanted very much to consume.

And of course, other men were going to look at her this way. Other men were going to dance with her.

Another man was going to marry her. Take her to his bed.

It was the plan. It was his salvation. Resenting it now… Well, he was worse than a dog in the manger, so to speak. Much worse.

He made a fox and a hen house look tame. Of course, if he were the fox he would devour her. He would have no one and nothing to answer to.

He was not a fox. He was a king.

And he could not touch her. He *would* not. He would honor that final request his father had made. To keep her safe. To see her married to a suitable man.

He was not that man, and he never could be.

Even if their relationship wasn't as it was, he would not be for her. He might have been, once. But that possibility had been destroyed along with so many other things. He had very nearly been destroyed, too. But as he had set about to rebuild himself, he had made choices. Choices that would redeem the sins in the past. Not his sins to redeem. But that mattered little.

He was the one who had to live with the consequences. He was the one who had to rule a country with strength and unfailing wisdom.

And so, he had purposed he would.

But that did not make him the man for her.

Thank God the ball was happening now. Thank God this interminable nightmare was almost over.

She would choose one of the men in attendance tonight. He would be certain of that.

He stood at the back of the room, surveying the crowd of people. All of the women dressed in glorious ball gowns, none of whom would be able to hold a candle to Sophia, he knew. None of whom would be able to provide him with the distraction that he needed.

"This is quite lovely." He turned to see his stepmother standing beside him. She had been traveling abroad with friends for months, clearly needing time away to process the loss of her husband. Though she was back now, living in a small house on palace grounds.

It suited her, she said, to live close, but no longer in the palace.

She had lost a significant amount of weight since the death of his father, and she had not had much to lose on that petite frame of hers to begin with. She was elegant as ever, but there was a sadness about her.

She had truly loved his father. It was something that Luca had never doubted. Never had he imagined she was a commoner simply looking to better her station by marrying royalty. No, there had been real, sincere love in their marriage.

Something that Luca himself would never be able to obtain.

"Thank you," he said.

"And all of this is for Sophia?"

"Yes," he said. "It is as my father wished. He wanted to see her in a good marriage. And I have arranged to see that it is so."

"Yes," she said, nodding slowly. "But what does Sophia think?"

"She has agreed. In that, she has agreed to try to

find someone tonight. And if she does not, she has six months following to choose the man that she wishes. But I have confidence that one of the men tonight will attract her."

"I see," she said.

"You do not approve?"

"I married your father because I loved him. And one of the wonderful things that came with that marriage was money. With money came the kind of freedom that I never could have hoped Sophia to have if we had remained impoverished. I hate to see it curtailed."

"This is not curtailing her freedom. It is simply keeping with what is expected of those in our station. I have explained this to Sophia already."

"Yes, Luca. I have no doubt you have. You are very like your father in that you are confident that your way is always correct."

"My way is the best for a woman in her position. You must trust that I am the authority on this."

"You forget," his stepmother said, "I have been queen for a sizable amount of time. I did not just leave the village. So to speak."

"Perhaps not. But I was born into this. And you must understand that it is difficult to marry so far above your station. That is not an insult. But I know that it took a great deal for yourself and Sophia to adjust to the change. I know that Sophia still finds it difficult. Can you imagine if she married someone for whom this was foreign?"

"You make a very good point."

"This ball, this marriage, is not for my own amusement." It was for his salvation. However, he would leave that part unspoken.

Suddenly, the double doors to the ballroom opened, and all eyes turned to the entryway. There she was, a brilliant flash of fuchsia, her dark hair tumbling around her shoulders. She was even more beautiful than he had remembered. Golden curves on brilliant display, her skin gleaming in the light.

"Oh, my," her mother said.

"She got a new stylist," he said stiffly.

"Apparently."

Sophia descended the staircase slowly, and the moment one foot hit the bottom of the stair, her first suitor had already approached her. The Swede.

Sophia would probably be disappointed he didn't have a sheep on a leash to entertain her. Or a sweater.

"You do not approve of him?" his stepmother asked.

"Of course I approve of him. I approve of every man that I asked to come and be considered as a potential husband for Sophia."

"Then you might want to look less like you wish to dismember him."

"I am protective of her," he said, straightening and curling his hands into fists.

"If you say so."

He gritted his teeth. He did not like the idea that his stepmother of all people would find him transparent. He prided himself on his control, but Sophia tested it at every turn.

And so he told himself that the feeling roaring through him now was relief when the man took hold of Sophia and swept her around the dance floor.

The other man's hand rested perilously low on her waist, on the curve of her hip, and if he was to move his hand down and around her back he would be cupping that lovely ass of hers. And that, Luca found unacceptable.

He will not stop there if he marries her. He will touch her everywhere. Taste her everywhere. She will belong to him.

He gritted his teeth. That was the point. The point was that she needed to belong to another man, so that he could no longer harbor any fantasies of her.

As the song ended, another man approached Sophia, and she began to dance with him. Another of her selections.

Luca approached a woman wearing royal blue, and asked her to dance. Kept himself busy, tried to focus on the feel of her soft, feminine curves beneath his hands. Because what did it matter if it was this woman, or another. What did it matter. Sex was sex. A woman's body was a woman's body. He should be able to find enjoyment in it. He should not long for the woman in pink across the room. The woman who was tacitly forbidden to him. But he did.

The woman he held in his arms now might well have been a cardboard cutout for all that she affected him.

But still, he continued to dance with her, knowing that he should not. Knowing that dancing with any single woman this long would create gossip. He didn't even know her name. He wouldn't ask for it. And tomorrow he would not remember her face until he saw it printed in the paper. She didn't matter.

Suddenly, Sophia extricated herself from her dance partner's hold, excusing herself with a broad gesture as she scurried across the ballroom.

"Excuse me," he said, releasing hold of his dance partner, following after his stepsister.

Sophia wove through the crowd and made her way outside. He followed. But by the time he got out to the balcony, she was gone. He looked over the edge and saw a dark shape moving across the grass below. He could only barely make her out, the glow from the ballroom lights casting just enough gold onto the ground to highlight her moving shape. He swung his leg over the edge of the balcony and lowered himself down to the grass below, following the path that Sophia had no doubt taken.

He said nothing, his movements silent as he went after her. To what end, he didn't know. But then, he had no idea what she thought she was doing, either. It was foolish for her to leave the ball. And it was foolish for him to go after her. All of this was foolish. Everything with her. Always.

And yet, he couldn't escape her. That was the essential problem. She was unsuitable because of their connection. She was inescapable because of their connection. And for that reason, he had never been able to master it.

He could not have her; neither could he banish her from his life.

And here he was, chasing after her in a suit.

He was the king of a nation, stumbling in the dark after a woman.

Finally, she stopped, her pale shoulders shaking, highlighted by the light of the moon. He reached out, placing his hand on her bare skin. She jumped, turning to face him, her eyes glistening in the light. "Luca."

And suddenly, he knew exactly why he had gone after her. He knew exactly what the endgame was. Exactly why he was here.

"Sophia."

And then he wrapped her in his arms and finally did the one thing he had expressly forbidden himself from doing. He claimed her lips with his own.

CHAPTER FIVE

LUCA WAS KISSING HER. It was impossible. Utterly and completely impossible that this was happening. She was delusional. Dreaming. She had to be.

Luca *hated* her.

Luca saw himself as being so far above her that he would hardly deign to speak to her if they weren't related by marriage.

He didn't want to kiss her. He didn't.

Except, with the little bit of brainpower that she had, she recalled that moment in the halls of the castle days ago. When she had gotten her makeover. He had grabbed hold of her arm and had told her he could not tell her how beautiful she was because it was pointless. Because nothing could come of it.

Did that mean he wished it could?

It had all felt like something too bright and too close then. Something she couldn't parse and didn't want to. Not when the end result would only be her own humiliation. Even if he didn't know what she was thinking, entertaining the notion that Luca might want her had always seemed horrific, even if no one ever found out.

It was so surreal a thought that she was still asking

it even as those firm, powerful lips thrust hers apart, his tongue invading her mouth.

She had never been kissed like this before. Had never received anything beyond polite kisses that had seemed to be a testing of her interest.

Luca, true to form, was not testing her interest. He was *assuming* it. And she imagined that if he found her disinterested, he would work with all that he had to change her mind.

Except, his assumption was correct. And she did not possess the strength to deny that. Not now.

Not when her most cherished fantasy was coming to life, right here in the darkened garden of the palace.

Luca cupped her face, large, hot hands holding her steady as he angled his face and took her deeper.

He kissed exactly like what he was. An autocratic conqueror. A man who had never been denied a single thing in his life.

A man who would not be denied now.

"I cannot watch this," he rasped. "I cannot watch other men dance with you. Put their hands on you."

"You said… You said you had to find me a husband." Her voice was wobbly, tremulous, and she hated that. She wished—very much—that she could be more confident. That she could sound sophisticated. As if this was simply another garden tryst of many in a long line of them. Rather than the first time she had truly, honestly been kissed by a man.

Rather than a girl on the receiving end of something she had desired all of her life.

She didn't want him to know that. She didn't want him to know how she felt.

But then she imagined that she betrayed herself with

each breath, with each moment that passed when she didn't slap his face and call him ten kinds of scoundrel for daring to touch her in that way.

Of course she betrayed herself. Because, though he had been the one to instigate, she had kissed him back.

She had been powerless to do anything else. She had been far too caught up in it, consumed by it. By him.

The story of her life.

Things went well, and then Luca. And it all went to hell. It all belonged to him.

"I am going to find you a husband," he said. "I swore it to my father." He dragged his thumb along the edge of her lip. "But I cannot pretend I don't want you. Not any longer."

"You… You want me?"

"It is like a disease," he ground out. "To want my *sister* as I do."

"I'm not your sister," she said, her lips numb. "We don't have the same parents. We don't share blood at all."

"But don't you see? To my father you were. And you would be to the nation. An affair between the two of us would have disastrous consequences."

She closed her eyes, swallowing hard. "How?"

"Think of the headlines. About how our parents were married, and I debauched you likely from the moment you were beneath my roof. As a child. Or, you seduced me to try and hold on to your place. The nation has accepted you as a princess, without a blood relation, but reminding them so starkly that you do not carry royal blood is only a mistake. Can you imagine? An affair between two people who must thereafter remain family? It would be a disaster," he reiterated.

"Then why did you kiss me?"

"Because I no longer possess the power to *not* kiss you. He had his hands on you," he growled, grabbing hold of her hips and drawing her up against his body. "You may have only ever wanted one man before me. But I will make you forget him."

She gasped. She could feel the aggressive jut of his arousal against her stomach, could feel the intensity in the way he held her. His blunt fingertips dug into her skin, and she was certain that he would leave bruises behind. But she didn't care. She would be happy to bear bruises from Luca's touch. Whatever that said about her.

And then, he stopped talking. Then, that infuriating, arrogant mouth was back on hers, kissing, sucking and tasting. He angled his head, dragging his teeth along her tender lower lip before nipping her, growling as he consumed her yet again.

Sophia didn't know this game. She didn't know what to do next. Didn't know how to use her lips and tongue just so as Luca seemed to do.

So she battled against inexperience with enthusiasm, clinging to the front of his jacket with one hand, the other wrapped around his tie as she raised herself up on her toes and kissed him with all the needs she had inside her. She found herself being propelled backward, deeper into the garden. There was a stone bench there, and Luca gripped her hips, sliding his large, warm hands down her thighs, holding on to her hard as he lifted her so that her legs were wrapped around his waist. Then he brought both of them down onto the stone bench, with her sitting on his lap.

Her thighs were spread wide, the quivering, needy

heart of her pressed hard against that telltale ridge that shouted loudly to her that this wasn't a hallucination. That Luca did want her. That no matter it didn't make any sense, that no matter it went against everything she had always believed about him, about herself, about who they were, it was happening.

He moved his hands back to cup her rear, drawing her even more firmly against his arousal. Heat streaked through her veins, lightning shooting through her body. She had never felt anything like this. Like the all-consuming intensity of Luca. That sure and certain mouth tasting her, the friction slick and undeniably intoxicating. Like those big, hot hands all over her curves. His length between her thighs. He was everywhere. All around her. Flooding her senses. It wasn't just his touch. It was his flavor. His scent.

Familiar and so unfamiliar all at the same time. She knew Luca. From a distance. He had been in her life for so many years. Part of so many formative feelings that she'd had. He had most definitely been her very first fantasy. But those fantasies had been muted. They had not come close to the reality of the man himself. Of what it meant to be held by him, kissed by him, consumed by him.

This was no gauzy fantasy. This was something else entirely. It was harsh, and it was far too sharp. She was afraid it was going to slice her in two. The feelings of pleasure that she felt were nothing like the fluttery sensations that had built low in her stomach when he used to look at her across a crowded room. Were nothing compared to the swooping feeling she would get in her stomach when she would allow herself to imagine something half as racy as him kissing her on the mouth.

No. This was pain. Sharp between her legs. A hollow sensation at her core that terrified her, because she didn't feel as though he had created it just now so much as uncovered it. That she was hollow until she could be filled by him. That if he didn't, she would always remain this way.

Luca.

This was a raw, savage uncovering of desire. Desire that she had always known was there, but that had been muted, blunted, by her innocence. By the sure certainty that nothing could ever happen between them.

But now he wanted her. And she didn't know if she was strong enough to bear it.

Because it wasn't just what might happen next. No. It was what would happen when it ended. Then it would end. He had said as much.

He might have confessed his desire for her, but there were no other feelings involved. He had spoken of nothing tender. No. It was nothing but anger in Luca's eyes. Anger and lust.

That was what had been on his face when he had chased her down in the corridor days ago. Anger. Rage. And lust. The unidentified emotion in his eyes. The one she had not been brave enough to identify.

He moved his hand up the back of her head, cupping her skull, then he plunged his fingers deep into her locks, curling his hand into a fist and tugging hard, forcing her head backward, pressing his lips to the curve of her throat. And she felt like wounded prey at the mercy of a predator. Her most vulnerable parts exposed to him.

And yet she allowed it. Didn't fight against it. Wanted it.

Needed it.

That was the worst part. This was something more than want. This was part of her essential makeup.

She had been exposed to Luca at such an early age that he had been formative to her. That he was part of her journey to womanhood. So maybe this was apt. Terrifying though it might be, maybe this was something that needed to happen.

This wasn't the Middle Ages. None of those men out in the ballroom had been promised a virgin princess.

She owed them nothing, for now. For now, it was only Luca.

For now.

And that would have to be enough.

"Dear God," he rasped, dragging his tongue along the edge of her collarbone, down lower to where the plump curve of her breasts met the neckline of her dress. "I've lost my mind."

"I…" She was going to say something witty. Something about the fact that she had lost hers right along with him. But she couldn't speak. Instead, she heaved in a sharp breath, bringing that wicked mouth into deeper contact with her breast. He growled, jerking the top of her dress down, exposing her to him.

She had never been naked in front of a man before. She found she wasn't embarrassed. Certainly, the darkness out in the garden helped, but she knew that with the aid of the moonlight he could still see plenty. But it was Luca. The only man that she had ever been prepared to have seen her naked body. The only man she had ever fantasized about. This was terrifying. It went far beyond anything she had imagined. But it was with him.

And that made all the difference. It made every difference.

He said some words in Italian that she didn't understand. She was fluent enough, having lived in San Gennaro for so much of her life, but she didn't know these words. Hot and filthy-sounding, even without the translation. He scraped his cheek along that tender skin, his whiskers abrading her skin. And then he drew one aching, tightened nipple deep into his mouth, sucking hard.

She arched her back, crying out as pleasure pierced her core like an arrow.

He brought one hand up to cup her breast, rough and hot. She wanted to ask him why his hands were so rough. Wanted to ask him what he did to keep his body so finely honed. Why a man who should have the body of any man with a desk job looked as he did.

But she couldn't ask. All of her words, all of her questions, were bottled up in her throat, and the only thing that could escape was one hoarse cry as he moved from one breast to the next with his mouth, sucking the other nipple in deep, teasing her and tormenting her as he did.

For a moment she had the thought that this was too much too soon. She wasn't ready for this. How could she be? She had never even kissed a man before, and now she was in the arms of King Luca, her top pulled down, her breasts exposed. Riding the hard ridge of his arousal. How could that not be too much? How could she possibly withstand such a thing?

But suddenly, perhaps in time with the flex of his hips upward—that iron part of him making contact with the place where she was softest, most pliant and most sensitive—perhaps it was that that crystallized everything for her. It wasn't enough. And she had waited a lifetime for it. It didn't matter what experience or lack of it she'd had before. Not in the least. What mattered was that it was him.

That she had longed for, craved, desired this very thing for what felt like an eternity.

Luca. Her stepbrother. The man who seemed for all the world to find her utterly and completely beneath his notice, was kissing her. And she could not deny him anything that he wanted.

She could not deny herself what she wanted.

Luca's large, warm hands slid down the shape of her body as if he was taking her measurements with those strong fingers. Then they moved down farther, to her thighs, finding the hem of her dress, already pushed up partway, and shoving it up farther, exposing her even more.

He made a low, feral sound. Hungry. Untamed. Perhaps he was like this with all women; that was a possibility. One that she didn't want to think about. At least not too much. She would like to be special. But she had no idea how she could be. Anything between them was impossible, and she knew it. She had always known it. That didn't mean her feelings disappeared.

"I have wanted you," he said, his voice rough, as rough as the scrape of his whiskers against the side of her neck as he dragged a kiss down her throat. "It is a madness. It is like a sickness. And nothing…nothing has ever come close to banishing it from me. You are like a poison in my blood."

The words sounded tortured. Tormented. And for a moment she wondered if he felt even the slightest bit of what she had felt over the past years. And if he did… Then whatever this could be, and she had no illusions that it could be anything remotely close to permanent, she knew it was the right thing.

Madness. Sickness. Poison.

Those words described what she felt for Luca far too closely. They resonated inside her. They were her truth. And if they were his…how could she deny it?

She was no longer content to simply sit on his lap and be kissed. No. She wanted him. She wanted this. And she was going to have him.

She returned volley with a growl of her own, biting his lower lip as she moved her hands to that black tie that held his crisp, white shirt shut. With trembling fingers she undid the knot and pulled it open, then made quick work of the top button of that shirt. Followed by the next. And the next. She pushed the fabric apart, exposing muscles, chest hair and hot, delicious skin to her touch.

She had heard people talk about desire. But they had never said that it was so close to feeling ill. So close to feeling like you might die if you couldn't have what you wanted.

So close to pain.

There was a hollow ache between her legs, running through her entire body, and she felt that if it was not filled by him she wouldn't be able to go on. It was as simple as that.

She traced her fingertips over his chest, across his nipple, gratified by the rough sound of pleasure that exited his mouth as she did so. He wrapped his arms around her tightly, lowering his head again, tasting and teasing her breasts as he did. She had never imagined that insanity could be blissful. But hers certainly was. Magical in a way that she had not imagined it could be.

She had not thought that there could be beauty in torment. But there was. In this moment.

In this world they had created in the rose garden, separate from the concerns happening in the ballroom. The concerns of their lives, real lives, and not this stolen moment.

There were men in there that she was expected to consider seriously as husbands. A whole raft of duties and responsibilities waiting for both of them that had nothing to do with satisfying their pleasure under a starry sky with only the moon as witness.

But she was glad they had found this. This quiet space. The space where only they belonged. Where their parents' marriage didn't matter. Where their titles didn't matter. Where—whatever that could possibly mean to a man like Luca—they simply were Luca and Sophia, with nothing else to concern them.

He kept on saying things. Rough. Broken. Words in Italian and English. Some of which she couldn't understand, not so much because of the language barrier but because of the intensity in his words, the depth of them. The kinds of things he said, talking about doing things she had never imagined, much less spoken about.

But they washed over her in a wave, and she found she wanted them all. That she wanted this.

Him.

Broken, and out of control in a way that she had never imagined it was possible for Luca to be. At all other moments he was the picture of control. Of absolute and total certainty. And in this moment he did not seem as though he had the power to be that man.

It made her feel powerful. Desired.

His hands moved between her thighs, sliding between the waistband of her panties and teasing her where she was wet and ready for him. For a moment she felt a fleeting sense of embarrassment, a scalding heat in her cheeks. Because certainly now he would know how much she wanted him. How much she felt for him. What woman would be like this if she didn't? And there, he found the incontrovertible evidence. But if it bothered him, he didn't show it. Instead, he seemed inflamed by it. Seemed to want her all the more.

"Perhaps later," he rasped, kissing her neck, her cheek, making his way back to her lips. "Perhaps later I will take my time. Will be able to savor you as you should be. But now… I find there is not enough time, and I must have you."

She wanted him to have her. Whatever that might mean. She needed it.

He shifted, undid the closure on his pants and wrapped his arms tightly around her, angling her hips so that she was seated above him, the head of his arousal pressing against the entrance to her body.

And then he thrust up into her, deep and savage, giving no quarter to her innocence at all. It hurt. But Luca didn't seem to notice. Instead, he began to move inside her in hard, decisive thrusts. She couldn't catch her breath. But then, she didn't want to. Even as she felt like she was being invaded, conquered, she didn't want him to stop. Even as it hurt, she didn't want him to stop. Gradually, the pain gave way to pleasure, an overwhelming, gripping sense of it that built inside her until she thought she wouldn't be able to take it much longer.

When it broke over her it was like a wave containing a revelation, pleasure like she had never known bursting through her. If she had looked up to find fireworks in the sky she wouldn't have been surprised. But the only thing above her was stars. The fireworks were in her.

They were the fireworks.

She and Luca together.

She held on to him tightly as she rode out her release, pulsing waves that seemed to go on and on crashing inside her endlessly. Then he gripped her hips hard, driving himself up into her with brute force as he found his own release, a growl vibrating through his chest as he did.

And then somehow, it was over. Nothing but the sound of their breathing, the feel of his heart pounding heavily against her hand, where it rested against his sweat-slicked chest.

The night sky no longer seemed endless. Instead, it pressed down on them, the reality of what had just occurred lowering the blackness but leaving the stars out of reach.

She felt dark. Cold.

She was cold. Because she was naked in a garden.

Luca moved her away from him, beginning to straighten his clothing. "We must go back," he said, his tone remote and stiff.

"How?" she asked. Because she had a feeling he did not just mean to the ball, but to the way things had been before he had touched her. Before that rock wall had broken between them and revealed what they had both desired for so long.

"It doesn't matter how. Only that it must be."

She looked at him, searching his face in the darkness. "I don't know if I can."

"But you must," he said, uncompromising.

The light from the moon cast hollows of his face

into light and shadow, making it look as though he was carved out of the very granite his voice seemed to be made of.

"You will go back into that ballroom and you will dance with the rest of the men you said you would dance with. Then you will choose a husband," he continued.

"Luca," she said, her voice breaking. "I can't do that. Not after I was just..."

"It is only sex, *sorellina*," he said, the endearment landing with a particular sharpness just now. "You will find a way to cope."

Panic attacked her, its sharp, grasping claws digging into her. "I was a virgin, you idiot."

That stopped him. He drew back as though he had been slapped.

"You said...you said you wanted a man."

She looked away, her shame complete now, her face so hot she was sure she was about to burst into flame. "Who do you think I wanted, you fool?"

The silence that fell between them was heavy. As if the velvet sky had fallen over the top of them.

"Not the choice I would have made my first time. But the choice was yours. You had every chance to say no. You did not." Suddenly his tone turned fierce. "Am I to assume you didn't want to? Are you trying to imply that you didn't know what you were doing?"

"No," she said. "I knew what I was doing."

"Then I fail to see what your virginity has to do with any of it. This is hardly Medieval times. No one will expect a virgin princess on their wedding night anyway."

"I suppose not."

"I must go back. I am the host, after all. Take all the time you need to gather yourself."

He said that as though she should be impressed with his softness. With his kindness. She was about to tell him how ludicrous that was, but then he turned and walked away, leaving her there, half-naked on a stone bench, having just lost her virginity to her stepbrother. To her king.

Her lungs were going to cave in on themselves. Collapse completely, along with her heart. It was shattered anyway, so it didn't matter where the pieces landed.

This was her fantasy. That bright little spot of hope that had existed somewhere inside her, a glimmer of what could be that kept her warm on the darkest of nights.

Now it was gone. Snuffed out. As dark as the night around her.

When she went to bed at night, she would no longer wonder. Because she knew. It had been better than she had imagined. Had transformed her. In more ways than the physical. He had been inside her. Joined to her. This man that had held her emotions captive for half of her life.

This man she'd spent nights weaving beautiful, gilded stories about in her head before she fell asleep. If only. If maybe. If someday.

But it had happened. And now there was no more rest in *if only.*

Nothing remained but shattered dreams.

He acted as though they would be able to go back to normal. But Sophia knew she would never be the same again.

CHAPTER SIX

SOPHIA HAD AVOIDED him for the past few weeks. Ever since she had gone back into the ballroom and proceeded to dance with every man he had commanded her to.

She had been pale-faced and angry-looking, but gradually, it had all settled into something serene, though no less upset.

But he did not approach her. Not again. And she moved around the palace as if she were a ghost.

He had failed her. Had failed them both. But there was nothing to be done. There was no use engaging in a postmortem. His control had failed him at the worst possible moment.

He had done the one thing he had purposed he would never do. And it had been all much more a spectacular failure than he had initially imagined it would be.

A *virgin.*

He had not thought she would be that.

She had gone to university. Had moved out in the world for quite some time, and she was beautiful. In his mind, irresistible. Hell, in practice she was irresistible. Had he been able to resist her, then he surely would have.

No man could possibly resist her. If his own ironclad control had failed…

So perhaps that was his pride. Because clearly she had somehow remained untouched all this time.

And he had failed at maintaining that particular status quo.

But that other man had been touching her. Holding her in his arms.

Perversely, he was satisfied by the fact that he had been the first man to touch her. It was wrong. And he should feel a deep sense of regret over it. Part of him did. But another part of him gloried in it.

As with all things Sophia, there was no consensus between desire and morality.

The only contact he'd had with Sophia had been for her to tell him that she wanted to speak with him today. And so he sat in his office, his hands curled into fists, resting on the top of his desk while he waited for her to appear.

The fact that she never failed to put him on edge irked him even now.

There'd never been a more pointless and futile attraction in the history of the world. Or, perhaps there had been, but it had not bedeviled him, and so, it didn't concern him now. No, it was Sophia who had that power over him.

And she was not for him.

There was no way he could reconfigure their fates to make it so. No way that he could switch around their circumstances. Even if she weren't his stepsister…

He was not the man for her.

The door to his office cracked slightly, and she slipped inside, not knocking. Not waiting for an announcement. Because of course she wouldn't. Of course she would break with protocol, even now. Not allowing the blessed formality inherent in royal life to put some distance between them when it was much needed.

"You wished to come and speak to me?"

"Yes," she said. "But I should think that was self-evident. Considering that I made an arrangement to come and speak to you, and now I am here doing it."

"There is no need to be sarcastic, Sophia."

"I'm surprised you recognized it, Luca."

For a moment their eyes caught and held, the sensation of that connection sending a zap of electricity down through his body.

She looked away as though she had felt that same sensation. As though it had burned.

"I recognize it easily enough. What did you wish to speak to me about?"

"I wanted to tell you that I've made my selection. I've decided who I will marry."

That was the last thing he had expected, and her words hit him with the force of a punch squared to the chest. So intense, so hard, he thought it might have stopped his heart from beating altogether.

"You have?"

"Yes. I hope that you value an alliance with Sweden."

He had not been aware that he possessed the ability to feel finer emotions. Until he felt a last remaining piece of himself—one he had not realized existed—turn to stone. "I'm surprised to hear you say that."

"That I selected him specifically? Or that I have selected anyone at all?"

"That you have complied at all. Rather than making this incredibly difficult."

She clasped her hands in front of her, her dark hair falling down into her face. The outfit she was wearing was much more suited to her than her usual fare. Tight, as that ball gown on the night he had first kissed her had been. A tangerine-colored top that shaped exquisitely to her curves, and a skirt with a white and blue pattern.

But the pattern was secondary to the fact that it hugged her body like a second skin. As he wished he could hug her even now. What he wouldn't give to span that glorious waist again, to slide his palms down to those generous hips.

Having her once had done nothing to eradicate the sickness inside him.

But this marriage… Perhaps it would accomplish what he had hoped it would.

And in the end, he would still have been the one to have her first.

Yes. But he will have her second, if he hasn't had her already, and you will have to watch the two of them together.

He had always known that would be his fate. There was no fighting against it.

"I had some very important questions answered the night of the ball," she said, making bold eye contact with him. "I have no reason to fight against this marriage. Not now."

There was an unspoken entreaty in those words, and it was one he could not answer.

He would have to marry, yes, that was certain. But it would never be a woman like her. It would be a woman who understood. One who didn't look at him with hope in her eyes.

One who wouldn't mind that the part of him that could care for another person, the part of him that loved, had been excised with a scalpel long ago.

That he was a man who ruled with his head because he knew a heart was no compass at all. Least of all his.

It felt nothing. Nothing at all.

"Excellent," he said. "I'm glad there's no longer a barrier."

Color flew to her cheeks, and he did nothing to correct her assumption that he had made an intentional double entendre. He had not. But if it made her angry, all the better.

"Let me know how soon you wish for the wedding to be, and I will arrange it."

"In a month," she said quickly. "We are to be married in a month."

"Then I will prepare an announcement."

Sophia's head hurt. Her heart hurt. Everything hurt. The depression that she had fallen under since the ball was pronounced. It made everything she did feel heavy. Weighted down.

The engagement to Erik hadn't helped matters. The courtship in general hadn't helped at all. And she felt like a terrible person. He was solicitous, kind. Their interactions had not been physical at all. The idea of letting him touch her so closely to when she and Luca had…

Though part of her wondered if she should. Like ripping off a Band-Aid.

The mystery was gone from sex anyway.

A tear slid down her cheek and she blinked, shocked, because she hadn't realized she had been so close to crying. She wiped it away and swallowed hard, attempting to gather herself.

She was currently getting a wedding gown fitted. That meant she had to look a little bit less morose. Though, right now, she was sitting in the room alone, wearing nothing but a crinoline.

Both the seamstress and her mother would be in the room soon, and she really needed to find a way to look as if she was engaged in the process.

But then, she felt as if she had not been engaged in the process of her life for the past few weeks, so why should this be any different?

It had been foolish, perhaps, to jump into marrying Erik, simply because she wanted to do something to strike back at Luca. Simply because she wanted there to be something in her life that wasn't that deep, yawning ache to be with him.

They couldn't be together. It was that simple. He didn't want to be with her. Oh, he had certainly revealed that he lusted after her in that moment in the garden, but it wasn't the same as what she felt for him.

And furthermore, he was allowing her to marry another man.

Another tear splashed onto her hand.

Was that why she was doing this? Was that why she was going through with the engagement? Because she wanted him to stop it?

That was so wholly childish and ridiculous.

And yet she had a feeling she might be just that ridiculous and childish.

The door to the dressing room opened, and the designer and her mother breezed inside at the same time.

Her mother was holding the dress, contained in a plastic zip-up bag, and the designer was carrying a kit.

"Let's help you get this on," the woman said briskly.

Sophia's mother unzipped the bag and helped Sophia pull the dress over her head as the designer instructed. There was much pinning and fussing and exclamation, and Sophia tried very hard to match those sounds.

"Are you okay?" her mother asked as the designer was down on her hands and knees pinning the hem of the gown.

"I'm…overwhelmed." She figured she would go for some form of honesty. It was better than pretending everything was fine when it clearly wasn't, and her mom wasn't going to accept that as an answer.

"It is understandable. This wedding has come together very quickly."

"It's what Luca wants."

"I see."

"It's what Father wanted."

"And what do you want, Sophia? Because as much as I loved your stepfather, and as much as I know he had your best interests at heart… I didn't marry him because I wanted to be queen. I didn't marry him for money, or status. I married him because I loved him. And I want nothing less for you. I understand that he did this because it is what he would have done for his biological daughter if he'd had one. You are not from this world. And you don't have to comply to the dictates of it if you don't wish to."

What was the alternative? Living life with Luca glowering down at her. Wanting him. Watching him get married and have children…

Well, it was that or cutting herself off from her family altogether.

For a moment she stood adrift in that fantasy. Blowing in a breeze where she was tied to nothing and no one. It made her feel empty, hollow. Terrified.

But at least it didn't hurt.

"I want this," she said, resolute. "It's the right thing. And he's a very nice man."

Her mother sighed heavily. "I'm sure that he is."

"You know that Luca wouldn't allow this if he wasn't suitable. If he wasn't good."

"Certainly not," she said. "I know Luca would never allow any harm to come to you. Not physical harm, anyway."

Sophia gritted her teeth, wondering, not for the first time, if her mother suspected that there was something between Luca and herself. If she did, she was not saying anything. Resolutely so.

And Sophia certainly wasn't going to say anything.

She looked down and kicked the heavy skirt of her dress out of the way, and then she straightened, looking at herself in the mirror. Suddenly, she felt dizzy, wobbling slightly as she took in the sight of herself wearing a wedding gown. A wedding gown.

She felt ill.

"Excuse me," she said, clamoring down from the stepstool and dashing into the adjoining bathroom, slamming the door behind her as she collapsed onto her knees and cast up her accounts into the toilet.

She braced herself, shaking and sweating, breathing hard. She had never been sick like that. So abruptly.

She felt terrible. Throwing up hadn't helped.

She pushed herself up, afraid that she had damaged the gown, but it looked intact.

There was a heavy, sharp knock on the door. "Sophia?" It was her mother. Worried, obviously.

"I'm fine," she said. "Just a little bit…nauseated."

"Can I come in?"

"Okay."

The door opened and her mother slipped inside, her expression full of concern. "Are you ill?"

"I wasn't," Sophia said.

"You just suddenly started to feel sick?"

"Yes."

"Sophia…" Her mother looked at her speculatively, "forgive me if this is intrusive… Is it possible that you… Are you pregnant?"

The tentative grasp that Sophia had on the ground beneath her gave way. And she found herself crumbling to the floor again.

"Sophia?"

"I…"

"Are you pregnant?" her mother asked.

"It's possible," she said.

"I suppose the good thing is that the wedding is soon," she said, bending down and grabbing hold of Sophia's chin, her matching dark gaze searching Sophia's. "Are you happy?"

"I'm scared," Sophia said.

She couldn't organize her thoughts. She was late. It was true. She hadn't given it much thought because she had been stressed out with planning the wedding. But she was quite late. And she and Luca had not used a condom that night.

One time.

She'd had sex one time.

With the last man on earth she should have ever been with, and she had gotten pregnant. What were the odds of that happening?

Of course, now she was engaged to another man, a man whose baby it couldn't possibly be, because she had never even kissed him.

But there was going to be a wedding. Invitations had been sent out. Announcements had been made. She was being fitted for a dress.

"Of course you are," her mother said. "It's a terrifying thing facing a change like this. But wonderful." She put her hand on Sophia's face. "You're the best thing that ever happened to me, Sophia."

Sophia tried to smile. "I hope I'll be even half as good a mother as you have been to me."

"You will be."

"I wish I had such confidence."

"You will have help from your husband," her mother said. "I didn't have any help. It will be so nice for you to start with more in life than we had."

Sophia's mouth felt dry as chalk. How could she tell her mother that it wasn't her fiancé's baby?

That it was Luca's.

She couldn't. So she didn't. Instead, she let her mother talk excitedly about the wedding, about being a grandmother. Instead, she went outside and finished the fitting.

When it was over, she walked down the empty halls of the palace, back in her simple shift dress she had been wearing earlier. Then she pushed the door to her bedroom open. She looked around. At this beautiful spectacular bedroom that it was still difficult to believe belonged to her.

She stumbled over to her bed, a glorious, canopied creation with frothy netting and an excess of pillows.

Then she lay across that bed and she wept. She wept like her heart was breaking.

Because it was.

And she had no idea what to do about it.

CHAPTER SEVEN

Ultimately, Sophia felt it was wisest to procure a test through the official palace physician. The princess was hardly going to go to a drugstore to acquire a pregnancy test. It would be foolish. Things like that could never stay secret, not for long. Not in a media-hungry society, always looking for scandal.

One of the many things she'd had to learn, because it wasn't ingrained. That anyone would be interested in the life and times of a girl like her. But they were now. Because of who her mother had married.

Because of who she was, all thanks to a piece of paper. Nothing more.

Oftentimes, she appreciated what had come from that marriage.

This was one of the times she appreciated it less.

Fortunately, she trusted the woman that she had seen for years, recommended to her by palace staff. And she knew that her confidentiality was in fact one of the most important parts of her role as the physician to all members of the royal family, and palace staff.

Unfortunately, no matter how good the doctor was, she could not change the test results with skill.

Sophia paced back and forth while she waited. She

knew pregnancy tests didn't take *that* long. Still, the doctor was certainly taking her time in the makeshift lab, AKA, Sophia's en-suite bathroom.

When the door finally did open, the doctor looked blank. Sophia couldn't read a plus or negative sign on the woman's face. "The test is positive," she said. "Congratulations."

Sophia didn't want to be congratulated. Why should she be? She'd made a massive mistake and put everything Luca believed in in jeopardy. She was risking public embarrassment, wasted money on a wedding…she… she deserved something. But it wasn't congratulations.

"Thank you," Sophia said, instead of any of the things she was thinking. "The wedding is soon at least, so all will be sorted."

Except, she had no idea how to sort it out. This wedding was happening. All of the moving parts were at critical mass.

Tomorrow. The wedding was tomorrow. People were coming from all over to attend.

She was going to have to go to him. She was going to have to see Erik and let him know exactly what transpired. Likely, he would want to break it off. But it was entirely possible that…

She had no idea what she was supposed to do. Was she going to hide Luca's child from him? And what would he think? There was no way he would believe that she had immediately gone to bed with another man. He would know the child was his.

Would he?

It was entirely possible she could convince him she had played the role of harlot. That she had gone straight from Luca, on a garden bench, to Erik's bed.

But Erik was blond, while Luca was dark, darker than she was. The child would not look like Erik.

"I just need some time alone," Sophia said finally. "That's all I need."

The doctor nodded, collecting things and leaving Sophia in her bedroom. Leading her to solve a problem that might well be utterly and completely unsolvable.

She walked over to the closet and opened it up, letting her hands drift over the silk fabric of the wedding gown that was hanging there.

She was carrying Luca's baby. And she was supposed to walk toward another man tomorrow and say vows to him. Promise to love him, stay with him forever. She was supposed to have her wedding night with him.

A violent wave of nausea rolled over her.

She had been lying to herself this entire time. Thinking that she could do this. Thinking that she could be with another man. That she could make all of her feelings for Luca go away if she only tried hard enough. That if she replaced him in her bed she could replace him in her heart, but she didn't know how that could possibly be.

She swallowed hard, her throat dry. There was no going back. Not now.

There couldn't be. There was so much riding on this. Luca was right. Deals had already been made with Erik regarding his holdings, based on this marriage. Luca's reputation…in the eyes of the people, of the world, it mattered.

San Gennaro's reputation depended on Luca's. And…this could potentially compromise that.

And she had to think of that.

It had nothing to do with her being afraid. With her

feeling raw and wounded. Nothing at all. It was the greater good. Not…not the fact that thinking of Luca hurt.

Yes, Erik she was going to have to talk to. Because she owed her future husband honesty if nothing else.

Luca…

She had a feeling it would not be a kindness to give him honesty.

Her head throbbed, her entire body feeling wrung out. She knew that her logic was fallible at best. She knew that she was wrong in so many ways, but she couldn't untangle it all to figure it out.

She picked up the phone, and she dialed the number she needed to call most.

"Hello?"

"Erik," she said, not sure if she was relieved or terrified that he'd answered. "There's something I need to tell you."

"You are not running out on the wedding, are you?"

"*You* might. When you hear what I have to say." She swallowed. "I'm pregnant."

There was nothing but silence for a moment.

"Well," he said, his tone grim. "We both know it isn't mine."

"Yes. We do. But…no one else has to know that. It would be for the best if the baby's father didn't know. And I can't have anyone… I can't have anyone knowing." She tightened her hold on her phone, her heart hammering so hard she could scarcely hear herself speak. "But only if that… If it doesn't offend you in some way."

"I cannot say I'm pleased about it. Though I appreciate the fact that you did not try to pass it off as mine."

"I wouldn't have done that," she said quickly. "Before we get married, you have to know the truth."

"Whose is it?" he asked.

She hesitated. "I cannot give you *that* truth. That's the one thing I can't tell. Trust me on this one thing. I know I made a mistake, but I told you this much. I'm not trying to trick you."

"I see," he said, his tone brave. "You didn't know you were pregnant before now?"

"I swear I didn't."

There was a long pause, silence settling over her, over the room, the furniture groaning beneath its weight.

"It is too late to turn back," he said at last. "I require this union with your country. The alliance and the agreements that were promised to me… I want to see them honored. And if we were to cancel the wedding at such a late date the resulting scandal would be a serious issue."

"Yes," she replied, her lips numb. "That is my feeling on it, as well."

"Then we will go ahead with the wedding."

She must have agreed, but she couldn't remember what she said the moment after she'd spoken the words.

Sophia hung up the phone, not feeling any sense of relief at all. She curled up into a ball on the bed as hopelessness washed through her. Tomorrow it would be finished. It would finally be over.

Except, it never would be. Because whatever the world believed, whatever anyone knew…

The child in her womb was Luca's. A part of him. A part of her. The evidence of their passion, of her love. A bright and shining thing that she would never be able to ignore.

But Luca had been clear. There can be no scandal. She would not subject their child to that. She would not subject him to it.

And so she would have to subject herself to this.

For the second night in a row, Sophia cried herself to sleep.

The morning of the wedding dawned bright and clear, and Sophia awoke feeling damaged. Empty.

Except she wasn't empty. She was carrying Luca's child.

That fact kept rolling through her mind on a reel all while her hair was fixed, her makeup done, her gown given its final fittings.

Her mother looked at her with shining eyes, pride in them. Misplaced.

So badly misplaced.

"Are you all right?" she asked.

"Nervous," she said honestly.

It echoed the exchange they'd had during the fitting. But it was all the more real now. Her tongue tasted like metal, her whole body like a leaden weight.

"Did you take a test?" her mother asked.

"Yes," Sophia said.

"And?"

"It's positive," Sophia returned. "I'm having a baby."

Her mother held her for a long time before letting her go finally. "Have you told Erik?"

"Yes."

If her mother thought something was amiss—and Sophia thought she might—the other woman said nothing. Instead, they continued readying themselves for the ceremony. Then, a half hour before everything was set to begin, Sophia was ushered into a private room where no one could see her. Where the big reveal of the bride would be preserved.

It was dark in there. Quiet. The first moment of reflection she'd had all day. Her veil added an extra layer of insulation against reality. And gave her too much time to think.

She resented it. She didn't want to reflect on anything. She wanted all of this to be over.

She wanted it done, so that there was no going back. She wanted her wedding night done.

Wanted that moment to pass so that Luca would no longer be the only one who'd had claim on her body. So that perhaps she could start building some sort of bond with Erik.

As if you believe that will work.

She had to. What other choice did she have? Tell her *stepbrother* she was having his baby? A stepbrother who didn't seem to want her as more than a physical diversion? Even if it wasn't for the potential scandal…

Luca had been more than willing to send her straight to the arms of another man out of his sense of duty, after taking her virginity in an open space where anyone could have caught them.

Yes, on some deep level she felt this was a betrayal of Luca, but she felt as if he had betrayed her first.

He had made no move to stop this wedding. None at all. He was truly going to let her marry another man.

Then she realized that all this time she had been hoping he would stop it. That he would step in. He said he could not stand to have another man touch her, as he had done the night of the ball.

In the end she had hoped, beyond reason, beyond anything, that he would make this stop.

But he had not.

The realization was like a hot iron through her chest. What a fool she was. She'd been clinging to hope, even now. Hope was why she was here. Because she kept imagining…

She squeezed her eyes shut, a tear streaming down her cheek.

She would be damned if she would go crawling to him. Confess to him she was pregnant with his child when he had already made it clear he did not want her.

And perhaps it was wrong. Perhaps she had no right to those feelings.

Perhaps, as the father, regardless of the fallout, he should be made aware of the baby.

But she couldn't.

Because what if he stopped it all then? What if that was the only reason?

How could she live with herself after that? How could she live with him?

Suddenly, the door to her little sanctuary burst open. His hands clenched into fists, his expression unreadable.

Luca.

CHAPTER EIGHT

RAGE ROLLED THROUGH Luca like a thunderstorm. There she was. His duplicitous stepsister. Her expression obscured by a veil, her figure a stunning tease in that virginal-looking gown.

They both knew she wasn't a virgin.

He had been the one to ruin that, to ruin her. He was well aware.

And then there was the other bit of evidence that she was not as innocent as she currently appeared to be.

"Are you here to give me away?" she asked, her tone maddeningly calm.

"Is that what you want? You want me to march you out of here and pass you off from my arm to his? Fair enough, as you seem to have gone from my bed and straight into his."

He waited for her to correct him on that. But she did not.

"It's a bit late to be acting possessive, *fratello*."

The word *brother* stabbed into him. Sharp. Enraging. The reason she was here prepared to marry another man in the first place.

"Is it now?" It did not feel too late. It felt altogether like just the right time.

She took a step back, stammering. Wondering if she had overplayed her hand. "I'm in a wedding gown. The guests have all arrived. I assume there is a priest."

"You know as well as I do that there is."

"Then unless you intend to give me to my groom, symbolically, of course, I suggest you step aside."

He crossed his arms, standing between Sophia and the door. "Absolutely not."

"I need to go, Luca," she said, her tone pleading with him.

"Answer me one question first," he said, taking a step toward her. His heart was pushing the limits of what a man could endure, he was certain, his stomach twisted.

"What question?" she asked.

"Have you slept with him?" He asked the question through gritted teeth, his entire body tense.

She turned to the side, the veil a cascade of white and bland separation, concealing her expression from him. "I don't see how that's any concern of yours."

"It is my concern if I say it is," Luca returned. "Answer the question, Sophia. And if you lie to me, I will find out."

Suddenly, her posture changed. She came alive. As though she'd been shocked with a live wire.

"Oh, no," she said, delicate hands balled into fists. "I haven't slept with him. But I intend to do so tonight. I would show you the lingerie I selected, but that would be a bit embarrassing. After all, you are only my very concerned stepbrother."

A red haze lowered itself over Luca's vision.

Anger was like a living thing inside him, roaring, tearing him to pieces. He had no idea what answer he would have preferred. One that proved she had been touched by another man, but might not be attempting to deceive them both…or this.

She was doing exactly what he had suspected. And by admitting that, she had also confirmed what he had suspected, his heart raging, when those lab results had come across his desk only an hour ago.

He had imagined…

He had imagined that she would come to him if the news was relevant to him.

She had not. But there was a chance. He had known that. Even if she had slept with Erik the day after she had been with him, there would be a chance.

And here, she had made it very clear, that there was only one possibility.

Still, she hadn't come to him. As if on some level she knew. Knew she should not bind herself to him. As if she could see the cracks in his soul.

If he were a good man, if any of his outward demonstrations of royal piety were deeper than skin, he would let her be.

Would let her go off and marry Erik.

But he had reached an end. An end to the show he had lived for the past two decades.

An end to anything remotely resembling *good*.

"We will have to send our regards to Erik," he said, taking a step forward.

"Why is that?"

"Because I…" He reached forward, grabbing the end of her veil, lifting it and drawing it over her head, revealing that impossibly lovely face that had called to him for years now. That was his constant torment. His constant desire. "I am about to kiss his bride for him."

Luca drew her into his arms; she was his now. There was no denying it. There was no other alternative.

When they parted, she was staring at him, wide eyed.

"And he," Luca continued, his voice rough, "is about to find himself without a wife."

Then he lifted her up and threw her over his shoulder, ignoring the indignant squeak that exited her lips.

"What are you doing?" She pounded a fist against his back.

They were turning into a bad farce of a classic film. And he didn't care. Not one bit.

"Well," he said, continuing to hold her fast. "It seems that we have skipped a few steps. Here you are, in a wedding dress, but our relationship has already been consummated. And it appears that you are pregnant with my child."

"Luca!"

"Did you think I wouldn't find out?" He carried her out of the chapel and across the lawn. It was private back here; paparazzi and guests both barred from coming into this section of the grounds, where the bride might be disturbed. And here, Luca had a private plane waiting.

Just in case.

Just in case of this exact moment.

It felt like madness. Like something that had overcome him in the moment. Strong enough he'd had to pick her up and haul her off.

But obviously some of his madness was premeditated.

Though he had not envisioned this exact scenario, it was clear to him now there had never been another possible outcome.

"Forgive me," he said, not meaning at all. "But I feel as though at this moment in time a wedding ceremony is a bit redundant. We are headed off on our honeymoon."

"We can't," she protested, beating against him again with one closed, impotent fist.

A rather limp, ineffective protest, all in all. When the poor creature could scarcely move.

"I am the king, *sorellina.* And I can do whatever I want."

Yes. He was king. And he could do whatever the hell he wanted. He had been far too caught up in being honorable. In being dutiful to his country. In doing as his father had asked. In doing as his country expected.

In protecting Sophia. Making sure she had the life that would best suit her, not the one that would best please him.

What the hell was the point of being king if you didn't take everything that you desired?

And he desired his stepsister. She was also carrying his heir.

That meant that she would be his.

Regardless of what anyone thought.

It was all clear and bright now. As if the sun had come out from behind the clouds.

"What if I refuse?" she asked.

He carried her up the steps, onto the plane, holding her still while his staff secured the cabin. None of them daring to question him. "You're not in a position to refuse," he said as he placed her in one of the leather seats and solicitously fastened her seat belt. "You are only in a position to obey."

She didn't speak to him for the entirety of the flight. He supposed on some level that was understandable.

She simply sat there and looked at him, radiating rage and tulle, resembling an indignant cake topper. Disheveled, from his carrying her out across the lawn and onto the plane, her hot eyes bright and angry, that lovely lace wedding gown making her look the perfect picture of a bride.

She would need a new wedding gown for when they married. As beautiful as she looked now he would be damned if she walked down the aisle toward him in a dress she had meant for someone else.

That was not something he could endure. He found that he was quickly getting to the end of his endurance where she was concerned.

Scandal was something to be avoided at all costs. It was something his mother had drilled into his head even after she had known…

She had protected the reputation of the family.

And now he was about to destroy that. Then it called into question a great many things.

But here was the point where he had to break from his desire to prevent scandal.

Because if there was one thing, one bitter shard of anger that existed in his chest that cut deeper than all the others, it was the fact that his mother had prized reputation over protecting her son.

Over pursuing retribution for him.

She had cared more for her marriage. More for her paramour.

He would not care more for a clean slate than for this child that Sophia carried. He had needed to marry. Had needed to produce an heir, and it seemed that he was halfway there already. Why should he preserve the nation, their sensibilities, and ignore the fact that this was a moment to seize on something that would be an important asset. Truly, he could not have planned this better.

Because there was only one way that he would be able to justify claiming Sophia as his own. Only one way he would be able to justify having her in his bed for life.

The child.

That, no one would be able to argue with. And yes, it would come at the cost of an ugly scandal. The things that would be written about them…

They would not be kind.

Those headlines would exist, and it was something that their child would have to contend with. Something they would have to contend with.

But in the end, the memory would fade, and they would be husband and wife longer than they had ever been stepbrother and stepsister.

In the end, it would work.

Because it had to.

He was not in the mood to allow the world to defy him. He was not in the mood to think in terms of limits.

He had, for far too long.

He was a king, after all.

And for too long he had allowed that to limit him.

No more.

"Do you want to know where we're going?" he asked, leaning back in his seat and eyeing the bar that sat across the cabin.

"I don't wish to know anything," she said, pale of face and tight-lipped with rage.

"Did you love him so much that this is an affront to you?"

"I tried," she said, whipping around to face him, her dark curls following the motion.

"I tried to do the right thing. I tried to do what you asked of me. I was willing to—"

He could not hear her lies. He held up a hand and stopped her speaking. "You were willing to try to pass my child off as another man's. For that, I cannot forgive you."

"You were willing to let me marry another man," she said. "Only when you found out that I was carrying your child did you try and stop it. You took my virginity in a garden. You gave no thought to protecting me. You took advantage of my innocence. You were going to let another man have me. For that, I cannot forgive *you*." She looked away from him again, pressing one hand to her stomach. "He knew it was not his child, Luca. Whatever you think of me, I would not try and convince another man that this baby was his."

"Does he know it's mine?"

She looked toward him, her dark eyes flashing. "I told him it was the one thing we could never speak of."

"I know you only found out yesterday," he said.

"How did *you* find out?" she asked.

"The palace physician reports directly to me, Sophia. In these matters, there is no privacy."

Her face drained of the rest of its color, her entire frame shaking with rage. And perversely, even in the moment, he found his eyes drawn, outlined to perfection by the sweetheart neckline of the gown, to the delicate swell of her breasts.

A sickness. Sophia would always be his sickness.

"How dare you?"

"I dare *everything*," he said, his voice like granite

even to his own ears. “I am the King of San Gennaro. You are pregnant with my heir. You would have me leave that to chance?”

“I was trying to prevent a scandal. And I don’t want your obligation, Luca.”

“You have it,” he bit out. “Endlessly, *sorellina*, and there is no way around that.”

“Would you have let me marry him?”

His throat tightened, adrenaline working its way through his veins. He closed his hands into fists and squeezed them. “Of course,” he said. “Because when it comes to matters of the flesh, you can hardly allow them to dictate the course of a country.”

“Except, apparently, when that flesh takes shape as a child.”

“Naturally,” he bit out. “I will hardly allow another man to raise my child. I will hardly sacrifice my son’s birthright on the altar of my reputation. On this you are correct, Sophia. I was careless with you. And that carelessness should not come back on our child.”

“It might not be a son. It might be a daughter. In which case, you might wish you had allowed me to marry someone else.”

“Never,” he said, his voice rough.

“You don’t seem overly happy.”

“Happiness is not essential here. What is essential is duty. What is essential is that I do what is right by my child.”

“Yes, I suppose it is what your father tried to do for me. Bundle me up and sell me off to the most worthy of men.”

“Yes, and sadly you seem to be stuck with me.”

She said nothing to that. He imagined she didn't think he meant it. He did.

He had his darkness. He had his trauma, and he would never have chosen to lock Sophia into a union with him. But the fact remained, it was unavoidable now.

And if that meant he got to sate his desire in her lovely body, then so be it.

"You will be my wife now, Sophia," he said.

"When?" She said it like a challenge. As if she didn't believe him.

"Oh, as soon as we can arrange it. We're going to San Paolo."

Her expression went strangely…soft. Very odd in the context of the moment, when before she'd been looking nearly feral. "Your father's island?"

"It is *my* island now." A soft, firm reminder that his father was gone.

That, though he would have strongly disapproved of this, he was not here to see it. No one was. Not now.

How easy it would be to lay her back on that chair, to push up that wedding dress and lose himself inside her. Talking was a pointless exercise when it was not what he wanted.

Heat lashed through him. He wanted her. Even in this moment, when all should be reduced to the gravity of the situation, he wanted her.

"This will not be easy," she said, her voice shaking.

"Denying me my child would have been simple, Sophia?"

"That isn't what I mean. Don't be dense, Luca. The world will be watching us. Will be watching and judging and we will be bringing a baby into that. It seemed kinder in some ways to try and avoid all of that."

Rage was like a storm inside him. By God, he couldn't cope with not having power. With having his choices taken from him. "You don't have a biological father of your own. The man couldn't be bothered to raise you. How dare you visit the same fate upon your child?"

"Biology doesn't matter," she snapped. "All that matters is that a man is good. Your father was the best father I could have ever asked for. My own father… He didn't want me. He didn't care for me. He didn't matter. Not when I had your father to call my own. He *earned* that place. He wasn't born with some magical right given to him by blood you can't even see. That's how I thought I could do it. Because I know full well that it's not genetics that make a parent."

"And what about me? You think so little of me that you think I am like the man who sired you? That I am like a man who could walk away from his child and never think of her again?"

"I figured what you didn't know couldn't hurt you. Or your goals. Or the country."

"How cavalierly you played with our fates," he bit out.

"How cavalierly you played with my privacy," she shot back.

"You don't deserve privacy," he returned. "You proved that with your betrayal."

Silence descended on the plane. Luca stood up and made his way across the space, heading over to the bar and pouring himself a measure of scotch.

"None for you," he said, his tone unkind. He was well aware of it. He didn't care. She did not deserve his kindness at the moment.

"You hate me," she said softly. "You always have. Or, if you don't hate me, it's a kind of malevolent indifference the likes of which I have never experienced. I would have said it was impossible. To dislike and not care at the same time. But you seem to manage it."

He shook his head, laughter escaping in spite of himself. Then he took a drink of scotch. "Is that what you think?"

"It is what I *know*, Luca."

"You are a fool," he said, knocking back his drink, relishing the burn all the way down to his gut. At least that burn was expected. Acceptable.

Then he stopped over to where she was seated, leaned forward, bracing his hands on the arms of the seat, bracketing her in. His eyes met hers, electricity arcing between them. His skin tingled with her being this near, his entire body on high alert. His heart was pounding heavily, his blood flowing south, preparing his body to enter hers.

He wondered if every time he was near her it would be thus. And concluded just as quickly that as it had been this way for nearly a decade it was likely not to change anytime soon.

"You think I hate you? You think I am indifferent to you? If I behaved that way, Sophia, it was only because I was attempting to protect your innocence. Attempting to protect you from my lust."

"Luca…"

He stood up, running his hands through his hair. "I have always known there was something wrong with me," he said. "That I could not trust my own desires. I proved it to be so the other night. But I quite admirably steered clear of that destruction for a very long time."

"You want me?" she asked, her voice small.

"Did I *want you*? I wanted no one else. Do you have any idea how many delightfully curvy brunettes I have taken to my bed and attempted not to make them you in my mind as I made love to them?"

Her face was white now, her lips a matching shade. "Am I supposed to be flattered by that? That you used other women and thought of me?"

"No one should be flattered by it," he said darkly. "But I feel strongly that no one should be flattered by my attentions, either."

"Why?"

The question was simple, and he supposed it was the logical one, and yet, it surprised him. He had not expected her to come back at him with the simplest and most reasonable question.

"It is not important."

"I think that it might be," she said.

"Truly it is not. All you need to know is that you will marry me. It is nonnegotiable. You will be my queen, and our child will be the heir. If you feel regret over it, you should've thought of that before you climbed on my lap in the garden."

"If you feel regret then perhaps you should've thought of that before you took me without a condom," she shot back.

Heat, white and sharp, streaked through him like a lightning bolt, and he had to grit his teeth, plant his feet firmly on the floor and tighten his hands into fists to keep from moving toward her. To keep from claiming her. To keep from doing just what she described now again.

"I have no regrets," he said. "I'm not so certain you'll feel the same in the fullness of time."

Sophia felt drained, utterly bedraggled by the time the plane landed, and she trudged off and onto the blaring heat of the tarmac. Her gown was beginning to feel impossibly heavy, but Luca had not offered her anything to change into.

Had she not just spent an extremely cool three hours on the plane with Luca, alternating between stony silence and recrimination, she would have thought she was in some kind of a dream.

An extremely twisted one.

It was far too hot on San Paolo for layers and layers of lace and chiffon. For the crinoline she had on beneath the gown.

The sky was jewel bright, reflected in the clear waters that stretched out around them, like an impassible moat, cutting them off from the world. The beach was bleached white by the sun, shrubby green grass and broken shells the only intrusion of color along the shoreline. And beyond that was the magnificent palatial estate that Luca's father had built just for their family. She had spent part of her childhood here on this island, and she had always thought it to be like heaven on earth.

Right now she did not feel so enamored with it.

But then, right now she did not feel so enamored with anything.

On the one hand…she had never been so relieved in her life. To have been carried out of that wedding before it had a chance to take place. Because truthfully, she did not want to marry Erik.

But it was difficult to think about marrying Luca. When she knew that he was only doing it for the child. When she knew that he would have let her walk down the aisle toward another man, that he would have done nothing to stop Erik from claiming her. Touching her. Kissing her. Joining his body to hers.

It was almost unimaginably painful. That full realization. That on her own she had not been enough.

It was that feeling of fantasy, of being in another time and space, that carried her through. That allowed her to breathe while they were driven from the landing base to the villa.

It was all white stucco and red clay roofing, brilliant and clean construction amidst the spiky green plants that surrounded the house.

The home itself was three floors, making the most of the fact it was built into the side of the mountain, that it overlooked the sea. She knew there was a large outdoor bathtub that faced out over the water, made of glass, as if to flaunt the exclusivity of the location.

She could not understand this as a child. It made no sense to her why someone would take their clothes off outdoors. Or why one person would get into a bath that size when there was a pool to swim in.

As an adult, she more than understood.

Because she could well imagine the hours she and Luca could spend in there, naked and slick, with nothing but the sea as witness to their time spent there.

She ached for it, shamefully. Even knowing that he did not want her. Not like this. Not forever.

They stepped inside the cool, extensive foyer, and Sophia looked around, nostalgia crashing into the present moment like a tidal wave. It was so strange. She could remember walking into this place as a girl. With her stepfather and her mother holding hands as a couple, with Luca the stormy and electric presence that made her feel strange and out of sorts. One that she wanted to run away from as much as she wanted to linger here.

That, at least, was the same.

She wanted to run from them as much as she wanted to run to heaven. Wanted his hands on her body, and wanted to shout and scream at him about how he was never permitted to touch her again.

He had devastated her.

And the worst part was, even as he had fulfilled the fantasy of rescuing her from the wedding she had not wanted, he had shattered her completely by doing so. Because of the reasons surrounding it.

She supposed it would be a wonderful thing if she could simply be happy to have Luca. If she could simply be grateful that he had come for her, regardless of the circumstances.

But she couldn't be.

Was it so much to ask that something be about her, and not someone else?

The fact of the matter was she hadn't been enough for her biological father. He hadn't wanted her. Not in the least. She loved her stepfather dearly, but she had been more of an impediment to his marrying her mother than she had been an attraction. He had certainly come to love her, and she didn't doubt that. But still…

She was loved circumstantially.

With Luca, she wasn't even loved.

How much more romantic that had seemed when he was out of reach.

"It seems my phone has… I believe they say blown

up?" Luca said, the words hard and crisp as he looked down at his mobile phone.

That felt strange. Wrong. Because she had been lost somewhere in the veil of fantasy and memory. And neither of those contained cell phones.

"Why?"

"Really?" he returned.

He had one dark brow raised, his handsome face imbued with a quizzical expression. And then suddenly it hit her. She had been so lost in her present pain that she had forgotten. Had forgotten that of course Luca's phone would be lit up with phone calls and text messages. With emails from members of the press, trying to find out what had happened.

By now, everyone knew that the wedding hadn't happened.

Suddenly, her arms felt empty, and she looked around. Realizing then that she had no purse, that she had not taken her phone. She had nothing. Nothing but this wedding dress for a wedding that hadn't happened.

"Luca," she said. "My mother is going to be frantic."

"Yes," he said, scrolling through his phone. "She is. She is deeply concerned that you've been kidnapped."

"I *have* been," she all but shouted.

"By me," he said simply.

"As if that doesn't make it kidnap?"

"I am the king of the nation," he said. "No one is going to arrest me over it."

"That is an extremely low standard to hold yourself to."

"I find at the moment I don't care overmuch."

"Are you going to tell her?" Sophia asked.

"Well, eventually we're going to tell everyone."

"Let me call my mother," she said.

Luca arched a brow. "I do not want your mother on the next flight here."

"You've kidnapped her daughter, what do you expect?"

"I don't want company."

"Why?"

Suddenly, she found herself being swept up off the ground once again. "You have made a bad habit of this."

"I don't find it a bad habit."

He began marching up the stairs, her wedding gown trailing dramatically behind her as they went.

"What are you doing?"

"Claiming your wedding night."

"There was no wedding. And anyway, it wasn't supposed to be *your* wedding night."

"It is about to be." He growled, and he leaned down, claiming her lips with his own.

The moment his mouth made contact with hers it was like the tide had washed over her. And she and her objections were left clinging to the rocks. With each brush that swept over her, she lost her hold on one of them. Her anger washed away. Her doubt. Her resilience. Her resolve.

Whatever Luca felt for her—and she didn't think it was anything tender at all—he wanted her. There was no denying that. He had said as much on the plane, hadn't he?

She had been so lost in her head over the fact that the baby was what had stopped him from letting the wedding go forward, that she hadn't fully taken that part on board. But it was real. It was true.

This was honest. If nothing else between them was. It was real, if the rest could not be.

This was why they were here. The electric, undeniable chemistry that existed between them, in defiance of absolutely everything that was good and right in the world.

She did not taste love on his tongue as it swept over hers. But she tasted need. And that, perhaps, could be enough.

His hold tight on her, he carried her all the way to the top of the stairs and down the landing toward the master bedroom, a room that they had certainly not stayed in before. Well, perhaps Luca had, but she had not. He all but kicked open the double doors, sweeping them inside and depositing her down at the foot of the bed.

"Where is… Where is everyone?" she asked, feeling like she was in a daze. She had only just realized that there seemed to be no servants present.

"I had everyone vacate. Supplies were left, including clothing for you, so you won't need for much. But we need privacy."

"Why?" Tears stung her eyes, an aching pain tightening her throat. She could not understand why he needed this.

This was all too much. She hadn't appreciated fully the protection that had been built into wanting a man she could never have. For her heart. For her body.

Now he was here. Looming large and powerful, so very beautiful.

It all felt too much. Like she would be consumed. Destroyed. Nothing at all of Sophia remaining.

"Because that bastard was going to put his hands on

you tonight," he said, his voice rough. "He was going to touch you. He was going to kiss you. Perhaps you were even fantasizing about it. But I will not have that. I will be the only man to touch you. No other. I will be the only man you want. The only desire in your body will be for me. I will be what you crave. Your body is mine."

"You didn't want me," she said, choked.

"No," he said. "I wanted… I prayed…to not want you. There is nothing that will take it from me. And so there is nothing but this. To take you in any way that I can. To have you. Fate is sealed where we are concerned. There is no reason now not to glory in it."

He reached behind her and grabbed hold of either side of the wedding gown, and he wrenched the corset top open. She gasped as it loosened, felt free as the fine stitching that had been so carefully conformed to her body came loose, and her breasts were left bare to him.

"So beautiful," he said, his dark head swooping down, his tongue like fire over one distended nipple.

How she ached for him. For this. Even as she hurt. Even as her desire threatened to destroy her, she wanted nothing more than to give in to it.

She breathed his name, lacing her fingers through his hair as he sucked her indeed. As he moved his attentions to her other breast, tracing a circle around one tight bud with the tip of his tongue.

"You're right," she said, her voice trembling. "This is madness."

"I knew it would destroy us, Sophia. I knew it could bring down an entire kingdom. But now here we are. There is nothing on earth I have wanted to be rid of more than this desire for you," he said, his voice low, tortured. "And good God I want to burn."

It was like fire. His touch branding her as he removed the layers of clothing from her body. As he left her completely naked except for her high heels, as he pushed her down onto the bed and spread her thighs wide, exposing the most intimate part of her body to his gaze.

He got down on his knees then, grabbing hold of her hips and forcing her toward his mouth.

"Luca," she said, shocked, appalled that he would do such a thing.

"This has been my greatest desire," he said. "Even more than sinking into your tight, wet body, I have wanted to taste you. I have wanted you coating my tongue, my lips. Sophia…"

He dipped his head then, that wicked, electric tongue swirling over the bundle of nerves at the apex of her thighs, tracing a line down to the entrance of her body and drawing the evidence of her desire from her. He added his fingers then, penetrating her, coaxing pleasure from deep inside her. It was too much. It was not enough. It was like a sharp pain that ran deep inside her. That could only be satisfied by him. Only him.

He pressed two fingers into her while he continued to lave her with the flat of his tongue, and she shattered completely. There were no thoughts in her head. Not about a wedding that might have been, not about the man who was supposed to strip this down off her tonight, not about scandal, not about anything. Nothing but this. The extreme heat bursting through her like light in the darkness.

He moved away from her then, his gaze predatory as he unbuttoned the crisp white shirt he wore, as he pushed his jacket from his shoulders and the shirt followed suit.

She could only stare at him. At the beautiful, perfect delineation of his muscles, the dark hair sprinkled there. Could only watch as his clever, masculine fingers made quick work of his belt, of his pants, as he left every last inch of his clothing on the floor, revealing powerful, muscular thighs and the thick, hard part of him that made him a man.

She'd had him inside her once. She would again. Even now, it seemed impossible.

If she had been able to see him the night she had been a virgin she would've been much more apprehensive.

At least now she knew that such fullness in size brought pleasure.

He growled, moving toward her with the liquid grace of a panther. Then he grabbed hold of her hips again, lifting her completely off the bed and throwing her back, coming to settle himself between her legs and thrusting into her with one quick, decisive movement.

Their coupling washed away everything. Like a cleansing fire, destroying the hay and the stubble, all of the temporary things, and leaving behind what was real.

This.

This connection between them that existed for no reason she could see other than to torture them. That remained.

Because whatever it was, it was real.

Each thrust of his powerful body within hers brought her to new heights, and she met each and every movement. With one of her own.

Until he shattered. Until, on a harsh growl, he spent himself deeply within her, and she was powerless to do anything but follow him over that precipice. When it was over, she held him. Because holding on to him was the only way to hold things together.

And she feared very much that the moment she let go, everything was going to fall apart.

Including her.

CHAPTER NINE

HE LEFT HER there in the expansive bed all by herself. Her dress was torn, past the point of fixing, and though he had mentioned there would be a new wardrobe supply for her here, she had no idea where said wardrobe was. Not that she had gone poking around.

She felt too…something. Sad. Bereft, almost, but also boneless and satisfied in a way she never had been before. Or, if she could compare it to anything, it was the way she had felt after their first time. Not happy, no. There was no room between them for something so simple as happy.

It was more like she was lying in the rubble of a building that had needed demolition.

That didn't make it easy. It didn't make it less of a pile of rubble. But there was something inevitable about all of it that made something in this a relief.

Even as it was a sharp pain, like being stabbed in the center of her chest.

She needed to call her mother. She knew full well that Luca did not want her to divulge their location. But he had left her. And there was a phone on the desk. Unless he had done something truly diabolical and cut the line, there was nothing stopping her from getting in touch with the one person who truly needed to know that she was okay.

She wrapped herself several times in the feather-soft white sheet, making sure it was secure at her breasts, before going to the phone and with trembling hands picking up the receiver and listening for the dial tone.

It had one. So, provided she could dial off the island, she should be able to get in touch with her mother.

"Let's see," she mumbled as she typed in the country code for San Gennaro followed by her mother's number.

The phone rang just once before her mother answered. "Hello?"

"Mom," Sophia said.

"Where are you?" her mother asked, panic lacing each word. "Are you safe?"

"Yes," she said.

It was true that she was physically safe. Emotionally was another matter.

"What happened? You were at the chapel and ready, and Luca went in to fetch you and… Is Luca with you?" her mother asked.

"Luca…" The rest of the sentence died.

"What is it?"

"Luca is the reason that I've gone missing," Sophia finished.

The silence on the other end was brittle, like a thin pane of glass that she was certain would splinter into a million pieces and shatter if she breathed too deeply.

"Is he?" her mother asked finally.

"There's something I have to tell you…"

"Oh, Sophia," her mother said, the words mournful. "I had hoped… I had hoped that you had put your feelings for him behind you."

"It's his baby, Mother," she said, the words coming out raw and painful.

More silence. But this one was full. Of emotion. Of words left unspoken. Sophia couldn't breathe.

"I see," the queen finally responded.

"We didn't mean for… I tried… He tried." She closed her eyes, swallowing hard. "We did try."

"Just tell me he never took advantage of you when you were younger." There was an underlying venom in her words that left Sophia in no doubt her mother would castrate Luca if the answer was yes.

Sophia shook her head, then realized her mother couldn't see. "No. Never. It was just… This time was the first time. The time that we…the pregnancy, I mean. That was the first time"

"I knew," her mother whispered. "But I hoped that it would pass. For both of you."

"You knew that he… That he had feelings for me?"

"I knew that he *desired* you. Far sooner than he should have. And I told his father to keep him away from you. There was no future for the two of you, Sophia. You have to understand that."

"I do," she said. "Why do you think I was prepared to marry another man?"

"Yes, well, that has created quite a scandal."

"Just wait until they find out what actually happened. I imagine my running off before the wedding is not half as salacious as the fact that I have run off with my stepbrother because I'm having his baby."

Her mother groaned, a long, drawn-out sound. "Sophia… The scandal this will cause."

Sophia cringed, feeling desperately sad to hear such

distress in her mother's voice. "I'm so sorry. So very sorry I disappointed you."

Her mother's voice softened. "I'm not disappointed. But it's a hard road, Sophia. Being married to a king. And that's simply when you're a commoner. I cannot imagine how difficult things will be for you and Luca. All things considered. I had hoped that you could avoid it."

"We did. Until we couldn't."

She was embarrassed to be talking with her mother in this frank fashion. Until only recently she had been a virgin, after all, and now she was confessing that she had been overwhelmed by a state of desire. Her mother knew full well what that meant.

"If it was love…" Her mother trailed off.

Sophia's shoulders stiffened, her back going straight, a pain hitting her in the stomach. "If it was love, I never would have pretended I might be able to marry Erik. Luca does not love me."

But she did wonder if perhaps marrying Erik had been about running away. Not from scandal, not even from this conversation with her mother.

From all that Luca made her feel. All he made her want.

"He is a good man," her mother said as if trying to offer her some consolation.

"I know he is. Too good for such a scandal."

"But too good to turn away from his responsibility. Still… I have to wonder if it would've been better if he would have allowed you to marry Erik."

Those words went through her like a lance. "Why?"

"If he can't love you…"

Her mother's choice of words there was interesting.

If he couldn't love her. Did that mean that her mother thought she was difficult to love, too? Or did she believe that Luca had a difficult time loving?

In many ways Sophia wondered if they were both true.

She didn't want to love him. That much was certain. Whatever she felt was far too bright and painful all on its own.

"I'm not sure I love him," she said truthfully. "I only know that whatever this is between us is undeniable. And he has chosen to make a scandal. I will only go so far to protect him. I'm not going to force him to disavow his child."

"Of course not. But, Sophia, it's going to be such a difficult life. Where are you? I feel like I should come and get you."

"I—"

The door opened and she turned sharply. Luca was standing there, regarding her with dark eyes. His expression was like a storm, his mouth set into a firm line.

"I have to go."

She hung up the phone, much to her mother's protests. And then Luca walked over to the phone and unplugged the power cord from the base. "I do not wish to be disturbed," he said. "How much did you tell your mother?"

"I told her that I'm having your baby."

He chuckled, bitter and hard. "I imagine her faith in me is greatly reduced by this news."

Sophia wrapped her arms around herself. "She said that she always knew. That you wanted me. That I wanted you."

"Fascinating," he said, not sounding at all fascinated. "But you had no idea, did you?"

"I didn't," she said truthfully. "I thought you despised me."

"You refused to be any less attractive to me, no matter how the years went on. You refused to shrink. You refused to be invisible. I certainly despised you, Sophia, but my desire for you is not exclusive from that."

"That's beautiful, Luca. Perhaps you should take up poetry."

"How's this for poetry? You're mine now." He took a step toward her, grabbing hold of the sheet that she had resolutely wrapped around her curves, and he pulled her to him, wrenching the soft, exquisite cotton from her body. "There is to be no doubt of that."

She stood there, naked and trembling, feeling hideously exposed in ways that went well beyond her skin.

"Then that makes you mine," she shot back, feeling run out and fragile after the day she had had. "Doesn't it?"

His dark eyes sharpened. "I'm not sure I get your meaning."

"If I belong to you, then I require nothing less. If we are to be married, Luca, I will be the only woman in your bed. You have all of me or you have none of me."

"I was never going to be unfaithful to whatever wife I took. I would hardly be unfaithful to you."

Electricity crackled between them, and neither spoke what was so patently obvious. So obvious that it lit the air between them with electricity.

That at least for now, there was no chance either of them would take another to their beds. They would have to exhaust the intense desire between the two of them first, and at the moment Sophia could not imagine it. Granted, she was new to sex, but she had a feeling that what existed between herself and Luca was uncommon in every way.

"What are you going to do?" she asked, her voice small, taking a step away from him.

"Tonight? Tonight I intend to take you back to my bed, spread you out before me and feast on you until you're crying out my name. Until my name is synonymous with *lover*, not *brother*."

His words set a rash of heat over her body. "I mean, about us. About telling the world about us. About our upcoming marriage. About…what we are going to do next."

"I'm going to make a press release to go out tomorrow morning. And you and I will stay here incommunicado until some of the furor dies down. Then I will marry you. Not in that dress," he said, looking at the scrap of white on the floor.

"I think that dress is beyond saving now," she mused.

He looked at her, his dark eyes suddenly bleak. "Who knew I would have something in common with a gown."

But before she had a chance to question such an odd statement, she was back in his arms, and he was kissing her again. And she had a feeling that there would be no more talking tonight.

The next morning Luca was full of purpose when he awoke. Sophia was naked, soft and warm, pressed up against his body, one breast resting at his biceps. She was sleeping peacefully, her dark hair a halo of curls on the pillow around her head. He had done it. He had destroyed everything.

It was strangely satisfying. A perfect and sustained string of curses directed to his mother even if it was going to have to make its way into the beyond.

A scandal she would not be able to squash.

He supposed it was unkind to think poorly of one's dead mother. But he could not find a kind thought for his own.

Strange, how he spent very little time thinking about her. He had already made decisions about himself, about his life, based on the events that had occurred in his childhood. He didn't have to think about them every day.

Truthfully, he didn't even have to think about them yearly. He spent a great deal of time not pondering the ways in which he was damaged, and even when he didn't think of it, typically in reference to why he had to keep his hands off Sophia—a horse that had well and truly left the barn now—it was only in terms of his scarred soul, not in terms of actual events.

This forced him to think of it. The fact that his responsible, pristine image was about to be destroyed, made him think of it.

No one can ever know about this. If your father knew about Giovanni our marriage would be over. And can you imagine what people would think of you? They would never forget, Luca. It is all you would ever be.

He gritted his teeth and got out of bed, staring out the window at the ocean below.

He had a press release to prepare.

He set about to doing just that, contacting his palace staff and letting his majordomo know exactly what had transpired. Exactly what would be happening from here on out. If the other man was shocked, he did not let on. But then, he supposed it was in the other man's job description to remain impassive about such things.

Luca also left instruction to keep his and Sophia's location secret.

With that taken care of, Luca decided that he needed to figure out what he was going to do with his fiancée. That was how he would think of her from now on. Until, that was, he was able to think of her as his wife. She was no longer first and foremost his stepsister.

In his mind, she never had been.

And that meant that he had to get to know her.

He had avoided that. For years he had avoided that. Of course he had. He had not wanted to foster any kind of attraction between them.

It had turned out that was futile anyway, because the attraction between them had been hell-bent on growing no matter what either of them did.

Now the fact remained, he was going to marry her, and he didn't know her at all.

That was not actually a point of contention for him, but he would have to be able to make conversation about her. They would have to be able to come to an accord on how they talked about their relationship.

And he had a feeling that Sophia would want to feel as if she knew him.

He had done what he had intended to do by bringing her here to the island. He had isolated her. And he had managed to get her into proximity with him. To keep her from marrying Erik. But he would not be able to keep her here forever. That meant that something other than kidnap was going to have to bind them. Eventually. Something other than sex would help, as well.

Although at the moment the sex was enough for him.

His staff had generously stocked the kitchen with a basket of croissants. Opening the fridge, he found a tray of fruit, figs and dates. Cheeses. Then, there was a pot of local honey in a small jar on the counter. He cobbled those things together, along with herbal tea, and brought them up to the bedroom. When he opened the door, Sophia shifted, making a sleepy sound.

She opened her eyes, and he could see the exact moment her vision came into focus.

She frowned. “Is that for me?”

“Yes,” he said, sitting down on the edge of the bed.

He was gratified to see that her gaze drifted away from the food and onto his chest, which was still currently fair. Her cheeks flushed, and she looked away.

It pleased him to see that she was not immune to him.

That someone so soft and lovely could be so affected by him.

He shoved that thought to the side.

“That’s…kind of you.” She shifted, pushing herself into a sitting position, holding her sheets against her breasts modestly. “What is this?” She opened up the pot sitting on the tray and frowned deeply. “This isn’t coffee.”

“You’re pregnant,” he pointed out. “I believe I recall hearing that pregnant women should not drink caffeine.”

“Not *too much* caffeine.” She sounded truly distressed. “That doesn’t mean I have to drink…herbs.”

“I was only doing the best I could. I’m not an expert.”

“That might be a first,” she said.

“What?”

She treated him to a smile that was almost impish.

Something he wasn't used to having directed at him. "You admitting that you don't know everything."

"Sophia..." he said, his tone full of warning.

"You can't tell me it isn't true."

"I was raised to be arrogant. It's part and parcel to being in charge."

"Really?" she asked.

"Nobody wants an uncertain king."

"Perhaps. But no one wants an insufferable husband, either."

Neither of them spoke for a moment. Sophia reached into the basket and procured herself a croissant.

"You like coffee," he said.

She lifted a shoulder. It was gloriously bare and he knew now from experience that her skin was as soft as it looked. He wished to lick her. If only because he had spent so many years not licking her. "Yes."

"I didn't know that."

"Almost everyone likes coffee. Or needs it, if it comes down to it."

"But we have never discussed what you like. Or what you don't like."

She looked thoughtful for a moment, and that should've been an indicator that this was not going according to plan, as he really should have guessed that Sophia was never going to be anything like compliant.

"Well," she said, "I like coffee, as established. My hobbies include getting fitted for wedding gowns that will eventually be torn off my body, and being kidnapped and spirited away to a private island."

Luca cast her a hard look. "Much more exotic than stamp collecting, you have to admit."

"Indeed. Although, my wretched dress is not going to increase in value. A stamp collection might."

"I beg to differ. By the time news of our union hits global media I imagine that torn gown will be worth quite a bit."

Sophia frowned, grabbing a strawberry from the fruit tray and biting into it angrily. "Global media," she muttered around the succulent fruit.

"There is no way around it. We are a headline, I think you will find."

"I tried *not* to find."

"Sophia," he said, suddenly weary of games. "There was no other alternative. No other outcome, and you know that. It was always going to be this."

He meant because of the baby. And yet, he couldn't escape feeling that there was something else in those words. Some other, deeper truths being hinted at.

"We tried," she said, sounding desolate.

"Not that night. Not the night of the ball."

She looked up at him, her expression quizzical. "Really?"

"You know it's true," he said. "Had I tried, I would never have touched you. But I didn't. It was simply that what I wanted became so much more powerful than what I should do. And I could not… Could not allow him to touch you."

"We would have allowed him to touch me last night," she said quietly, picking at a fig.

"He didn't," Luca said. "That's all that matters."

"Luca," she said, looking up at him, her expression incisive. "Why is reputation so important to you? I mean, beyond the typical reasons. Beyond the reasons that most rulers have. You have never been… I knew your father.

I loved him. As my own father. He was the only father I ever knew. He was serious, and he treated his position with much gravity. But it's not like you. You do everything with such gravity. And I… Truthfully, whether you believe me or not, part of the reason I didn't tell you is that I didn't want to put this on you. I know how much your country means to you…"

"Not more than my child," he said, fire rising up in his chest, bile in his throat. "Nothing matters more than my child, Sophia, you must know that. The moment those test results came across my desk I had to know. I will not sacrifice my child on an altar with my country's name stamped onto it. With my reputation on it. My name is only a name. The baby you carry is my blood." He took a deep breath. "What good is a legacy if you don't defend the ones who are supposed to carry it out when you die?"

"I'm sorry," she said, and she sounded it. "You're right. For all that we…" She squeezed her eyes shut. "For all that I have carried a certain fascination for you for a great number of years, I don't know you." She opened her eyes, tears glistening in them. "If I could guess at this so wrong, then it is apparent there are things I don't know."

"You're not wrong," he said, the word scraping his throat. "On any score with this, I would have protected the name. But not at the expense of a child."

It was the breaking point. Because if the name didn't matter, then what he had endured, then the lack of action his mother had taken to defend him, would be null and void, and that was unfathomable to him in many ways. This was where the corner turned. Where it became far too close to what had been done to him. And that, he could not allow.

"What are we going to do today?" The question was open, honest, and it made him feel strange.

"I had not given it much thought."

That was a lie. What he wanted, what he wanted more than anything, was to strip her completely naked, rip that sheet right off her as he had done last night, and keep her that way for the entire day.

"Your wardrobe should arrive soon," he said instead of that. "And then of course, there is the beach, and the pool."

"Badminton," she pointed out. "We used to play badminton."

"You cannot be serious."

"We're rather cut off here, Luca," she said. "I was thinking of all the things we used to do to entertain ourselves."

He treated her to a scorching look, and he watched as her face turned scarlet all the way up to the roots of her hair.

"We can't do that the entire time," she protested, her hand flinging out wide like an indignant windmill.

He leaned forward, gripping her chin with his thumb and forefinger. "Why not?"

Her eyes widened. "Because… Because… We can't." Her protest was beginning to sound weak.

"I'm going to need a better reason than that, Sophia. As we have spent years not doing it, and I feel that we have much time to make up for."

"Well," she said, sniffing piously. "It's not done."

"I assure you, *cara*, that it is done quite frequently."

"You would *die*." She sounded entirely certain of this assessment.

He couldn't help himself. He laughed. "That's a bit overdramatic, don't you think?"

"No," she protested. "There is nothing dramatic about it. You've been there both times we've, well, you know. I can't breathe for nearly an hour afterward. If we did it all day…"

"It would be different," he said. "But no less impacting."

"Is it always like this, then? Does it just naturally shatter you less and less each time? Is this how it's been with all your lovers?"

He could lie to her. But then, a lie would neither bring him joy nor accomplish anything. Truth was the best option.

"It has never been like this with any of my previous lovers," he said. "I already told you that you have been my obsession for far too long. And there has been nothing that I could do to put a dent in that hunger. And before you… I didn't know such hunger at all."

"Oh," she said, sounding subdued.

"I wished often that it was simple enough to just want another woman," he said. "But it is not."

He shook his head. "There is no way around it. We must go through."

"Perhaps after badminton."

"If you get out a badminton racket, I will break it over my knee." Possibly, he could break it over another part of his body, given how hard he was at the moment.

It didn't take much. He was held in thrall, just for a moment, as the sunlight broke through a crack in the curtains, streamed onto Sophia's lovely upturned face, catching the light behind her wild curls. Sophia was naked in his bed. After so many years of lust.

She was his. There was triumph in that, to be certain.

He was Nero. Fiddling while Rome burned, he supposed. But Rome was going to burn no matter what at this point. He supposed he might as well play away.

"There is one thing I'm curious about."

"Whether or not I take cream in my coffee?"

"No. Why were you a virgin, Sophia?"

She drew back, pressing her hand to the center of her chest, the expression almost comically missish. "Does it matter?"

"The very fact that you would ask that question says to me that it must."

"I never found anyone that I felt… Luca, if no other man could make me feel what I felt just looking at you, if he kissed me, if he touched me, what was the point of going to bed with him? I would be thinking of you."

He was humbled by that. Shame. A familiar, black fog rolling over his shoulders and down his spine. Yes, shame was his constant companion. And sex was…

It never occurred to him to deprive himself of sex. His introduction to it—such as it was—had not been his choice. And he had set out to make a choice after that, and every time thereafter.

It had become a way of putting distance and bodies between that first encounter.

To prove to himself that in truth, the two experiences were not even the same. But what had been done to him against his will that night was something dark. Something ugly.

Control. A deep contempt for another person's autonomy.

"I was with other people and thought of you," he pointed out. "Unless I made it a point not to. And then,

I made sure it was someone who was quite different to you."

"I suppose that's the difference between men and women, then," she said.

"Or simply the difference between you and me," he responded. "Sophia… There are many reasons that I never allowed myself to touch you for all that time."

"Your reputation."

"My reputation, the reputation of San Gennaro, is only a piece of the puzzle."

"Then tell me what the puzzle is, Luca. I feel like I should understand since we are supposed to be married. I feel like I need to understand you."

"We have a history," he said slowly. "One that has been difficult. I cannot… I cannot adequately express to you the way it was when I first noticed you as a woman. The way that it hit me. You were always…reckless and wild in a way that I could not fathom, Sophia, and yet the fact that it bothered me as it did never made any sense. Until you turned seventeen. And suddenly…everything that you were, this vivacious, irrepressible girl, crashed into what you had become. I knew I couldn't have you. I knew that it was impossible. And so, as much as there was never closeness between us, I pushed you away. I don't regret that. It was my attempt at doing what was right. I failed, in the end. And so, those years, that history, is useless to us. Let us forget who we were in the past and why. We have to make a way forward, and I don't think there are answers lurking behind."

She narrowed her eyes, looking at him with total skepticism. He could see that she did not agree with him, not remotely.

But there was no point talking about the shadows

in the past. He didn't want her to know him. He didn't want anyone to know him. They could have a life, like this. One where they made love and she teased him. Frankly, it was a better life than he had ever imagined for himself.

He had not ever fathomed that his duty could be quite so pleasurable.

He had resolved himself to a life without the woman that he wanted most. Now he had her. There was no point dragging skeletons out of the closet.

"You have an objection, *cara*?"

"You want to act as though we haven't known each other for most of our lives? You don't want to go back and try to understand who I was?"

"Isn't it most important that we understand who each other is now?"

"Can we do that? Can it be accomplished if we don't actually know what each other was built with?"

"There are no surprises in my story. I was born into royalty." He shrugged his shoulders. "Here I remain."

"You lost your mother when you were sixteen. I suppose that was very painful for you."

"Yes," he responded, the word sharp like a blade.

It was painful. But perhaps not in the way she meant. Not in any way he could put into words.

Losing someone you were meant to love, someone you had grown to hate, was its own particular kind of pain. There had been guilt. Such guilt. As if it were the hatred in his heart that had poisoned her to death. As if he had somehow caused her car to go off the road that day.

He knew better than that now.

But that, too, was a discussion they would not have.

"Today I thought we might have a walk on the beach," he said. "What do you think of that?"

She nodded slowly. "That sounds nice."

Though she still didn't sound convinced.

She would see. It would be better his way.

And if Sophia wanted to share herself with him, he was more than happy to allow it. In fact, he found he was quite hungry for it.

But he would not poison her with the stories of his past.

The poison in his own veins was quite enough. He refused to spread it.

On the score of protecting the family reputation, of protecting her from a life with him, he had failed.

He did not have to fail when it came to everything else.

Sophia was hot and sweaty after spending an afternoon combing through the white sand beaches, finding seashells and taking breaks from the sun to soak her feet in the water.

True to his word, her clothing had eventually arrived, and she had found a lovely white dress that seemed suited to the surroundings. They had walked together, and he hadn't touched her.

It occurred to her that Luca had *never* touched her without sexual intent. Nothing intentional anyway.

There had been no casual handholding. He'd never moved to touch her with affection, only to strip her of her clothes.

Which was why when they had been on their return trip to the estate she had looped her fingers through his and taken control of that situation.

She had almost immediately wished that she hadn't. It had been so impacting. So very strange. To hold Luca's hand. Like they were a couple. Not just secret, torrid lovers, but something much gentler and sweeter, too.

Strange, because there was no real gentleness in their interaction.

Although, it had been quite a nice thing he'd done this morning with the fruit. The herbal tea notwithstanding.

When they returned to the villa, dinner had been laid out for them on the deck that overlooked the sea. A lovely spread of fresh seafood and crisp, bright vegetables.

All a little bit healthy for her taste. Though that concern was answered at the end of the meal when Luca went into the kitchen and returned a moment later with the truly sinful-looking dessert made of layers of cream, meringue and raspberry.

Sophia took a bite of the decadent dessert and closed her eyes, listening to the sound of the ocean below, the sun still creating warmth, even as it sank down into the sea. A breeze blew gently through her hair, lifting the heavy curls off the back of her neck, cooling her.

For a moment she had the horrible feeling that if she opened her eyes she would find that Luca wasn't really there. That she had somehow hallucinated all of this in order to survive the wedding.

That in reality she was on her honeymoon with Erik. Because of course it had to be a fantasy that Luca had come to claim her. That he had whisked her out of that waiting room in the back of the chapel and spirited her off to a private island.

But no. When she opened her eyes there he was. Regarding her closely, his dark, unfathomable eyes assessing her. The remaining light of the sun shone brilliantly on his razor-sharp cheekbones, highlighting the rough, dark whiskers that had grown over his square jaw. She did not think he had shaved since they had arrived.

She suddenly had the urge to watch him shave. To watch him brush his teeth.

To claim all those little intimate moments for herself. Those routine things that were so easy to take for granted. She wanted to be close to him.

That was the sad thing. She had made love to him a few times now, and still, she didn't feel…like they were close.

Physically, they had been as close as two people could be. But there was still a gulf between them. She wanted to know what had created him. This good, hard man who clung to his principles like a mountain climber holding on to the face of a rock.

He fascinated her, this man. Who only ever let his passion unleash itself in the bedroom. Who was otherwise all things reserved and restrained.

That he had been hiding his desire for her for so many years was a revelation.

But he didn't *want* her to know him. He had made that clear.

She understood now why her mother had sounded so upset on the phone. It wasn't simply the issues that they would have with the press. But the pain she would experience, having feelings for her husband that far outweighed the feelings he had for her. Of wanting more of him than he would ever share. Luca desired her. He wanted her body. He'd had it. But sex and intimacy were not the same things.

That fact had become clear when they held hands on the beach and it had rocked her world in a wholly different fashion than being naked with him had.

One thing was clear: sex was certainly the way to reach him.

Because it was the only time when his guard was down. Of course, hers was equally reduced when they were making love. He did things to her… Made her feel things… Things she had not imagined were possible. And she wanted more. She had never thought of herself as greedy, not really.

How could a woman who had been born into poverty and become a princess overnight ever ask for more out of life? And yet…she wanted more. Being with him, finally having what she had held herself back from for all that time, had only made her more greedy.

There was something about today, about the beautiful afternoon spent walking on the beach that ended with holding hands, and this magical dinner, that made her feel a sense of urgency. Or maybe it wasn't the dinner, or the handholding. Maybe it was simply the fact that they were to be married. And if they were going to get married then it meant this was forever. And if this was going to be her forever…

It had been a certain kind of torture, wanting Luca and not having him. But having him in some ways, but never in others, was worse.

Or if not worse, it was simply that it was closer. She couldn't pretend that there was nothing between them, not when she was sharing his bed.

He was beautiful. And physically, he made her feel so very much. It wasn't enough.

And maybe she was so perfectly aware of how not

enough it was in part because she knew full well that it could be more.

She had seen that passion. She had felt it. Had been over him, beneath him, as he had cried out her name and lost himself completely in their lovemaking.

She wanted *that* man out of bed, too.

But in order to reach him, she imagined she had to appeal to him first in bed.

Not a hardship as far as she was concerned.

But it would perhaps require her to be a bit more bold than she had been previously.

After all, she had been a virgin until only recently. But the fact remained that what she had told Luca earlier was true. She had been a virgin because of him. Because of the way he had made her feel.

That meant he could have any of her. All of her. Because he was the one her body had been waiting for, so truly, there was no reason for her to be timid. Not where he was concerned.

"Just have some business to attend to," Luca said, rising from his chair. "I will meet you in our room."

The meaning behind his words was clear. But if Luca thought he was going to be in control of every interaction between them…well, she was about to prove to him otherwise.

CHAPTER TEN

LUCA WAS QUESTIONING the wisdom of checking the way their story was being played out in the headlines before he and Sophia left the island. What was the point? He could have simply left it all a mystery. Could have spent this time focused on her.

But no, the ugly weight of reality had pulled on him, and he had answered. So he had done some cursory searches to see if they had been splashed all over the tabloids yet.

He had underestimated the intensity of the reaction.

The headlines were lurid. Bold. Scandal in the palace. A borderline incestuous love affair between step-siblings that had been going on for… God knew how long.

A good and handsome groom had been left at the altar, the King of San Gennaro finally snapping and claiming his illicit lover before she could marry someone else.

There were one, maybe two, stories that shed a more romantic light on the situation. Forbidden lovers who had been in crisis. Who had not been able to choose to be together until it had been decided for them by fate. By a pregnancy.

The truth was somewhere in the middle. He and Sophia certainly weren't in love.

He looked out the window, at the clear night sky, the stars punching through the blackness. It reminded him of being with Sophia. Little spots of brightness that managed to bring something into those dark spaces.

There was so much more darkness than light. And it was amazing that the blackness did not consume it.

For a brief moment he felt something like hope. Like perhaps it would be the same with her. That *his* blackness would not cover her light, but that her light would do something to brighten that darkness.

But no.

It could not be. Not really. He was not fool enough to believe it. Hope, in his experience, was a twisted thing.

Was for better men than him.

Suddenly, he was acutely aware of the pitch-dark. Of the way that it stretched out inside him. Yawning endlessly.

He needed to get back to her. Needed to have her hold him in her arms.

A wretched thing. Because he should be the one carrying her.

It was amazing, but somewhere, amidst all the granite inside his chest, there was softness for her. A softness he had never allowed himself to truly focus on before. He had been too obsessed with pushing her away. With keeping his feelings for her limited.

It was over now.

He had her. So he supposed…

The headlines once again crowded his head. It wasn't fair. That Sophia should be subjected to such a thing. Already, there had been many unkind things written about her mother and about her when she was young. And yes, gradually, the tide had turned in their favor. And even then, most had seen it as a fairy tale. He doubted very much that people would ever see this as any kind of fairy tale.

In that world stepsiblings were always wicked. And they certainly didn't get a happy ending.

Least of all with the princess in the story.

No. Theirs was not a fairy tale.

Theirs was something dark and frightening, obsession and lust creating a cautionary tale.

One he certainly wasn't going to heed. It was far too late for that.

He turned and walked out of the office, heading down the long hallway toward the room he was sharing with Sophia.

She might be asleep. She might not have waited up for him.

He pushed the door open without knocking, and did not see her in bed. In fact, he did not see her anywhere.

He frowned. And then he looked up and saw her standing in the doorway of the balcony that contained the large bathtub he had built several fantasies around.

She was wearing nothing more than a white gown, diaphanous and insubstantial. He was certain that—even in the dim light—he could make out the shadow at the apex of her thighs. Of her nipples.

"What are you doing?" he asked.

Her dark brown hair was a riot of curls, those generous curves calling to him.

Every time they'd been together it had been frantic as if they were both afraid one or both of them might come to their senses and put a stop to everything. This was different. There was a look in her eye that spoke of seduction. Seduction certainly hadn't been involved in any of their previous couplings.

He swore, beginning to undo the buttons on his shirt, until Sophia held up a delicate hand. "Not so fast."

"You will not tease me," he growled, taking a step toward her.

"I don't want to tease you."

"Then why are you stopping me from ravishing you? Because you know all I can think of is ripping that dress off you."

"You keep doing that to me," she scolded.

"Perhaps I think white isn't your color. Or perhaps I think the clothing doesn't suit you. But then, the conclusion could be drawn that I simply don't think clothes in general suit you. I've often wondered why I never cared for the image that the palace stylist had cultivated for you. And obviously the new one has done better. But I think the real reason is quite simple. I like you better naked. And part of me always knew that I would."

She looked down for a beat, those long, dark lashes fanning over her cheekbones. The only sign that she was perhaps not as confident as she appeared.

But then she looked up at him, those brilliant, defiant eyes meeting his. Sophia. Always there to challenge him.

"I'm happy to get naked for you, Luca," she said, the way her lips formed the sounds of his name sending an illicit shiver down to his manhood, making him feel as though she had licked him there.

"But what?"

"I require a forfeit."

"A forfeit?" He paused for a moment, the only sound

coming from the distant waves crashing on the rocks below, and the thundering of his heart in his ears. "Well, now, that is very interesting. Do you wish me to get down on my knees and worship at the cleft of your thighs? Because I'm more than happy to spend an evening there."

"No. That would be too easy. For both of us. I will take off this gown in exchange for one thing."

"What is that?"

"You have to tell me one thing you have never told another soul. It might be enough for you to pretend that we only just met, Luca, but it is not enough for me."

His stomach curdled. Going sour at the thought. Because there was only one thing that sprung readily to his mind. There was no other living soul who knew what had happened to him, even though at one time someone certainly had known.

Well, perhaps there was another living soul who knew. Whether or not Giovanni was dead or alive wasn't something Luca was privy to. He didn't want to find out. He hoped the man was dead. If he wasn't, Luca would be far too tempted to see to his demise himself.

Though, considering the scandal that had just erupted, perhaps murder would be surmountable. Or at least not so glaring in the face of all this.

Still. He was not going to tell Sophia.

He gritted his teeth, casting his mind back to something… Anything that he might be able to tell her. So desperate was he to have her naked.

"I was rejected by the first girl I ever cared for," he said. "Though I use the words *cared for* euphemistically here, considering I didn't know her at all."

That wasn't something he often thought about. What

had happened the night of the ball. Before he had been violated. When everything had been simple and he had been innocent in many ways.

"What?"

"There was a girl who came to a ball that my father threw. There were dignitaries from all around the world." Which was what had allowed his mother to sneak her lover into the palace.

A man that Luca had met on a few occasions and had gotten a terrible, sick feeling in his stomach whenever he spoke. He had sensed that he knew the relationship between Giovanni and his mother. But then later he wondered if really that disquiet that he felt had to do with the fact that Giovanni was a predator. A predator who had set his sights on Luca.

"There was a girl called Annalise. She was beautiful. Her father was a dignitary in Morocco and they were visiting the palace for our grand party. I was entranced by her. She refused to dance with me. But then we spoke for a while. I led her out to the garden, and I tried to kiss her. She dodged me, and I ended up kissing a rosebush instead."

Sophia laughed, clearly not expecting the story. "You were a prince."

"And she was unimpressed with me."

"How old were you?"

"Sixteen. I believe she was eighteen."

"Oh, no," Sophia said, laughing. "You were punching above your weight."

"I had imagined that being the prince in the palace in which her family was staying might lend me an edge."

Sophia giggled, ducking her head, the expression making her look young. Making him feel young. As if perhaps he were that boy he had been that night. Innocent. Full of possibilities. To love, to be loved.

Living a life that would not ultimately culminate in the moment when his mother proved her lack of care for him.

But perhaps living the life that his head appeared to be at that point in time. Golden. Glittering. One of a privileged, infinitely fortunate prince who had the world at his feet.

Though, in this moment, he would give the world in place of Sophia.

"I like her," Sophia said. "A woman who was not impressed with you just because of your title."

"The same can be said for you, I think," he said, taking a step toward her. She took a step back.

"If anything," Sophia said, "I have always found your status to be a hindrance. Imagine what it would have been like if we would have met under different circumstances."

"You would still be younger than me," he said. "So it would still take time for me to see you differently."

"All right. What if you met me at seventeen, instead of at twelve?"

"Perhaps I would have asked you for your phone number."

She laughed. "That's so startlingly benign. You and I have never been afforded anything quite so dull."

"No, indeed."

"I must warn you," she said. "I don't intend for tonight to be dull, either."

"I believe we have started as we mean to go on."

"I suppose so."

"Your dress," he said. "I have given you my forfeit. You owe me mine."

She said nothing. Instead, she raised her hand, brushing the thin strap of her dress down so that it hung loosely over her shoulder. And then she did the same to the other side. The diaphanous fabric barely clung to her body, held up by those generous breasts of hers. He wanted to wrench it down, expose her body to his hungry gaze.

But this was her game. And he was held captive by it. Desperate to see what her rules might be.

He had grown into a man that most would never dream of defying. That was by design. But Sophia… She dared. And he wanted to see what else she might dare.

"I believe it was for the entire dress," he pressed. He stood, curling his hands into fists, his heart thundering so hard he thought it might burst through a hole in his chest.

She made him…

She made him wild. And he had not been wild for a very long time.

"I suppose it was," she returned. "Though I see that you are standing there fully clothed. And it doesn't escape my notice that the first time we were together you were also mostly clothed, while I…"

"Your dress was still on. Technically."

"I was exposed."

"All the better to enjoy you, *cara*."

She shivered, and he was gratified by that response. "Well, I want to enjoy you. I want you naked."

She lifted her chin, her expression one of utter defiance. Defiance he wished to answer. Though he had a feeling that his little beauty's boldness might end if he actually complied with her request.

For all that she was playing at being in charge here, for all that she was a responsive and generous lover, she was still inexperienced.

He wondered how long it would take for that to not be the case. How many times. How many kisses. The number of moments he would have to spend in her bed in order to strip that inexperience from her. That innocence. Until she would look at him boldly when he removed his clothes, until she would no longer blush when he whispered erotic things in her ear.

He looked forward to the progression, but he was not in a hurry. For now, he would enjoy this.

More than anything, he looked forward to the fact that there would be a progression, rather than a one-off and a garden alcove, like he had imagined it would be.

He gripped the hem of the black T-shirt he was wearing and dragged it over his head, casting it to the floor, making similar and quick work of the rest of his clothes. Until he stood before her with nothing on.

She did shrink back, only slightly. He had been correct in his theory that she might still find the sight of him without clothes to be a bit confronting.

He spread his arms wide. “And here I am for you, *cara mia.* Where is my reward?”

She turned around quickly, and if it wasn’t for the heavy rise and fall of her shoulders, he might have thought it an extension of the game, rather than a moment where nerves had taken over.

But then she lifted her arms, taking a slow, indrawn breath, the fabric of the gown slipping, falling to her waist. Exposing the elegant line of her back, the twin dimples just below the plump curve of her ass. Still covered by that flowing dress.

He gritted his teeth, holding himself back. He wanted nothing more than to move to her. Than to take control. He ached with it.

But he waited. Still, he waited.

She placed her hands at her hips, pushing the fabric down her slender legs, revealing the rest of that tempting skin.

And then, his control was lost.

He walked up behind her quietly, careful not to give her any indication of what he planned to do next.

Slowly, very slowly, he reached out and swept her dark hair to the side, exposing her neck. And he kissed her. His lips pressed firmly against the center of the back of her neck, careful not to touch her anywhere else.

She gasped, a sharp sound of need winding its way through the breath.

He drew back, pressing the back of his knuckles to that spot between her shoulder blades, following the indent of her spine down low. She squirmed, wiggling her hips, and he gripped her left side with his hand, holding her still as he followed his journey down all the way until his fingers pressed between her thighs, finding that place where she was soft and wet just for him.

He moved his hand back upward to cup one rounded cheek, squeezing her hard as he slid the hand that gripped her hip around her stomach, pulling her up against him so that she could feel the evidence of his arousal pressing against her lower back.

"I'm growing impatient of games," he whispered into her ear, capturing her lobe between his teeth and biting her gently.

She arched against him, her lovely ass pressing into him.

She wiggled.

"If you keep doing that, Sophia," he said, "you're going to push me to my limit."

"Perhaps I want to find it."

"I'm not sure you do."

"I don't want your control," she said softly. "I don't want you to be solicitous and careful. I know that you are a man of honor, Luca. But I feel that there is no place for honor between us just now." She arched even farther into him. "Indeed, there's not much room for anything between us. It's just our skin, our bodies, pressed against each other."

He pushed his hand down toward the apex of her thighs, those downy curls beneath his fingers the filthiest pleasure he'd ever experienced in his life.

He pushed down farther, brushing his fingers over that sensitive bundle of nerves, through her folds, finding the entrance to her body and pressing his fingers inside her. She let her head fall back against his shoulder, relaxing on an indrawn breath.

"Is this what you wanted?" he asked. "You want me uncontained? You want me out of control? As if it has not been so from the moment I first laid my hands on you in that garden?"

"You are far more controlled than I would like," she gasped.

"Control is a good thing," he said. "I think you will find."

He swept his free hand up to cup her breast, teasing her nipple with his thumb. "You will benefit from my control," he rasped, drawing his cheek down the side of her neck, over her shoulder, well aware that his whiskers were scraping delicate skin. She moaned. A clear sign that she quite liked his control in the right venue.

"But I don't have any," she whispered.

"Is that what you think? Sophia, you have had control of me for far too long. My thoughts turn on the sway of your hips, my focus shifting with each breath you take in my presence. How can you not know this?"

"You said I was your sickness," she breathed.

"And indeed it is true." He kissed her shoulder. "There is no cure. I am a terminal case. But I have accepted this."

"I'm not sure how I'm supposed to—" she gasped, her breath hitching as he pressed his fingers deeper inside her "—feel about that."

"Feel this," he said, thrusting his hips against her backside again. "And feel the pleasure that I give you."

She reached up, grabbing hold of the hand that was resting on her breasts, as though she was trying to get him to ease his pleasuring of her. As though it was too much. He collected that wrist, holding it in his hand like an iron manacle, and then he took hold of her other hand, bringing them around behind her and holding them fast, pinning them to her lower back as he continued to toy with her between her legs with his free hand.

She shifted her hips. "You're holding me prisoner now?"

"It seems fair. I've been held captive by you for years now."

"Luca," she breathed his name, total capitulation to what was happening between them. He worked his fingers between her legs faster, stroking her slickness over her clit before bringing his fingers down to the entrance of her body again, delving deep. The waves of her release seemed to come from deep within her, her internal muscles pulsing hard around his fingers as she found her pleasure.

He propelled her out onto the balcony, up to the edge of the bath. He tightened his grip on her stomach, lifting them both down into the water, prepared by her already. And there they were calm out under the stars again, only this time, there were no people. Nobody in a nearby ballroom to come out and discover them. No one at all.

He sat on the edge of the tub, whirling her around to face him, wrapping her legs around his waist, the slick heart of her coming into contact with his arousal.

"Out here," he said, "if you scream no one will hear you. Only the stars."

Those stars. That brightness. Her brightness.

"Then I suggest you do your part to make me scream."

He moved both hands down to cup her butt, freeing her wrists as he did. She moved her hands to his shoulders, gripping him tightly as he moved them both across the tub, the slick glide of the water over their skin adding a sharpness to the sensuality of the moment.

"You want to scream?" He moved them over to the glass edge of the tub that overlooked the sea and turned her, maneuvering her so that she was in front of him, facing the water, the reflection of the silvery moon over the waves.

"Hold on to the edge," he commanded.

She did so without arguing, though there was a hesitancy to her movements that spoke of confusion. She would not be confused for long.

He pressed one hand to her hip, and with the other, guided his erection to the entrance of her body. He pushed into her in one decisive thrust, grabbing both hips and pulling her back against him, the motion creating ripples in the water.

She gasped, leaning forward, her breasts pressed against the glass, her hands curved around the edge like claws. She bowed her head over the tub. He reached forward, grabbing hold of her dark curls and drawing her head back, none too gently, as he found her throat with his lips, kissing her, then scraping it with the edge of his teeth.

He rode her like that, one hand gripping her hip tightly, his blunt fingers digging into her skin, the other holding her hair as he thrust into her in an endless rhythm that pushed fire down his spine and sent pleasure through him like a river of molten flame.

He felt when her thighs began to quiver, when she got close to release. And he slipped his hand to her furrow again, brushing his fingers over where she was most sensitive, not stopping even as he felt her release break over her. Not stopping until she was screaming herself hoarse into the night, out over that endless ocean, up to the stars.

Into the darkness.

Into his darkness.

And when his own control reached its end he grabbed hold of her with both hands, holding her steady while he poured himself into her. His despair, his need, his release, nothing like a simple achievement of pleasure, but the sharp edge of a knife, cutting into him, making him bleed.

Reducing him. Right there in front of her. And there

was nothing that could be done about that. Nothing he could do to fight it.

He reached out, holding on to the edge of the tub, bracing himself for a moment while he caught his breath. She looked over her shoulder, those eyes connecting with his. She looked… She looked as undone as he felt, and he could not ignore the question in them. The need. To be held.

He gathered her up in his arms and carried her across the tub and they stepped out onto the balcony. There was a large, fluffy towel folded up on a shelf adjacent to the tub and he grabbed hold of it, wrapping it around her and holding her against him as he brought her back into the bedroom, depositing her onto the center of the bed.

He didn't bother to dry himself, coming down beside her completely naked as she wrapped the edges of the towel more firmly around her body.

She rolled onto her back, letting out a long, slow sigh. She had the towel pulled over her breasts, but it parted just above her belly button, revealing that delicious triangle at the apex of her thighs. He was not going to disabuse her of her illusion that she might be covered.

"Luca," she whispered. "Why do I get the feeling that it isn't the secret of Annalise that stands between us?"

CHAPTER ELEVEN

"I DON'T FOLLOW YOU."

"That's not your secret. You may not have ever told anyone about it, but I think you never told anyone because it wasn't important. I think there's something important. Something you don't talk about because of the heaviness."

She rolled to her side, looking at him, her dark gaze much more insightful than he would like. He felt… Well, he felt naked. A ridiculous thing, because he had been naked this entire time. But suddenly, he felt as though she had cut into him and peeled his skin from his bones, giving her a deep look into places that he had been so certain were hidden. And yet, she had seen. Easily and with accuracy.

"I'm not talking about this now."

"Then when? It's a wonderful thing, a beautiful thing, to have you out of control when we are together like this. But what about the rest of the time? What about what comes after? When we have to live a life together."

He growled, rolling over, pinning her to the bed, pressing his palms into her shoulders. "The dark things that live in me… It will do you no good to know about them." He felt a sick kind of shame roll over his skin like an oily film, as if he had not just been made clean by the water in the bathtub. As if he had not just been made clean by joining to her.

He realized, with a sharp sort of shock, that there was an element of fear buried in his deep reluctance to never speak of his past. Luca was an attractive man, and he well knew it. Not just physically; the women responded to his looks, to his expertly sculpted body and to his sexual prowess. But also, he was a man with money, a man with a title. It would be disingenuous for him to pretend he presented absolutely no attraction to women.

But he realized that the words his mother had spoken to him after that night had taken root deeper than he had imagined. That it would make people think things about him. That it would repulse and appall Sophia if she knew the truth. If she knew the things that had been done to his body, would she want him at all? Or would she find him damaged in some way?

It was an unacceptable weakness. To worry about these things. To care at all.

And that was the real problem. He wanted to pretend that it didn't matter. That he didn't think about it. That it only shaped him in good ways. In ways that he had chosen. But these feelings, this moment, made it impossible. An illusion he could no longer cling to. If he resented Sophia for anything, it was this, most of all.

"Do you want to know why reputation is so important to me?" The words scraped his throat raw on their exit. He didn't want to speak of this, but the very fact that it had become such a leaden weight inside him that it had become something insurmountable, meant it was time for him to speak of it. Because if there was one thing he couldn't stand more than the memory, it was giving it power.

It was acknowledging all that it meant to him.

He wanted it to be nothing. Which meant speaking of it should be nothing. But the ugly turn of that was if it meant something to Sophia… If he had to see disgust or pity in her eyes…

But suddenly, that luminous gaze of hers was far too much for him to withstand. And he thought that perhaps, as long as she wanted him in the end, a little bit of distance was not the worst thing.

"My mother had lovers," he said. "I imagine you didn't know that."

Sophia frowned. "I've never heard my mother or your father speak of his first wife."

"Yes. Well. It is not because he was mired in grief. Though I think he felt some measure of it, they were no longer in love by the time she died, if they ever were. I think…" Suddenly, a thought occurred to him that never had before. "I think your mother was his first experience of love. I think perhaps that is why the connection was so powerful there was no care given to propriety. Not when he already knew what could happen when you married someone who was supposed to be suitable."

"You… You knew that she had lovers. But you must have been…a boy."

"I was. Very young. At first, I did not question the presence of men in the palace and my father's absence. We had many people stay there at many different times. But it was clear, after a fashion, that they were…special to my mother. It could not be ignored. Mostly, they ignored me. But there was one… He often tried to speak to me. Attempted to cultivate a relationship with me. I was sixteen."

"That was just before she died," Sophia said softly.

"Yes. Giovanni was the last one. It was as if everything came to a head at that point." He hesitated. "Remember that ball I told you about?"

"The one with Annalise."

"Yes. I think perhaps the reason that my memory of her is so sharp is because… Sometimes my life feels as if it's divided into before and after. I know that many people would think I mean my mother's death. But that is not the case. Before and after the night of that ball. I was a different person then. A boy. Protected from the world. That is the function of palace walls, after all. They keep you insulated. And I was, for certain."

He didn't want Sophia to touch him while he spoke of this. Didn't want there to have been any contact between them. He rolled to the side, putting a solid expanse of bedspread between them. She seemed to understand. Because she didn't move. She stayed rooted to the spot he had pinned her in a moment ago.

"That night, after the ball ended… Giovanni had gotten me a drink. It was slightly unusual as he took pains in public to pretend he didn't know me. Why hint at a relationship with my mother? But still. I took the drink. I felt…very tired. And I remember I left early. I assume he then took advantage of the fact that people were moving around. The fact that people were walking through the halls… It was all normal. And anyone who was in attendance had certainly been vetted and approved by the royal family."

"Luca," she whispered, "what happened?" He could hear both confusion and dawning horror in her voice.

And he knew that she had not guessed, but that she felt a strong sense of disquiet. Of fear.

He took a breath, closed his eyes. "He violated me."

The words were metallic on his tongue. There were uglier words for what had happened to him. More apparent. But they were still too difficult to speak, because *victim* lay on the other side of them, and that was something he could not admit. Something he could not speak.

"He…"

He did not allow her to speak. "I think you know the answer."

She said nothing for a moment, silence settling heavy around them as flashes of memory replayed themselves in his mind. Flashes were all he had. A blessing of sorts, he supposed. A strange, surreal state brought about by whatever drug he'd been given.

"Why wasn't he arrested? Why weren't you protected?"

"It never happened again," he said gravely. No. He had gone straight to his mother. Because there had been no one else to speak to about it. How could he tell his father what had happened, at the hands of his mother's lover? To do so would mean to uncover her. But surely, she would protect her son.

She had not.

Not really.

Her version of protection had been to ensure that Giovanni didn't come to the palace anymore. She had cut off her association with him, but she did not, would not, push punishing him. For her own reputation.

"The reputation of the nation," he said, his throat tightening. "It was the most important thing."

"How can you say that? Of course it wasn't. Your

safety was the most important thing. Justice for what had been done to you."

Her lip was curled upward, an expression of disgust. Likely directed at what had been done to him, and not at him. But still, somehow it felt all the same.

"What does that mean in context with an entire nation of people?"

"You were raped," she said.

The words hit him like the lash of a whip. "And how is a nation supposed to contend with that? A future king who has been…victimized. Who was held down in his own bedchamber… It could not be. My mother explained why."

"Your mother?"

"There is no point having this discussion. She was correct. It would follow me, Sophia. It would be the story of who I was. Something like that cannot be forgotten. Admitting a weakness on that score…"

"You are not weak," she protested. "There is nothing weak about… You were drugged."

"So easy it would be to destroy the throne then. To attack the kingdom. See how vulnerable I am?"

"No," she protested.

"I don't believe that," he said. "To be clear. I was there, and I'm well aware of what I would have been able to fight and what I could not. But that would be the speculation, Sophia. And there is a reason that this does not get spoken of."

"Luca…"

"I have trusted you with it. You asked for this. You pushed for it. Don't you dare betray me."

He felt some guilt at saying that. As if she would. Of course she wouldn't. She was looking at him with the truest emotion he had ever seen. His mother certainly hadn't looked at him like that. She had been horrified, too. But not about what had been done to him half as much as what the fallout could be. The fallout for her.

He hated this. He hated thinking of it. It was best left buried deep, with the lesson carried forward. There was no point to this. Because there was nothing that could be done. It was dragging out dead bodies and beating them. And there was simply no reason for that.

You could not spend your life punching at ghosts. That much he knew.

"Am I a strong king, Sophia?"

"Yes," she said softly.

"Would I be so strong in the eyes of the people if they knew?"

"You should be," she said.

"But *would I be*? We cannot deal in what should be. If what should have happened had happened I would not have been violated. But I was. I can only deal in reality as it is. And I cannot take chances. Why do you think I did my very best to stay away from you? I have a reputation. Our country has a reputation. And what exists now? It has been built on the back of my silence. And now I've blown it all to hell."

"Luca, you cannot carry all of that. You're a man. You cannot control what people think of you. You're a good man, that's what matters. Not what people think. But what you do for the country."

"So you say. But our standing in the world would greatly be affected by the way the people perceived me. By the headlines. And when it came to my child… There was no choice. In that I would choose him."

"You should have chosen yourself," she said softly.

He bit back the fact that it was his mother who hadn't chosen him. So why the hell should he?

He had already stripped his soul bare, had already confessed to the kind of weakness and shame that made his skin crawl to even consider. The last thing he was going to do was go further into mommy issues.

"I chose San Gennaro," he said instead.

"Luca..."

He got out of bed. "I have some more work to see to."

"It's late."

"Yes," he said. "But it will not wait."

There was no work. But he needed distance. Feeling like he did, he could not allow her to touch him. He needed a chance to get distance from this moment. To forget this conversation had ever happened.

He had expected... He had expected her to pull back, and she wouldn't. Damn her. She surprised him at every turn.

He collected his clothing and pulled it on, walking out of the bedroom, ignoring Sophia's protests. He pushed his hands through his hair and paused for a moment, only just now realizing how quickly his heart was beating. But he had done it. He had spoken the words. Maybe now... Maybe now it wouldn't matter.

He walked down the hall toward his office, and when he entered the room his phone was lighting up, vibrating on his desk.

It was his stepmother. He picked up the phone. "It's late," he said.

"You need to come home," she said.

"I'm busy at the moment."

"Luca," she said, "I would not tell you to come home if it wasn't absolutely necessary. This is all getting out of hand. And you cannot simply leave the country to take care of itself."

"What about Sophia? This is for her benefit, not mine."

"Then leave her there alone. Wherever you've spirited her off to, leave her in peace while you come here to deal with the fallout of your actions."

"I assure you that your daughter has culpability in the situation."

"Oh, I have no doubt, but if your only view is to protect her, then leave her behind and come back and address your people."

"You know I can't do that. If we step out, we must do so together."

"That is likely true. But… Luca, I beg you, don't hurt Sophia. She is not from your world. No matter how long she has lived in it… It is not ingrained in her the way that it is in you. That duty must come first. For her, love will always come first."

Yes, and he knew that. Because for her, what his mother had done was unfathomable. While to him… He might resent it, but… In the end, could he truly be angry about it? What he had said to her was true. He would be defined by that experience if the world knew of it. It was difficult to be angry about the fact that he was not.

"I won't," he said.

"I wish I believed you."

"I will marry her. I will not abandon her."

"That's my concern. But you seem to think that is all that is required of you. There is so much more, Luca."

"What else is there?"

She said nothing for a moment. "Come home."

"I will ready a plane for an early morning departure."

CHAPTER TWELVE

WHEN SOPHIA AWOKE to see Luca standing at the side of the bed, wearing nothing but a pair of dark slacks, his arms crossed over his bare chest, his expression forbidding, she knew something was wrong.

"What?" She scrambled into a sitting position and pulled her sheet up to her chest.

Suddenly, last night came flooding back to her. His confession. What had happened to him at the hands of his mother's lover. He had left after that. And it had hurt that he had pulled away, but she had understood that it had been required.

Still. She wanted to hold him. She wanted to…offer him something.

She knew that he wouldn't let her.

"We need to leave," he said, his voice stern.

He walked over to the closet and took out a crisp white shirt, pulling it over his broad shoulders and beginning to button it slowly.

"Why?" She shook her head, trying to clear the webs of cotton from her brain. "I thought we were going to stay here until everything died down."

"We were. But your mother called. She convinced me otherwise." His jaw firmed, his expression like iron.

"It is not going to be easy. But she is correct. I have left the country to burn in my absence, and I cannot do that. She suggested…that I leave you here."

"I don't want to stay here. I want to go with you."

He seemed to relax slightly at that. But only slightly. "I feel it would be best for you to come with me. It would be good for us to present a united front. However…"

"There is no however," she said, pushing herself up so that she was sitting straighter. "You're right. If you return without me the rumors will only get worse. Whatever you say. I need to be there. I need to be there, speaking for myself. There is no other alternative that is acceptable."

"You are very brave, Sophia."

Was she? She had never felt particularly brave. A girl who had tried once to gain the attention of her father, only to fail. Who had then spent a life infatuated with a stepbrother who didn't even like her.

Suddenly, it all became clear, as if the clouds had rolled back, revealing a clear sky and full sun. She had spent those years infatuated with Luca to protect herself. If she had ever fancied herself in love with him, she had been wrong. Because she had not known him.

He had never even been kind to her. Had never demonstrated any softness toward her. Had taken no pains to make her feel welcome in the palace.

He had been the safest.

Until the moment he had touched her in the garden, and it all became painfully real.

But until last night, she had never really known him.

She had been attracted to the untouchable quality he had. To the safety that represented. And more than that, to his strength. The integrity that he exuded.

She had admired that, because she had known men without it. Her own father being one of them.

But that wasn't enough to be love.

Suddenly, as he stood there, putting himself back together, after making himself so vulnerable the night before, putting the king back on over the top of the wounded boy, she fully appreciated what that integrity meant. What that strength cost.

That the granite in his voice, the hardness in his eyes, the straightness in his stance, the way he held his head high, had all come with great difficulty.

Anyone who knew his public story would think he was a man who was exactly as he had been raised to be. A man who had never faced any real adversity, beyond the loss of his mother. And what famous, handsome prince these days had not experienced such a thing?

But they didn't know. Not really.

Until last night she hadn't, either.

Suddenly, it felt as if someone had reached inside her chest and grabbed hold of her heart, squeezing it hard. Feeling overwhelmed her. There was no safety here. There was no careful divide created by his disdain, no distance at all. This wasn't simple attraction, wasn't fascination. It was more. It was deeper.

It was something she had not imagined possible. Something she hadn't wanted.

Love, for her, apart from her family, had always been a simple word.

This was more. It created a seismic shift inside her, incited her to action. To open herself up and expose herself to hurt.

The very last thing that love was was a feeling. It was so many other things first.

She understood that then.

Because until then, she had not loved Luca.

But she did now. Deeply.

"I must get myself presentable," she said. And then she rose out of the bed, not covering herself at all, and walked over to the closet, where, at the moment their clothes were mingled. Would it always be like this? With their lives tangled together?

She imagined that Luca fancied a royal marriage to be something based on tradition. That they would carry out their separate lives, in their separate quarters.

But their parents hadn't done that. His father, and her mother, had shared everything. Space. Life. Breath.

That was what she wanted. She didn't want to be the wife of his duty. She wanted to be the wife of his heart.

She turned to face him, whatever words on her lips there had been dying the moment that her gaze connected with his. With the heat there. He was looking at her with a deep, ferocious hunger that made her feel… both happy and sad all at once.

Luca wanted her. There was no denying that.

But whatever else he felt…

He was perfect. A man perfectly formed, with a wonderfully symmetrical face, classically handsome features that his aristocratic air pushed over into being devastating. His physique was well muscled, his hands large and capable. So wonderful to be held by.

But he was scarred. Inside, he was destroyed.

And no one looking at him would have any clue.

She wondered…

She wondered if there was any way to reach past those scars.

Any way to touch his heart.

She turned away from him again, concentrating on dressing herself. She selected a rather somber black sheath dress, not one that would be approved by the new stylist, but one that would best suit their return back to the country. She had a feeling they would be trying to strike a tone that landed somewhere between defiance and contrition. Not an easy thing to do. But they would have to be resolute in what they had chosen, while being mindful of the position the nation was put in due to the scandal.

He was distant the entire plane ride back to San Gennaro, but she wasn't overly surprised by that. He was trying to rebuild that wall. Brick by brick. Oh, not to keep out that physical lust. Not anymore.

But that new emotional connection that had been forged last night…

He wanted badly to turn away from that. And she didn't know how to press it. She had always imagined she had lived the harder life. She was from poverty, after all. She had a father who didn't want her. She knew what it was to go to bed hungry. She'd been fortunate enough to come into a wonderful life at the palace, but it had been foreign to her. Filled with traditions and silverware that were completely unfamiliar to her.

But now she knew different.

Now she knew that incredible strength could mask unfathomable pain. The walls of a palace could not keep out predators when they had simply been let in.

When the plane descended it felt like a heavyweight was pushing them down toward the ground. Or perhaps that was just the feeling inside her chest. Heaviness.

She wished they could stay on the island. That they could stay in a world where rigorous walks on the beach and lazy lovemaking sessions in a tub were the most pressing things between them.

She had to wonder… If they had not spoken last night…would he be ready to fly back today? Would he be so dead set on their need to return home?

She wondered if he wasn't facing his duty so much as running from her.

No, that wasn't fair.

If there was one thing Luca was not, it was a coward. He would forcefully tell her he didn't want to speak of something, that was certain, but he would not run.

"Prepare yourself," he said, the first words he had spoken to her in hours as the plane door opened.

And indeed, his words were not misplaced. Their car was down there waiting for them, but it was surrounded. Bodyguards were doing their best to keep the horde at bay, but camera flashes were going off, blinding Sophia as they made their way down the stairs and toward the limousine.

Luca wrapped his arm tightly around her and guided her into the car, speaking firmly in Italian before closing the door behind them.

"We will have to speak to them, won't we?" she asked as the car attempted to maneuver its way through the throng.

"Eventually," he said. "But I will do it on my own terms. I am the king of this nation, and I will not be led around by the dictates of the press. Yes, we have answers to give. Yes, we must return and create a solid front for the country. But I will not stand on the tarmac and give an interview like some fame whore reality TV star."

She examined the hard line of his profile, shiver working its way down her spine.

Everything he believed in was crumbling in front of him, and still, he was like granite. Protecting his image had been everything, because if it wasn't…

She felt like she'd been stabbed in the chest as she realized, fully, deeply, the cost of all this to him. How it linked to the pain of his past, and the decisions that had been made then.

It made her want to fix it. To fix him. Because she had been part of this destruction. But she hadn't understood.

"Luca," she said softly.

"We don't need to talk," he said, firm and rigid. "There will be time later."

"Will there?"

"We will have to prepare a statement."

Preparing a statement was not the same as the two of them talking. But she wasn't going to correct him on that score right now.

Later, when she was installed back in her normal bedroom, alone, she wished she had pressed the issue.

But Luca had been forceful and autocratic like he could be, and he had determined that the two of them should not do anything wildly different from normal until they figured out how they were going to handle the public fallout.

She wished that she was in bed with him.

But then, maybe it was good for her to have some time alone.

She tossed and turned for a few moments, and then got out of bed. She crossed the large room, wearing only her nightgown, and padded out to the balcony. She leaned over the edge, staring out at the familiar grounds below, illuminated by the moonlight. She looked in the direction of the garden. Where all of this had started.

She wouldn't take it back. She simply wouldn't.

Not when being with him had opened the door to learning so much about herself.

To learning about love.

The discovery that she had been protecting herself all those years was a startling one, and yet, not surprising at the same time.

The breeze kicked up, and she could smell the roses coming in on the wind, tangling through her hair. She closed her eyes. And for a moment she thought she might be able to smell Luca's aftershave. His skin. That scent that had become so beloved, and so familiar.

"Here you are."

She whirled around at the sound of his voice, only to see him standing in the doorway of the balcony, looking out.

"Did you think I had jumped?"

"I rather hoped you hadn't."

"I thought we weren't going to talk tonight."

"I couldn't sleep," he said.

He pushed away from the door frame, and came out onto the balcony. He was wearing the same white button-up he'd had on earlier, the top three buttons undone. She could imagine, so easily, what his muscular chest would look like. What it would feel like if she were to push her hand beneath the edge of the shirt and touch him. His hair was disheveled as though he had been running his hands through it. Her eye was drawn to the gold wristwatch he was wearing. She didn't know why. But it was sexy. Maybe it was just because to her, he was sexy.

"I couldn't sleep, either." She frowned. "But I suppose that's self-evident."

"Perhaps."

"It's dark out here," she said, lifting her shoulder.

"What does that mean?"

"We can talk in the dark." She hadn't meant to say that. But she wondered if it was true. If this balcony could act as a confessional, like their bed had done last night.

"We can talk in the light just as well," he said, his tone stiff.

"No," she said, weary. "I'm not sure we can. At least, I think it doesn't make things easier."

"What is it you have to say?"

"I hope that you have some things to say to me. But…"

She wasn't quite in a space where she wanted to confess her undying love. But she did want him to know… She wanted him to know something. "You know," she said slowly. "After our parents were married… I saw my father. He found me. Actually, all of the press made it easy."

Luca frowned. "You were protected by guards."

"Yes. But they were hardly going to stop me from meeting with my father."

"I didn't know about it."

"Well, you wouldn't have. You were away at university by then. We saw each other for a while… Until your father refused to give him a substantial sum of money. I was so angry, Luca. I thought that your father was being cruel. Because after that my father took himself away from me. He didn't want me. He never did. But I couldn't see that. Not then. I was only thirteen, and it felt immeasurably awful to have my father taken from me simply because yours wouldn't give him what he needed."

"What a terrible thing," Luca said, his voice rough. "To be so badly used by a parent."

"But you know about that, don't you? I didn't think you did. I thought… I thought for you things were so easy. I admired you. Even when you weren't nice to me. I admired how certain you were. How steady. You were all of these things that I could never be, wearing this position like a second skin. But now I know. I know what it costs you to stand up tall. And it only makes me admire you all the more."

He ignored her, walking over to the balcony, standing beside her. He gripped the railing, and she followed suit, their hands parallel to each other but not touching. Still, she could feel him. With every breath.

"How did you come to be close with my father? After all that anger you had toward him?" Luca asked. He quite neatly changed the subject.

But she didn't mind talking about this. She wanted to tell him. She wanted to… Well, she wanted to give no less than she took.

Or, what she hoped to take.

"He proved to be the better man," she said.

"How?" He seemed hungry for that answer.

"My father quit seeing me after your father refused to pay him off. Meanwhile, I was a wretch to your father. I was rude. I was insufferable. And he never once threatened to remove himself from my life. No. He only became more determined to forge a relationship with me. He refused to quit on me. Even when I was a monster. He could have… He could have simply let us exist in the same space. There was no reason that he had to try to have a relationship with me. But he did. He proved what manner of man he was through his actions. He showed me what strength was. What loyalty was." She swallowed hard, her throat dry like sandpaper. "He demonstrated love to me. And I had certainly seen it coming from my mother. But not from anyone else. He made me feel like I was worth something."

Yes, the king had pursued her. Her affection. He had made that relationship absolutely safe for her before she had decided to give of herself. But when it came to Luca…it wasn't the same.

When it came to him, she might have to put herself out there first. And she…

That was terrifying. She wasn't sure she could.

It wasn't something she was sure she could do.

If only he would…

She bit her lip. "I was very grateful to have your father. He did a lot to repair the damage that my own father created."

"I can only hope to be half the father he was."

"Well, I hope to be as good of a mother as my own."

It was the first time they had really talked about the baby in those terms. It had all been about blood, and errors and duty. But it had been real. It had not been about being a mother and a father.

"Your mother has always been good to me," he said. "She never had a thing to prove, you know. Not a thing to hide. Not like my own mother did. She is a truly kind woman, who had many things said about her by the media. Cruel, unfair. But she held her head high. You are the same, Sophia. I know you are. You will show our child—son or daughter—how to do the same."

She ducked her head, her heart swelling. "I hope so."

"If it had to be that our child was born in scandal, there is no one I would trust better to teach him to withstand."

Suddenly, Luca released his hold on the railing and turned away from her. She felt the abandonment keenly. As if the air had grown colder. Darker.

"Wait." She held up her hand, even though he couldn't see her. But he stopped, his shoulders held rigid. "I don't… I'm not sorry. So you know. I don't regret this."

Only the slight incline of his head indicated her words had meant something to him. The pause he took.

"Good night, Sophia," he said.

She wanted to say more. The words gathered in her chest, climbed up her throat, tight in a ball like a fist. But she couldn't speak them. So instead, she issued a request. "Stay with me. Tonight."

Then he took her by the hand, and led her to bed. And he did stay, all through the night.

It was surprising how quickly a royal wedding could be put together. Certainly, the wedding that they had assembled for Erik and Sophia had come together quickly enough, but this had been accomplished in lightning speed. They had handled the press a few days earlier, making a joint statement from the grounds of the palace, that had been streamed live over the internet and television. They had spoken about their commitment to San Gennaro, and to each other. And unsurprisingly it had been met with somewhat mixed reviews. But he had expected nothing less.

There was no way they were going to have a universal buy-in from the public. Not given the state of things.

They would have to win them over through the course of time. He had a feeling the baby would help.

Babies often did.

They were to be married in two days' time, and truly, he couldn't ask for things to be going much better than they were. He had Sophia in his bed every night, in spite of his determination that they would not carry on in that regard once they were back at the palace, and everything was going as smoothly as it possibly could. In terms of his lack of control when it came to bedding her…

She was his weakness. That was the simple truth.

He was a man who hadn't afforded himself a weakness as long as he'd been a grown man. Sophia had always challenged him. Had always slipped beneath his resolve and made him question all that he knew about himself.

He didn't like it. But he rather did like sleeping skin to skin with her.

Sacrifices had to be made.

There would be a small gathering tonight, of the guests arriving for the upcoming union. Nothing large, like it would have been with more time. Like it would have been if there wasn't a cloud hanging over the top of them.

It would fade. Surely, it would fade.

And if it didn't? An interesting thought to have. He had been so wedded to his reputation, to guarding what everyone thought, the idea that he had no more control over it was…

He frowned. He wasn't even certain he cared.

Sophia was the mother of his child. She was to be his wife. There was no arguing with that. And as she had said to him just the other night…whatever people thought of him, he could rule. And he could do it well.

The rest didn't matter.

"How are you finding things?" he asked as Sophia was ushered toward him at the entrance of the dining hall.

She was wearing a dress of such a pale color that the sequins over the top of it looked as though they had been somehow fastened directly to her pale, smooth skin. It glittered with each step she took, and the top came to an artful V at her breasts, showing off those delicate curves in exquisite fashion.

She took hold of his arm, looked up at him. "Entertaining dignitaries' wives is a strange experience."

"But it is your life now," he pointed out.

She wilted somewhat at that.

"I am sorry, *cara mia*," he said, "but it cannot be ignored that being queen does carry its share of burdens. Your mother, I'm certain, knows all about that."

"Yes," she said, though somewhat hesitant.

He wondered what the caveat was, because there was one. He could hear it. Unspoken, deep down her throat. But they were walking into a dining room crowded full of people, half of whom were hoping they would be witnessing some sort of glorious meltdown, he was certain, so he was hardly going to broach the topic now.

He sat at the head of the table, and Sophia had departed from him and made her way down to the foot.

Tradition, he mused, was such a fascinating thing. Things like this… They formed from somewhere, and that demonstrated that humans could clearly create them out of thin air. On a whim. But there were certain points in history where tradition had simply been followed, and not created. As though someone else had made those rules, and human beings were bound to them. As though they could not be broken.

Tradition. Appearances.

Those things had been paramount to his mother, even while she had lived in exactly the fashion she had wanted. And he… He clung to it because it gave him a sense of purpose. Because it made him feel as if what had happened to him—and the lack of fallout after—had been unavoidable.

It was the reason that he was seated across the room from Sophia now, when he would like her at his side.

All of these fake rules.

He was a damned king, and yet there were all these rules.

The rules that kept him from receiving any sort of justice. The rules that prevented him from acting on his attraction to Sophia in the first place.

And the rules that kept him from sitting beside her now. The rules that had kept them from spending the day together.

A strange thing. All of it.

Those seated around him directly had been artfully chosen people. Selected carefully by members of his cabinet. People who would only speak highly of him, and certainly not call into question his union with his stepsister. He was certain the same could be said for those who had been seated directly around Sophia, and those in the middle could fling poison back and forth across the table to their hearts' content, for he and his bride could not hear it.

When the meal was finished he rose, nodding his head once and signaling Sophia to follow suit.

She looked up at him with slightly cautious eyes, but she followed his lead. She had watched his father and her mother do this many times. She knew that she was simply to follow his lead.

They met at the center of the table and he took her arm again, then they turned toward the doors and made their exit.

The guests would follow shortly, but they had a moment, a quiet moment there in the antechamber.

"Are you all right?"

"Yes," she said. "I do understand how these things work."

"But it's only just dawning on you that your role in them has changed. Am I correct in assuming that?"

"It's a lot of things. Marrying you. Becoming a mother. The fact that I was going to be queen was low on my list of things to deal with."

"And yet, you will be my queen. Tomorrow."

Her skin looked a bit waxen, pale, her gown and her necklace glittering in the dim light, which was helpful to her, as she herself did not glitter at all at the moment.

"It's too late to go back," he said.

She jerked her focus toward him. "I didn't say that I wanted to."

"You don't seem happy."

"I'm overwhelmed. I have been overwhelmed from the moment that you kissed me in the garden all those weeks ago. I don't know how you can expect me to feel any differently than that."

"Well, I suggest that by the time we are in the chapel tomorrow you find a way to feel slightly less overwhelmed."

She lifted a brow, her expression going totally flat. "As you command, sire."

He had no opportunity to respond to that because their guests began to depart the dining room and fill the antechamber.

"With regrets," Luca said, "I must bid you all goodnight. As must my fiancée. With the wedding tomorrow we do not wish to overextend her."

He wrapped his arm around her waist, breaking with propriety completely by engaging in such an intimate hold in public, and propelled her from the room. She was all but hissing by the time they arrived in her bedroom.

"Luca," she said. "We have guests, and I spent the entire day on my best behavior, not so that you could ruin it now."

"My apologies," he said, his tone hard. "I am ever ruining the reputations of others."

She looked ashamed at that. And he felt guilty. Because he knew that wasn't what she meant.

"Luca, I didn't mean…"

"I'm aware. I apologize for using that against you."

She didn't seem to know what to say to that. "Don't apologize to me," she said finally. "We're going to have to learn how to make this work."

She looked thoughtful at that.

"We don't have a lot of practice getting along. Not outside of bed anyway," he said.

"That is very true." She clasped her hands and folded them in front of her body. Then she let out a long, slow breath and lifted one leg slightly, towing her high heel off, before working on the other. It reduced her height by three inches, leaving her looking a small, shimmering fairy standing in the bedchamber.

"I know how they made it work," she said slowly. "I know why it was easy for them."

"Why is that?"

"They loved each other. They loved each other so very much, Luca. It wasn't a child, or the need for marriage or money that brought them together. They risked everything to be together. Not because they had to, but because they wanted to."

Her words were soft, and yet they landed in his soul like a blow. "I don't understand what you want me to do with that. I don't understand what you want me to say. You're pregnant. Your mother was not pregnant. I cannot change the circumstances of why we are marrying."

"I know," she said. "But I've found that over the past weeks my reasons for marrying you have changed." She looked up at him, her dark eyes luminous. "Luca, I imagined myself half in love with you for most of my life but it wasn't until after that night in San Paolo that I realized that wasn't true."

His stomach crawled like acid. Of course. She had realized she didn't love him after she found out that he had been such a weak victim of such a disgusting crime. That his body had been used in such a fashion. Of course she was repulsed by him. Who wouldn't be? He was repulsed by himself most of the time. Questioning a great many things about him. Questioning his attraction to Sophia herself. If it was something inside him that had been twisted and broken off beyond repair. Something that had caused him to want a thing that was forbidden to him.

"I am sorry to have destroyed your vision of me."

"No," she said. "That was when my vision of you became whole. Luca, you were a safe thing to love. I couldn't be with you. You were my stepbrother. How could it ever happen? You could never hurt me, not the way my father had done. And all the better, as long as I was obsessed with you, no one else could hurt me, either. You were a wall that I could build around myself. A thing to distract my heart with. The minute that you touched me that wall was destroyed. I didn't know you. How could I love you if I didn't know you? I admired things about you. I admired your strength. I admired what an honest man you were. But I didn't know the cost of those things, Luca, and knowing that… That was when I began to love you for real. I love you, Luca. I didn't want to say it. Because I wanted so badly to protect myself. I have been rejected before. I loved my father, and he only wanted to use what money your father could give him. I could not face being the one who tore themselves open and revealed their whole heart, only to be met with nothing. And I almost did… The other night I almost did. But I was afraid. I'm not going to be afraid anymore. I don't want to be. You deserve more than someone hiding and protecting themselves." She swallowed hard. "I love you."

Everything inside him rebelled at her claim. Utterly. Completely. There was no way it could be true. No way in heaven or hell.

"You don't love me," he said, his voice hard. "You want to make all of this a bit more palatable for you. You want to make it easier. But you don't love me."

"I do."

"Fine. Think what you wish, but that doesn't mean it's going to change anything."

"Why not? Why can't it change anything?"

"Because I don't love anything," he said. "Nothing at all."

"That can't be true, Luca. You loved your father. You care a great deal for my mother..."

"Family. Is different."

"How? Your mother was family..."

"I'm going to marry you, Sophia," he said. "I don't see why we need to get involved in an argument regarding feelings. I have committed to you. Why should you want anything else?"

"Because it's not just something else. It's everything else. Love is vital, Luca, and without it... It's the glue. It's not about lust. It's not blood. It's love."

"There we disagree. Because some days it's the promises that will be all that hold us together. That is how life works. Sometimes it's simply the things you have decided that keep you going. You cannot make decisions in desperation. You must make them with a cool head, and only then can you be certain you will act with a level of integrity."

"Fine. I can accept that you feel that way. In fact, it's one of the things I admire about you. You're a good man. You always have been. There is no doubt about that. But there has to be more. We cannot have one without the other. I don't want commitment without love, Luca. I can't."

"Why not?"

He could not understand why she couldn't let this go. Love was nothing. Love was...

Love failed. It left you bleeding on the ground. He had heard it said many times that love did not seek its own, but that was not his experience.

His mother cared only for herself.

He had been a casualty in her pursuit of pleasure, in her pursuit of protecting her own comfort.

He hadn't mattered.

Why should Sophia feel that he did? And why should she try to demand that he…?

It didn't matter. It didn't matter as long as he promised to stay with her.

"Because don't I deserve to be loved? Don't I deserve to be at the forefront of whatever action is being taken? I have been loved, richly so in my life. But… I've never been chosen. My mother loved me in spite of the fact that having me plunged her into poverty. Your father loved me because he loved my mother. My own father didn't care at all. He wanted money. And you want the baby. Is it so much to ask, Luca, that I be wanted for who I am? That I be loved for who I am?"

"I have told you a great many times that you are a sickness in my blood. If I didn't want you then we wouldn't be here at all. There would be no baby."

"Being your sickness isn't the same as being your love, Luca, and if you can't sort that out, then I'm not sure we have anything left to say to each other."

"So you'll just storm away from me?" he asked, anger rising up unreasonably inside him. "If you can't have exactly what you want the moment you want you're going to leave?" Of course she would. Why would she stay with him? That was the fundamental issue with all of this. She could profess to love him, and she might even believe it. But when it all came down, that would not be so. It couldn't be.

Because he was a man who had been used and discarded. The violation he had experienced at the hands of his mother's paramour not remotely as invasive as the one he had experienced when his mother had chosen to maintain her reputation over protecting him. Seeking justice for him.

And he had no idea how to feel about it. Because she was dead. Because he wasn't entirely certain he wanted his pain splashed all over the headlines, and had they sought legal action against the man who had harmed him, he certainly would have been in the headlines.

He didn't know what he wanted. He didn't know what he was worth.

But he knew he wasn't worth Sophia and all of the feelings she professed to have for him now.

She had tried to explain to him how her feelings for him had shifted, but she didn't truly understand. She couldn't.

"I told my mother what was done to me," he said, his voice low. "I went to her. Trusted her. I had been drugged. I had been violated. Abused. And I told her as much. That she had let that man into the palace, and that he had sought me out and harmed me in such a way. She was upset. And she was fearful. But it was not for me. It was for her own self. She could not have my father finding out she had been conducting affairs. She could not have the public finding out that she had been engaged in such a thing. And if we were to bring him before the law, then of course he would expose my mother for what she was. She couldn't have that. She didn't care for me, Sophia. Not one bit. My own mother."

"She was broken," Sophia said. "As my father is broken. You cannot possibly think that I deserve the way my father treated me, can you?"

"That's different."

"It isn't. You're just too afraid to step out from beneath this."

"Because on the other side is nothing. Nothing but the harsh, unending truth that I was nothing more than an incidental to the person who should have loved me simply because of the connection that we shared."

"Luca," she said. "I love you."

Suddenly, the emotion in his chest was like panic. Because she kept persisting even though he had told her to stop. And the monster inside him was growling louder, and he couldn't drown it out with platitudes. Nothing about promises or duty, or about standing tall in the face of an unfriendly press. About being a king and therefore being above these kinds of emotions, needing to rule with a cool head and a steady heart, rather than one given to things such as this. But he could not speak those words. He could not even feel them.

"You cannot love me," he said. "You cannot love me because I do not love myself." He gritted his teeth, despising the weakness inside him. "The man I could've been was stolen from me. I had to rebuild myself out of something, because God knows nobody was going to do it for me. I was broken open. All that I might have been poured out. And when I put myself together I did not make an effort to replace those things within me that were weak. Those things within me that had… That made me seem as though I might make a good victim."

"No," she said. "That's not fair."

"There is no fair in this. I was chosen for a reason. The boldness that it takes to do to me what that man did. Did you ever think of it that way? I was the future King of San Gennaro, and he felt as though he could take advantage of me, and he knew that he would not be punished. He knew that my mother would protect him. He knew that I would not be able to come forward and speak out against him. My hands would be tied. I refused… I refused to be remade in the same fashion that I had been born. I despise what I was, but I like the man I am now a little more. You cannot…"

He turned away from her, closing his eyes and gathering his control once again. "You cannot."

"Luca," she said, sounding broken, and he hated that, too. She deserved something else. Something different. A chance to be with a man, to want a man, to care for a man, who was not…broken in this way.

"Do you know," he said. "I have often wondered if there was something inherently sick inside me."

"You keep saying that word."

"I know. Because I wonder if it's why I've wanted you so badly for so long. Because there was something in me…"

"No. Stop trying to push me away."

"I'm not trying to push you away. I'll marry you. But I'm never going to love you in the way that you want me to. I can't. That part of myself is gone. It's dead. I had to cut it out of me so that I can survive all that I went through." He shook his head. "I will not change it for you. I cannot."

To change now would be to open himself back up to the kind of pain that he wanted gone from him forever, and he wouldn't do it.

"But you are pushing me away," she said.

"Sophia…"

She took a step away from him. "I'm sorry, Luca. I love you. And I'm not going to marry you simply because of duty. I would marry you because I loved you but I want you to marry me for the same reason. It would be so easy…" Her words came out choked, her brown eyes filling with tears. "It would be so easy to simply let this be. To take what you're offering, and be content with that. But I… I cannot. Luca, I can't. Because I think we could both have more. It doesn't have to be a sickness. It can be the cure. But only if you let it. And if I stay, and I allow you to have me without risking anything…"

His stomach tightened, turned over, and he ceased hearing her. Stopped listening. "If you don't want a man who's been raped, *cara mia*, all you have to do is say so."

"*Don't.* Don't make it about me being scared. I am scared, but I'm doing the brave thing. The hard thing. I refuse to let us live our lives as broken pieces when we can be whole together."

"What are you saying?"

"That for the second time, Princess Sophia is not going to show up to her wedding."

And with that, Sophia turned and walked out of the room, not bothering to gather her shoes. And he simply stood there, looking at them. Thinking this was the strangest interpretation of a Cinderella story he had ever heard of.

But after that came a strange pain in his chest like he couldn't remember feeling before. And he didn't even try to stop it from dropping him to his knees.

CHAPTER THIRTEEN

SOPHIA RAN UNTIL her mind was blank. Until there was nothing but her bare feet pounding down on the damp grass, the blades sticking between her toes, mud giving way and creating a slick foothold as she prayed her legs wouldn't fail her. Prayed they would carry her far away from Luca. From heartbreak.

She was still on the palace grounds, for they extended vastly, and she knew that she was going to have to stop running and get in a car. Get on a plane, to truly escape Luca. But for now she couldn't stop. For now she could do nothing but run.

She stopped when she came to the edge of the woods, and then she took a cautious step forward, the texture of the grounds changing to loose dirt and pine needles, the heavy tree cover protecting her from the pale moonlight. It was cool, almost frigid, there beneath the dark trees.

She shivered. She wrapped her arms around herself, trying to catch her breath. She took another step forward, and another, her dress shimmering in front of her, catching stolen beams of moonlight, flashing in the darkness.

She didn't know what she had just done. Didn't know what her plan was.

To walk into the forest and die?

No.

That was hardly the solution to dealing with a man not returning your affection.

She had been right, in what she had said to him. She couldn't go through with a marriage to a man who didn't love her. Not just for her own sake, but for his.

She had the feeling that many people—herself included until recently—thought love to be a beautiful, quiet thing. A force that allowed you to be yourself. And while that was true…it didn't mean the self that you projected to the world.

Real love, she fully understood now, challenged that identity. It forced you to reach down deep to your essence, and ask yourself who you were *there*. Real love was not about being comfortable. Not about being protected. Real love was about being stripped bare. Was about revealing yourself, unprotected to the other person, trusting that they would not use your tender and vulnerable places against you. That they would protect them for you, so that you didn't have to.

Real love was the difference between hiding in a darkened forest, or standing in the light.

Right now she was hiding in a forest.

She closed her eyes, a tear tracking down her face.

And it was then she realized where her feet were carrying her. She pressed on through the forest. Through and through. Until she found the paved drive that wound through the trees.

Her mother had moved into the dower house some time ago. It was an outmoded sort of thing, surely, as the palace was so large, but her mother seemed to like it. Liked having her own house rather than standing on ceremony in the massive palace.

It gave her a sense of peace. Gave her a small slice of her simple life back. Although the cottage, with its impeccably tended garden, bright pink roses climbing up the sides of the walls and exquisite furnishings was far grander than anything possessed by Sophia or her mother in their former lives.

It was dark now, the white stucco of the cottage shining a pale beacon through the dimness, the roses fluttering slightly against the wall as the breeze kicked up.

The gravel in the driveway cut into her feet, but she didn't care.

She walked up to the door and knocked.

It opened slowly, and then more quickly when her mother realized it was her.

"Sophia," she said. "What are you doing here?"

"I…" She swallowed hard. "I didn't know where else to go. I didn't even know I was coming here until… Until I realized where I was."

"What happened?"

"Luca and I fought. I… I called off the wedding."

"Come inside," her mother said, ushering her in.

There, Sophia found herself quickly wrapped in a blanket and settled on the couch, and before she knew it, a cup of tea was being firmly placed into her hand.

"Tell me."

"He doesn't wish to love me," Sophia said. "Which I feel is very different to not loving me at all. He doesn't want love. It… It frightens him." She would not reveal Luca's secrets to her mother. Because though she trusted her mother to keep confidences, they were Luca's secrets to tell. “He is very wounded by some things in his past, and he doesn’t want…”

“He doesn’t want to be healed?”

“Yes. Was his father like that?”

“No.” Her mother shook her head. “I was. Your father hurt me deeply. Years of being shunned for being a single mother. The casual judgment I faced every day leaving the house. Collecting assistance so that I could feed you. It all left me scarred and hardened. And then I met Magnus. He charmed me. And yes, when we met, seduced me. I’m not going to dance around that, Sophia, since I know you know full well about those things.”

Sophia felt her face heat. “Indeed.”

“It was easy for him to tempt me into his bed, but into his life was another thing entirely. And I did my best. To work my job, to keep my liaisons with a king private. To continue to be a good mother to you. I thought I could keep all those things separate. That all of those parts of myself didn’t have to be contained in one woman. That I could put walls up.” She smiled softly. “But I couldn’t. Not in the end. But I was hanging on very tightly to my pain. And I realized I was going to have to open my hands up and drop that pain if I was going to grab hold of what he was offering me. But when your pain has been fuel for so long, it is a difficult thing to do.”

“I think that’s how it is for him. I think his pain has kept him going, because without it…”

“Without it there’s only despair. Anger is much easier. Do you know what else anger is preferable to?”

“What?”

“Hope. Learning to hope again is a terrifying thing. And when you have been harmed, you don’t want it.

You resist it. Those little bits of light creeping back into the darkness are the most terrifying thing. You cannot hide in the light, Sophia. Darkness is a wonderful concealment. But it conceals everything. The beauty of the world. All that we can have around us. But it reveals us, too. The light. I suspect that is what Luca is resisting."

"What should I do? Should I go back to him? Love him even though he doesn't love me?"

"I can't tell you what to do. I don't want you trapped in a loveless marriage. But…"

"If I love him it isn't loveless," she said softly.

"No. It isn't." Her mother sat down on the couch next to her, clasping her hands in her lap. "The king loved me all the while when I could not love him. But he also didn't compromise. He did not want a mistress. He wanted a wife. And as far as he was concerned, if I didn't love him, even if we took vows, I might as well be a mistress."

"So he gave you an ultimatum."

"No. He just made it known he could not fully bring me into his life without love."

"Well. Luca and I can't exactly have that sort of arrangement. We are going to have a child together. And I live in the palace half the time."

Her mother laughed softly. "I'm not telling you what to do, Sophia. I feel there is the potential for heartbreak at every turn with this situation."

"That's not very encouraging."

"It isn't supposed to be encouraging. It's just the truth. I guess the question is… If he's going to break your heart either way… Would you rather be with him or be without him?"

"I don't know."

Except she did know. She wanted him. She wanted to be in his life, in his bed, but it felt like a potentially dangerous thing to do. The wrong thing. Like it would damage…

Her pride. Her defenses.

Perhaps she was more like her mother than she imagined.

Claims of love were bold, but quite empty when the action was withheld until the other person performed to your specifications.

His mother had given up on him. Had put herself before him.

Sophia realized she could not do the same.

Luca was not a man given to drink. He was not a man who indulged in anything, particularly. But he was drunk now. There was nothing else that was going to calm the pounding ache in his head. In his chest. He had sat there, for hours, on the floor of Sophia's bedroom, pain biting into him like rabid wolves. And then he had gotten up and gone back to his own quarters, and proceeded to drink the contents of his personal bar.

Now the pain was just swimming back and forth inside him, hazy and dull and no less present.

And he had even less control of his thoughts now. Chasing through his mind like rabid foxes after their own tails.

He was worthless. Worthless. A king of an entire country, worth absolutely nothing.

He did not allow himself those thoughts. He never did. But in this moment, he not only allowed them, he fed them. Like they were his pets. He allowed them to rain down on him, a black misery that coated him completely.

He embraced, wholly, his misery. His self-pity.

Sophia had spoken of how he stood tall in spite of everything. But here he was, on the floor. Prostrate to the sins that had been committed against him, and to what remained of his own soul. Black and bruised like the rest of him.

Dark.

He was a night without stars.

Sophia was the stars.

He rolled onto his back, the earth spinning on its axis.

He was worthless because he had been treated like an object. Worthless because his own mother had not cared to seek justice for him.

And yet, in the midst of those thoughts, in the midst of that darkness, there came a glimmer.

Sophia did not see him as worthless. Sophia thought he was strong.

Sophia thought he was worthy of love.

And in an instant, as though the sun had broken through storm clouds, he felt bathed in light.

Why should his mother, Giovanni, be the ones who formed his life? Why should they decide what he was?

Perhaps, in withholding what had happened to him from the media, his mother had protected him from having the public form an opinion on who he was, but within that, he had allowed her to form his opinion of his life. Of what he could be. Of what he could have.

He had escaped the press defining him by that night, but he defined himself by it. By his mother's response.

Had trained himself to believe that if he did not act

above reproach in every way at all times, that he would be as useless as he had long feared.

Sophia saw more than that. Sophia saw through to the man he might have been. She made him think that perhaps he could be that man again.

And he had sent her away, because he didn't feel worthy of that.

But she thought he was. She mattered more. She mattered more than Giovanni. She mattered more than his mother.

She mattered more than all the stars in the sky.

If Sophia could love him…

Pain burst through him, as brilliant and blinding as the light from only a moment before.

He loved her. He loved her. And he had hurt her. He had sent her away to protect himself. Which was truly no different than what his mother had done, in many ways.

Putting himself before her.

He would not.

He didn't want to marry Sophia because of the baby. He didn't want her because he was sick.

He wanted her because she was her.

Undeniably, beautifully her.

When he closed his eyes, it was her face he saw.

And then, he knew nothing else.

CHAPTER FOURTEEN

THE DAY OF the wedding, Sophia stayed in her mother's house until clothing could be sent. Then she was bundled up and whisked off to the palace, where she checked to see if anything had been canceled.

It had not been.

Perhaps it was Luca's ferocious pride not able to come to grips with the fact that she was going to defy him.

Perhaps he had a plan to try and win her back.

Or perhaps, he had simply known that in the end she wouldn't leave him to be humiliated.

Whatever the reasoning, she would find out later. With the help of her stylist, she got dressed in her wedding gown far earlier than was necessary. And then she began to make inquiries of the staff.

"Where is he?" she asked.

"The king?"

"Yes."

"In his rooms. But you know it is bad luck for the groom…"

"I already had the bad luck to fall in love with my stepbrother. I think I have reached my limit." She picked up the front of her dress and dashed across the palace, making her way to Luca's chamber.

But he wasn't there. Dejected, she began to make the journey back to her own. The halls were remarkably empty, the staff all seeing to preparations for the wedding that might not happen, it seemed to Sophia.

So she was surprised when she heard another set of footsteps in the corridor.

She looked up and saw Luca standing there. He was wearing black slacks and a white shirt that was unbuttoned at the throat. For one blinding second she could hardly fight the impulse to fling herself across the empty space between them and kiss him there. Right at his neck, right where his heart beat, strong and steady.

But she remained rooted to where she was, her breathing shallow.

"Luca," she said.

"I was searching for you," he said.

"Here I am."

He frowned. "You're wearing a wedding gown."

She swished her hips back and forth, the dress swirling around her legs. "Yes."

"You said you wouldn't marry me."

"I changed my mind."

"Well. I have decided that I changed my mind, as well."

"What?"

"I do not wish to marry you simply because you're having a baby, Sophia. You're right. That would be a terrible thing. A terrible mistake."

Sophia felt crushed. As if he had brought those strong hands down over her heart and ground it into powder.

"You don't want to marry me?" she asked.

"I do want to marry you," he said. "But I'm happy to not marry you. We can live in sin. We can have a bastard. We could create scandal the world over and forget everyone else."

Sophia was stunned. She blinked. "No. Luca, your reputation… The reputation of San Gennaro…"

"It doesn't matter. If I must court scandal to prove my feelings for you, then I will do so. It is nothing in the face of my feelings for you. My love for you. And if I have to burn all of it to the ground to prove to you that what I feel is real, believe me, Sophia. My reputation is nothing, my throne is nothing, if I don't have you. I would give all of it up. For you. That was the real sickness in my blood, my darling girl. That I wanted so badly to hold on to this thing that I believed was more important than anything. Was the only thing that gave me value. While I fought with what I really wanted on the inside. You. It was always you. But I knew that I was going to have to give up that facade of perfection that felt as if it defined my very existence if I was going to have you. Please believe me, *cara mia*, I would gladly leave it all behind for you. For this. For us."

Then Sophia did cross the space between them. She did fling her arms around his neck. And she kissed him there, where his pulse was throbbing at the base of his throat. "Luca," she whispered. "Luca, I believe you. And I want to be married to you. Because I want it to be real. I want it to be forever. We could make vows in a forest, and I know it would be just as real, but we might as well give our child legitimacy, don't you think?"

"I mean, I suppose it would make things easier. With succession and everything."

"You're a king. We could bend the rules. But I feel like perhaps we should just get married."

"I kept thinking there were more rules for me because I was a king. But all those chains were inside me. And all the darkness… It's because I refused to let the light in. I stood there, on the island, and looked up at the stars. And I marveled at them. And wished very much that I could… That I could be more than darkness. That you could be my light. The only one stopping that was me. All along. The only thing stopping it was…"

"Fear. I understand that… That hope is the most frightening thing there is."

"It is," Luca agreed. "Truly terrifying to want for more when you simply accepted all the things you would never have. When you've told yourself you don't need it."

"Luca," she said softly. "You're not broken. You are not damaged. The people who hurt you… They are the ones who are broken."

"I was broken," he whispered. He grabbed hold of her hands and lifted them, kissing her fingertips. "I was broken for a time. But not now. You put me back together."

"We put each other back together."

"I love you," he said.

"I love you, too."

"I did not think I would get my happy ending."

"You didn't?"

He shook his head. "Stepsiblings of any stripe are always evil."

"Well, then I could just as easily have been evil, too."

"Of course not," he said. "You're the princess."

"And you happen to be my Prince Charming, Luca. Stepbrother or not."

"Am I very charming?" He grinned at her, and the expression on his face made her light up inside.

"Not always," she said, smiling slightly. "But you're mine. And that's all that matters."

"That makes you mine, too."

"I choose you. I choose you over everything," she said. She pressed a kiss to his lips, and he held her for a moment.

"I choose you, too," he said. "Over everything."

And though they spoke their vows later that day, it was those vows that she knew would carry them through for the rest of their lives.

EPILOGUE

SHE WAS ABOVE him in absolutely every way. A radiant angel of light, his wife. And never had he been more certain of that than when he looked at her, holding their daughter in her arms.

He had been right about one thing, the scandal of their union had settled quickly enough once the excitement over the royal baby had overshadowed it all. A new little princess was much more interesting to the world over than how Sophia and Luca had gotten their start.

Luca knelt down by his wife's hospital bed, gazing in awe at the two most important women in his life.

"What do you think, Your Majesty?" she asked.

"I think…" He swallowed hard. "I think that with two such brilliant lights in my life I will never have to be lost in darkness again."

* * * * *